BELLES & BRATVA
BEASTS

SIRE RUTLEDGE
IS A PASTOR.
THE DEVIL'S FRIEND.
AND MY FIRST SIN.

SIRE

KELLY FINLEY

SIRE

KELLY FINLEY

Sire: Belles & Bratva Beasts, Book Three

Kelly Finley

© 2025 Kelly Finley Publishing, LLC

Visit the author's website at kellyfinley.com

ISBN: 979-8-9916399-2-7 (eBook)

ISBN: 979-8-9916399-8-9 (paperback)

Interior Formatting by Kelly Finley

Cover design by Lori Jackson

Cover photo by Michelle Lancaster @lanefotograf

Cover model: Kallym Grimmond

ALSO BY KELLY FINLEY

Belles & Bratva Beasts

Nash

Axel

Sire

Loch

Jace

Interconnected Books

Shameless Play

Shameless Game

Make Him

Tempt Her

The Six

Holiday For Six

Halloween For Six

After Him

With Him

CONTENT ADVISORY
WARNING: THESE ARE SPOILERS, TOO

This book, like all in this series, contains a very spicy plot with swoony angst and witty snark set in an ex-mafia secret society. Congrats if this is your kind of romance.

It also contains topics that readers may be sensitive to. If you have any questions about this list, please message me on my social media platforms @kellyfinleybooks (Instagram, TikTok, and Facebook).

- A morally grey pastor who takes some liberties at the pulpit. Is it sacrilegious? She does moan, "Oh God," so you decide
- A strong FMC, virgin, and proud woman of color
- She's a survivor of sex trafficking, rescued before being violated
- He likes to take the heads of evil men, implied, not graphic
- They're soulmates, but
- He's bisexual with a breeding kink
- MM+F scenes are featured

- Age-gap love (He's 43. She's 19. They're consenting adults)
- Detailed sex scenes that feature virginity "loss," exhibitionism, group sex, extreme dirty talk, breeding kink, male bisexuality, anal, cunnilingus, fellatio, an audience … you get the idea
- He only loves his wife, but she celebrates who he is
- Is it a why-choose? Not really. It's a bi-annual thing. You'll see…
- There's a taboo initiation into a secret society involving other men
- Kings, who prove their love for their Queens (in front of each other)
- They're brothers, too. But never brother-on-brother
- A plot surrounding a betrayal and a child taken
- A voluntary organ donation to save a child
- A badass woman who survived abuse and being a child bride, and built an empire of revenge
- References to physical and psychological parental abuse
- It's a book in a series about men who escaped the mafia, so they're not big Bratva fans. Instead, they're like the ex-mafia avengers
- And a guaranteed HEA

If this has only piqued your interest, this book is for you.

THE KINGS & QUEENS

ORDER OF THRONES

Ruslan Kholodov	Nadine Faye "The Queen"
Axel King	Ruby Jones
Nash Allen	Vale Monroe
Sire Rutledge	Wren Chapel
Grant Moultrie	Delphine Laurent
Jace Ryan	Vivian Tate
Nick Barinov	Zar Rollins
Loch Waring	Alena Allen

PLAYLIST

Chapter 1
"angel," Camyilo

Chapter 2
"You," by Ari Abdul

Chapter 6
"Touch Me Like a Gangster," Jessie Murph

Chapter 7
"Islands in the Stream," Dolly Parton, Kenny Rogers

Chapter 12
"Sin So Sweet," Warren Zeiders

Chapter 15
"Worship," Ari Abdul

Chapter 20
"you should see mine in a crown," Billie Eilish
Chapter 21
"God Needs The Devil," Jonah Kagen
Chapter 23
"With the Devil I'm Going Down," Steelfeather
Chapter 24
"Skin and Bones," David Kushner
Chapter 27
"Dear god," Tate McRae
Chapter 30
"Darkerside," David Kushner
Chapter 31
"Born Again," LISA, Doja Cat, RAYE
Chapter 35
"Fast," Demi Lovato
Chapter 38
"DEVIL YOU KNOW," Tyler Braden
Chapter 42
"Indigo," Sam Barber, Avery Anna
Chapter 48
"Thank God," Kane Brown, Katelyn Brown
Chapter 50
"God Went Crazy," Teddy Swims

To all smutty readers who deserve to scream,
"Oh, God"
with the Devil in bed

PROLOGUE
SIRE

This moment.

This is how I wish I'd met Wren, not the dark and disturbing way we did.

She had been through enough. She deserved a meet-cute, as if this were the first time I set my eyes on her.

This moment is happy, ballsy, and so hilarious, it's fucking beautiful.

"If you like bean enchiladas! And getting caught in the rain!"

Wren belts the famous 1970s song, smacking her chest like she's Celine Dion on the bow of the Titanic ... when really ... she's the tipsy, future sister-in-law of the bride, with a voice that sounds a fuck-ton better screaming my name when she comes than entertaining me and her big family of in-laws at a wedding rehearsal dinner.

"Did she just..."

Axel, my brother, marvels, staring up at my stunning wife, who's standing on the bar in front of us and singing into an empty tequila bottle.

She has a habit of massacring lyrics. It's one of her many adorable flaws.

My flaws? They're a lot darker and way more murderous.

Axel's dumbfounded. "Does she really think those are the lyrics?"

"She *sure* does." I grin like a love-struck puppy, gazing up at her.

Wren's white minidress is giving a mouth-watering view of her pink lace panties, and she gives zero fucks.

Yeah, I'm hopelessly in love with this tiny woman who stole my heart and pinky.

"But it's 'The Piña Colada Song'." Nash, my other brother, sits beside me, sounding equally amazed. "I mean, everyone knows it."

"Actually..." I'll always defend my wife. To the death. Done. Proven. Prefer not to do it again and get blood on my white Nike Killshots. "The song's title is 'Escape' and that's what I'll need to find if I tell my beautiful wife she's fucking songs up."

"But she's just kidding, right?" Jace, my most colossal brother, sits on the other side of Nash, defending her. "She does it for laughs. She's gotta know those aren't the lyrics."

Hell, Jace is like all of us. He defends our queens, no matter what. Gazing up in awe at Wren, who's shrieking about making love at midnight, he's allowed to stare up her dress, too. All of my brothers can. It's not like they haven't seen her panties before.

They just can't fucking touch her. Not anymore. After this wedding, it's back to me, getting her pregnant.

"She's not joking." I can't take my eyes off her. "When she screeches 'Living On A Prayer,' she thinks Bon Jovi is singing, 'It doesn't make a difference if we're *naked* or not.'"

Nash slaps the bar, rolling with laughter. He's the silent,

deadly one, but that has him wiping his eyes. "*Naked* or not? Goddamn, that's *so* Wren."

"It's *so* Vale, too," Jace chimes in about Nash's wife. "She answers your front door topless. Naked is a constant state for her."

Nash laughs, "That's because it's you, her second king, at our door, and she believes clothing optional was one of our marriage vows."

Our wives are our queens, and we're their kings, their husbands. We'll die protecting them, and when we do, one of our brothers has taken a vow to be their second king, to protect our queen and family.

Together, we've initiated our queens. They belong to us. They're bound to us.

It's an intimate and powerful, albeit taboo tradition that saved our lives years ago, and now I'm praying it'll save Wren's life.

Because mine?

I'm about to risk it for my family.

"Hmm. Clothing optional?" Axel smirks. "I'll be amending my wedding vows with Ruby tomorrow."

Nash sips his whisky. "Like fuck you'd let Ruby answer the door topless."

Jace huffs, "Like fuck he could stop her."

I preach, "Because we're all so goddamn in love."

Our entire family is here in Mykonos for Axel and Ruby's wedding, and this is how I wish I had met my wife: absolutely gobsmacked at how fucking amazing this brave woman is.

But that's not the lethal life my brothers and I lead, and I can't tell anymore if we were born into danger, or if we choose it.

Tough to say.

We just do it.

We escaped the Bratva as boys, only to make our own

mafia of vigilante justice seekers as men, led by our badass mom, and I wouldn't change a thing.

In two days, I may lose my family and life over what I did to save them, and I'd do it again.

The chorus returns. Wren bends down, kissing me before her smiling lips sing, "If you love bean enchiladas…"

And why am I smiling back? Why do I know all hell will break loose?

Because I know hell.

I'm the son of the devil.

But as a pastor now, I believe in heaven, too.

I smile because I have my Wren, my wife, my heaven on Earth. She's my soul's salvation because I met her, like this…

CHAPTER ONE
SIRE

A year ago...

You know the saying, "Give the devil his due."

It's to acknowledge the good qualities of an evil person.

Why, thank you. I appreciate it.

Because I am the Devil looking at this Angel.

"Girls, turn around. Full circle. Come on! Show them the goods!" The seller barks, and the girls cry, shaking and obeying...except...

This one.

"Yeah," I gloat. "This one's mine!"

She's no girl. She's a young woman with pert breasts, rouge nipples, and a dark mound, peeking through her white silk slip.

I can't tell her maturity by her body because some of the underage girls in here have mature-looking bodies, too. But it's their eyes betraying their innocence. They're way too young for the hell they're being sold into.

Okay, being trafficked and sold is hell at any age, but I can tell this one is wiser beyond her years. Her eyes don't shake in terror. Her half-naked body doesn't tremble. Her tawny cheeks are dry.

She's the only one not crying.

No, she looks straight ahead, and if looks could kill, every man in this room would be dead.

These girls and young women are being sold, and I'm buying them.

Settle down.

Don't worry.

I won't lay a hand on them, and neither will my brothers, posing as other buyers in the room. They're making us sit in a circle of chairs around the girls.

This fucker, the seller, a hedge fund manager by day, rented a swanky house in Palm Beach, and he has us sitting like we're getting ready to dine. Like we're about to make an evil meal of these innocent girls.

So, the Lord wants me to use the gun strapped to my ankle and hidden under my jeans to kill the seller.

The sloppy pat-down I got at the door missed my Glock.

Amateurs.

But the Devil in me knows if I kill this fucker now, we won't bust his entire network, and that's what we want.

"What's your name, sweetie?" Some old, sick fuck addicted to self-tanner reaches for the youngest girl.

She sobs, and I growl, "Yeah, she's mine, too."

"You can't have them all," he whines.

"Like you can stop me, mother fucker?"

I'm not dressed like a forty-something pastor; I'm dressed like a twenty-something dealer. Guess I look like one, too. Ink on my face. Neck. Hands. My entire body. Most people can't see past my menacing exterior to my tortured soul inside, and fuck yes, that's how I want it.

"No." My brother Axel glares at me. "I'm taking three of them."

"Fuck you." Grant, my other brother, acts along. "I'm not going home empty-handed. I want two."

"I'm taking the blondes." Nash, who's like our brother, fights his rage. He's a father to a daughter, and this shit is eating him alive, but he plays the part. "All three of them."

That leaves the youngest girl ... and this one.

This iron angel belongs to me.

"You know the price, gentlemen." The seller enters the circle. "The bidding starts at a million each."

"You said a hundred *K* each." The old orange man whines again, "That's not a good deal."

They go back and forth, and it doesn't matter. My brothers and I came to get these girls. To get them the fuck out of here and the help they need.

Our brother Jace and our mom are waiting in a van five miles away. They'll take these girls and get them somewhere safe.

This is what we do, and we don't fuck around. In fifteen minutes, we've bought them all, and they're starting to leave. My brothers won't blow their cover.

But this last one?

The Iron Angel?

"I've grown quite fond of her." The seller caresses her long raven curls. "She's special. Such a rare little bird. Right, Wren?" He grabs her breast, and I clench my jaw as he sneers, "She'll fight back, and that makes it sweeter."

He throws her down on the marble floor. Crashing on her backside, she muffles her cry, her tattoos revealed.

Stigmata tattoos.

Two blood red marks on the inside of her wrists. Two on the tops of her bare feet. They look like the nail wounds of Jesus Christ on the cross.

Days from now, I'll realize her tattoos are my sign. My greatest temptation and salvation.

Right now?

I get in his face. "Don't fucking touch my property."

"She's not yours yet. Maybe I should have her first. We've been saving them all, ten little virgins. But this one? I think I'll break her before you buy her."

"Two million." My lip curls.

He tilts his head.

Fuck, that was too much. He's suspicious.

"If she's worth so much to you..." He pulls a knife from the pocket of his khaki pants. "How about I take a pound of flesh, too?"

A sob breaks the youngest girl, burying her face in her shaking hands.

Dragging herself up, the Iron Angel reaches for her, protecting her like a big sister.

God, save her. The youngest girl barely looks fourteen. The same age as my mother when she was kidnapped and trafficked to my father.

But my Iron Angel? She acts wiser than her years. *Dear Lord, she's brave.*

"What do you want?" I stare down the seller.

"How about I take a pound of flesh from her," he points his knife at the youngest girl, "and the virgin flower from her."

He grabs the Iron Angel, and something in me snaps.

I did this for my brother. I sacrificed myself.

And I'll do this for her—a complete stranger.

From as young as I can remember, a spirit has moved through me. I can't describe it, and I don't need to. It speaks and I listen.

The problem is.

Is it God?

Or the Devil?

"Take a piece of my flesh." I don't care. My spirit speaks, using my mouth, "Take a piece of me and give me these girls."

"Why?"

Yeah, he's suspicious.

"Because I like blood." I'm not lying. "I like mine. I like theirs. I like cutting and breeding, and let's start the fun now."

Quoting scripture, I hold out my left hand, "I remind you to fan into flame the gift of God, which is in you through the laying of my hands."

"What the fuck?" The seller scoffs.

But the Iron Angel…

Her eyes widen, not knowing what she's seeing, staring at me, but she knows scripture. She must be wondering, *Why is God's word spewing from the Devil's mouth?*

"I'm not fucking cutting your hand off, man." The seller gestures to the opulent house. "I don't need a mess and the heat on me."

It doesn't matter.

Tomorrow, Nash will drain this evil fuck's accounts of the money we paid for the girls, and then Axel and I will kill him, the orange buyer, and the hired guns behind him. It's only six men. It won't be hard.

It'll be fun. I'll make sure of it.

"You want flesh or not?"

"Theirs." He points to the girls.

"Nah, they're my toys and I don't share. So, take my fucking pinky and let's roll."

I slam my hand down on a glass table, strewn with tumblers of whisky. Giving a pinky isn't a Christian custom. It's *Yubitsume*, a Japanese mafia thing. My Russian mafia father admired their discipline and rituals. Growing up, he took a lot from our flesh, too.

But the seller keeps eyeing my Iron Angel.

"Come on, man." I keep my voice flat. "Three million and my pinky, and it's a deal, and I get to take my girls home to play. I have a dungeon waiting for them."

He likes the sound of that way too much. In three steps, he presses the blade, poised over my splayed digits.

"No!" The Iron Angel cries out, "Don't hurt him!"

I wink at her. "It's alright. I won't feel a thing."

But goddamn, I do.

At first, the shock hits me, even though I expect it. Numbly, I stare down at him doing it, my blood pumping as flesh and bone are severed. It spills over the glass table, but he wipes it up with a towel one of the gunmen throws at him.

Then it's a throbbing, nauseating pain from my severed finger to my stomach, to every nerve in my body registering the unnatural trauma—the permanent loss.

But I hide it.

I don't want to scare the girl and the Iron Angel any more than we need to get the fuck out of here.

"Done."

I make myself breathe while the seller lifts half of my pinky, holding it to the light like a goddamn diamond.

"Careful," he warns. "With your appetite for torturing virgin pussy, you'll run out of fingers."

No, dumbass, you're out of time.

In twenty-four hours, I'll cut your head off.

With a blood-soaked towel wrapped around my left hand, I signal to my angel with the right. Shockingly, she follows me without resistance and gets the girl to come, too.

I guess the Iron Angel believes I'm the lesser of the evils in the room.

Maybe she's wrong.

When we get to my rented Hummer parked in the driveway, I clock Axel in his rental, acting like he's on his phone when really, he's waiting for me.

His eyes shock wide at the bloody towel around my hand, but I lift my chin. *I got this.*

Yanking the back door open, I bark, "Get in."

The youngest starts to sob again, so I drop my voice to as true as I can make it sound.

"I won't hurt you. I'm taking both of you to a woman who protects girls in your situation."

"Come on." The Iron Angel urges the youngest one to climb in. "It'll be okay. We're safe now."

I don't know where this angel gets her conviction, but she follows it. Holding the girl in the back seat like a sister, she protects her again, while glaring at me through the rear-view mirror. "Who are you?"

I smirk. It's fitting. Fated. "A fallen angel."

"Don't bullshit me. Who are you, and where are you taking us?"

Fuck it. I don't hide this part of me.

My mom has a safe place for these girls. She'll get them all the resources they need, and I'll go back to my cursed soul.

"I'm a pastor at a church that helps trafficking victims like you. I'm taking you to a woman who spends all her money helping girls and women get safe."

Her glare in the mirror's reflection confronts my soul. *Huh.* Only my brothers are brave enough to look at me that way. "You can trust her."

Her eyes narrow. "Can I trust you?"

"No." I don't lie.

"Why not?"

"You have stigmata tattoos. You know what a fallen angel is."

"An angel who rebelled against God, and was cast out of heaven, and now waits in darkness until judgment day."

I wink. "Nice to meet ya."

She gets the idea, and I take the next interstate exit, my heavy heart already lighter after that confession.

"What did you do?" Damn, she's brave. "What's your sin?"

I glance in the mirror again. The youngest girl looks asleep. Or passed out in shock. *Fuck, I need to get her to my mom.*

"Tell me," the Iron Angel insists. "You gave a pound of flesh for me, and I want to know."

Fine.

I'll never see her again.

And I need to confess my sins.

"I lay with men. I lay with women. I have some very dark needs when I do, and while I help everyone else, I don't help myself. I sold my brother to the Devil, and I'll be paying for it for the rest of my life." I pause. "Amen."

She studies me, her topaz eyes never breaking their glare in the mirror, her breath stealing all the oxygen in the car. It's like we're in the presence of something powerful, but I don't know its name as a heavy minute claims the space between us.

"My name is Wren."

"It's *not* nice to meet me, Wren."

"What's your name?"

"It's best you don't know."

This is me, protecting her. That's half of my DNA. The other half? It's wired for destruction. I could rip her to shreds.

So why do I sense she's doing the same for me? Like she was brought here to protect me, too? How can a creature so small make the molecules around me feel so ... *so right?*

For another potent minute, she's silent before warning, "Lay a hand on this girl and I'll poison you."

Poison? What a biblical way to go.

"You should."

I spot the passenger van up the road in a hotel parking lot. My brother Jace waits beside it. My mom, as well. My brothers, in their rental cars with their victims, have arrived, too. They'll take the girls from here, and I'll never see the Iron Angel again.

It's best that way.

You should only glimpse the Devil, not take a road trip with him.

I park beside the van.

Of course, the Iron Angel fears what's about to happen, so she vows again, "And if you ever lay a hand on me, Pastor—"

"Yeah, yeah…" I meet her gaze in the mirror. *What the fuck?* She makes me smile. "You'll poison me, too."

"No," she answers sweetly. "We'll fall in love."

CHAPTER TWO
WREN

"You're not gonna change your mind about him, are you?"

"Nope," I answer the mountain of muscle beside me. "I'm five feet tall. Stubbornness serves me well."

Standing by the doorway of a kids' playroom in a historic Charleston church, I've made the right decision about the man we're staring at.

I haven't stopped thinking about The Pastor.

How could I?

He's the fallen angel who sacrificed his flesh for me.

And if I'm making the wrong decision about him—*which I'm not*—how much more fucked up can my life get?

I trust my instincts. They're all I have left, and they've gotten me this far.

I also trust this total snack standing beside me. He's the one who drove the passenger van to the fancy beach house where my life, and the lives of nine other girls, went from savage to saved.

It's been a whirlwind of a week since then, but my heart

has been like the eye of a storm. Calm. Certain of where I need to go next.

Staring at the back of the man God sent to me, I ask the other, "He's your brother, isn't he?"

Mr. Muscle doesn't answer. We just watch the back of the jacked and tatted man in a tight, white T-shirt and jeans, who looks eerily like him.

Giggling kids surround The Pastor, but my stare falls to the white bandage wrapped around his left pinky. Or what remains of it. The rest? He sacrificed for me.

It's why I'm here.

It was a sign.

I side-whisper, "What's he doing?"

"Entertaining the kids while their parents take an English class."

"But what are they doing to *him*?"

"Adding to the tattoos on his face." Mr. Muscle leans against the doorjamb. "Hopefully, not with Sharpies this time. That shit was too funny, literally. He had a poop emoji on his forehead for a week."

A giggle erupts from my throat, imagining it.

Before the hell of this past year, I was a happy person. It was a conscious choice. When you have nothing and no one, you can at least own a positive attitude.

And whenever my joy would waver, I'd ask myself, "*WWDD?*"

What Would Dolly Do?

Sorry, Jesus. You and I are tight, but Dolly Parton is the mother I never had. She's taught me that smiles and kindness open doors if not hearts, and it's how I've survived so far. Smiling and praying someone will open their door to me.

And here I am, doing it again.

The Pastor sits on a red plastic children's chair. With a

soulful voice and slight Southern twang, he sings a song about a bullfrog and "Joy to the World."

He's enchanting the kids who laugh with markers in their little hands, scribbling over the flesh I admire, too. Innocent, colorful doodles over black, ominous ink. On his face. His neck. His arms.

"So those markers will wash off?" I worry.

"He wouldn't care if it didn't." I glance up at Mr. Muscle. He beams at the sight, revealing, "He'll do anything for kids."

Meeting my stare, Mr. Muscle's blue eyes sparkle. They ease the threat of his menacing form. Otherwise, this guy is a snow-covered volcano—peaceful, beautiful, and huge until he blows.

"Like he did for you, little one." He sounds worried, too. "But I'm not sure about this; me, bringing you to him. He has a good soul but an evil temper. Be warned."

"Well," I shrug, "I'm sure about him."

Defiance edges my voice. The sound of it makes The Pastor turn his head. In an instant, his indigo eyes widen, surprised, before they narrow with fuming recognition.

"It's me! Hi!" I sing out, yes, sounding like the Taylor Swift song, so I add to the awkwardness. *WWDD?*

I smile.

I wave.

Mr. Muscle huffs a chuckle, "*This* should be interesting."

Fluent Spanish rolls off the tongue of The Pastor, slowly rising, tension rippling the muscles under his T-shirt. Pointing to an older woman, holding a book and sitting in a rocking chair, he must be telling the kids it's story time. Eagerly, they circle her, but one little boy won't leave his side.

The boy is two or so.

It's my informed guess. Foster siblings surrounded me for the first sixteen years of my life.

The Pastor glances at the crying boy, tugging at his jeans,

so he gently scoops him up in his inked arms ... and ... there go my ovaries. Content, the toddler rests his head on The Pastor's chest.

But his sexy face, aimed at me?

It's not giving Content.

No, common sense tells me to run from a man with tattoos on his face; he got them for a reason. They're giving *Fuck off or Die* vibes. Even on a hot face like his.

But how can I be afraid of a dangerous man with rainbows doodled on his forehead?

He stares at me, and I stare at him. New, sparkling sensations plunge my depths, and I don't know what to name them.

Even as he storms our way, his voice growling low at both of us, "What in the hell are you doing here?"

"She told me to bring her to you." Mr. Muscle folds his beefy arms across his chest. "And she's like a cute mosquito. Tiny and light. Biting and the most dangerous insect in the world. The fuck if I'll say no to her."

Smiling, I elbow him. "Jeez. Thanks, Mr. Muscle."

In the past week, I've grown attached to him. His name is Jace. When our van arrived at the beach house, I heard the doctors, there to treat us, greet him with warmth.

Jace brought us meals, but never introduced himself, and I was a little busy recovering from shock.

I keep recalling what the therapist said to me after I was rescued. "Trusting another person may seem unimaginable right now, and that's okay."

She's not wrong. Trust has been a gamble for me; a game I've lost until now.

But I'm right about The Pastor.

I more than trust him.

I belong with him.

Even though I don't know his name.

The therapist's name was Rachel, and I know the woman who saved us, who Jace works for, is Ms. Nadine Faye. She introduced herself in the van while she gave us blankets to wrap around our shivering flesh, and in a matter of hours, Ms. Faye felt like our mama bear.

I felt safe; a rare emotion for me.

And I don't know why Luck has finally found me, too, but I'm not giving it back.

I *am* a mosquito.

Little, light brown, buzzing, and yeah, cute until I bite. I gotta survive, too.

"You can't be here." The Pastor cups the boy's downy curls, his tenderness at odds with his menacing appearance and simmering rage. "You're safe now. You need to go home."

Be brave.

I don't care he's the most beautiful man I've ever seen; he's a beast right now, and I'm used to his kind.

"I don't *have* a home."

"Well, then, go back to wherever you came from."

"That's the *last* place that's safe for me."

"Then go to your family," he seethes. "Parents. Grandparents. Aunts or uncles somewhere."

I swallow. "I don't *have* a family, either."

And it's all I've ever wanted.

There's not a word for the hole in my heart. It just aches, empty and lonely, a void I smile through until I close my eyes every night and fill it with tears. It's been there since I was days old and left on the steps of a chapel.

"The fuck, man?" The Pastor aims his ire at Mr. Muscle. "You got the intel from the girls. You took them back to their families. Why is *she* still here?"

My fists land on my waist. "Look, Crayola King, *she* can speak for herself. As I told Mister Muscle and Miss Faye, I have no home, no family, and where I came from is not safe, so I'm staying here..." It's hard to breathe with the way he's looking at me, but I insist, "I'm staying with *you*."

A bomb drops in his deep blue eyes, but I'm right. I feel it in my soul. You recognize a prayer when it's been answered.

Though he thinks I'm as wrong as sour milk. He flares his pierced nose at me like...

No.

Fucking.

Way.

Sure, I probably didn't help my cause the first time we met. I told The Pastor we'd fall in love if he ever touched me.

Yep, that scared the shit out of him. It kinda scared me, too, but I couldn't help it.

Sometimes...

Okay, almost *every* time, I don't think about it. The truth just pops out of my mouth. I'm allergic to lies.

And after what The Pastor did for me? A man doesn't need to be nailed to a cross for me to know he's my salvation.

Some way, somehow, I'm meant to be with this man.

This menacing man, wrapped in ominous ink, who hates that I've invaded his sacred world. Yeah, *him*. He's my answered prayer.

I suspect he won't judge me for what I've done to survive, even though we're painfully opposite people except for this...

"Thou hast made for thee to dwell in a Sanctuary, O Lord," I shock The Pastor, "which thy *hands* have established." I quote scripture, aiming my eyes at his bandaged hand.

Point.

Made.

"See what I mean?" Mr. Muscle gestures. "She's all yours."

He turns to leave, but The Pastor seethes, "Take her with you."

He turns back. "You heard her, bro. She belongs with *you*. You're two biblical peas in a pod."

Yep, I knew it: brothers.

"Take her back to the safe house."

"No can do." He arches a thick brow. "*Ms. Faye* said to bring her to you. It's what she wants."

She? Does he mean the gorgeous mama bear who saved us? Or me? Or both?

Either way, Mr. Muscle said the name as if it's a lie. Like, *Ms. Faye* isn't who she really is. But she is a woman you'd best obey. That truth is crystal clear.

It's in the eyes of both men; eyes that suspiciously look like Ms. Faye's. They're so ocean blue, you want to dive into their depths, even if it kills you.

"*Padre.*" The toddler starts poking his finger, fascinated by the diamond stud in The Pastor's nostril. It amuses the boy and doesn't annoy the devilish man who's too busy glaring down at me.

Our eye contact feels like a standoff.

Like a battle has begun.

A war of heat, fire, and fate.

And I belong right here, holding my ground and fighting for my future. It's all I've ever known.

His nostrils flare. "How old are you?"

So, I flare mine back. "Old enough to know when a man cuts his finger off for you, you belong with him."

He seethes, "I did that so you wouldn't belong to *any* man. You're free to go."

"I'm equally free to stay."

"You can't stay with me. I'm a pastor. Pretty, young women can't live with me."

Not true. He confessed in the car when he rescued me, *I lay with men. I lay with women. I have some very dark needs when I do.*

That means he's not celibate. Quite the opposite.

And *pretty?* Oh, God, it wets the part of my body that's been imagining him all week.

After the hell I'd been through, I closed my eyes at night, needing to fantasize about the heaven we could share. The Pastor's hot body, tangled with men. His lips, his fingers, his ... *God yes,* every part of him claiming me, too.

Sure, I'm a virgin, but I've watched porn. It's been my only exposure and education, and now all I can do is picture this man doing every sweet and salacious thing to me.

For the rest of my life.

Standing so close to him, my cheeks burn. The intense way he stares at me, heat drips down my body. Pooling wet and warm, between my thighs like never before.

I force them not to shake in his holy presence.

The Pastor is the hottest man I've ever seen, and that's saying a lot considering his smoldering sibling beside me.

"This isn't a monastery." I glance around. Mr. Muscle led us through buildings and hallways. This church takes up a city block. "I'm sure there's a room for me somewhere. I can cook, clean, pull weeds, and babysit kids. I can also get a job nearby and save money. I just need to stay *safe* and stay with you."

"Me?" He steps into my air. "Why? Who's after you?"

His cologne—amber, oak, and musk—grabs me. He's so close, I discern the tattoo on his high cheekbone, too. A small, broken heart. And his indigo eyes are changing, softening. He's worried.

"It's not safe to say." I soften, too. "The less you know, the better."

"Ahem." Mr. Muscle mutters, "Sounds familiar."

"This isn't a monastery *or* an apartment building." The Pastor ignores his brother. "Parts of this church were built centuries ago. No one lives here. It's a historic landmark."

"But you live *behind* it." Mr. Muscle pushes from the door-jamb. "On the other side of the old graveyard."

"Why, thank you, Charleston tour guide," he mocks his not-so-little brother, who doled out the deets. "Wanna give her a horse-drawn carriage ride while you tell her *all* my shit? Maybe point out where I grocery shop, too?"

Okay.

Now they're colossal *and* cute, and I suspect The Pastor wouldn't curse if the playful boy in his arms understood English. He keeps calling him *Padre* and poking his face.

And what a face.

Strong brows. Perfect nose. Full lips. Especially that bottom one. The dark brown scruff on his angular jaw threatens to be a beard. It mirrors his dark brown hair, kissed by the southern sun. Black ink crawls up his thick neck, snaking down his thick fingers, too. His thin T-shirt can't hide his wide, ripped form. He's tall, but everyone's taller than me. That's not amazing.

But it's his eyes.

They're amazing.

They remind me of my favorite flowers—blue hydrangeas. How they draw from their roots, changing their color depending on how they're nourished.

So, can I change his mind, too?

Hopefully ... because I won't change mine.

"Keep me safe." I step into his shadow. "You're my gift from God. You said it yourself before you let some asshole cut off your pinky for me. Don't tell me something didn't speak to you then."

"Yeah," he snaps, "an evil sex trafficker spoke to me, and it was the only way to get you and that little girl out of there."

"And *this* one won't tell us where she was kidnapped," Mr. Muscle adds, frustrated by my silence this past week. "All the other girls? We found their families. They're from every rural town across Appalachia. But her? She won't tell us where she's from, just that she's not a kid. She's nineteen, and not safe if she goes home, so she's staying here. With *you.*"

I feel vindicated.

Mr. Muscle is on my side.

"You have a spare bedroom," he continues. "You know *why* we do *what* we do, so protect her."

"Until when?" The Pastor fumes, "Until the truth sets her free?" His glare slices to me. "When will you tell us how you wound up trafficked? What happened, and who's after you? And how long will you need my protection?"

"When will you tell me who you really are?" I point between them. "Both of you. No church does what you did for me and those girls. It was a group of you guys working for Ms. Faye. I counted five of you when we got in the van. So, who are *you?*"

Silence turns their stunning faces to threatening stone.

Common sense would tell me to stop asking questions. These men look like they could kill me in one smack.

But we know my record with common sense.

"Okay, fine." I tap my foot. "Names. At least give me those and I'll finally give you my full name."

Mr. Muscle offers his bear paw, his smile dazzling. "Jace Ryan."

I shake his hand. "Nice to meet you, Jace. But can I still call you Mister Muscle?"

He winks, nodding yes.

Next to these two, I'm a Polly Pocket doll, but they won't break me. They won't even toy with me. They're not like the men who tormented me for a year.

The Pastor comforts the boy in his grasp with a pat on his back. But I don't miss the demonic tattoos smoking over his corded forearms. Or how he stares at me, his gaze flicking to my exposed waist in this crop top, before he rips it away, forcing his glare back to mine.

He doesn't want me here.

But he doesn't want me hurt.

He doesn't want me to stay.

But ... *he wants me.*

Yes, that's this feeling making everyone else in the room disappear while his eyes lock with mine. There's something powerful between us. It's making my pulse race, too.

We feel it.

And I won't break our standoff.

Yes, stubbornness serves me well. I've stared down too many people who had the power to help or hurt me. I'm not afraid to let the silence get so powerful between us, he finally breaks.

"I'm Pastor Sire Rutledge." He nods. "And you're *Wren...?*"

Hope makes me smile. I haven't told anyone my last name yet, and Sire wants it so he can send me back to where I belong, but...

"I'm Wren. Wren *Chapel.*"

I'm not going anywhere.

The Pastor's lips part, realizing I'm right.

I belong with him.

CHAPTER THREE
SIRE

"Bed's there." I point to it. "Extra sheets and towels are in the closet." I point to those. "You got your own bathroom there." I point to everything like Captain Fucking Obvious.

Why? Because I need someplace to look that's not Wren.

Wren *Chapel.*

Jesus, Jesus. Way to make it obvious this is a divine intervention. Or a test of my faith? I don't know yet, but I know I've been thinking about her since we met last week.

"We'll fall in love."

"We'll fall in love."

That luring mantra was the last thing Wren Chapel said to me, and it's echoed through my mind daily.

Okay ... hourly.

Fine. Sometimes more.

Wren said if I touch her, we'll fall in love. It scared the shit out of me—*and I don't get scared*—because it made no fucking sense.

Love doesn't happen like that: with one touch. At least, it

hasn't for me. I just marry other couples, blessing their unions, while denying myself one.

I don't fall in love.

I don't deserve it.

Try as I might, I told myself not to think about the Iron Angel, and ... I didn't listen.

I thought about her all the time.

How she was brave, seeming wise beyond her years. How she had the tattoos of a savior, able to stare down a devil like me. How she wanted to protect me as much as I protected her. How she made me want to confess to her. I never felt so right sharing my wrongs.

I couldn't stop thinking about her beauty, either. I thought about her in ways no man my age should. The urges of every wrong thing I wanted to do to her felt so goddamn right flowing through my cursed veins.

And hard dick.

I've been praying about her all week.

I knew she was safe. My mother would never let anything happen to her, and I don't usually obsess over the victims we help. I focus on the criminals who hurt them and make their lives hell before ending it, promising to meet them there, where I'll do it all over again.

But Wren kept taunting my mind. With worry. With want.

The phantom, throbbing pain where my finger used to be didn't help. I unwrapped my bandage, cleaned my stitches, and didn't regret it. I can still feel my pulse where a part of me should be.

And now that missing part of me has a name.

Wren Chapel.

A name almost as pretty as the small woman standing beside me, proudly wearing it well.

"Put your things in that dresser, use that lamp if you need

it, and give the water a few minutes to heat up before you take a shower. It's an old building."

More obvious shit. More thoughts about her. More prayers I'll be saying for my sanity—and celibacy—for as long as she's here because now I'm wondering...

What would she look like naked in the shower with my cock pumping deep inside her.

Jesus, what did you get me into?

She's a test, isn't she? One my dick fails every time I glance at her. The damn thing spots her little waist peeking between her baggy jeans and that little top, barely revealing her pert tits, too, and the devil in my jeans twitches.

Sure, I was going to hell anyway, but not for this.

Not for wanting her.

"Okay, thanks." She reaches for the handle of her suitcase, all the clothes and toiletries my mom bought her, but half of me isn't depraved. I beat her to it and, like a gentleman, set it on the bed for her. "How can I thank you?"

Banish these damned thoughts from my mind. The ones imagining my tongue licking your wet, virgin pussy.

"You don't need to thank me. Just—" I wave to the simple white room. White paint. White sheets. White linen head-board. Jesus, Jesus. It's like you knew a virgin would move in with me. "Just keep it clean."

Because, clearly, my mind isn't.

"But I have to thank you somehow. I'll earn my keep." She glances at the hardwood floor, laughing, "Do your pet dust bunnies have names?"

I see one hopping by. "Yeah, sorry about that. I really only sleep and eat here. I try to keep it clean, but—"

"Perfect. I'll cook and clean for you and—"

"I don't need a maid."

"But you need to eat." *You.* "So let me cook, and I can babysit the kids at the church, too."

"You like kids? Aren't you practically one yourself?"

That's a cute scowl she makes at my sarcasm. "I love kids and no. I'll be twenty this September eighth."

A smile smacks my face, a chuckle erupting from my throat.

"What did I say?" Her eyes widen. "Why are you laughing?"

"I'm not laughing."

I am. It's rare, and I'm laughing at God.

September 8. Really? The Virgin Mary's birthday?

Okay, God, sign received. I haven't stopped thinking about her since she took my breath away the night I met her, and she has a holy birthday.

Got it. Build a shrine for Wren Chapel and worship her forever. Copy that.

Question is ... if I fuck her, too, will I explode into flames? Probably. But why do I suspect loving her would be worth burning in hell?

"No, you're laughing at me." A smile plays with her luscious lips. "So, be careful when you do because you're cracking that tattoo by your eye."

"That's not a crack. It's a wrinkle. I'm forty-three and I'm laughing because only youth look forward to their next birthday."

"Forty-three?" She scoffs, "You look so young. I pegged you for thirty or so."

Fuck, don't say peg.

Don't say anything that makes me regret being a holy man —half the time.

"I'm way past thirty, and you're all set." I turn toward the door. "Unpack and join me in the kitchen. We'll make a grocery list for tomorrow and ... whatever."

Just get me out of her new bedroom. Get me away from her smelling like pure soap and sin.

No one has ever done this to me. Not my adoring parishioners, throwing themselves at me. Not a hot woman at a coffee shop, twirling her hair. Not a flirting young man, buying me a drink at a bar.

No one, in years, has ever tempted me like Wren Chapel has...

In minutes.

Aiming toward my kitchen, I'm too disciplined and damned, I don't let myself get tempted into—

Fuck, what is this feeling?

Lust. Yes.

No.

No. It's lechery because she's so young.

Maybe her age is why this tight feeling in my pounding chest feels like more. It's why I agreed to let her stay here. I want to protect Wren. I want to keep her safe, and I'll give anything to do it. My pinky. My life.

That's natural. Right? It's noble.

I want to save everyone, and Wren's no different.

I've been this way since I was a kid. One of my first memories is of my brother, Axel. I'm the oldest, and he was born next. I must've been three or so, and I could hear our father hitting our mother, and for the first time, I didn't run to her, begging our father to stop. Unfortunately, those nights are my first memories, too.

But that night, I ran to my brother. He was the most vulnerable, and I stood by his crib, watching him sleep, ready to soothe him if he awoke, scared like me.

It's the first time I remember praying, too. I asked God to protect us from our father, the Devil.

Eventually, he did. We escaped him and the Bratva.

Eventually, the Devil came back for us anyway.

Pressing the button on the machine, I brew a pot of

coffee. My soul is so malformed compared to others; caffeine calms me.

While it brews, I wipe the kids' scribbles off my face with a wet paper towel. Once enough drips into the carafe, I pour a mug full. Black, like my soul, that's how I like my coffee. I sip, praying for an answer.

What can Wren do while she's here? While I find out who's after her, so I can kill them, and let her go home safely, because with the urges I'm fighting, she's not safe with me.

But she says she has no home.

No family either.

I can't imagine. My family *is* my home. My brothers. My mother. They're where I belong. Even though they'll hate me one day. They'll cast me out when they find out what I did, though I did it to protect them.

How was I to know that—

"Ahem."

The gentle noise lifts my gaze from the floor.

Wren's standing on the other side of the white marble island separating the kitchen from the living room.

I love my open-concept loft. It's a modernized, converted space atop a historic, brick mercantile building. An old grave-yard separates the back of this building from my church. My penthouse is in the perfect location, and it's been all the space I've needed.

Until now.

Now, there's not enough space between me and Wren. A continent separating us wouldn't be enough for the forbidden thoughts I have about her.

"Do you have a garbage can?" she asks.

"Is something wrong? Are the dust bunnies that bad?" I take a sip.

"Dust doesn't bother me, but..." She shrugs, smiling. "I'm on my period and I'd prefer not to walk across your pretty place with my used Always Ultra Thin pad wrapped in a bloody wad of toilet paper."

I almost spew my coffee.

"Oh. Okay. Um…" I point toward the sliding door across the kitchen. "There's a little trash can in there, beside the dryer. Use that and, sorry. I'm used to male guests."

She tilts her head. "Boyfriends?"

"No boyfriends. No girlfriends, either." *Don't think it. Don't think it.* "My brother stays here sometimes."

"Jace?" She beams. "He's sweet."

"Yeah, he's sweet until he's not, but he has a place. My baby brother, Loch. He doesn't live here anymore and would crash with me sometimes, but now he has a girlfriend, so…"

Why am I compelled to keep confessing to her? Hell, I already told her my darkest secrets, thinking I'd never see her again.

What are the odds she doesn't remember everything I said?

With her mention of my boyfriends *and* girlfriends? With the way she's looking at me? All cute and cunning?

Not a hot virgin's chance in horny hell.

No, Wren doesn't stare back with her topaz eyes, all innocent and sweet, even though I know she is.

Pure perception. That's what she has, and she punches me with it, so I lean against the countertop.

It's either that, or I start squirming. And do people make me squirm? Fuck no. That's how odd this is. Odd and … interesting.

Nonchalantly, she strolls toward my laundry room, calling over her shoulder, "While I'm here, if you need me to vacate while you add to your body count, just lemme know."

"I'm not *adding* to my body count."

Lies. *I want to add you. Only you. In countless, filthy ways, and with every part of your innocent body.*

Hell is naming a street after me now.

"That's not what you told me in the car." She grabs the garbage can. "You said you fuck men and women, and you need to get kinky about it, and I'm not judging."

"What do YOU know about kink?"

Yep, she does remember, and ... Dick, I can't believe you just asked that. You're going to get us in trouble.

"I'm a virgin, not a prude." She turns back, hugging the small white pail to her chest, dangerously stepping my way. "I'm not shook over your bisexuality. I mean, maybe I'm bi, too. I don't know. I haven't tried anything yet, but when I get really horny, I watch hard core porn and masturbate to all kinds of kinky fantasies and—"

Holy.

Fucking.

Hell.

Her mouth.

Is heaven.

And I'm dying for it.

"Jesus," I sigh, "do you know what a filter is?"

She smiles, nodding toward my machine. "For coffee, yes. For my mouth? Sorry, I've tried, but they don't exist. Why? Am I offending you? Are you like closeted or...?"

Her face falls, disappointed. "Please don't tell me you're one of those hypocritical, hateful pastor pricks. I grew up around them, and I *really* liked you, but if that's who you—"

"I'm not. Our congregation is inclusive."

"Are you out with them?"

"I'm their *pastor*."

"And?"

"And it doesn't matter. I don't fuck my flock. That would be a moral failure."

"So, who do you fuck?"

Jesus, Jesus. "Again. You, needing a filter."

Her brows lift. "And you, being a grown-ass man. Why be ashamed? You have needs. We all do."

"Yeah, I need to know who you're running from."

"I'm not running." She tilts her head, winking. "I'm relocating."

My molars clench. Wren might seem wise beyond her years, but this? She has no fucking clue how dark the world can be.

"Don't play games with me, Wren. I said you could stay, and I'll protect you until you're safe. But you make it hard if I don't know who the threat is."

Really hard.

Shut up, Dick.

"Just consider all men, but *you*, a threat and kill them if they come for me." With a swish, she walks across the living room to the hallway leading to our bedrooms, which are—fuck my life, not her—right next to each other.

"Where are you going? We need to make a grocery list."

I need not watch her sweet ass sway.

"Just a sec," she chirps over her shoulder. "My pussy is about to be a bloody crime scene if I don't change my pad."

Dear Lord, please strike Dick down, and her mouth closed. You know what I just thought ... and the Devil is proud.

A few minutes later, Wren returns to the kitchen, and I have to force the most taboo thoughts out of my mind, focusing on something else.

"Coffee?"

"Sure." She opens my refrigerator. In my periphery, while I grab a mug, I catch her pulling back, shocked. "You said you grocery shop."

"I do. Three times a week."

"Milk, vegetables, salad greens, and half of a rotisserie chicken carcass? These aren't groceries. They're farm supplies."

She makes me laugh. "No, they're healthy choices. Milk and sugar?"

"Lots of sugar with a cup of milk and a splash of coffee, please."

I prepare her cup, phantom pain throbbing in my pinky, taboo thoughts throbbing in my dick. Damn, it's like a horny demon possesses me as she starts jotting items on the pad of paper I set out. And she keeps jotting. And jotting. And...

"I don't usually get that hungry." I hand her a steaming mug of cavities.

"Who would? No one is starving for a salad." She takes the mug, smiling. "Thank you."

Innocently, her fingertips brush my bandage.

But it's the soft, intentional way she pauses, gazing down at my wound for her; it does something to my heart.

It flips.

I didn't know it could fucking do that. I didn't know I could feel every right and wrong thing for a person so goddamn fast—forget my world—it's making my soul spin.

Before she takes a sip, she offers, "I think you'll love the taste of my recipes."

Mind: don't even.

I glance down at the grocery list. Apparently, I'm opening a restaurant. "Who taught you how to cook?"

Slowly, I'll gather the intel on her and where she came from, so she can go right back, before I do something I'll always and never regret.

"YouTube, necessity, and Nannie."

"You said you don't have grandparents."

After a tentative sip, she shares, "I don't. I was raised in foster care. I've been placed in over eleven homes, and my last one was with Nannie. I was seventeen and she was going to adopt me. But then..."

Her voice trails.

"Then what? She changed her mind?"

"She died."

The soul-lifting smile Wren's worn since she exploded into my life tonight falls with her gaze to the floor.

Arousal abandoned me the moment she said *foster care*, and now all that remains thundering through my veins is compassion for her.

This is where it comes from. Her wisdom. Her strength. Her sadness. Her habit of smiling through the pain.

The Iron Angel.

"I'm so sorry, Wren."

She grins, swiping a tear away. "Nannie wouldn't want me wallowing."

"But you're allowed to grieve her."

"I did. That was two years ago, and I celebrate her by cooking her recipes."

But I'm doing the math, and it's heartbreaking. "How long were you in foster care?"

She steps away, shaking her head. "You can't send me back into the system. I aged out. I'm on my own now. No one can make me—"

"Wren, I'm not..." *Fuck this.* I set my mug down and surrender my hands. "I won't send you back to wherever. I promise. You can stay here, and I'll protect you, but from who? I need to know. How did you end up with *that* man in *that* auction? He sells to the most powerful men in the world. Politicians. Royalty. CEOs. You're lucky I was there."

I stare at the bottom of her white mug while she stares at me, draining her cup. *Fuck, she's doing it again.* She's seeing way too much about me with those stunning eyes.

Lowering her mug, she licks her lips. "You killed him, didn't you?"

I cross one ankle over the other—that's my answer.

"I hope you killed him," she adds. "I hope you killed all of those men."

"You hope you're living with a killer?"

"A killer who kills men like that? This is my cup of care." She flips her mug over. "Oh, look. It's empty."

She mirrors me, leaning against the island countertop, crossing her arms and ankles.

"So," she grins. "Here we are."

"Here we are." I grin, too.

"So, now what?"

"Now. *What?*"

Her eyes narrow. "Who are you *really*, Sire?"

"Who are you really, *Wren?*"

"My lips are sealed."

"Teach that to your mouth. It needs a filter."

The way she twists those plump lips, half amused, half annoyed with me...

Damn, if she weren't so young, I'd claim that gorgeous, fucking mouth. I'd take every virgin inch of her, inside and out, and never give them back.

She'd be mine.

All mine.

To show off.

To fill.

To breed.

These are not the thoughts of a holy man. But there's been a hole in my dark heart for as long as I can remember, and my evil father is the one who dug it so fucking deep.

I've prayed for a way to fill it.

That man, with his dark heart, thanks to his evil father, wants to deflower and defile this young woman in every filthy way possible. He's a beast. He shouldn't be let out of his cage. He shouldn't be near her.

But *this man?*

The one who prayed and found another father in God? The one whose mother taught him how to love and protect, how tenderness is strength? The one whose brothers give him a family he fights for?

This man can see that he's staring down at the most stunning woman he's ever seen. Poems and proverbs are written for the way he feels looking at her.

She rips his breath away.

Long, thick, dark, curly hair, sweeping to her tiny waist. Deep olive, or is it tawny brown skin? Thick, striking brows. A button nose. Her light freckles, a constellation across her high cheekbones. Pink pillow lips and an elfin chin.

Wren's beauty belongs in an ancient century, a testament to a sacred world long ago, her thick eyelashes shrouding an old soul.

Sure, there's a wounded child in her topaz eyes, but he has one too.

Maybe we all do.

So, this man?

He uncrosses his arms and ankles, closing the distance between them.

She's so small, gazing up at his approach, her lips parting, unsure of what he'll do, but her eyes staring, unafraid of him.

The electricity between them, undeniable. The pull to her, magnetic. Their worlds, divined to collide.

Pecking her forehead, this man says, "Welcome home, Wren Chapel."

And then I turn to go to bed before the beast regrets ever touching her again.

CHAPTER FOUR
SIRE

Harboring an innocent woman should give me peace.

Right?

Wrong, and welcome to my world.

Especially after thoughts of Wren kept me and Dick up all night, only to find another manila envelope on the floor by my locked, steel door this morning.

My fucking father.

This is how he communicates with me, and he's not even the one leaving the envelopes.

No, Ruslan Kholodov, the head of Russian Bratva, is probably kicking back in his compound in Moscow while I have to deal with this shit. He gets one of his soldiers to leave me a note, like we're some goddamn pen pals and not mortal enemies.

I could kill my abusive father a million times, but he has my mother in his crosshairs. He has my brothers, too. He's found us, and I'm the only one who knows, so I play along.

I keep us safe.

Swiping the envelope from the floor, I rip it open. It's a clipping from *The Palm Beach Post* newspaper from four days ago. An article about a headless body found washed ashore on South Palm Beach. The remains have been identified as those of a hedge fund manager from New York City, who was renting a vacation home nearby.

Yep, this was my work. My rage. I'm usually not so sloppy, but that man touched Wren. He wanted to violate her before selling her, and Axel couldn't stop me.

No one can when I want vengeance.

Under this article, there's another about a golf tournament on Hilton Head Island in three months.

The client list.

The powerful, predatory men trafficking girls, and the ways they hide their evil enterprise.

Don't ask me why my father sends me clues. Why, when he kidnapped and trafficked my mother, is he sending me intel about monsters like him?

Is he gloating?

Or feeling guilty?

I don't give a damn; innocent girls are at stake, so I follow the clues.

Sometimes, I get intel from my parishioners. A few are undocumented, the most vulnerable to exploitation, and they give me names and ways to help others like them. Other times, I get these taunting letters from my father, likely delivered by his Sovietnik, Viktor.

Viktor is my father's advisor, and it's as if they're praising my work. Like my gruesome vengeance is a kid's drawing you proudly hang on your refrigerator.

I rip it to shreds before washing it down the sink with dish soap and the metallic whirl of the disposal.

This is how I found Wren. My father sent me an article about a golf tournament in Palm Beach, sponsored by the hedge fund manager's firm. I put the rest together.

How did Wren get mixed up with those men? She's been

in my home for less than twelve hours, and I'm ready to wage a war over her.

Grabbing my phone, I don't care that it's just after five in the morning, I call Axel.

"Yeah." He sounds annoyed, not awakened.

"You already up?"

"Yeah, I'm going for a run."

"Since when do you run and not lift?"

"Since I fucking feel like it. Hurry up. It's five twenty. I gotta go."

"Where?"

"Where you stop asking me so many fucking questions. What do you need?"

To annoy the shit out of my little brothers. Especially Axel. He's in charge because I didn't want it, but I want this. Giving him hell is fun.

"Careful. Penis chafing is common when you run. Especially if you're running with a third leg, I should know."

"Goddamnit, Sergei. *What?*"

When he uses my real name, I've really pissed him off. *God bless him.* I laugh. "When you're done being Usain Bolt, come to the church, and bring Nash."

"I have court at nine."

"After that."

"Copy." He hangs up.

But I need more than Axel and Nash to help me protect Wren. I hate doing this, but I have to get to church before the preschool opens, and I can't leave her at risk.

Gently, I knock on her bedroom door. "Wren? It's me ... Sire."

No shit, Dick. Who else would it be?

"Wren?" I repeat.

"Just a sec." Her voice sounds rushed before her door swings open. "Yeah?"

I'm going to hell.

The blood surging to my dick is instant. It swells so fast, I'm dizzy. Hastily, she's holding a white bath towel around her naked body, her hair a sexy, untamed mane, her eyes wide and worried.

She should be.

For a second, I'm not a pastor who'll protect her. I'm an animal, and she's my mate; the instincts are overwhelming.

"Is something wrong?"

"Pajamas" is all I can utter because they're all that's missing in this moment. Everything else is here. Everything I want to take and fuck and own.

"I don't have any," she sighs, "and I need to do laundry because my bras and panties are dirty and—"

"Fuck," I mutter, turning around. "Hang on."

Dick, I swear, if you think about her panties and how dirty you can make her. You just did. *Shut up.*

Storming toward my closet, I snap one of a dozen dress shirts off a hanger. "Here." I shove it at her when I meet her back in the hallway.

"Uh, thanks." She takes it. "What's going on?"

"I'm going to work, and you need a phone."

Her face falls. "Okay, um. I can save up for one as quickly as I can and—"

"Fuck," I mutter, turning around again. "Hang on."

Stupidity is an affliction, and I have the virus around her. Usually, I'm ten steps ahead in any game, but around Wren's naked body in a bath towel, I want to drop to my knees and rip that towel open, losing the rest of my mind and mouth in her pussy.

Fishing through my nightstand's drawer, I grab a white box. There's enough charge on this new phone for me to enter my number, Jace's, and who else? Axel? No, he gives off dickish vibes when really, he's a giant kitten.

So, who?

Nash! He's a dad. Alena, his daughter, is twenty-something. If Wren's in trouble, Nash will know what to do because I feel like a stallion and Wren's the filly in heat, brought into my barn stall to breed. Only my body works around her, not my brain.

"Here." I hand her the device.

"An iPhone?" Her eyes widen like it's Christmas. "And it's *new?*"

"I put my number and Jace's in there. Also, Nash. He's one of us. Call us if you need anything while I'm gone."

She considers the gleaming gift before her narrowing stare meets mine. "A new iPhone? And you just happen to have one in your bedroom?"

"Yeah."

"How many do you keep?"

"Too many for you to ask about."

"Do you have guns?"

"Do you like living?"

While I was loading contacts in her new phone, she put on my dress shirt. I know some pills make a man's dick hard for hours, but I'm hoping there's one that makes you flaccid for days because Wren's tawny skin in my white shirt is the goddamn sexiest thing I've ever seen. And I belong to a fetish factory in Atlanta. I've seen everything.

"So, you have burner phones, guns, and probably bags of cash lying around." She crosses her arms. "Do you have an extra AR I can use?"

"First, don't burn that phone. Apple has enough of my money. Second, I'll leave you a hundred dollars a day. Let me know if you need more. And third, who taught you how to shoot an AR?"

Her voice lilts. "YouTube?"

"Wren."

"What? They even have videos teaching you how to sneeze."

I raise a brow.

She raises hers.

"Do you know how to use a Glock?"

Her eyes light up. "Yes."

"Can you do it without turning my sheetrock into Swiss cheese?"

"Run a zig-zag pattern and I'll show you."

Goddamn, she's hot when she's a smartass.

"Alright. I'll leave you a phone, a gun, and some cash. Try not to start a drug empire while I'm gone."

"I'm going with you."

"You're cute when you're mistaken."

"You're crazy when you think I'll stay here all day."

I shake my head, torn between keeping her safe by my side or relocating her to a remote convent on a cliff in Italy. "You can't go to church with me. How will I explain who you are?"

"I'll be a family friend."

I laugh. "My family doesn't *have* friends."

"Liar," she scoffs. "I've met Jace. He could make a corpse catch feelings."

She's right about my brothers—most of them. Jace, Grant, Nick, and Loch could charm a teenager into giving up their phone. Forever. While me, Axel, and Nash? We'd just take the damn thing and tell them to quit finger-fucking it. Either works.

"Look," Wren sighs. "Honestly, I'm a little afraid to be left by myself until I know my way around. So, just give me the lay of the land around here and I'll be fine."

"Escape routes." I nod. "You're always looking for them, aren't you?"

"I can't sleep in a room with no windows, or with my back to a door. Not since I was nine."

Letting Wren see how she wraps around my heart with each tiny confession of her story would be a big risk. A reveal. A regret I don't want to have because each one pulls me even closer to her.

"Okay. We leave in thirty."

"What's my story if someone asks?"

"Our moms are best friends. They went to college together, and ... uh ..." Fuck, I've never done this. To most, I have no family. The less I say, the better. "And you're visiting Charleston, deciding if you want to go to college here."

Her head tilts. "There's no way our moms could be the same age."

"Say you're adopted. Always use parts of the truth to sell a lie." She glances away. "Wren, we have to come up with something. No one can know how we met."

"Or who we *are*," she mutters, and I don't answer. After a deep inhale, she chirps, "Okay. What's your mom's name?"

"Nadine."

"Ms. Faye?" Her eyes widen. "I knew it!"

I don't answer that part, either. "Use my last name with hers; Nadine Rutledge from Pickens, South Carolina. It's my cover story. And your mom and origin?"

"Dolly," she blurts. "Dolly Parker from Chattanooga. That's my mom."

"Tennessee? Is that where you're from?"

"Close enough. I've been there before, so I can bullshit the rest."

I search her eyes, trying to figure out her tell. For such an honest creature with no filter, how will I know when she's lying? And when will she trust she doesn't have to lie to me?

Mine are much worse.

On the way to the church, I show her the code to my

door, the iron gate to the graveyard behind my building, and the prettiest path through the historic headstones.

Does it grab my heart again how she names the flowers and comments on the families buried together? Yeah. Because I can't bear to think of her lying alone under blue hydrangeas for eternity.

By the time we emerge on Church Street, cars are queued for the preschool dropoff, and Ms. Davis, our director, stands on the sidewalk with worry written across her brow.

"What's wrong?" I approach her with Wren on my heels.

"I'm down an assistant in the infant room."

"Again?"

"It's that stomach bug," she answers. "It's going through everyone, and I need one staff per five infants, and we have two for twelve."

"I'll do it," Wren chirps. "I'm CPR trained. Even did a Red Cross babysitting class years back."

Ms. Davis darts her eyes from me to Wren. I make the introductions, but she's too stressed to question Wren's origin. She just worries, "Thank you, dear. You're sweet to offer, but I need licensed providers."

Wren's shoulders fall, and we have a line of parents in their cars looking pissed off. Childcare is the biggest source of revenue for the church, and I wouldn't wish angry moms on hell's demons.

"Just for today, let her help," I suggest. "I can vouch for her until we can find someone by tomorrow."

Playfully, Ms. Davis backhands my arm. "You and the rules, Pastor Rutledge. You sure do like to bend them."

I wink. "Just as long as we don't break God's rules, we're good."

I leave Wren in the capable hands of Ms. Davis while I assist the teachers with the older kids as they settle into their rooms for the day.

Then, I duck into the chapel and meet with our Music Director. We review the run-of-show for my Sunday sermon while I tune my guitar and practice a few songs before heading to my office to answer emails.

While drafting my sermon, I'm tempted to check on Wren, but it would insult her. She's an adult. She's made it this far on her own. But how?

ONE

Outside

It's Axel's text. We use numbers on phones, not names. I walk outside to find him and Nash, number two, leaning against the iron fence outside the chapel.

Axel smirks. "Heard you have a new roommate."

Nash mirrors him. "Heard she only wanted *you*."

I scowl. "And you heard she's nineteen and won't tell us how she wound up in Palm Beach. But she says it's not safe for her to go home, wherever that is, and I want to know who the fuck kidnapped her."

I'm getting aggravated. I know my family and I can protect Wren from anyone.

Anyone, except the one in our family who's the most vicious man I know, and why did he point me in the direction of Wren?

"There's a golf tournament in Hilton Head in three months," I tell them. "Somehow, it's connected to Palm Beach."

"What's your source?"

Axel always asks. He's a lawyer. He's also my brother, who trusts me, though he shouldn't. He's the reason for the broken heart on my face, the brother I betrayed.

This wicked game I play with our father is eating my soul alive.

"A parishioner," I answer. "She has a sister in Hilton Head, cleaning rental properties, and that's how they're running the girls. Through men, staying in rentals, under the guise of golf tournaments."

It's not a total lie. I did get that intel last month, but now, thanks to the Devil, I know they're connected.

"Claude Owen Turner the Third." Nash nods. "Hilton Head was his ring until he was busted along with that piece-of-shit Senator Gentry Evans, and now Turner's son has taken over. The Queen told me she heard about him through a source at the club."

The Queen is our mother, Nadine Faye.

The club is the exclusive sex club she owns north of town.

And we, her sons, the kings, honor her by hunting down men like our father.

"So, Turner and Palm Beach are connected," Axel adds it up. "Alright. We took out Palm Beach; Turner's next."

Dear God, I feel a murderous rage. Mix our father with sex traffickers touching my Iron Angel, and no living being with a pulse is safe near me.

I seethe, "I want to know how *Wren* got caught in their net."

"*Wren?*" The smile on Axel's face is rare. "What a pretty name for a hot woman."

"You hear how he says it, too?" Nash elbows him. "I hear wedding bells."

I swear, these fuckers timed that. The bell on my church's chapel chimes eleven times while their shit-eating grins eat up every strike.

"No," I snarl once it's done. "That was my soul being eternally damned for the way I can't stop thinking about her."

Nash huffs, "We're already damned. Might as well get what you want before you go to hell."

His hypocrisy amuses me. "Will you be taking your advice, Mr. Allen?"

Nash's face falls. We all know he's in love with Vale, his daughter's best friend, but he won't lay a hand on her. It's been years, and Vale's almost thirty, and Nash still lusts for her from afar.

"Besides," I add. "I just met her."

"Yeah, and in ten minutes, you sacrificed a finger for her," Axel corrects. "Sometimes it happens that way. You meet a woman and in an instant you know she's your future queen."

Your queen.

His certainty speaks to me.

Each brother must find one; that's our tradition. Axel tried, but his first queen betrayed him. She left him.

While me? I used to believe I'd find my queen, but my father found me first. So, I made a deal with him, and now I don't deserve a queen. Especially one too innocent to claim.

No, Wren deserves to be safe.

I give Axel the intel I have on her. "Search child services in Tennessee for the past eighteen years. Find her records. Check the Pigeon Forge area." Axel looks confused. "Just do it. She sort of mentioned Dolly Parton, and I have a hunch."

"And you." I turn to Nash. "Look into this Turner fucker in Hilton Head. Check everyone who played in the Palm Beach tournament to see if any trace back to Tennessee."

"And you," Axel slaps my back, "look in the fucking mirror, because I've never seen you this worried for a woman."

Nash slaps my back, too. "You mean ... we've never seen him falling in love with his future queen."

My glare shifts between them. "Do not regard him as an enemy, but warn him as a brother that—"

"*And* he's quoting scripture." Axel pulls away, laughing, "I'm out."

"See ya." Nash laughs, turning away, too.

For the rest of the day, my thoughts are swimming. My

confusion deepens. I'm searching for an answer to what it means as I work my way toward the preschool building, ready to help with pick-up.

But I'm stopped in my tracks at the sight on the sidewalk, standing in the dappled sunlight, under an oak draped in Spanish moss.

Wren Chapel.

Holding a swaddled infant in her arms.

In an instant, I'm convinced Axel was right—you know your queen, your wife, when you see her.

The light flooding my dark heart is like none I've ever felt. This is stuff prayers beg for, and it can't be real.

It can't be this simple.

Easily, Wren chats with Ms. Davis. Naturally, she bounces, soothing the baby. Quickly, she must feel me staring as she turns my way ... and smiles.

Jesus, Jesus.

Okay, you're convinced she's the one, but I'm not.

CHAPTER FIVE
WREN

HOME.

I haven't stopped thinking about that word. That moment. That soft peck on my forehead.

That was last night, and I swear Sire's innocent kiss still ghosts my skin. *Welcome home, Wren Chapel.* He'll never know what that meant to me.

Everything.

Like everything I lost.

He chomps on an apple he grabbed in the produce section. "Do you need more Always pads?" Smiling, he casually points down the personal-care aisle of the grocery store.

Uh, what made Mr. Grumpy suddenly so sweet?

I haven't seen him all day. It flew by while I took care of babies, and I loved it. I was in my element.

But this? It's weird. It's like he's been smoking heavenly weed. He's all smiling and shit.

He's been looking at me that way since he met me in the preschool pick-up line. Sweetly, he took the baby from my arms like it was his, too, and I don't want to read into it.

But I do.

"I'm good," I answer.

"Motrin?"

"Got it. But I need this." I grab a container of feta cheese. "It's for your salads."

"I don't put cheese on my salads."

"You do now."

He chuckles. "Just keep it healthy."

"Peach cobbler is healthy. Right?"

"Wrong."

I reach for a box of butter sticks. And another. "If it's fruit, it's healthy. If it's covered in butter, it's even better."

He grins, eyeing the baking goods I've loaded in the grocery cart. But don't think I missed all the eyes on him today.

It's not like you can ignore Sire. His height. His ink. His broad shoulders tapering to his narrow waist. He can't hide the muscles under his hot combo of tight, grey dress pants, a loose V-neck T-shirt, and bright white sneakers.

He's got a style you can't ignore.

A body demanding your eyes.

A face possessing your soul.

People on the sidewalk greeted him on our stroll here. Cashiers waved when we entered the store. The manager rushed over to shake his hand. "Evenin', Pastor Rutledge." The lady in the bakery offered him a sample of salted brownies ... and silently, her pussy if she could serve it on a platter, too.

Everyone knows him. Most want him. All worship him and eye me with suspicion, even though he's politely introducing me as "Wren, a family friend."

"Guess we should keep your last name hush-hush." He teases, "Since you're in hiding and all."

From the bottom shelf, I grab the cheapest bag of sugar. "Puhlease. Like you aren't hiding, too." Not answering, he takes it, puts it back, grabs a bag of organic sugar, so I chuckle, "*And* that's what I thought."

From the middle shelf, I select the cheapest bottle of vanilla extract and add it to our cart. He puts it back, grabbing the most expensive kind, with his question, "Where did you get good instincts?"

"Nice try." I use the bottom shelf as a step to reach the baking chocolate bar on the top shelf. "I'm not telling you where I'm from. Remember?"

But it's my constant struggle. I'm too short, and who puts shit up this high? Stretching, I use sheer will to make my fingers grow two inches longer, my toes teetering on the edge of the shelf.

"Let me grab that."

His big hand steadies my waist, making me gasp. His touch, warm and soft, his masculine scent wrapping around me. His gruff voice tickles my ear as he reaches over me for the chocolate bar. "You're going to tell me everything about you, Wren Chapel. Because you know too much about me, and your instincts are right; that's a dangerous thing."

Instantly, he pulls away, leaving my heart racing from his threat, his touch.

I step off the shelf and whip around to find his indigo eyes warning me.

"Fine." I glance down the aisle. We're alone, but I lower my voice. "You want to know something about me? Okay. A social worker named me. It's in my records. She wrote that I looked like an abandoned baby bird and named me Wren. And I got my last name because that's what they usually do with orphans. We're named after where we're found. Dix Chapel. Thank God I got the second name."

His brows bend. "You were left in a chapel?"

"Yep. Wrapped in a blanket and left on a pew, and no one's ever claimed me, and I don't know where I'm from.

Brazil? Morocco? Lebanon? I've heard it all. 'You're so pretty. Are you Cherokee?' and I can't answer because I don't know, which makes for really sad conversations because it's none of their damn business that no one wanted me, so yeah. That's me, in an unknown nutshell." I fold my arms. "Your turn."

He swallows the last bite of his apple, his eyes darkening, but I don't back down. I arch a brow.

"My father was an abusive and powerful man," he shares. "When I was thirteen, my mom finally escaped him, and my brothers and I have been hiding here, with her, under different names ever since. That's me, in a hidden nutshell."

"*Was?* Is he dead?"

"I'll kill him one day."

"That's not very godly of you."

"Oh," he smirks, "God *wants* me to kill him. He deserves it."

I'm not shocked or scared. Oddly, I've never felt as safe as I do, standing in Sire's shadow. "Is your father the Devil? The one you mentioned when you rescued me?"

"It doesn't bother you? That I'm going to kill another man?"

"Way to change the subject and no. It doesn't bother me. Grow up like I did—unwanted—and you realize there are no rights or wrongs. Just survival."

"Damn, Wren." He shakes his head. "With every minute you talk, I want to kill whoever hurt you. You know that, right?" His voice drops, ominous and lethal. "I'm going to *kill* him. Whoever tried to sell you into that hell. God has told me to do it."

"I know and that's why I'm not telling you his name." Rage curls his lip, but I chirp, "So, where did you get *your* name?"

"Way to change the subject."

"Tit for tat. So, what are you? An equestrian?" I scan his

impressive form. "A sire is a stallion, right? One used for breeding, and you were named after one?"

With a sexy laugh, his rage evaporates. "*Sire* is also what you call a king."

There's a new, electric edge to him tonight—I don't know what's changed between us in twenty-four hours—but I want to dance on it.

With the extreme way we met, this feels fated, even fun, our layers quickly falling away. I'm not hiding where I'm from to play games with him. It's to honor the one good person in my life so far.

The one good person ... before I met Sire.

I'm not afraid to be with him. In fact, something tells me to tempt him if I have to.

"But *stallion* fits you, doesn't it?" I let him witness my stare, boldly dropping to the bulge in his pants, my eyes groping his size. *God, is it growing?* I bite my lip. It scares and seduces me. "You *are* a sire."

I lift my eyes from his swelling package and meet his evil smirk. It's like he's two men—a pastor and a predator. It's so hot and haunting, that sweet spot between my legs tingles.

The heated look in his eyes traps me against the shelves. It reaches down between my clenched thighs, covered by jeans, grabbing my sex.

He leans forward, looming over me. "Oh, my innocent angel." The deep timbre of his voice finds the tiny bud on my body I love to play with. "You don't want to know how *hugely* fitting my name is."

"What if I *do*?"

There.

I said it.

I know what he did last night. The walls between our bedrooms are paper-thin. Same as our bathrooms. I could hear him in the shower, and again, an hour later, in his bed. His muffled, manly grunts of lust made my insides flutter.

The need rushing through my body was unbearable. My legs opened, and I did the same thing, but I couldn't be as quiet. The pillow couldn't muffle my scream. I've never had a huge orgasm like that.

Did he hear me?

I never had a man in my mind. *Sire*. A name on my lips. *Sire*. A desire so painful, I had to satisfy it. *Sire*. He was all I could think about while I came so hard, it hurt.

It only made me more certain I belong with him.

"No way, Wren." His face suddenly softens, his voice, too. "You don't want me. You're too young."

I glare. "Funny, I'm not too young for other things. Like joining the Army and killing people or dying for my country. Let me ask you something personal."

"In the middle of a fucking grocery store?" He grins. "Shoot. It hasn't stopped you so far."

"Do you believe I have a right to choose what happens to my body? If I get pregnant? If I get cancer? Good or bad, do you believe I'm capable of making those decisions for myself?"

He steps back. "Of course, I do."

"Anything and everything because it's my body, right?"

"Right."

"Then don't insult me and all women and treat us like a cafeteria line."

"A what?" He half chuckles.

"A cafeteria line where you pick and choose when I get to make decisions for myself. It doesn't work that way. It's not logical. A woman either has complete power over her body or none. Otherwise, it's patriarchal bullshit."

His eyes sparkle. "So, you're a feminist?"

"A woman is a fool not to fight for herself, and Nannie was

a feminist, too. Old school. She marched for me to be able to stand here and tell you to go fuck yourself if you try to tell me what to do with my body. Which ... by the way ... wants to fuck you. I want you to be my first."

"Jesus, Jesus," he mutters.

"Amen."

The pause he gives, searching my eyes, gives me hope.

I know this is right. I've felt it every moment in his presence; *I belong with Sire.*

And maybe this is the mark of my youth; I'm impatient. My lonely heart won't survive a slow burn. Or maybe, I've been adrift my whole life, and he's my shore. You don't wait to save your life; you grab safety the moment you have it. Or maybe I want Sire so much, my stomach falls as he shakes his head.

"It can't happen, Wren, and there are a dozen reasons why." Pain creases the line cracking the already broken heart by his eye. "Sorry."

"Fine," I sigh. "Just don't tell me I don't know what I want. I heard what you did last night, twice, so don't insult me and tell me you don't want it, too."

He doesn't look mad, and I'm not angry, either. It's odd. Honestly, it's like neither one of us has the power to decide; it's been decided for us. We belong together.

"What I *want* is on the next aisle." He turns, walking away. "Right by the coffee, I want to find a filter for your mouth."

But I wait by our cart.

Not embarrassed.

Not shy.

Not wrong, either.

I wait for him to turn around and smile. "What are you waiting for?"

Sweetly, I smile back. "You."

He has to feel this. I know he does. He says it can't happen when it already has. We're already together.

He pulls up short, breathing like he's silently praying on what to do next.

Then...

He beckons with his bandaged hand. "Come with me, Wren Chapel. God knows I want that, too."

CHAPTER SIX
SIRE

THIS WOMAN IS GIVING ME SIGNS EVERYWHERE, DESIRES I can't handle, and dreams I never want to wake from.

But I do.

The sun hasn't risen, but something startles me awake—a noise. From under the empty pillow beside mine, I grab my Glock.

With my gun held low, I open my bedroom door. Across the hallway alcove, I spot hers is closed, so I peek around the corner into my living room.

Who the fuck is in here?

The pendant lights over my kitchen island glow. I left them on in case Wren woke up. There's a rustling by my front door. So help me God, if it's one of my father's soldiers with a note.

It draws me nearer...

My finger on the trigger...

My vision, tunneling...

The moment she steps into view, I heave an exhale, "God-damn, it's you."

Wren looks my way, not even startled. "Of course, it's me. I'm cooking you breakfast. Oh, and doing your laundry."

No, she's barefoot and wearing my shirt with her hair twisted in a messy bun, tendrils falling. It's a ravishing sight that pisses me off.

"It's six in the morning." My stomach growls with me, "I'm not hungry. And *stop* doing my laundry."

"It's just your underwear." She shrugs. Grabbing a spatula by the stove, she points to a barstool at the island. "Sit. Your eggs are almost ready."

"If you're out here, why is your bedroom door closed?"

She looks away.

It's odd, so I follow my instincts. Pushing her door open, I find her bed made, her room immaculate. Her suitcase is open on top of it, with her clothes neatly packed. She's even washed the bath towel she used and left it folded on the closet shelf.

I storm back her way. "Why is all your shit packed? You going somewhere?"

She wears an innocent face. "No, I just never unpacked."

"Why?"

"Lesson learned the hard way. Several times."

It never ends with her, the falling I feel. "You can unpack. I won't make you leave. This is your home now."

"It is until I make you mad."

"Too late. I've been royally fucking fuming since you returned, but you don't see me kicking you out because you won't tell me who's after you."

"Yeah." She waves her spatula at the gun in my hand. "I won't tell you because you'll go all gangster on him."

"Who?" I seethe, and she rolls her eyes.

"Like I'll crack like an egg. Speaking of..." She points at the barstool again. "Sit or yours will get cold."

I don't know what it is, but I'm drawn her way. I take a

seat and set my gun down, waiting for my pulse to lower, but it won't.

No, everything rises around her, so I'm thankful to hide it under the marble countertop.

First, her scrambled eggs are the best I've ever tasted. Then, she hits me with bacon that I never eat, so I devour seven pieces. Finally, she puts a nail in my culinary coffin with a warm muffin, a pat of butter melting where she sliced it open. It goes great with the perfect cup of coffee she brewed for me, too.

"Zucchini muffins with shredded carrots and organic, dark chocolate chips," she shares with a bite of muffin in her mouth. "That's healthy, right?"

"It's fucking delicious." I spew crumbs before using the napkin she hands to me. "Nannie's recipe?"

"Yeah, but I added the carrots for you." She peers at my loaded gun on the island, not afraid, curious.

"Nannie teach you to shoot?"

"No. She kept a loaded shotgun but hated it."

"So, who taught you?" Taking my empty plate, she won't look at me. "Wren." Gently, I grab her wrist. "*Who* taught you how to shoot?"

"What makes you think I can shoot?"

The way her skin is so goddamn soft in my grasp sends a hot jolt through me.

"You said you could." So, I let her go. Sliding my gun her way, I command, "Clear the round in the chamber, release the clip, then reload it." Her eyes narrow. "Show me you know how to handle a weapon, and I'll answer a question."

Lightning fast, she sets my plate down and grabs the gun. I've never been so aroused in my life watching a woman handle a weapon as well as she wields a spatula, too.

Holy hell, she's fast, deft, and smiling as her hands pop the round out of the chamber, her trigger finger releasing the clip. Checking it, she slams it back in before racking a fresh round and setting the ready weapon before me.

"There." She smiles. "Now ... how did you lose your virginity?"

Laughter explodes before I can stop it. "*That's* what you want to know about me?"

She flits her hand at my Glock. "You're a man of God *and* a gangster. A good gangster, and so is your brother. Mystery solved. I want to know about sex. *Your* sex."

"Where did you learn how to handle guns?"

She puts my plate in the sink. "Answer my question first, and I'll tell you. Oh, and tell me both. Your first with a woman *and* a man."

God, you're laughing, aren't you? It's amusing she wants to know this. That she has the lady balls to ask. That I'm getting even harder telling her.

"I was sixteen, and it was at the same time." She blinks, confused. "I mean, it was the three of us together. They were a couple. He was my best friend, and she was his girlfriend."

She needs to stop chewing her lip like that.

Covertly, I adjust myself.

"She came on to me," I continue, "and he didn't get mad. They'd talked about it. They were seniors and eighteen and had more experience than me. We were at her house, her parents weren't there, and she started making out with me. It got me hard and he started giving me a hand job, so I started kissing him, too, and—"

"Did you know you were bi before that?"

"Tough to say. If you knew my life before, I didn't have time to think about sex. I was too busy surviving."

The way she nods, understanding. These surging feelings for her swell my heart even bigger.

"So, I had my first with her, and an hour later, my first with him. Honestly, I was so excited just to have the chance to fuck, I didn't question why I wanted both of them; I just did."

"Were you top or bottom?"

I chuckle. "How do you know about that?"

"How can I not? That's the difference between our generations. I'm not uptight about sex. All sex. It's everywhere online. I'm used to it."

"I'm not uptight, either. Never was." I point between us. "But there's a big difference between watching a screen and sharing something real."

"Okay, so do you top or bottom when it's real? I mean... with a man?"

"Funny, how people always want to know that, and... that's sounding like a second question when it's your turn to answer mine."

She starts washing the dishes. "The home I was placed in before Nannie; they were preppers. They believed only God, guns, and canned goods could protect them from Armageddon or the Russians."

I snort. I can't help it. *If she only knew.*

"So, we homeschooled, hunted, and went to church. Every day."

"How long were you there?" I want to help her wash up, but Dick won't deflate. He sees her hard nipples under my shirt.

"Five years."

"Huh." I pull back. "All that time, and they didn't want to adopt you?"

She shakes her head. Now, I'm the naive one. "If you're lucky, you get a family like that. For the rest of us, it's about the state's check and the free childcare we provide. I was the babysitter of four in that house until..."

She cuts herself off, putting the iron skillet back in the cabinet.

"Until what? Why did you leave?"

"My turn." She turns around. "Have you ever been in love?"

You mean other than now?

That has to be the name for this avalanche of emotions. Care tumbling with awe, admiration colliding with lust, warmth and want sliding into protection, possession, passion: I don't want to feel them, but I do. I don't want to call it *falling in love*, but goddamn, I think I am.

"No, not really."

She tilts her head, not believing. "Forty-three years and you've never been in love?"

"I love God. I love my family and my flock. I fuck people, and I don't hate them, but no. I've never been in love. I've been busy."

I've been cursed.

"Busy helping women like me?"

I nod.

"Have you ever been with one? A woman you rescued?"

"Fuck no," I snap. "Damn, why would you think that?"

"Why else would you risk everything to help us?"

I don't confess this part about me. It's not only my past and secrets. It's my family's lives at risk.

"My turn."

"Fine," she sighs, turning to fill her coffee mug. Then, she gives me way too many feelings, pouring me another cup, too. "Your turn. Ask away."

I spot them on her wrists as she's pouring. "Why did you get stigmata tattoos?"

It's been taunting me. The reason why. The way she appeared in my life. Is it a sign from God, or the Devil, because I get visions of holding Wren's tattooed wrists, bound above her head while I fuck her so hard I make her bleed, with her marked feet, digging into my pumping ass, my dick filling her with every inch, every drop I have. Over and over.

Now I know why people need exorcisms.

I knew I could be evil, but with her, I feel possessed.

She falls quiet. Like something dark possesses her, too. "If I tell you," she pauses, "will you promise to answer my next question?"

"Yes."

She sets her mug down. "The last home I was in before Nannie's: the preppers. The father started giving me *that* look. When you're a teenager, you know it. I'd seen it before and knew I was in trouble. And I knew there was one thing that'd protect me, one thing he feared above all—God." She swallows. "He wouldn't touch me if I had his marks."

I clench my teeth, certain plans for that man's death forming in my mind.

"There was a woman in our town who owned a tattoo parlor," she explains. "She gave me the tattoos, no questions asked, except she asked if I needed help. I told her I needed a safe place to go, and she told me to go to the library, to ask for Nannie, that she'd help me, and she did. After two weeks, I was placed with her."

There's so much to unpack, but I ask, "Do you regret the tattoos? Why you got them?"

"No," she says flatly. "I have two parents: Jesus and Dolly."

I fight my smile. "Dolly?"

"Dolly Parton." *I knew it*. "She's like my mom. I listen to her songs every night. I love butterflies like Dolly does. I even got one tattooed right here..."

Nonchalantly, she starts to unbutton my shirt she's wearing. "I get the idea." But I stop her. I worry. "Wren, if Nannie's home was so safe, how did you wind up where I found you?"

"My turn." She lifts her chin, controlling this game of

truths, too. "You said you have dark needs when you lie with men and women. What are they?"

Hey, God. You win.

Because I won't lie to Wren, she's earned my respect. Yes, I'll lie to protect my family, but myself? I'm not worth protecting. If I can be saved, it's up to you or someone else.

I open my mouth to tell her, but my gaze falls on her lips. Lush, soft, pink lips. I suspect they've never been kissed, and I can't.

"You're too young to know."

She braces her fists against the countertop, her shoulders drawing up. Like a young lioness, she practically growls, looking ready to pounce and rip my throat open.

Fuck, I'm falling.

"We had this fight last night, and I won," she says. "I'm a virgin, but not innocent. *I'm* old enough to know the difference. Are *you*?"

"Why are you still a virgin? Are you waiting for marriage?"

Her gaze burns into mine. "No, I've been waiting for a man I can trust. I've been waiting for *you*. And you feel it, too. I know you do. God. Fate. Destiny. Whatever you want to call it, it put us together."

"You're too young to know your fate. How can you be so sure?"

"Joan of Arc was seventeen when she led the French army to victory. She was my age, nineteen, when she was burned at the stake, and she's a saint now. You want to tell me she was too young? That she wasn't sure God had a plan for her?"

Damn, I don't know yet who hurt her, but I won't be like him. I won't be like any man who's preyed on her.

I'll protect her.

She's right.

God's telling me to do it.

"Wren, you can trust me, and goddamn, I'm honored

you're asking me. You're brave, but you don't want me to be your first."

"You're right." She rests her chin in her palm. "I want you to be my whole lot of times, too."

Dick firmly agrees. He's aching to take care of her, but my mind argues. "You can't know that. You need more experience with a guy your age."

She smirks. "A guy my age who lives with his parents, plays video games all day, jerks off all night, and then wants to mansplain how, in his sheltered world, he knows more about life than me? No, thanks. I'd rather experience death by masturbation. Which, by the way, I heard you again last night."

I suppress a laugh because it's maddening how right she is, how wrong this is supposed to be, and how refreshing it feels that we can talk about it.

"So when I jerk off or mansplain, it doesn't bother you?"

"No. It turns me on because I know you've had sex, I bet you're good at it, and you've lived a lot more than me. You're a grown-ass man, but I've lived, too. Way too much for my age, actually, so let me *she*splain..."

She leans even closer. I can see the smart wheels turning behind her eyes. I can feel the chains holding me back, snapping free.

"You've met your match, gangster, and yes, I'm *much* younger than you." She narrows her mesmerizing eyes. "So, tell me. Are *you* mature enough to handle it?"

CHAPTER SEVEN
WREN

He smirks back, slanting his eyes like a predator.

It makes my knees knock. If I didn't know better, I'd say Sire is going to attack me.

But I do know better; I trust him. I'm not afraid when he probes, "Are *you* woman enough to handle my answer?"

"Yes."

He licks his lips. "You sure, little angel, because I'm the devil in bed?"

My pulse may be revving faster than a doe being chased, but my feet won't move.

I want Sire, and I want to know. I want to join the godly devil in his bed and burn with him forever.

And did I mention that Sire's been sitting there in grey, cotton pajama pants, with no shirt on, this whole time?

When he stormed into the room, all gun, ink, and muscles, Jesus took the wheel and my mouth because I couldn't function.

I don't know how I managed to serve up scrambled eggs when I could barely breathe at the sight of him.

Dark crosses and angels cover his thick neck, arms, and

hands. Lions with bloody fangs pierce his swole pecs. They prowl over his broad, sculpted shoulders, too, but his shredded abs are bare. No ink. No hair. Just muscle after ripped muscle leading down to...

Dear God, I wanted to drop to my knees.

My mouth watered.

What's that line on a man called? The one he has that looks like a thick, angled belt of abs pointing straight to his...

Yep, I saw it hanging.

He *is* a stallion. That's why I asked about his first time because I don't know how any woman or man can fit him inside, but I want to try.

I trust him to try.

I trust we're *destined* to try.

"I'm not afraid of you or your dark needs." I stare into his eyes. "Try me."

"You want me to *try* you, Wren?" His glare narrows. "Is that what you think about when you touch yourself, Angel? I've heard you, too, moaning my name. Such a horny little virgin, trying to tempt me. Is that what you want? My dick, opening every tight, wet part of you for the first time?"

The flush to my cheeks is hot, the slick flood between my thighs uncontrollable. "Yes," I boldly answer. "Open every part of me, Sire."

Like a dark shadow up a wall, he rises. He wants me to see every manly, menacing inch on him, as if he's warning me to stay away, to stop tempting him.

Grabbing the countertop, he leans toward me, tension vibrating off his flexing muscles. "I will *never* try a woman I rescue or any man I save because it's not right. And I want them *right*. I want them bent over and open for me. I want them wet or hard and in heat. I want to see it, taste it, smell it, touch it, and take it. I want them begging me to breed them because *that's* what I do, little angel."

Shockwaves pulse to my clit, my core clenching, my instincts responding.

He growls, "I *am* a sire. I'm an animal made to breed people who beg for every inch of my hard dick, every drop of my sweet cum. I fill them, breeding them so hard and so many times, what's so natural and right feels so fucking wrong and dark and dirty, and I love it. I don't want to stop. I *don't* stop, and they don't stop begging for more."

"You... You have a bunch of kids?"

Why do I want the answer? Why do I *fear* the answer?

"No," he seethes. "I'm always protected because I don't deserve kids. I'm a fucking beast who's just like my evil father. I want to take and claim and breed, and I want the whole world to see me do it because I *CAN*. I can fuck that hard and ruin anyone who loves me."

"But..." Suddenly, my heart hurts. "But you said you've never been in love."

"I haven't. I mean, my family. I mean, anyone who trusts me. I betray them. I ruin their lives." He's deadly serious. The light in his eyes, gone. "You don't want me, Wren. After everything you've been through, you deserve far better than me."

"But I—"

I'm stopped by a text pinging his phone. Across the open loft, we can hear it in his bedroom.

"Shit," he mutters, quickly turning away to answer it.

With shaking hands, I finish putting away the dishes.

It's not fear that has me trembling. It's desire. It's fate. I want everything Sire described. The visions he's put in my mind of his dark needs; I want to feel them.

I'm meant to fill them.

"Lunch." He startles me. I whip around. "My mother wants to have lunch with us."

"Your mother?"

"Yes. Ms. Faye." His bare chest heaves like he ran a marathon, and it's over. "She wants you to wear the dress she bought for you. She said it's in your luggage, which, by the way, you *will* unpack to stay in *our* home while I go to church and come back for you at noon."

SIX HOURS LATER, I'VE SHOWERED AND GOTTEN READY, after I scoured the kitchen, mopped the floors, and dusted furniture. *Our home* is spotless.

I got the sweetest feeling folding Sire's T-shirts. The headiest sensation lifting his clean black boxer briefs to my nose: amber and musk. I left them neatly stacked on his bed, resisting the impulse to snoop around.

I may tempt him, but I'd never betray him.

And if I'm supposed to be embarrassed about wanting him this much and being honest about it, I'm not. I'm too flooded with other potent feelings.

I believe in him. I know we're supposed to be together. I don't care what he's done or who he's betrayed, so I unpack my clothes. It's not much, but the gesture means a lot.

"Our home," he said, and I keep hearing it.

I almost had one. I almost had a safe home with a loving mother, a cute dog, and simple happiness. I almost had what many take for granted, but I lost it all in a single, cruel stroke of bad luck and bad people.

"Wren?"

I like my name in his low, gruff voice. I like stepping out of my bedroom to greet him. I like the dark grey suit, tie, and vest he's wearing. I like how Sire looks so handsome right now, how he's staring at me in that high and smiling way again.

I blink back tears.

Happy tears.

"I'm ready, just..." I turn, hiding them as he walks my way. "Can you zip me up, please?"

I lift my hair so it won't get caught in the zipper. Ms. Faye gave me a cream tweed Chanel sleeveless minidress with a scalloped neck and hemline. I've never worn such luxury against my skin. I've never felt so pretty and like a fool, too, because I can't reach the zipper in the back.

"You look..." His voice chokes. His heat blankets my back. "You look beautiful, Wren."

Slowly, too slowly, he pulls the zipper up, his fingertips brushing the nape of my neck. His touch, racing innocent goosebumps down my skin, breathless desire igniting even deeper below.

"Thank you," I sigh. "But I don't have any heels. I only have these flats Ms. Faye gave me. I hope they're okay."

"My mom never had daughters." He steps back as I turn around. "Let her spoil you. Trust me. She loves it."

The flats Nadine gave me are Chanel, too. They're white ballet slippers with a black, silk toe. I'm both awkward and honored wearing clothes I could never have dreamed of affording. And next to Sire, I feel like a tiny princess, too.

His intense stare drinks me in. His fists clench, then unclench, before they gesture for me to walk with him.

Escorting me to his black Mercedes sedan parked outside, he opens the passenger door for me. It's like I'm being whisked away to meet the Queen, but Sire seems oddly quiet about it.

"Music?" I chirp.

"You'll have to play new music on my phone." He pulls it

out of his suit pocket. "This is a nineteen ninety-five classic. It only plays cassette tapes."

"Cassettes? Do you—"

Interrupting, he mocks, "You're too young to know what those are, aren't you?"

"*No.* You didn't have to see the pyramids being built to know what they are. Jeez. I was gonna ask if you have any tapes we can listen to."

He points to the glove compartment. I open it and search through the cases, reading aloud, "Radiohead. Alanis Morissette. Pearl Jam. TLC. Wow. Did these come with the car?"

"No," he huffs. "It was a good year for music."

"I agree."

"You weren't even *born*." More sarcasm.

The breeding beast, turned sweet escort, has become Mr. Grumpy again, and I don't know why. All I've done is his laundry.

"Yeah, and they invented bread before I was born, too, but I know how to bake it. Some things are ageless." I pull out a shiny, new case with a handwritten insert. "What's this?" I don't recognize the titles.

He glances at it, wincing. "Don't play it."

"What is it?"

"Something *WE* are *NOT* playing," he barks.

"Speaking in plural for me?" I pop the cassette in. "That's mighty male of you."

While he glares at the interstate before us, there's a crackling sound, a cough, the strum of a guitar, and then it's him. I'd recognize his voice anywhere after hearing him sing to the kids. But this song is darker, in his deepest register, like the pain he's singing about.

I watch his face. Every heartbreaking wince and agonizing flinch. I know not to ask him about the haunting lyrics. Not now. Not like this.

"You have a beautiful voice." I just share the truth. "Really beautiful."

He swallows. "Thank you."

"Sorry." I press the pause button. "I shouldn't have played it when you asked me not to."

"Sorry. I shouldn't be a dick and speak to you in that tone. It's just..." He glances at me. "You look breathtaking, Wren, and I don't know how to feel about it."

"Thank you. You look really handsome, and I know *exactly* how I feel about it."

He shakes his head, a smile playing with his lips.

I eject the tape, trying to lighten the mood. "Got any Dolly?"

"Actually," he grins, "check the eighties love song mix."

I fish through the cases. "You know, I'm dying to make old man jokes right now." I find the case and Dolly's song number on the insert.

"Tell you what..." He checks the rearview mirror. "For a handsome, older man who gets grumpy, and a breathtaking, younger woman who keeps asserting her power, maybe we should stop talking about age."

"Deal." I press the cassette in and click the forward button until it starts playing the best love song ever, in my very biased opinion.

It's a duet with Dolly, featuring Kenny Rogers. I belt his opening lyrics, and Sire laughs, pressing pause.

"*What* do you think he just said?"

"Duh..." I scoff. "He says, 'Baby, when I met you there was peace on earth'." Laughter shakes Sire's chest. It's contagious. He makes me laugh back, "What? That's what he's *saying*."

"Uh, no, it isn't but sing it with me anyway. Be Dolly, and I'll be Kenny because you're fucking cute fucking up the song."

"I'm *not* fucking up the song."

He winks. "Whatever you say, Angel."

But it is cute, if not the happiest moment of my life, belting the duet with him.

Sire's voice is sexy, the lyrics feel prophetic, and each time he snickers, I know I fucked them up again, but he doesn't correct me. He sings with me and smiles even bigger, which I didn't think was possible.

By the time our duet is over, he's pulling into an almost empty parking lot beside a three-story brick building with its big windows painted black. I glance around and see a wide river in the distance, along with other huge buildings with no signs on them.

"Where *are* we?"

"The old Naval yard." He kills the ignition, turning to me. "Listen, you need to know a few things before we go inside."

Can he be more ominous? "*Oh-kay.*"

"Ms. Faye is my mother, and this is her club: a private sex club." *Hey, Pulse, calm down.* "She uses the money she makes here to save people like you."

"And you and your brother help her."

"Bro-*thers.*"

"How many do you have?"

And do they all look as hot as him and Jace? God help me if they do.

"I have six brothers. There's seven of us who work for her because we believe in what she does."

"Why?"

"That's not my story to tell."

"So, what can you tell me?"

"That the club isn't open right now, otherwise, no way in hell would I let you in."

"Because I'm under twenty-one?"

"No." He shakes his head like it makes him mad. "Because you're about to see things you never have."

"Hmm." I study him. "I'm not shook by taboo things, so why are you worried about me seeing them?" I lower my brows, teasing, "Is it because you *breed* here?"

His nostrils flare. "Never. One, it's my mom's club, so hell-no, I don't let her see me fuck. Two, I can't risk being seen here. My flock is progressive. Some are even members here, but not me. Because three, I don't get the same freedom. I'm held to a different standard."

"Because they'll judge your sexuality?"

He nods.

"So, where do you fuck?"

"Where do you get off asking me?"

I bat my lashes. The pun is too easy. "Because I get off knowing."

Half-amused, he rolls his eyes. "I belong to a fetish club in Atlanta, and sometimes, I use an app. But it's been a minute, and I've been busy." He pauses. "Busy finding you. So, come on." He opens his door. "If you have a death wish, be late for a meeting with my mom."

Before I can open my door, he's doing it for me. He's offering me his big, inked hand, and I take it, my heart fluttering under my butterfly tattoo. He's a brutal gentleman, gently shadowing me with his protection, as he escorts me into...

A sex club.

Inside, the house lights are on. I'm sure it's usually dark in here, setting an erotic mood, but right now, it's swarming with worker bees, cleaning every surface.

Glancing around, I can't take it all in.

Concrete floors and ornate rugs. A large stage. Velvet sofas. Acrylic stools. Plush chairs. Tufted ottomans. Leather benches. Chains and padded crosses hang on the wall. Ropes and shackles sway beside them. Glass jars full of condoms, wipes, and packets of lube are everywhere.

Sandalwood scents the air. Sex toys are for sale next to the gleaming bar.

Oh, my God.

It's fucking heaven.

Literally.

For a minute, I can't breathe. I just stare like a kid in a candy store, my clit tingling so sweet.

From behind the long bar, where staff in black T-shirts and pants diligently clean, Ms. Nadine Faye walks our way in a Chanel pink skirt suit with her arms held open for me.

"There she is." Her blue eyes sparkle like her son's. "My dear, you look like a modern-day Audrey Hepburn."

A blush hits my cheeks as she pecks them. "Thank you," I beam.

She gives me the warmest hug, too, before Sire gives her one, along with a quick peck on her cheek. "Hey, Mom."

But he sounds mad, and she picks up on it. "What's wrong?"

He gestures to me. "She shouldn't be in here. It's inappropriate. I don't know why we're meeting here."

The wise smile that lifts her lips makes me worship her. Nannie did the same thing when someone questioned her power.

Arching one of her groomed brows, Ms. Faye calmly answers, "If I didn't think Wren could handle being in my club, she wouldn't be here."

She turns to me. "Wren, dear, look around. Explore. Ask my staff all your questions. They're professional and informed. And please excuse us while I talk the ears off of my stubborn mule of a son."

CHAPTER EIGHT
SIRE

"Look at her," Mom admires Wren. "She's like a swan to water."

We stand by the one-way glass window in her third-floor office overlooking the main floor below. I loom beside her, watching Wren sip a soda at the bar while animatedly talking to Lucy, the head bartender.

It looks perfectly innocent ... except there's a new shipment of giant boxed dildos on the bar beside Wren.

I say flatly, "She's too young to be in here."

In return, I expect a dose of Southern sass from my mom. She's the queen of it, an art she perfected to blend in.

But she sighs, touching my arm. "I love how protective you are of her, and I love how you saved her, too. That's why I wanted to meet here."

She glances down at my hand. I'm not wearing a bandage. My stitches have dissolved. The scar on my partial pinky is raw, making tears well in her eyes, as if my wound is hers.

I guess, for a mom, it is.

"Sergei, you've always been the one who hurt the most and—"

"No, mom. *You* did."

As her eldest son, I have the most memories. Many horrific. A few, sweet. Mom and I were so close in age, I became like her best friend, too. I could always make her smile.

"Yes, I did," she answers, "and I was years younger than Wren is now when I had you. In this world, perhaps fourteen is too young to become a mother, but Wren is like me; we were girls in a world where our innocence was taken from us so we could survive. I was married to an evil monster who gave me three sweet sons by the time I was her age, and the only reason we survived," she points between us, "is because every girl is born with an army of women inside her who will fight back, so do *not* underestimate her."

I swallow the lump in my throat, remembering every black eye my mom had, every sweet song she'd sing to me, despite her pain.

"So, what are you saying, my Queen?"

I mean it. I worship my mother. All of my brothers do.

She's wise and warm, a badass and brutal. I know this "lunch date" is Mom trying to set me up with Wren...

And it's working.

It was either love or a heart attack that seized my chest so fucking hard at the sight of Wren in that white dress. I couldn't breathe standing so close to her. I wanted to *unzip* her dress.

And then our duet in the car? Belting Dolly and Kenny and *those* lyrics? I don't do shit like that. I don't smile like that. But it was like hanging out with my best friend.

Who's hot.

Who makes my dick raging hard.

Fuck, this is happening too fast, and I can't stop it, especially when my mom says...

"I'm saying follow your heart."

"My heart isn't the problem. I'll never hurt her. My dick on the other hand..."

She cuts me a look. "While you're grown and require no lectures from me about ethics versus erections ... get over it."

"What?"

"Get over whatever it is that's been bothering you for years. You think I didn't notice? How you were hell-bent on finding your queen in your twenties. Woman or man. You know I'd love either. But then, like a switch when you turned thirty, the light in you died. You stopped believing in love."

Thirty?

That's when my father found me. He found us. And that's when he said either I provide him with a legitimate heir for his criminal empire, a grandson with a woman of my choosing, or he'll kill my mom.

While my brothers and I are powerful, trained, and ruthless when needed—we escaped one of the world's most powerful criminal organizations—if my father doesn't kill my mother himself, the hundreds who work for him will.

So, it was a deal—a deal I made with the Devil. I'd give him an heir, and he'd let us live.

But he didn't keep the deal.

"I still believe in love, Mom, I just don't have the time for it."

She sniffs. "What's that smell?"

I roll my eyes; she always does this. "Bullshit."

"That's right." She points to Wren, who's—*fuck me*—inspecting a new ponytail anal plug Lucy is showing her. "Because you *will* make time for her. And you will tell her everything about us and earn her trust."

"Everything?"

"Yes, *everything*. I spent a week with her and instantly trusted her. There's something about her. I want her to be safe, and so do you. And the only way she's going to tell us who sold her into that ring is if she trusts you."

"She thinks I'll kill him."

She deadpans. "Then don't." I make my face stone. "*Sergei.*" But fuck, she's my mom. She sees straight through me. "Young man, when I tell you not to do something, you'd best listen."

I snort. "I'm not young, Mom."

"The hell you aren't. You're young enough to let yourself fall in love with her, marry her, make her your queen, and give me some beautiful grandbabies. And you and your brothers will make your vows to protect her, and keep her safe, or I will whoop your ass into next week. Understand?"

Has my mother ever laid a violent hand on me? If yanking my earlobe counts, yes. But she owns too many guns, and I respect her too much to disobey her.

"Yes, ma'am. I'll tell her everything and try to earn her trust. We'll find out who sold her. But marry her?" I shake my head. "Mom, you know I can't."

She flits her jeweled hand. "Just get to know her and you'll realize I'm right."

"Wren has no filter. Give us four more days, and I'll know everything about her. But they won't accept us. My flock. They'll say I'm a cradle-snatcher or a manther."

"A what?" she scoffs.

"Like an older woman with a younger man is a cougar or a panther, a *manther* is an older man who goes after much younger women."

"Hmm." She smirks. "Well, *They* can walk a mile in my heels and kiss my ass. Judgmental people either need to be loved or laid. Honey, don't listen to them."

"I'm their pastor. It's my job to listen to them."

"Listen, yes. Go your whole life denying yourself love?" Laughing, she points to Wren, who's straddling a BDSM breeding bench like she's riding a pony carousel outside a grocery store. "Darlin', it's too late. Your love is sitting right there."

Mom takes us to lunch at a place by the river and introduces Wren to Oysters Rockefeller. It's obvious Wren wants to puke, but she won't do it. She's too polite, and she and my mom have too much fun, laughing over stories about me and my brothers.

"Tell her the poison ivy story," my mother insists.

I sigh—*God, kill me now*—as I look at Wren, who's smiling at me with those pink lips I want to devour.

"We lived on a farm when we first moved here, and to earn our keep, we picked peaches and did yard work. One day, guess I was seventeen or so, we cleared the weeds growing behind the farmhouse and thought nothing of it until we started itching the next day."

"Itching where?" My mother taunts.

Now, God. Now would be a good time.

"Itching on our penises because we'd been pulling our puds with poison ivy hands all night."

Wren snorts her sweet tea, and my mom grabs her hand, laughing, "Darlin, *four* of my boys had poison penises. What a proud day for a mother."

"Who?" Wren smiles, and Mom's right.

My love is sitting right in front of me.

I raise my hand. "Me, Axel, Grant, and Jace. Nick and Loch were too young, and I hadn't met Nash yet."

"Sweet Jace?" Wren looks shocked, asking me, "How old was he?"

"Barely thirteen and a threat to anything that would hold still."

"My Lord," Mom shakes her head, "my sweet Jace used to hump the sofa cushions."

I throw my chin up, laughing. "Until Axel caught him and told him to quit fucking the furniture."

We spend hours with my mom, who takes Wren shopping for more clothes, handbags, heels, makeup, and my favorite, painfully awkward moment *ever*—expensive lingerie.

I have to wait outside the sexy store while praying to God to give me restraint.

With my mother's blessing, Wren's angelic lure, and every sign being thrown in my face, I feel like a caged demon who's been set free. My urges are too strong.

Driving back to my penthouse at night, I switch the mood to an emotion I can control. I tell Wren more funny stories of life on the peach farm. For me, my mom, and brothers, it was the first time we were safe, so damn if we didn't laugh at almost everything.

"Tomorrow at two," I ask Wren as I park my car, "would you like to come to my service?"

"Are you singing?"

"Yeah. A few songs. But sorry, no Dolly."

She exaggerates a pout, and I stare at lips I'm dying to kiss.

It would be the perfect end to an almost perfect day.

"Tell you what," I say instead. "I'll print the lyrics to the songs I'm singing so no one will hear you fuck them up."

"Uh!" She laughs, yanking her door open. "I don't fuck up lyrics."

I can't get out to open her door fast enough, but I have a feeling I'll be saying it for the rest of my short life, "Whatever you say, Angel."

Laughing together, we walk side-by-side, my hand on the

small of her back, our bodies brushing. Every urge tells me to take her sweet face in my hands and kiss her, but—

"Ahem."

A deep voice from the shadow by my door makes me step in front of Wren, my hand reaching for the gun in my back holster.

"It's me, holy fucker."

Axel steps out of the shadows. Wren grabs my jacket. Like me, my brother is a menacing sight at first glance.

"It's okay," I tell her. "He's one of the poison penises."

Axel cocks a dark brow, and Wren switches gears from frightened to a fairy.

"Hi, Sire's brother." She sticks her hand out. "I'm Wren, and I believe we met before you murdered those dickheads. Thanks, by the way."

"Hi, Wren." Axel grins, shaking her hand. "It's nice to meet you. And yes, I'm Axel, we've met, my penis has amazing properties, but poison ain't one, and you're welcome. Glad to see you've invaded my brother's monkish life."

Wren smiles my way. "I like him."

"Don't." I scowl. "He's a dickhead wrapped in gangster's clothing."

But really, he's not. Axel has a caring heart. It's just buried under all the shit we survived as kids.

"Wren," he asks, "can I steal Pastor Prick for a minute?"

"Sure!" She likes that nickname too much. Pointing to my car, she asks, "Should I get my bags now or—"

"I'll bring them up."

"Okay." She turns toward my door, entering the code.

But I draw my gun. "Wait. Let me go up with you and clear the place."

I'm disturbed that Wren seems unfazed by this. Dutifully, she stands behind me until I've checked every room.

"So, who's the oldest?" she asks, opening the container of muffins in the kitchen.

"Me." I holster my gun.

"But Axel talks like he's in charge." And she talks with her mouth full—another irresistible trait.

"He is."

"Why aren't you? You know, patriarchal birth order and all."

"You sure know a lot about patriarchy."

She gestures to the air. "We all have its cancer."

"Exactly, and I was the first male heir my father always wanted, but fuck him; I didn't want the power. I just never expected he'd turn his wrath on Axel next."

Her brows bend. "Then why don't you take over now?"

"Trust me, Axel's better at it. You don't want me in charge."

"Why?"

"Because when I'm mad, heads roll."

Her head tilts, curious, not afraid. I'm beginning to love that trait, too. "What do you mean?"

"I mean..." I turn for the door. "When I get back, I have some answers for you." I glance back. "And Wren?" She looks up. "You'll have answers for me, too."

CHAPTER NINE
SIRE

Opening the door at the bottom of the stairs to my penthouse, I step back, shocked to find Axel *and* Loch waiting for me.

"Hey, man." I give Loch a quick hug and back slap. "Didn't expect to see you so soon."

He cups my shoulder. "Came home early for the initiation. Got some errands to run and ... um ... some shit to take care of."

My youngest brother gives me a knowing look. He matches my height and build, but my baby brother is anything but. His job has put more brawn on him—his job *and* love.

I've never seen Loch so happy and healthy. The shit he has to take care of is that he's in love with Alena Allen, Nash's daughter, even though Nash is going to fucking kill him when he finds out.

Nash told Loch to protect Alena, to be her colleague and secret bodyguard. With the evil circles we run in, more like with the vile fucks we kill, Axel ordered it, too.

Alena has no idea who we are and the danger she's in.

But Nash and Axel sure as hell didn't expect Loch to fall in love with her, and all the kinky shit Loch and Alena are into.

Yeah, I know about that, too.

I'm the oldest—the pastor. My brothers confide in me about everything, and I keep their secrets. You'd think I'd be against keeping them, but I have my own.

Axel explains, "I told him to meet us here because we're going to need him."

"Need him for what?"

"I'll need Loch to hold you back when I tell you what I found out about Wren."

Cue my pulse skyrocketing, red rage starting to bleed over my eyes. "*What* about Wren?"

Sympathy bends Axel's face. "Man, I don't know how she made it this far and can still smile like an angel."

Axel sees it too; the light that sparkles off of Wren like goddamn glitter in the darkest world. I'm drawn to it. I'm starting to fear ever losing it.

"Just tell him." Loch sounds sympathetic, too.

Fury burns through my constricting throat, worry biting at my eyes. "Tell me *what* about Wren?"

"I got a copy of her child services file," Axel explains. "You're right. She's from Tennessee and was bounced from home to home. As a baby, it was because she cried. Her foster parents said she wouldn't sleep and wanted to be held too much."

Oh fuck. The biting at my eyes gets worse.

"As a little girl," Axel swallows, "some foster parents said she was weird or mentally ill. That she'd smile and talk to God or the sky and butterflies like they could hear her."

Yep, my eyes start leaking.

Axel grabs my arm. "Her file said there's no evidence of abuse. Not the worst kind, but it's like no one ever wanted her. In some placements, they didn't keep her a week before they wanted her to leave. They told her she was too different. She didn't fit in. Fuck," he seethes, "who would do that to a kid?"

Through clenched teeth and blurred vision, I demand, "Tell me about her second-to-last placement."

"She was placed with some family in Maryville, Tennessee. Nothing bad's on the record, but for some reason, Wren was moved and placed with Nannette Banks in Happy Valley, Tennessee, until she was eighteen."

Happy Valley? I suspect it didn't end that way for Wren.

"Those places are idyllic but remote as hell," Loch adds.

"Why does that matter?"

I can't think clearly. I can't reason. I just see Wren as a little girl who needed to be held and loved. She wanted a family, but she was rejected from home to home, and made to feel bad that she believed in God.

And now, God, I want to burn the fucking world down for her.

"Because," Loch answers, "that's what makes those places perfect for drug trafficking. Rough terrain. Remote. Low population. You can get away with murder on those mountains. I would know."

"I think that's what happened." Axel won't let go of my arm, and I don't want him to. He's right. Someone needs to hold me back.

"I have a new paralegal: Ruby," he adds. "She's smart as hell with good instincts. She obtained Wren's DCS file but dug a little deeper. She found out that one month before Wren turned eighteen, Nannette Banks died from a stroke, and she had left her home to Wren. But eight months later, Wren's home was the site of the largest meth bust in the county. Two days after the bust, it went up in flames."

"Who was busted?" I rage.

"Not Wren," Axel huffs like the wicked side of him is amused. "Three men were taken into custody. One was an unidentified minor. He was released, but the other two died hours after their arrest." Axel smirks. "They had been poisoned and—"

"And the ringleader remains at large somewhere in those mountains," Loch adds.

Now, my brain is working.

Now, I can see it.

Meth? Death and drug trafficking? *Not Wren.* Fire, poisoning, and vengeance? *Oh, my Iron Angel.*

I reason aloud, "Somehow those bastards turned Wren's home into a meth lab, but she fought back. They underestimated her. She probably collected enough evidence to turn them in, but she poisoned them to be sure they wouldn't be a threat, and then she set their operation on fire."

Axel grins, impressed. "Like a fucking queen, she did."

"And that's why you're here, right?" I turn to Loch. "Thank fuck you didn't join the Marines, because I need a forest ranger who can help me hunt that ringleader down."

Loch nods. "We will."

"That ringleader?" Axel pulls away like I'm about to blow. "The one who probably sold Wren into that trafficking ring?"

"You mean the man whose head I'll take?"

"Yeah," Axel answers. "He's Nannette Banks's son."

CHAPTER TEN
WREN

I can't sleep. Growing up, I never really could. I guess the hole in my heart was too big.

But at least here, in Sire's home, *our home*, my eyelids grow heavy. I can almost close them, but Sire's still downstairs talking to his brother, Axel.

Is it the buzz from the best day ever, or something else that's making me wait up for him?

Finally, I hear Sire open and close his front door. I listen to him set the shopping bags down before his footfalls thud over the wooden floors. I hear him close his bedroom door, and minutes later, he's taking a shower.

But I don't hear his erotic, muffled groans that do something to my body. I don't hear anything until a soft knock on my door startles me.

"Wren? You awake?"

"Yeah." I sit up and turn on the lamp beside my bed. "Come in."

He opens the door. Standing in the threshold with his damp hair, he's wearing a white T-shirt, light grey sweatpants, and a worried look. "Can we talk?"

"Uh, sure." I reach to throw the sheets off.

"No." He signals for me to stop. "Stay there. Let's just, uh…" He gestures to the corner of my bed. "May I?"

"Sure."

He's acting weird. He sits quietly for a long time, keeping his distance with his hands clasped together. His distant stare is locked on the wall in front of him, and I think … he's praying?

He makes me worry, "Sire? What's wrong?"

A soft smile lifts his lips as he glances at me. "That's the first time you've called me by my name." He huffs, "And it's not even my real name."

"Is this when we start giving answers? Like, what is your real name?"

"My birth name is Sergei Kholodov, the first son and heir of Ruslan Kholodov, the head of the Bratva, the Russian mafia, but let me go first."

My shock lasts two seconds because he hits me with…

"Nannie's real name was Nannette Banks. Right?" he asks, and I nod, feeling my world start to unravel. "And her son's name is Waylon Banks? Right?" Tears well in my eyes. "And he's the meth dealer who funneled you into the human trafficking ring where I found you?"

"Where you rescued me," I mutter, letting my first tear fall.

"Wren…" He reaches for my foot under the blanket, gently grabbing it like he'll never let me go. "I know about your child services file. I know all the cruel reasons you never had a home, how you were never held, how you talked to God and butterflies when you were a little girl."

Tears blur my vision. "I still do."

Barely, he smiles before his face falls. "I know that after Nannie died, her home was involved in a meth bust, and then it went up in flames." He squeezes my foot. "Did you set that fire?"

I lift my chin, tears spilling down my cheeks. "Damn right I did."

"But Wren, it was your only home. You had no place else to go."

"Nannie never would have wanted her home used like that. She loved her son but wouldn't enable him. She had a restraining order against him."

"But he took possession because you weren't eighteen when she died, though her home had been left to you." Sire pauses, searching my eyes. "Did he kill his mother?"

I can barely speak through the rocks choking my throat. They burn. "Technically, no. But they fought about her leaving the home to me and not him, and I think it caused her so much stress that it was my fault that she..."

A sob breaks my voice. Embarrassed, I cover my face with my hands.

"Come here." Sire gets up and sits beside me. Pulling me into his strong arms, he holds me against his chest. The compassion is so new to me that nineteen years of pain break me into a thousand pieces.

I'm a girl in his arms and a grown woman, too. Everything I've held in for so long collides, and I don't know how long I cry. I just finally let it out. I finally have someone who doesn't yell at me to stop crying, who's not pushing me away.

Nannie was loving, but she wasn't affectionate. She was mountain-strong and gave that gift to me. She taught me to fight back.

But in Sire's warm arms, I don't have to fight. With my cheek on his chest, and his big hand caressing my head there, even though I'm snotting his T-shirt, I hug him, too, and he holds me even tighter.

"You have a home now, Wren," he whispers into my hair. "This is your home, too."

I pull back, my vision blurred, my breath huffing, "But you just met me."

Gently, his thumb brushes a tear away. "We both know we've just begun."

My heart stutters, happy, but, "You don't know what I did."

"Oh, Angel." A sweet smile plays on his lips. "You have no idea about me, either."

"You're a mafia man of God. Got it."

"And you poisoned Waylon's men, didn't you?" He's grinning at me like he's impressed, not appalled. "How did you do it?"

I force a smile through tears. "You need to marry me first."

"Oh?" He raises a brow, amused. "Do I?"

"Yeah, so you can't testify against your wife."

Gently, he brushes another tear away. "Damn, you're a sweet, sharp surprise around every corner, aren't you?"

"I'm not always sweet. Yes, I did some things to survive, but I don't want you to kill him."

"He deserves it."

"Not Waylon, I mean Alan."

"Who's Alan?"

I swipe my wet cheeks. "Alan is Nannie's grandson. Waylon's son. The minor who was busted, too. He's caught up in that life with his dad, and it's not his fault. Alan has an addiction. He needs help. But if you go after Waylon, you'll find Alan, and I worry he'll be so high he won't know what he's doing. He's always worked for his dad, and..."

It's no use drying my cheeks. More tears fall. "It would kill Nannie. Like her heart in heaven would break. I already feel like it's my fault she died, and if something happens to her grandson because of me…"

"Okay." He wraps around me again. "No one is dying tonight. Let's catch our breath. We'll talk about this tomorrow."

"Okay," I mumble against his chest. His *really* hard chest. For a minute, I soak him in until I sigh, "God. You're like a hot, marble statue."

His chuckle rumbles against my cheek. "Oh, Angel. You have no idea how hot and hard I am touching you."

The rushing tickle to my core is instant. I'm not shy, not with him holding me and every emotion flooding my senses. "I'm making you hard?"

"You're making me everything."

"Did you mean it?" I linger my hand down his back, wishing he wasn't wearing a T-shirt. "That we've just begun?"

I should stop doing his laundry so he'll have nothing to wear.

"Listen to me, Angel." His voice sounds gruff; his lips pressed to my ear. "With everything I know about you now, you're mine, Wren Chapel."

I want to surrender to the burst of hope his claim gives me, but "You're not judging me for what I did?"

"Never. I realize now, we're a lot alike."

"Hmm. It's kinda like we belong together." I trace my fingertip over his pec. "What brilliant, young woman said that recently?"

He chuckles. "Yes, argument won. Signs received. Prayers answered. I just need to tell you some things. And I need to go slow with you."

"Why?" I try to keep the impatience out of my voice. "Can't we speed things up?"

I'm wearing his dress shirt. But it's thin enough for him to feel how hard he makes my nipples. I arch into him, rubbing them against his abs, my lips steaming over the thin cotton covering his nipple, too. "I want you. Please fu—"

"*Fuuuck*, Wren." His hold on me tightens. Fisting my hair, he yanks my neck open, his hot lips trailing down my flesh, making a moan crawl up my throat. His whiskers tickle, following the same path back to my ear. "Angel, don't tempt me. I want to hold you tonight."

"Hold me?"

"I read your file, and everything you never had. Wren, I'm going to give it to you; everything you want."

I rise, pressing my lips to his ear. "I only want you, Sire. I'm yours."

His growl is instant. His strength, overwhelming. He forces our bodies back until we're lying on the bed, and he's braced on top of me, my heart racing in this position, my legs opening for him, but he nuzzles his furrowed brow to mine.

"I'm serious, Wren. Don't make me lose control. I've been praying for restraint with you. Give me at least one night to hold you. That's all we'll do."

I cup his face, tears welling in my eyes. "But I'm afraid, because holding me means *everything* to me."

Softly, he kisses my palm. "I know. I've never done it, either."

"You've never spent the night with someone?"

"No." He stares down at me, his voice rich with depth. "I've never held someone knowing that I'll never let them go."

Now they fall. The tears and my heart. "You'll never let me go?"

"Never, Angel." He kisses a tear trailing from my eye. "If you ask me anything in my name, I will do it."

He quotes scripture, and I smile. "Sire, don't ever let me go."

"Wren, don't lose faith in me."

"Never, I promise."

Softly, he kisses my cheek before he says firmly, "Now, roll on your side and stay under the blankets."

"Why?"

He reaches over and turns off the lamp. "So, I won't feel your soft skin against mine, and completely lose control, and do every dirty thing I want to do to you."

I chew my lip, joy dancing through my veins. Flipping to my side, I know I won't sleep, and I don't need to. I only need this—Sire, gently wrapping his big arm around me, his warmth, his manly scent, his heavy muscles engulfing me. His lips brush the top of my head, his nose nuzzling into my curls.

I could cry right now, at what this means to me, for Sire to hold me, but I fear if I do, I'll never stop, and as a child, I cried enough.

I'm a woman now who deserves this joy. Smiling, I sigh into the pillow, "I feel you."

He kisses my hair. "I should think so. I've got seventeen inches on you."

He means our height, but I wriggle my ass against his erection. "You sure do, Stallion."

"*Wren*," he growls lowly.

"That's what I'm going to call you: my stallion."

"Shut up," he says softly. "That's what I'm going to tell you to do right now."

"Why?" I tempt.

"Because I'm going to make you mine, and when I do..." He grinds into me, and I gasp, feeling his full, frightening size pressing against my ass. "I want to breed you, Wren, not break you."

CHAPTER ELEVEN
SIRE

It's true. The Lord works in mysterious ways.

Because it's a mystery to me how we slept at all. How I didn't hold Wren down, suck her hard nipples, and spread her willing legs, so I could fuck her all night long.

Good God, I wanted to. The urge was maddening, but the need to hold her was stronger.

In the Bible, the world was created in six days. In my arms, I fell in love with Wren Chapel in one night.

She mumbled in her sleep, like she was having bad dreams, then she snuggled into me, and stilled, quiet and peaceful.

Fuck, what that did to me. I melted, holding my future wife.

There's only one problem.

Isn't there always?

My angel would be marrying the Devil. The deed to make her my queen, dark. The world I live in, dangerous. The deal I've made, deplorable.

I'll never forgive myself.

Her body stirs, writhing against mine, and I groan, hit by a sudden wave of lust. One rolls in every minute with her.

"Wow," she yawns. "All night?"

I mutter into her hair. "Yes, I held you all night."

"I know, and I slept like a baby. Thank you." She wriggles against my aching hard-on. "But what about this?"

I try to reason it away. "The average man has three to five erections a night."

"Does the average man wake up with a baseball bat between his legs?"

I laugh. "They do call it 'morning wood' for a reason."

She rolls over in my arms, more breathtaking than every dawn rising over the ocean. When did she get golden flecks in her eyes?

They sparkle. "Can we score a homerun this morning?"

I brush a twirly lock off her face. "It's the Lord's Day, Angel."

"Even better. I promise I'll moan 'oh God' lots of times."

"I promise we have a lot to talk about before that can ever happen."

"Okay." She wedges away from me, getting cutely serious. "I have many godly qualities, but patience isn't one of them. Let's talk, so we can move on."

"Well, good morning to you, too."

She flicks my nose. "Good morning, and you're right. We need to talk. Last night was about my secrets. So, this morning, tell me yours."

Jesus, I'm calling on you.

Help a love-struck brother out.

"I told you about my brothers, and you've met our mother. I told you how we escaped our father, and what an evil, powerful man he is. Because we escaped him, he's been hunting us. He wants revenge."

"Russian mafia and murder." She nods. "Check."

I huff a laugh. "And you don't flinch at it?"

"I dealt with country cartels. They may not have millions like the mafia, but they have no mercy either."

"Okay, so you appreciate what my father and his soldiers will do if they seek their revenge. Torture. Rape. Murder. Threatening our family, too. That means us and everyone we love."

"I would be at risk. Got it, and used to it."

Fuck, the more I tell Wren, the more I realize we *were* meant to be together.

God couldn't have painted a more perfect woman for me.

Except...

"Because we're at risk, we have a tradition, and in the past, like for my mom, it was barbaric. But we do it now with consent, as an intimate bond to keep us and our loved ones safe."

Curiosity, not fear, dances in her eyes.

"Way back," I explain, "a king would take a wife, a queen, but his queen would accept two kings on her wedding night: one, her first king and husband, the other, her second king, who vowed to protect her and her children if something happened to her first husband. It's how power stayed with the elites."

"Yep." She doesn't bat an eyelash. "Polyandry: one wife with multiple husbands, often brothers. They do it in the Himalayas because farmland is so scarce."

I'm stunned silent.

"What?" She grins. "Nannie was a librarian. I read tons of books, especially anything about sex and marriage. And you're saying that you and your brothers are polyandrous and..." Her smile fades. "And you have a *wife?*"

"No." I cup her cheek. "I've never had a wife, and my brothers wouldn't share their wives, either. It's one night, one initiation. Back home, we were considered princes. We would've been kings who made our queens together, and we kept the tradition here because my mom's second king rescued us. He died so that my mom, my brothers, and I could escape my father."

Her brows furrow. "That happened to your mom? All of that?"

"All of that and worse. My father kidnapped and forced her to marry him when she was fourteen. He forced her to take a second husband, too, but over time, she fell in love with him. His name was Maxim, and sometimes I wonder if he was my true dad, because I hate my father so much."

"Your father was abusive?"

"To all of us."

I reach over my back and tug off my T-shirt. Her eyes widen at my naked torso so close to her, but I take her fingertips and touch them to my chest, over the ink covering my scars.

"He'd burn me with a cigar lighter. He'd say since I loved God more than him, he'd give me the Devil's burns, too."

Tears well in Wren's eyes. Fuck, it kills me when she cries, especially for me.

I don't want her pity. I don't deserve it. I need her to understand how cruel my father is. Why I'd do anything for my brothers. I never meant to betray them.

"Axel suffered much worse," I share.

"Worse than burns?"

"I guess all abuse is horrific. When my brothers were babies, I'd hear my mom begging my father to let her take care of her sons, but he'd yell at her and say we needed to be tough. So, I did it. I always held my little brothers when they cried."

"That's why."

"That's why, what?"

"That's why you looked so natural holding that little boy." She smiles. "You'll make a great dad."

The lump in my throat is sudden. I don't have to tell Wren this, but I *want* to. I did a horrible, wrong thing. But with her, if I get a chance, I'll do everything right.

"Wren, I don't deserve to be a father."

She touches my cheek. "Of course, you do."

"No, I don't. I need to tell you something no one else knows. And I need to trust that you'll never tell anyone."

"I won't."

"But your mouth has never met a filter."

"But I've met you." She lifts my left hand, reverently kissing my partial pinky. "And you have my loyalty. Always."

And you have my heart, always.

And if I can ever fix this, it starts now.

It begins with her.

"My father has found me. He did it because I was arrested at nineteen for breaking into a pharmacy to get pain pills for a lady on our street who was undergoing chemo. He said it was a matter of time before I had a criminal record, and it took him eleven years to show up at my door."

She pulls back, shocked. "Does your mom know?"

"No one knows, because he's threatening to kill her and my brothers if I say a word."

"So, what did he want?"

"A legitimate heir. He's obsessed with pure bloodlines and that bullshit. My mother is descended from the Russian Czar, and my father's organization respects her lineage. And since my brothers and I escaped him, we hate him; he has no heirs. It's a disgrace for him."

"So, he wants you back?"

"I'd rather kill him and die, but I don't want my mother or brothers dead, either. So, I made a deal with him that once I married a woman, I'd give him our first son so he'd have an heir, and he'd let us live."

Horror hits her beautiful face.

"I never meant it," I rush. "I figured as long as I never married and had a kid, death would take him first."

She's doing it again. I can feel her looking at me and reading my soul. I find it comforting now.

"But?" she asks gently.

"But I should've known better than to make a deal with the Devil. I played the game too long, so once again, he set his sights on Axel."

She sits up, her hair the sexiest, long mane of curls. "What did he do to Axel?"

"He found a Russian woman, from a noble line, to move here and secretly seduce him. To marry Axel. And then she got pregnant and left him."

"Poor Axel." She touches her chest. "He must hate your father so much."

"He does, but he has no idea what he did."

"How's that possible?"

I sit up beside her. Scrubbing my hand down my face, I won't stop now. I can finally take a breath of relief, confessing everything to Wren.

Bear one another's burdens, the Bible says, and I've finally found a woman strong enough to bear mine.

"I have no proof this happened, only a gut instinct," I explain. "Katya was Axel's first wife, and when we made her our first queen, she wanted me, too. She came on to me all the time. She wanted me and Axel together. No condoms and in their bed. A permanent threesome. She begged me to breed her, too."

Wren asks painfully, "*Did* you?"

Fuck, she looks hurt. Wounded. Jealous. Even betrayed, and I want Wren to be possessive over me. I'm hers now.

"Never, I promise. I may have a dark kink, but I have control. I'd never betray my brother, and I don't fuck people who give me evil vibes, and that was Katya—evil. Just like my father."

"So, she married Axel, and you and your brothers made her a queen, but then she left him?"

"Yeah, with a note and a broken heart. And I suspect it was because she was finally pregnant and never told him. She went back to my father, while Axel has no idea he has a child, and that's why I don't deserve one."

"When was this?"

"Over three years ago, and I repent every day. I feel sick every day. *I* should've sacrificed my child, not Axel."

"But..." Her eyes search mine. "Could you *do* that? Give a child to that monster?"

"No. But what other choice did I have but to at least say I'd do it?"

"Why haven't you told Axel?"

"Because if I'm right, nothing will stop him. He'll get his kid and kill our father, and Katya, too, and he'll start a war we won't win. Kids, moms, wives: everyone will die."

She reaches for my left hand. "So, you keep the peace, don't you?"

I nod, rage and regret burning behind my eyes.

"You're a true man of God," she sighs. "You're trying to protect everyone, and you'll sacrifice yourself to do it."

"I don't care what happens to me. I'll fix this somehow, but I care about you now. You can stay here. I'll sign this place over to you, put some guards outside, and I'll leave you safe and at peace."

She squeezes my hand. "Or?"

I've preached about revelations, and now, I'm experiencing one. It's not a blinding light, like Paul on the road to Damascus.

It's the most beautiful woman I've ever seen, an orphan from Tennessee, who was left in a chapel, and *thank you, God,* I found her.

"Or you're mine, Wren. Forever. We're in this together. We never let go, and we never lose faith. That was our promise last night."

She kneels in front of me. It puts us nose to nose, lips to lips. "You made a deal with the Devil, but now, you'll make a deal with an Angel. All I ask is if you ever have to choose, you choose me."

I lace a hand through her hair. "There's no *if*, Angel. I'll always choose you. I did it the moment I laid eyes on you."

"Deal." She inches closer. "Now, lay your lips on me."

Our eyes lock, and it *is* a light. It's white, hot, electric, and blazing through my veins. It surges through me, igniting my instincts. I'm meant to have her, breed her, but I won't destroy her.

I nuzzle her nose. "Have you ever been kissed?"

"No. You get every first with me, Sire. Even love."

"I'll kiss you, Angel. I'm falling in love with you, too." I brush my lips over hers. "But I won't be inside you until you're my wife. I know it's patriarchal bullshit, but I don't care. I need to do everything right with you, Wren. You deserve it."

"Can we do everything right the first time?" She nips my bottom lip. "Then, everything wrong together? Forever?"

I'm holding back. I'm raging hard. "You don't know what you're asking for, Angel."

"Then, by God, show me."

CHAPTER TWELVE
WREN

SIRE CUPS MY FACE, HOLDING MY GAZE. HEAVEN OR HELL, I don't know what to call the light in his eyes, but I'm drawn to it.

Slowly, he kisses my lips. Tender. Tasting. Tempting. And I whimper for more.

So, he does it again. Faster. Wetter. Hotter. His tongue teasing the seam of my lips, and I let him teach me.

I part my lips open for him, and he groans. His breath falls heavy, his tongue exploring mine, and I get dizzy. I don't want lucidity; I want his lush lips. I want everything they're making me feel, from my racing heart to the wet rush between my thighs.

He tilts his head more, his hands weaving into my hair. When he gets fistfuls, he groans even deeper, his tongue more demanding, and I answer his mouth with a moan.

"Fuck, Angel," he huffs into our kiss. "Is this okay?"

"Yes," I pant. "Am *I* doing it right?"

"Do you want me to kiss you more?"

"Please."

"Then we're doing it right."

He kisses me until my world is spinning and my lips are swollen. My flesh is on fire. My panties are soaked. My empty cunt pulses. Desire keeps making my belly flip and flutter.

Good God, and it's only his kiss.

Imagining what even more will feel like with him makes me hungry. I moan into his mouth, my hand skimming his silky, hard pec, over his hidden scars, to his hard nipple.

Instinct tells me to pinch it gently, and he grunts, nipping my bottom lip before he pulls back like we have to stop. Like we have to be chaste, or else.

Maybe I'm too aroused. The way he looks is too tempting. The way I need him, too strong.

I'm supposed to slice my words up into sweet, passive, bite-sized pieces for any male ego to consume but fuck that. Nannie called that *the patriarchy*, and my desire agrees.

"More, Sire. Now," I demand. "Breed me. I want you to."

"Fuck, Wren." His grip in my hair tightens to the point of sweet pain. "Don't tempt me. You have no idea the dirty, perverted, fucking fantasies I have about you."

"So make them real with me."

He searches my eyes, and I watch his do that flip. From a man of God to a mafia king. From a pastor to a predator. From holding back, to oh-fuck-here-he-comes.

He smirks, evil and electric. "You want something dirty, little angel?"

Pleasure jolts through me. "Yes."

"You said you've watched porn. Are you ready for a real show?"

"Very ready."

"Lie back and unbutton your shirt for me," he demands. "You're going to be my private porn."

I lie across the bed as he throws the pillows on the floor. I can't find my breath, staring at the sight of him shirtless and kneeling between my spread legs. All his ink and muscles. His whole body is huge. But it's what's hard and thick between his legs that rips my breath away.

"Oh my God," I sigh as he reaches in, adjusting himself under his light grey sweatpants. The pants are so thin, I can see the outline of his swollen tip. He lifts his penis from pressed hard and long against his leg, to jutting, straight out, and so far that it pulls the elastic band inches away from his shredded waist.

"You like that, Angel?" He taunts, staring down at me, "You like seeing how fucking hard I get for you?"

"Yes," I pant. "You're huge."

He smirks. "How would you know, little virgin?"

"You have a huge, porn dick; that's how I know."

"Have you ever touched a real one?"

"I've never even *seen* a real one."

I guess that turns him on. His eyelids drop with lust, his hand giving one stroke to his covered erection.

"Show me," he demands. "Unbutton my shirt that you wear around our home and fucking tease me in. Show me what the sight of my hard dick does to your little nipples."

I release one button, then another, until all are undone, before I sweep the white, starchy cotton away, revealing my naked breasts and white cotton panties.

"Fuck, Wren," he groans as a dark spot appears at the tip of his dick under his light grey pants. "Fuck, Angel. Show me what you did, thinking about me in this bed."

"I did this." I circle my nipples until they're hard. Until they're ready for me to pinch, and I do. But I've never done this with someone watching me, with *Sire* watching me, and it's so intense, a slick flood soaks my panties.

"That's it," he urges. "Keep playing with your nipples. Fuck, you have perfect, little tits."

"Shouldn't they be bigger?"

"No, they should be in my mouth, and they will be one day soon."

"Are you..." I pant, lightly tugging at my excited nipples for him. "Are you going to touch me? Please?"

"No, Angel. Not today. If I touch you, I'll fuck you. I held you all night, and fucking died kissing you just now; I don't have much control left. Just show me what's going to be mine."

He licks his lips, another spot blooming in his pants. "Take your panties off for me, Angel."

I comply, tugging them down to my thighs. "Should I shave next time?"

Almost all the women I've seen in porn are hairless, and I've groomed like them, but I don't have the money or the will to get a full wax.

I guess I don't need to because he stares at my exposed pussy, his breath deepening as another dark, wet spot soaks his pants. He hisses, "That's *my* fucking pussy. Do whatever makes you feel beautiful because you are. Goddamn, Wren."

He yanks my panties off, pressing them to his nose. "Fuck, your pussy smells sweet, so wet and ready." He glares down at me. "Spread your legs open again. That's it. Show me that tight little pink hole I get to open and fill."

This time, I reach down and spread my lips for him, too. "I do this, thinking of you." With my fingertip, I circle my glistening clit. "You're the only man I've ever wanted. I came so hard, thinking about you."

His stare is locked on my pussy. "Any women?"

"No. Only you."

"Show me what you did the first night here, why I heard you coming so hard. It made me jerk off for you all over again."

"I did this." I start flicking my clit, my gaze devouring his gorgeous body. "I imagined my finger was your finger. Your tongue. Your gorgeous, huge dick. I imagined us doing so many dirty things together."

From his eyes, craving my pussy, to his parted lips, thirsty for my show, to his abs, subtly flexing, making his hips slightly thrust. His dick is huge, hungry, hidden, and dripping...

My Lord, his name is fitting.

He is a sire.

The ultimate male specimen, made to breed a woman like me.

But he's not touching himself. His hands are balled tight by his side, one fist clenching my wet panties.

It's like, if he touches himself or me, he'll lose control, and I'm loving this about him. How I know he can be brutal. I can only imagine how many men he's killed, but he won't hurt me. He won't touch me. He won't even fuck me until ... *I'm his wife.*

That's what he said, so I brace my feet against the mattress and rub my clit while I lift my hips, opening and thrusting, showing him how ready I am for him. "Pastor Rutledge, please. I really need you to fuck this wet pussy."

"Fuck, when you say that, Wren," he grunts, looking tortured. "Fuck, Angel, you're so swollen and pink and opening for me. Goddamn, your virgin pussy looks pretty."

It always felt like a burden or a barrier, my virginity. But it never felt beautiful. Not until now. Not until I see myself through Sire's gaze. He's so aroused that more dark spots saturate his sweatpants.

"Pastor, is that your cum?" I ask.

"Pre-cum, little angel." His voice sounds so gruff, his breath getting heavier. "And if you keep touching your pretty pussy for me, you'll make me come for you. And you're going to watch my dick do it while you come for me, too."

"I'm getting close." I strum my finger faster over my tinging clit. Letting him watch me touch myself has that luscious sensation growing even deeper and tightening my core. "So close," I pant.

"What was your dirty fantasy?" He demands, "Tell me what we were doing together that made you come."

If I weren't so aroused and on the edge of an orgasm, I'd suddenly find a filter. I'd be too shy to confess, "I imagined you, fucking me hard and deep, while we sucked another man's cock together."

"*Fuucccckk, Wren.*" He throws his head back. His thigh starts shaking. "Angel, you're too innocent for that."

"No, I'm not. I want every sweet first with you, then every dirty thing together. I want you and your brothers to initiate me. I want to be your wife. I want everything, Sire, as long as it's with you."

"Show me." He glares down at me, his hips thrusting faster, like he's fucking me, not thin air. "Show me how you made that pussy come, imagining me fucking you, and sucking a cock for you. Do it. Come with your fingers inside your tight cunt."

"I... I..." I rub my clit, my thighs trembling. "I've never fingered myself."

"What?" he pants.

"No fingers. No tampons. Nothing's ever been inside me." I'm right on my edge, telling him everything, showing him everything, playing with my clit for him while I spread my legs as wide as I can so he can see. "You, Sire. You'll be the first inside me."

"Fuck, Wren! Fuck!!" He doesn't touch himself, letting his thighs shake so hard, his hips pumping, his thick cock pulsing, before a creamy spurt of his cum shoots right through the thin cotton of his soaked pants. He watches it paint my mound before another creamy spurt escapes, while he grunts, staring at me.

With a silent scream, I come in front of him, too. At the

sight of him coming on me. The promise of him coming inside me. The convulsions are so strong, my legs violently shake, so I snap them closed with a groan, my eyes rolling back.

"No, Angel," he growls, "eyes on me while I eat your ripe pussy. I need a fucking bite."

"What?" I babble. I don't understand. Before I have a chance to get my bearings, his face is between my legs, his big hands pinning my trembling thighs open.

"Look at me," he demands. "Watch your pastor while I suck your virgin clit and make your sweet cum drip down my chin."

He does it so perfectly, powerfully. I've never felt this before, a mouth on my pussy, a tongue on my clit, his whiskers tickling my tender lips.

The hungry groans he emits as he sucks my tender nub for the first time make me thrash with another orgasm. It hits me so fast and hard, this time my scream shatters the room. "Oh God, Sire!"

"Yes, Angel. I'm your God. Do it again. Make your pussy come for your Lord."

"Please." I grab the sheets. "Please, Sire, I need you inside me. It hurts; I need you so bad."

"Not yet. Watch me." I lift on my elbows. In a euphoric daze, I marvel as he laves his tongue over my engorged clit, as he makes my thighs shake again. "You're so wet and ready for me," he praises. "So fucking ready to breed. Want to see what it will feel like?"

"What *what* will fe—"

I don't get a chance to finish.

Gently, his tongue licks at my opening, softly penetrating my cunt, and I collapse on the bed, falling into a need I've never known. "Please, Sire," my back bows with my beg.

"Quit fisting the sheets and fist my hair, Wren. Come on."

He guides my hand. "Grab my head and smear your pussy all over my face. Be my dirty little angel and do it until you're pouring your virgin cum into my mouth."

"Oh my God," I groan. I obey. I clench a fistful of his silky hair between my legs and shamelessly thrust my hips, trying to get his tongue to fuck me. It's barely inside, but it's enough to make me buck while his nose rubs my desperate clit, too. It's enough to make me come so hard, I see stars. I see heaven, and we're fucking forever in it.

I don't know what I moan, say, or do. Time ceases. Pleasure explodes. Light takes my vision until Sire's mouth is on mine.

He's kissing me and glossing his tongue over mine. He's making me taste my first real cum. It's tangy, tart, and sweet how he made me do it, and I moan into his mouth.

I wrap my legs around him, my arms, too. I make him groan and sink his body weight, most of it, on top of me until I can feel his sticky, semen-soaked pants against my flesh.

He sighs over our lips. "We're in trouble, Wren."

"Why?" I pant, gazing up at him.

"Because I need to marry you, Angel, real damn fast."

CHAPTER THIRTEEN
WREN

L ATER IN THE AFTERNOON, I'M STILL GLOWING. M Y BELLY does this yummy tickling flip every time I recall this morning with Sire.

Is that normal?

I guess I'll burn in hell because my memories find me chewing my lip while I watch him captivate his flock with his Sunday church service.

He's not wearing his sexy, dark grey suit as he preaches, and it's probably for the best. At this rate, I'll go through four pairs of panties a day, just staring at him.

Today, he wears faded jeans and a loose, V-neck T-shirt. His pristine white Nike Killshots add to his street style. His afternoon service is the contemporary kind. Music. Video screens. He doesn't even give a sermon, not like what I'm used to—all hellfire and brimstone.

No, he's like Moses, leading his people into the community. He's urging his followers to volunteer at least one hour a week.

"It is not enough to be compassionate, you must *act*," he says, holding his microphone like a rock star. "The Dalai

Lama said that, and I think he and Jesus would be friends. I think Jesus wouldn't be on his phone, posting memes about change. No, he'd be in his community, making that change *happen*. Will you?"

I sit on the front pew and glance back, wondering if everyone is as inspired as I am.

Every spot on every pew is full, with more standing at the back to watch. All eyes are on him. Heads are nodding, voices murmuring praise. They're enraptured.

Then, I notice a blonde woman two rows back, staring at me. Her smile is so fake, it looks like AI made her. Clearly, she disapproves of me. *But sorry, Karen, I'm used to women like you.*

Proudly, I smile back.

Then, another blonde woman, across the aisle, catches my attention. She's not fake. No, she winks at me, and I scan the man sitting beside her, stifling my gasp.

It's not Jace, but it looks like his twin.

No! He looks like one of the men who was there the night Sire rescued me.

Another brother!

It has to be.

So, that makes the winking woman, proudly sitting beside him, his wife? His queen? Instantly, I like her. I smile back, genuinely this time, and feeling sorry for every kind woman named Karen, before I turn back, lest my gawking gets weirder.

Once his sermon is over, Sire slings an electric guitar over his shoulder. Sorry, panties. Time of drench is now. That man could sing a drive-thru menu and win a Grammy. Instead, he sings a Christian rock anthem about a lion named Judah.

I glance back again, and the entire congregation is standing, some with their eyes closed and swaying with their hands in the air like it's a rock concert.

But fake Karen? She's chewing her bottom lip and obviously soaking her panties like me.

The blonde queen?

She's hugging Sire's brother by his waist. They look so in love and proud of him.

But I dread the end of the service, when I know Sire will have to spend minutes, if not an hour, talking to his adoring parishioners while I sit awkward and alone.

I'm used to it, so *WWDD?*

Whenever I feel out of place—which is usually all of the time, few in Tennessee or here look like me—I hum Dolly's "Little Sparrow" to keep me company.

But Sire shocks me.

As soon as he finishes with a closing prayer, he leaves the pulpit and walks my way, his beaming smile aimed at me.

He takes my hand, giving me goosebumps. "What did you think?"

I lift on my toes, whispering in his ear, "I'm so inspired, I'm walking on the water in my panties."

He snorts, laughing, before he leans down to whisper, "Behave, or I won't spare the rod in my pants tonight."

"Pastor Rutledge!" Why am I not surprised to turn and see AI Karen gushing? "I just loved your sermon today. I've decided to spend more time volunteering at my son's prep school. Right, Dan?" She backhands the man, busy on his phone beside her. "We're donating more to Cooper's school."

"Uh, yeah." Surprised, Dan glances up. "More money to the school. Got it." He winks at Sire. "Great sermon today, Pastor."

"Thank you." Politely, Sire shakes their hands. "I know a couple of other county schools that could use some generous donations, too. Let me know if you want their information."

"Yes, we do." Karen whips her plastic smile at me. "And

who's your friend, Pastor? She must be new. I'd never forget a face like hers."

Oh, I know a coded insult when I hear one.

"*She* has a name and a voice." I smile, speaking for myself, "I'm Wren Chapel. It's nice to meet you."

"And she's more than my friend." Gently, Sire squeezes my hand. He won't let go. "Wren is my girlfriend. I hope you and the parish will welcome her warmly."

"Girlfriend?" Karen looks aghast. I'm shocked, too, but in a heart-melting way. "Why, isn't that a little unbecoming for a pastor?"

Sire opens his mouth to speak, but—

"I am sure it is *very* coming for them." A rich, French accent turns our heads toward the winking blonde, who's sneering at my new enemy, "God believes in love. Yes? So why should our pastor be denied love, too?"

Inwardly, I'm fist-bumping the queen I don't even know yet. Without a formal introduction, she's already stabbing a back that's trying to stab mine.

And I love her accent. Even her insults sound elegant.

"Why, I just mean she looks too young for him," Karen drawls. "A May-December romance is highly inappropriate for a man of God."

"Meh." The sweet blonde shrugs. "It is better than having a cold, dry January for a marriage. No?"

Eyeing Dan, Karen's tuned-out husband, who's back on his phone, the blonde queen scores another point for me.

"Mrs. Cabot," Sire interjects. "I appreciate that you want what's best for me, and I can assure you, I've prayed on this; *Wren* is what's best for me. Despite our age difference, we have a lot in common."

It flies all over me that Sire has to be the better man right now. I'd rather have him take out his Glock and tell her to stick her December up my May ass.

"What could you two possibly have in common, other than one immoral sin?" Mrs. Cabot, apparently that's Karen's name, isn't backing down.

Clearly, she can't have Sire, so no one else can.

I glance and see others gathering around. Sire's brother, of course. Ms. Davis, the preschool director. A crowd of parishioners, whose eyes volley like they can't decide which side to take.

Sire saved me, and my instinct will always be to save him, too. I won't let him lose his parish because of me, because of *us*. In fact, I'll be his partner in Christianity and crime.

I softly reply, "Judge not, lest ye be judged. The Book of Matthew. It's one of my favorites. It teaches us to have compassion and self-awareness." I smile. "God, Mrs. Cabot. Our Lord is who the pastor and I have in common. God is who we all have in common. Let us rejoice in him."

Truth is, I know God is a woman. Watch a baby being born, and it's obvious. But I'm playing the patriarchy card for the win.

"Amen," Sire's brother crows, and the others nod, agreeing.

"Why, of course." Mrs. Cabot blushes. "Welcome, dear. And praise the Lord." She grabs her husband's elbow, hissing, "Come on, Dan. And put your damn phone away."

Others approach me with warm greetings, but I'm floating. I'm smiling through a haze.

His girlfriend.

I guess Sire is serious. He meant it. He's all in. It means everything to him to introduce me to his parish, so I remember my manners, shaking hands, and giving warm hugs.

Even Ms. Davis whispers to me with her hug, "I knew it, and I approve. If you get your childcare license, dear, I'd be honored for you to work with me."

"Thank you, and I will."

That would be my dream. I love kids. I love giving them all the hugs I wish I had gotten as a child.

Finally, it's just Sire and me, standing with his brother and the blonde queen.

"Wren," Sire lowers his voice, "this is my brother, Grant, and his badass queen, Delphine."

"Well, hello, our little Phoenix." Grant hugs me. He's as big and warm as Sire. "You are a little bird, aren't you? All rising fire and no bullshit."

I shrug, smiling. "Mess with me and I'll burn your ass."

"*Oui!* I love you already." Delphine yanks me into a tight hug. "Finally, I have another queen with me."

"What about Zar?" Grant asks.

Sire winces, muttering, "Shit. I forgot that's tonight."

"What's tonight?"

Grant cuts Sire a look. Delphine purses her perfect red lips like she can't say. And I sense something going on.

"Sire?" I tilt my head. "What's tonight? And who is Zar?"

CHAPTER FOURTEEN
SIRE

IT BECOMES CLEAR I NOT ONLY UNDERESTIMATED WREN, I underestimated myself.

"So, you're not mad?" I ask her. "You're not jealous? Or furious? Or even pouting?"

I'm shocked because Wren's mature acceptance of what I'm doing tonight arouses me in ways that are way too early for our relationship.

"If you want me to throw a tantrum, I can try," she jokes with a mouth full of red velvet cake.

Delphine laughs. "There. It is settled. She is one of us. She celebrates our initiations. *C'est magnifique.*"

"But think about it," Grant warns. "If we're all in an initiation tonight, who's watching Wren?"

She scoffs, "I don't need a babysitter."

"But you do need a bodyguard," I insist. "No fucking way will I leave you unprotected."

"Unprotected while you initiate a *man*?" She licks frosting off her top lip. "You sure I can't *come* with you?"

Oh, my angel, teasing me with your dirty pun.

"*Oui.* Why can't she come?" Delphine asks. "She can sit

beside me on a queen's throne. She can see how queens are made. She'll love it."

"Because only kings and queens are allowed to watch an initiation," Grant explains.

"Then blindfold me," Wren offers.

"Fuck no," I sneer lowly, thankful there aren't many here for an early dinner in the restaurant. "I can't focus on being a second king tonight, while my future queen sits blindfolded, and listening to me do it."

"Yeah." Grant nods, sympathizing, "That'd be too hot. You'll bust a nut too soon."

"That and..." I pause, trying to use logic, not lust. "This isn't about us tonight. It's about Nick and Zar and their love. It's their ceremony. It means a lot to them. To all of us."

"It means a lot that you're *doing* this," Grant adds. "I'll always try and help a brother, but I can't get it up for a man, even one as buff as Zar."

I'm not usually surprised like this, but I am by how Wren softly looks at me. It's not the same look as when she feared I already had kids or a wife.

No, when I told Wren we're initiating a queen tonight, and for the first time, the queen is a man, and I'm vowing to be his second king, Wren looked touched, even happy about it.

Zar is my brother Nick's future husband. We love our brother, and we love Zar, and it's not like Zar needs my protection. He has the build and billions to defend himself.

But this is about our bond and our survival. If a brother isn't really our blood, like Nash. If a brother is gay, like Nick. If a brother is bi, like me. Or if a brother can be a royal dick-head, like Axel. It doesn't matter.

If we stick together and stick to our traditions, we survive.

When Nick said he wanted Zar to be his queen, to be

honored like the other spouses, we agreed. It was obvious that I would be Zar's second king. With the way Zar looks—tall, tan, and handsome—it's not a sacrifice. I was honored, and honestly, aroused to do it.

But now, I have Wren.

She's flipped my world upside down in days, and I don't want it back. I want her, and she wants this.

"You're changing your traditions to honor Zar," Wren points out. "So, why can't you change your tradition so I can be there?"

Delphine raises her glass of Champagne. "*Tchin-tchin!*"

I reach for Wren's hand on the white linen tablecloth. Holding it, I get damn honest with her. I'm starting to count on it.

"Because I'm not ready for that, Angel. First, I want our wedding night when I make you mine. After that, we can do everything else."

"Promise?"

I lean over, kissing her cheek. "Promise."

"When did you get so traditional?" Delphine asks, amused.

"When I met *her*." I lift Wren's hand, kissing it.

"Bullshit, you've always been this way." Grant leans back in his chair. "You'll break every damn rule, but not a tradition. Watch out, Wren. He'll sneak and unwrap his Christmas presents under the tree to see what they are, then wrap them back, like no one can tell. But then he'll make you wait until New Year's Eve to open them."

Wren looks perplexed. "New Year's Eve?"

"It's Russian Orthodox tradition." Grant winks at her. "Your holy fucker is a complicated man."

I laugh. "Amen."

"So," Wren asks, "if I can't be at the initiation tonight and you won't let me take care of myself, which I can, by the way. Give me a Glock and Netflix, and I'll be fine. Who's going to..." she air quotes, "protect me?"

CHAPTER FIFTEEN
WREN

"So, what's the difference?" I ask. "They all taste like gasoline to me."

Nash taps the glass shaped like a tulip. "Whisky is made of grain and aged in barrels." He's turned Sire's island into a bar. "Scotch is similar but made in Scotland, and bourbon is produced here, and mostly made of corn."

"And *she* is going to be drunk if you keep this up!" Sire calls out from his bedroom.

"*She* has to start sometime, my brother!" Nash shouts back, grinning.

"Here." He offers me a glass. "This is a Van Winkle twenty-five. Rare and how bourbon should taste."

I sip and I like him. I feel safe with Nash. Sire's family is changing a tradition for me, too. Though Nash is a king, all decided he'd miss Zar's initiation tonight, so he can stay here and protect me.

At first, I was annoyed. I felt infantilized, as if I needed a babysitter.

But then Nash showed up, all inked, jacked, and wearing sexy glasses like the Clark Kent of the mafia. He started pouring us drinks from Sire's fancy liquor cabinet and treating me like an adult, and I was sold on his brand of protection.

I'm getting an education on fancy liquor, too.

"Not. *Ahem*. Bad," I cough at the sip of fancy bourbon.

Sire roars across his penthouse, "Brother, I will kick your ass if she pukes!"

Nash winks at me. "You'd better go check on him before he pops a blood vessel. Oh, and..." He hands me the glass of bourbon. "Take this with you. It'll piss him off."

I sip it once more, admitting, "It is kind of like fancy brown moonshine."

Nash bristles. "You just made every corpse in Kentucky roll over in their grave."

I laugh, making my way to Sire's bedroom. "Knock, knock," I say to his closed door.

"Come in." His voice sounds garbled.

I push open his door and gasp, "God! Stop looking like that!"

"Like what?" he asks with a frothy toothbrush in his mouth.

"Like *that*." I close the door, flitting my hand at his tight, black boxer briefs. Can we thank Calvin Klein enough for those?

Sire glances down, grinning. "Like what you see, Angel? Or are you drunk?"

I set the glass of bourbon on his dresser. "I'm perfectly sober and I want to *touch* what I see."

Standing in the doorway to his bathroom, he gets that animal look. It makes my heart hammer. It tells me to run or be ravaged.

Of course, I'm feeling ravishing.

"Can I?" I sound breathy. "Can I touch you before you're with a man tonight?"

"Wren, I won't do it if it upsets you. Just say the word."

Worried, he said those words with minty suds in his mouth before turning to spit them in the sink. He rinses and sets his toothbrush down before turning back to me.

"I'm serious, Angel. Always be honest with me." He points to his heart, then mine. "That's how we'll work."

"Did you honestly mean it today?" I meet him at his bathroom vanity. "That I'm your girlfriend?"

"Yes. That's where we'll start, and quickly progress to you being my wife, because I've waited long enough. I prayed, and here you are, and I'm not letting you go. I want *you*, and I want you protected."

His fingers brush my cheek. "That's all this is tonight: us, protecting a queen. I don't have feelings for Zar. Not like I have for you."

"Okay, if I'm being honest." Softly, I rest my hands on his firm abs. He flexes like it tickles. "I think it's sweet what you're doing for Zar and *Nick*, right? Nick's your brother's name? Sorry. It's hard keeping track."

"Yes, Nick's my brother. The second youngest." He leans against his countertop, but I don't move my hands. I like touching him too much. "And Zar will be his husband, as soon as they can come out."

"Why aren't they out?"

"Because Nick plays for the NFL."

I nod. "That makes it even sweeter. At least they're out with their family."

"You'll be my family, too, Wren. So, don't hide your truth from me."

"Okay, truthfully?" My fingertips glide to the band of his boxers. "I think it's hot, too. I know it's a sacred ritual for you all, but I'd be lying if I said that I don't find the thought of you with a man *very* arousing."

"Why?" He gazes down at where I'm touching him, at where he's getting rock hard.

"Because it's *your* truth. It's who you are and what you desire, and the world is shitty and lonely enough. We all deserve the love we need to survive."

He cups my jaw. "You deserve it, too, Wren. You deserve love and whatever you want."

"All I know is that I want *you*." I tickle my fingertips under the elastic. The way I can make him softly flinch excites me. "I want to see you, Sire, and touch you and taste you before you're with Zar tonight."

"Fuck," he sighs, staring at me, then his swollen erection. "Fuck, Angel, you're killing me."

"Will you let me kill your cock in my mouth?"

"Goddamn, Wren." He grabs the marble countertop behind him. "I'm going to fucking lose it when I feel you touch my dick, you know that, right? You've never done it. You've never seen a real cock or touched a hard dick or ever tasted cum, and it drives me fucking insane that I'll be the first for you. Maybe that's perverted as hell, but it's how I feel: dirty, filthy, and perverted for you, and I love every fucking thing I plan to do to you."

"Like what?" My hand is trembling, teasing and tugging at the elastic of his boxers.

"Like, I've been there, done that, and I don't want other women. I'll be faithful and devoted to you. Yes, I'm traditional that way, and I can't help it. You'll be my wife and queen. But other men? Fuck, I'll never share you. You belong to *me*. But I'll initiate you. I'll let you explore a little. It's only fair since I got to do it."

I'm overwhelmed and dizzy, imagining it, but I anchor to him, grabbing his flexing abs. "I only want to explore *you* right now. Please?"

His voice is gruff and strained, "Touch what you want, Angel."

I gaze down, and his length is so rigid. Pressed at an angle in his tight boxers, his tip reaches his hip bone, and I don't know what to do, so I let curiosity fuel my desire, my first touch as I wrap my hand over his shaft. *Oh my God. It's so hard and warm.* I squeeze it and it twitches.

"Shit, Wren," he hisses.

I gasp, jerking my hand away. "Did I hurt you?"

"Fuck, no," he growls. "Do it again, Angel. Put your hand on my dick and stroke it."

I obey, stroking his shaft over his boxers, and when I use both hands, he groans, watching me, "Fuck, yes, my little virgin. Are you getting wet touching my hard dick?"

"Yes." My voice trembles. I'm not nervous, I'm too aroused. "Yes, I'm wet."

I'm still wearing the cream Chanel minidress I wore to his church service, along with a new pair of pink lace panties, and now they're so slick from touching him, I love it.

"Pull my boxers down." He's still grabbing the countertop behind him. "Let me watch you wrap your hands around your first hard dick."

I tug at his elastic, but his erection? His tip? What if I hurt him?

"Do I just..."

"Pull them down," he urges. "It won't hurt. I'll get off watching my dick spring so fucking hard for you."

I tug them down, shocked at the sight. "My God, it's a thick, curving snake!"

Oh shit. I said that aloud.

He chuckles, his rigid dick bouncing with delight. "Yes, Angel. I have a slight up curve. Your pussy's going to love it one day. It'll hit the perfect spot inside that tight little cunt of yours."

I don't know what he means, but I believe him.

"Do I do this?" I glide my fingertip under his swollen tip, lifting his pearly drop to my lips. Gazing into his eyes, I suck my first taste of him off my fingertip. "Mmm," I moan. "Salty."

"My dirty little angel." A grin curls his lips. "Taste my cum again."

"But how do I..." I wrap both hands around his hard, naked shaft, squeezing tight and slowly stroking it. "Do I make your dick drip like this?"

"Oh God." He throws his chin up. "Oh, fuck, yes, Wren, you do. Jerk it like that."

Suddenly, I'm thankful for porn. I wouldn't know how to do this otherwise, and Sire seems to love it. He gazes down, his lips parted, his hips thrusting his dick into my tight, stroking grasp.

"You like this, Angel?" His voice sounds so guttural. "Do you like milking my thick cock?"

I swipe another drop from his tip and suck it off my finger for him to see. "I love your thick cock. Or is it your long dick?"

"Fuck, Wren, it's both with you," he pants. "It's everything with you."

"I want to suck you. I want you in my mouth."

I lean down, hinging at my hips to put his tip in my mouth, but he huffs, "No. Not like that, Angel. It won't be comfortable for you."

I look up. "On my knees?"

He shakes his head. "You're too petite. It won't be the right angle." He nods toward his bedroom. "On my bed. Sit on my bed."

In five steps, I'm eagerly sitting on his bed while I watch him kick off his boxers.

Menacing and so manly, Sire stalks my way, and my pulse triples as confusing edges of fear and lust scrape at my insides. His cock juts so huge and hard, I'm afraid. I don't know what to do with it. What urge to listen to—want or worry—but then he cups my cheek, lifting my chin.

"We don't have to do this, Wren. We can slow down. We can work up to this."

It's all I need to hear: decision made. "I'm so worked up and wet, I *want* to do this."

"Show me." He drags his thumb over my bottom lip. "Lift your dress, and pull your panties aside, and prove to me that your pussy is wet to suck my cock."

I keep my eyes locked on his. It feels dirty and delicious, exposing my pussy to him. "See, my stallion?" It makes me bold. "See how wet my little pussy is to suck your big dick, Pastor Rutledge? Now, make me your dirty girl and put your thick cock in my virgin mouth and christen me with your cum."

He fists his base, his other hand fisting my hair. "God-damn Wren, don't you ever find a filter for that filthy mouth." He aims his tip at my lips. "Lick it. Now."

Gazing up at him, I lick the creamy drop off his tip. His primal grunt is the hottest thing I've ever heard. Licking his crown, I explore his swollen penis like a lollipop. I don't know the proper technique, but I love it because he looks evil and entranced.

"Now, open wider, Angel. Wrap those virgin lips around my tip and taste your first cock."

I stretch my lips open, gliding them over his slick, salty, smooth tip. It's new and naughty. Natural and not what I expected. I like it because I make him groan, "Oh, fuck, yes. That's it. Look at your mouth full of your first cock. Such a pretty virgin face to fuck."

I moan, rolling my eyes at his praise, at the pulse in my cunt. With one hand, I shamelessly play with myself. With my other hand, I eagerly wrap it around his shaft, right by my mouth, sealing it to my lips like I've seen in videos, and I do my best to please him.

"Fuck, Wren." His grip in my hair tightens. "Fuck, my angel. You like sucking my dick, don't you?"

"Yes," I gasp with spit webbed from my lips to his tip. "Yes, I like being dirty for you." I pump my hand over his shaft, and he matches my tempo with his hand at his base. "Do you like watching me suck your dick, Pastor?"

"Fuck, yes."

"Do you like fucking my virgin mouth? It's all yours to fill with your seed."

"Goddamn, Wren," he snarls, pumping his base faster.

"Come in my mouth." I don't know what's making me feel this way. His desire or mine? Or both? But it's overwhelming. "Please. Please let me taste your cum, Pastor."

"Fuck, Angel." He removes my hand from his shaft and guides it between his legs. "Here. Touch me here and you'll make me come fast." He presses my fingers to the tender spot behind his balls, close to his anus. "Rub right here. Like a massage. In firm circles."

The moment I touch him there, pressing two fingers in circles, he groans, his right thigh shaking. The sudden power it gives me. The pleasure too. To control him. To please him. To have a massive man like him about to fall apart at the touch of my little fingers?

I wrap my other hand around his shaft and glide my lips over his tip, taking as much of him as I can without gagging.

"Oh fuck, Angel," he grunts, watching me, his hands cupping my head. "Oh fuck, Wren, you're making me come. That's it. Take what you can. Let me fuck that virgin mouth. That's right. Drool for me. Stretch those lips and cry. Moan and play with my ass and suck my dick, you sweet, dirty little thing."

I'm lightheaded and lost to lust. I love this. I love the sight of him. I love watching his lips shake until he's huffing and panting, "Fuck, Wren, fuck. Angel, you can't swallow it all..."

He tries to warn me, but I try anyway because ... *he's mine.*

I hold what I can of him in my mouth and squeeze his shaft while I sneak my finger to his ass, teasing it, and he explodes.

He doesn't even roar or shout. He violently jerks, grunting and forcing his eyes to lock on mine while his eyelids flutter and his dick pulses against my lips. I moan at him filling my mouth, all creamy and salty, until I can't take any more. I pull back and let some spill over my lips.

"Don't swallow," he barely speaks. "You don't have to swallow."

But I do. I let him watch me do it before I lick my lips. "I'm yours, Sire."

He pants, catching his breath, "Fuck yes, you are, Wren. Forever. Now, lie back."

I fall back on his bed, and he quickly drops to his knees, ripping my soaked panties to the side. I don't protest or resist. I let him feast on what belongs to him.

Sucking my hard clit, he moans into my pussy. I'm so wet and aroused by sucking him off, it won't take me long. I want to come for him, too.

I fist my hands in his hair like he taught me to, and I'm so close. I'm shaking ... but then there's a knock on the door.

"Bro." It's Nash. "You're going to be late."

"Come in," Sire commands. "Come in and see why I don't give a damn if I'm late."

I'm too shocked, then suddenly, aroused. I don't object when Nash opens the door. I hear it and close my eyes with a moan.

"I'm eating her sweet virgin pussy before I go anywhere,"

Sire taunts, then licks my exposed clit. "She just sucked her first cock, *my cock*. Didn't you, Angel? Weren't you such a good girl for me that you swallowed my cum?"

"Yes," I pant.

"It made her really fucking wet and a sweet slut for me; aren't you, my angel?"

"Yes, Pastor." My thighs shake.

"Show another king how much you like it, how I'm teaching you to come for me." With a wicked flutter, his tongue assaults my clit, and I cry out. "That's it, Wren. You can't be shy around us. You'll be our queen, too. You'll learn to come for us. *All* of us."

I've never known this depth of lust, but I want to drown in it. I'm loving it.

Gently, Sire sucks my clit again, and I writhe at the sensation, the taboo. I know Nash is watching us, and like Sire can read my mind, he insists, "Open your eyes, Angel. Look at Nash. Look at another king, while I eat your pussy, and then look at me, and come for *your* king."

I turn my head, my dazed focus finding Nash. While I stare at him, witnessing the lust in his eyes, I feel Sire's lips sucking my clit. Sire's naked and eating my soaking pussy in front of Nash, and I convulse.

I struggle to look at Sire next, and when I do, when I meet his devilish eyes gazing at me from between my legs while another man watches him make me come, and I do it with a back-breaking scream.

I lose my mind and minutes to my orgasm until I'm huffing for breath, and opening my eyes, realizing that Nash has left and Sire is braced over me, waiting until I find my focus.

Tenderly, deeply, he kisses me. I taste my cum on his tongue, and he must taste his in my mouth, too.

"You, Wren," he sighs. "You'll be my wife and the queen

we initiate next." I open my mouth to speak, but his kiss stops me. "Don't answer me, yet. Just wait up for me tonight, because I'm always coming home to you, I promise."

CHAPTER SIXTEEN
WREN

POURING KETTLE CORN INTO A BIG BOWL, THERE'S NO WAY around this, so I might as well ask Nash, "Has Sire ever watched *you* have sex?"

"Well, shit." Nash half-chokes, half-laughs. "Sire's right. You're damn cute, and have no filter, and yeah, he has."

Sire left an hour ago. So, I took a shower, slid into the white pajama set Nadine bought me, twisted my wet hair into a bun, and refused to be embarrassed about what happened.

It was too hot, too intimate to care, and now ... I'm curious.

"When did he see you fuck?"

"Years ago, we'd go to clubs together. Recently? Only during initiations."

I guess Nash refuses to be embarrassed, too. I plop on the other side of the sofa and put the popcorn bowl between us. "What kind of clubs?

He grabs a handful. "Kink clubs."

I twist my lips, dying to ask, and he laughs, "No, I don't have the same kink as Sire, not that I don't love him and whatever he does. We're very different and a lot alike. We'd go to a club and find partners. I'd be with women; he'd be with women and men. We usually fucked side-by-side, but we never loved them."

I curl my legs under me. "You've never been in love?"

"Oh, I've been in love for over ten years."

"Wait. What?" I lean forward, excited for this story. "With who? Are you married? Do you have a queen?"

"No," he shares. "I had a daughter when I was sixteen, and it took me a while to get my shit together and be a good dad. Now, it's my priority, being a dad, and Alena's a grown woman. She's amazing ... *and* ... so is her beautiful best friend."

My eyes widen, intrigued. "Alena's best friend? You're in love with your daughter's best friend?"

"She's almost thirty now and has no idea."

"Does she have a name?"

"Vale Monroe."

"So." I stuff popcorn in my mouth. "What are you gonna do about it?"

He does it, too, talking with his mouth full. "Decide if I should reply to her text."

Playfully, I nudge his leg. "Oh, so Vale *texted* you?"

"Yeah, she needs help with some accounting where she works, and *I* need help because I'm seriously considering doing it."

"You're an accountant and *mafia*?"

He laughs. "Yeah, and you know we don't go around calling ourselves that."

"Then why wouldn't you help her?"

"The same reason why Sire treated you like kryptonite for the first two days you were here. Once we touch you, it's over. We're done and in love."

My heart flips. "You think Sire's in love with me?"

Nash turns my way, lowering his eyes. "I *know* he's falling in love with you. I've known Sire since I was seventeen, and we met in juvie. He's been my family ever since, and I've *never* seen him this way with anyone."

I ask him something that's been on my mind. "Do you think we're going too fast?"

He raises an eyebrow. "Do you?"

I pause. "If I listen to some people? Yes, I guess. But if I listen to my heart? No. I have this instinct, like God is telling me that I belong with him."

"Damn." Nash shakes his head. "See? You're perfect together."

"But some people at his church are judging us because of our age difference." I shrug. "Or maybe it's because I'm brown. Or both."

"Fuck them," he scoffs. "They'd judge if Sire were with a White man. They'd judge if he were with a Black woman his age. Judgmental people want everyone to be miserable like them."

"So, what's keeping you from Vale?"

"Vale is my daughter's best friend, and I'll die before I hurt my daughter. And me being with Vale? It'd hurt Alena. But if they weren't best friends?" He shakes his head. "Vale would be mine. She'd drive me bat-shit crazy with her snarky mouth, and I'd be the happiest man alive."

"I think you should go for it. Help Vale with her accounting. What's the worst that can happen?"

"A lot." His tone gets serious. "The worst that can happen is exactly why I'm sitting here, honored to be protecting you." He pauses. "You need to let us go after the man who sold you into that trafficking ring, Wren. I'm fucking serious."

I glance away.

I'm really torn on this.

"Wren?" Nash touches my arm. "Men like him don't stop at hurting one girl. He won't stop until *he* is stopped."

I turn back. "Can I think about it?"

"Yeah." He winks. "And you can pick what we watch."

We go through a bag of popcorn while we watch *John Wick*, and I impress Nash with how many times I notice when a gun fires more shots than its magazine would allow.

We're like two peas in an ammo pod, until he starts to doze off and I curl up beside him and close my eyes, too.

Hours must've passed because I wake up in Sire's arms, carrying me across the room.

"You're home," I sigh happily.

"Yes, Angel. I came home for you."

I glance over his shoulder into the living room. "Where's Nash?"

"He left thirty minutes ago."

"I like him."

"Good." He lies me down on his bed. "You'll need to pick a second king, and Nash is available."

"A second king? Like you two will—"

"Shhh." He kisses me. "Let's sleep. We can play Q&A tomorrow."

Through heavy eyelids, I watch him loosen his tie. "I like you in a suit."

"Do you?" He grins, hanging his jacket in a neat row of a dozen dark ones that match. "I would've thought you'd liked my younger, Gucci look."

"No." I joke, "I like your whole lusty, oh my Lord look."

He laughs, unbuttoning his starched shirt, "Well then—" But his phone on the nightstand buzzes.

"Shit," he mutters.

I glance over and see FIVE on his screen. "Who's Five?"

"Jace," he tells me before answering, "Yeah?"

His eyes narrow while I can hear the angry boom in Jace's voice, but I can't tell what he's saying.

"Goddammit!" Sire roars. "Don't let them kill him! I'm on my way."

He hangs up and looks at me. "Get dressed, Angel. I can't leave you here, and I've got brothers trying to kill each other."

BRISKLY, WE WALK DOWN THE MIDNIGHT SIDEWALKS OF Charleston. The bar scene is alive, and it puts Sire on edge.

"Keep your hand on my arm, Angel. Always let me know you're there."

His head is on a swivel, his hand ready to grab his holstered gun.

We rush past a crowd outside a bar, and I almost stumble in my sandals. "Where are we going?"

"Axel's office." Ignoring the pedestrian light, he holds my hand while we jog across a street.

"Axel's fighting one of your brothers?"

"More like Axel and Nash are about to kill Loch, our baby brother."

"Why?"

"Because he's in love with Alena."

"Who? Axel or Loch?"

"Loch. And I'm the only one who's known. But it seems Loch thought tonight, of all nights, would be a good time to fess up to Nash."

"I mean..." I glance up at the three-story building with arched windows, while Sire enters a code for its door. "Given how Nash is Alena's father, and y'all probably go gangster about your women, would there ever be a *good* time for Loch to tell Nash that he's fucking his daughter senseless?"

"Well, when you put it that way..." Sire holds the glass door open for me. "Nash will *definitely* kill Loch."

Rushing up two flights of stairs, we can hear their shouts before we enter what must be Axel's personal office.

"Why Alena?" Axel roars. "You can have any woman. Why her?"

With a right hook, he punches a really hot, beefy guy who must be Loch.

"Because, Dick!" Loch uppercuts Axel's gut. "I love her!"

I look and see Nash pacing like an angry lion who just fed; his knuckles, lips, and nose are covered in blood. It seems like he's already had a round with Loch, but he's not bleeding as badly as the gusher pouring from Loch's eyebrow.

"She deserves better, you fucking..." Axel lunges for Loch, tackling him to the carpet.

Loch twists, rolling on top of him, cocking his fist back to punch Axel, who's moving his knee to kick Loch in the balls when...

"Hurt my brother, and I will strike you down!" Sire booms like God above.

Like the God who wiped out humanity with a flood because he was mad. Yeah, that God. The one you don't mess with—Sire's looking and sounding like him.

Loch glares up at him. "You're defending Axel? He fucking started it!"

Sire snarls, looming over them, "I'm defending *both* of you, and I will fucking *finish* both of you if you don't stop this shit right now."

Loch drops his fist.

"Jesus." Jace leans against the window, rolling his eyes. "They'll listen to you but not *me?*"

Sire leans down, getting in Loch's face, then Axel's. "Because they know I'm fucking crazy when I'm mad and nothing pisses me off more than our family fighting." His finger thumps Loch's head. "Get the fuck off him."

Loch crawls up.

"And you." Sire puts his finger in Axel's face. "You should know better. *I* make the heads roll in this family, not you."

"Did you know?" Axel spits blood on his carpet before confronting Sire. "Did you know about him and Alena?"

"Yes." Sire stands and looks at Nash. "I've known Loch has been in love with Alena since *before* you told him to guard her."

"What?" Nash charges toward Sire. "You fucking knew?"

"Yes." Sire stands in front of Loch, protecting him. Not that Loch looks like he needs defending. He's huge. Like Sire, Jace, Axel, Grant, and...

Damn, what do they put in the water in Russia?

"Because he loves Alena." Sire holds his hand up to stop Nash. "And that's all you should want; a good man who loves your daughter and—"

"I'd never let anything happen to her," Loch interrupts, blinking through the blood trickling into his eye.

"Um, guys." I raise my hand. "Can we press pause on this beefy brawl while someone points me in the direction of a first aid kit?"

Axel lies on the floor, suddenly smiling. Pointing to the open office space behind me, he says, "In the break room, on the right, under the sink."

Sire winks. "Thanks, Angel."

"No problem. You know, it's gonna be a bitch getting that blood out of the carpet."

I aim toward the break room while I hear Jace laughing, "She's the smartest one of us all. She's trying to fix this shit while y'all keep fighting about it, which is fucking dumb because you can't help who you fall in love with."

This is true.

Quickly, I find the big red box under the sink and over-hear Axel yelling at Loch, "You *will* marry her! I won't let you break her heart!"

Which is weird because, isn't that Nash's line? Why does Axel care so much about Alena?

"Fuck you!" I return to Axel's office and find Loch shouting back at him. He plops down on a desk; must be Axel's desk. "I already bought her an engagement ring today. So, don't turn this into some arranged marriage bullshit where you think you can tell me what to do and I have to listen. I guarded her because I *wanted* to. I was already in love with her, but then she fell in love with me, too, and now, we're getting married."

Nash seethes, "When were you going to ask my permission to marry my daughter?"

"Um," Loch mocks, "after you punched my bleeding eye, but before you tried to break my nose."

"Here. Use this. Apply pressure." I rip open a pack of gauze from the kit and hand it to Loch. "I'm Wren, by the way."

"Thanks, Wren." He softens toward me. "I'm Loch."

I wink. "I figured."

"How were you going to do this without our support?" Axel stands, brushing the carpet lint off his black suit. "How are you going to marry Alena without her finding out about us?"

I walk over and hand Axel some gauze for his bloody lip. I advise, "That's gonna need some ice, too."

Axel looks oddly amused, patting his swollen lip. "Thanks, Wren."

I smile. "No problem."

"He'll marry her," Nash proclaims, "and we'll never tell Alena who we are and—"

"Here." I hand Nash some gauze, too. "Lean forward and

pinch your nose. Don't tip your head back. That's a misconception."

"Uh..." Nash pinches his bloody nose with the gauze. "Thanks, Wren."

"You're welcome," I chirp.

Suddenly, Jace snorts, and Sire starts laughing.

"What?" I ask the room of bullheaded men.

Sire grins at me. "Want to tell us why you won't stop shaking your head at us?"

"Was I?"

"Uh, yeah," Jace huffs. "Because they're dumbasses, right?"

I shrug. "Any man's a dumbass if you think you can keep a secret from a woman for long. From what I gather, Alena doesn't know who you are? That you're ex-Bratva?"

Axel sneers at Sire, "And just how does *SHE* know who we are?"

"Okay, first." My fists land on my waist. "If y'all don't stop talking *over* women instead of *to* us, your beds will stay as cold as cast-iron commodes. We want to fuck dicks, not marry them. And second, you're as dumb as a barrel of hair if you think ignorance is protection. Tell that to the parents who used the pull-out method. Alena needs to know who you are. *That* keeps her safe."

I turn and grab a packet of antibiotic ointment.

"And besides," I talk with my back to them, cutting the packet open. "Sire told me who y'all are because take it from a country girl who's dealt with swinging dicks before; I'd rather know and duck than get blindsided by one."

I pause, the sudden image of all these swinging dicks in the room invading my mind. But in my imagination, they're hard and hot, so I clarify, "I mean, warn us about flaccid, floppy dicks. The big, hard ones, we like."

Loch starts laughing while Jace howls, "Can we marry her now, please?"

Sire shakes his head, grinning. "I'm working on it."

I chew my lip, excited for what that means, before I turn to Loch with ointment on my fingertip. "Hold still."

"Yes, ma'am." He bends down so I can reach him.

"Can we talk about Alena? And who's marrying her?" Axel brings everyone back to the argument.

"Next weekend, I'm proposing to her," Loch proclaims while I dab his eyebrow. "And I'd like your blessing, Nash. You know I would, but either way, you can't stop me."

"Did you buy her a big diamond?" I whisper to him.

"Sorta," Loch whispers back. "She likes simple stuff. So, it's a band of small diamonds."

"Nice choice." I nudge him before covering his cut with a sterile bandage.

He nudges me back as Nash seethes, "She's my daughter, and my responsibility above all. Yes, you can marry her. And no, she will not find out who we are. And Wren?"

I turn his way.

"I'm talking straight to you because I respect what you said," Nash addresses me. "In most cases, yes, it's best to know. But in the circles we run in, and the ones we rescued you from, if they think you or Alena know something, and they get a hold of you, they will traffick and torture you and—"

"Been there, done that," I calmly argue. "I love you guys. I know I just met you, but after what you did for me? Done. I love you. You have my loyalty. But ultimately, you can't protect us. Safety is an illusion."

"But we *did* protect you, Angel." Sire steps toward me. "Yes, you've been through some shit, but it would've been a lot worse if I wasn't there. And you're right. We can't always protect you, but we will die trying. Together."

He cups my cheeks, giving me a deep kiss before he huffs over our lips, "Goddamn, little woman, you're amazing."

Then he turns to his brothers. "And we're not fighting anymore. Nothing tears us apart. Understood?"

They nod.

"Let us do it, Wren." Loch arches his bandaged brow. "Let us go up into those mountains and go after that man for you."

Jace crosses his arms. "We promise we'll get him."

"We promise your home may be gone, but we'll get your land back, too," Axel adds.

"And we won't hurt Alan," Sire assures me. "We'll get him the help he needs, but his dad?" Sire narrows his eyes. "He's going to lose his head for laying a hand on my woman."

"Aw, fuck," Jace mutters. "Sire's about to go all biblical again for her."

CHAPTER SEVENTEEN
SIRE

JESUS, JESUS. I THOUGHT THE BIBLE HAD DRAMA, BUT MY family is running a close second.

"So, tell me about Zar's initiation." Wren sits on my island countertop, sipping tea. "And my initiation. What will it be like?"

No, wait. We're about to be tied for the dramatic lead.

I've brewed chamomile tea so I could calm the fuck down after that fight, but apparently, Wren's excited, too. For all the tempting reasons.

Setting my mug beside her, I stand between her legs. It's an ungodly hour in the early morning, but my angel always looks like heaven.

"Before we discuss initiations, give me the green light to kill him."

We stare at each other before she's slitting her eyes. "Do you really think Waylon's hurting other girls?"

"I know he is."

"How?"

"My brothers don't know this. It's part of my damning secret about my father, but he sends me clues."

"Clues?" She shocks back. "What is this? 'CSI'?"

"I don't know why he does it, but people are at stake, so I follow them, and that's how I found you. That youngest girl that I rescued with you?"

Her face bends, heartbroken. "Kelsey?"

"Yeah. She was from Chilhowee. Waylon's part of a ring, grabbing girls from rural towns." Her breath changes. "How did he grab you? You'd burned down his lab, his crew was dead, so how did he kidnap you?"

With resignation, she sighs, "I was camping, trying to hide and hunt, and it worked for months, until he tracked me down and got me while I was sleeping. The next thing I knew, I was in the back of a semi-truck with nine other girls."

The images I conjure of him hurting Wren, of him hurting all those girls, make me snarl, "*Give* me the green light, Wren."

"Don't hurt Alan."

"You have my word."

"Okay," she sighs. "But I'm going with you."

I huff, "The hell you are, Annie Oakley."

She huffs back, "The hell you can find him without me, city boy. That's the deal. You want vengeance, and I want Alan in treatment. Deal or no deal."

She jabs her hand out, raising an eyebrow. Her lips are sealed, which is fucking rare.

This is my lesson: never negotiate with terrorists when you're falling in love with them.

"Deal." I shake her small hand.

She lifts mine to her lips, sucking my middle finger before tempting me, "Now, tell me about the initiation tonight."

Gently, I grab her hips. "I can't tell you about Zar's initiation. I'll never lie to you, but initiations are sacred, and the kings don't talk about them. We do it out of respect for our queens. If you want to know what happened, you'll need to ask Zar."

Her voice rises. "Did you just *trick* me?"

"No. No matter what, I can't tell you about initiations."

"But I don't know Zar."

"You will soon, I'm sure."

"Where was he tonight? And everyone else?"

"Grant and Delphine took Nick and Zar out to celebrate. Probably to my mom's club, while the shit hit the fan with the rest of my brothers."

"So, your *mom's* involved with the initiations?"

The disgust on her face matches the urge I have to puke.

"Oh, hell, no. Never. She leaves that for us. She just insists that all queens are honored, so she bakes a Korovai for the initiation."

"What's that?"

"Russian wedding bread."

Her eyes widen. Each word, a shock to her system. "Your mom. Bakes bread. For your. *Orgy?*"

Fuck, she makes me laugh, and goddamn, I need it. "It's not an *orgy*. It's a... Well..." I falter, remembering what happened tonight and not wanting to lie.

"Come on." Her shoulders sag. "What can you tell me about the initiations?"

I cup her cheek, stroking my thumb over her soft skin. "They're a lot like a wedding. First, the king makes his vow to his queen. Then, they consummate their union. Next, the second king makes his vow to honor their new union and to protect the queen before they consummate their shared bond."

Wren smirks, believing in that like flying unicorns. "You mean ... you fuck, and then have a threesome in front of the other kings and queens?"

"Yes. They bear witness."

"Is that all they *bare*?"

I tongue my teeth. "Often, they bare more."

"So..." Holy hell, the way Wren's eyes look aroused by this stirs Dick. And here I thought he'd be exhausted. "Are only the first and second kings involved in initiating the queen?"

I squeeze her hips, loving the handfuls I get with her, loving the images I'm getting *with* her. "We give our queen whatever she or he demands."

"How many queens are there?"

"Right now? Two. Delphine and Zar, and if you want, you're next."

"If I *want*?" She chuckles, amazed. "I haven't even tasted the first flavor yet, which is you, and now you're telling me there are seven flavors? And you'll let me try them all?"

I stare into her topaz eyes, and *oh fuck...*

Here comes the storm.

Arousal and anger whip inside me like the winds forming a tornado. The hottest thoughts of the most taboo pleasures I can give Wren collide with the cold reality that she's just begun ... and it makes me want to destroy something.

I've enjoyed years of kinky sex, indulging my darkest desires, while Wren hasn't even been opened. She hasn't explored all she'll crave, and as a man who craved breeding women and men, I know what's fair. She should have an equal chance.

But tell that to my heart.

I'm a deviant devil who wants a godly marriage with her.

I crave dirty things with my pure woman.

I want all to see my claim, but I only want to do it with her.

I believe in freedom, but I want to control her sex.

I'm well aware of the contradictions.

They'd amuse me if I didn't feel them splintering my soul.

"What?" Softly, Wren touches my cheek. "What did I say?

You look upset. Was it the seven flavors thing? I'm sorry. I was joking. I only want *you*."

I don't have an answer, and she blinks, tears welling in her eyes.

"I mean it. *You*, Sire. You're all I want. You're just so honest with me, which I love. So, when it comes to sex, I want to share it with you, whatever that looks like, as long as it's me and you. *Together*."

With my heart pounding, I softly kiss her. I can destroy this delicate creature, while all I want to do is rip apart anyone who hurts her—even myself.

This must be love: this vortex of emotions.

Nature's most powerful storm.

I nuzzle her forehead. "I only want you, too. All my years faded the moment I saw you, Wren. You became my now and my future. I know it because I *have* a past, and you don't when it comes to sex. And I feel like a complicated, hypocritical, selfish man because I have pure feelings for you, like now, but then I get dark urges with you ... like what we did with Nash."

She nibbles her lip. She can't control her reaction to the salacious memory, and I murmur, "You liked it, didn't you? You came so hard when Nash watched me eat your pussy."

"Yes," she sighs. "It made me feel beautiful and powerful and dirty at the same time. I loved it, and I'm not ashamed to tell you that I want to do it again. I want to do *everything* with you."

This woman is a war I don't give a damn if I win, just as long as I'm with her until the day I die.

"I want it, too. But then..." I brush my lips over hers. "I want to make you my wife and the mother of my children. You're sacred to me, Wren."

She rests her hands over my thundering heart. "I feel the same about you. Would it scare you if I told you that afternoon on the sidewalk, when I was holding baby Isaac, and waiting for his mom to pick him up, and you came over and held him, too: it felt like fate. I knew we'd have babies together, too."

Fuck, I'm fighting tears. It's moments like this that I believe in God and heaven and love … and … now *us*.

"I had the same vision. It scared me, but it also made me happy. How is that possible?"

"Because, Sire," she pauses, "we're meant to be *everything* together."

Age becomes another contradiction we share, because in moments like these, Wren's the wiser one.

She won't back down from our stare. She believes, "I think we can be sacred and sexy, complicated and committed, hypocritical and hot, selfish and—"

Jesus, Jesus.

She's the one.

The only one.

I grab her lips with a passionate kiss—a kiss like none I've ever had.

Wren's first kiss felt like mine, too. Humility and hunger overwhelmed me, claiming her lips and tongue for the first time. I just kept kissing and kissing her, and going deeper, and finding my home. And I feel it now: home with her. And really … *really* fucking hungry for her, too.

She tastes like the sweetest sin, panting over our lips, "That was a helluva interruption."

"You make a helluva good argument."

"Did I win?"

"I'm losing my heart to you, Angel. We're both winning."

Trailing my lips down her neck, I inhale a new scent on her flesh: daisies, caramel, and sexy musk. Before, her scent was pure soap, but now, it's pure seduction.

"Fuck," I growl, "when did you get perfume?"

She opens her neck for me. "In the lingerie store, when I went shopping with your mom."

I nibble her flesh. "Never say 'mom' and 'lingerie' to me in the same sentence."

She giggles. "Did you just get soft?"

I steam over her ear, "Hardly."

Reaching down, she squeezes my aching cock, and I groan, "Careful, Angel. You're making me nineteen again."

"Is that a bad thing?"

"It is for your virgin pussy, because I'm *not* nineteen. I'm forty-three and I know exactly how to fuck you and make you come all night like you deserve."

I pull back and she gazes down, admiring my erection, before meeting my eyes.

"I want you to have what you deserve, too," she insists. "Make me a wife and a mom, and a complicated, hypocritical woman, too. Because I won't share you with other women. I'll get too jealous. But I'll share you with men." She chews her lip. "It kind of turns me on, too."

My hard cock twitches. Excitement lights up her eyes, making me warn, "Not yet, Wren."

With the sexiest pout, she strokes my heavy dick. "You're such a wet pussy tease, Pastor Rutledge."

Fuck, when she calls me that, I lose it.

I fist her hair. "I'm not teasing. I'm in charge."

Cupping her hand, I force our palms to stroke my dick together, our moans mingling with my vow over our heated lips.

"I'll tease your virgin pussy and make you come, and I'll let you play with my hard cock like it's your favorite toy. But I mean it, Wren Chapel. You'll be my wife before I open you. You're mine, the right way, before we do every wrong thing together."

CHAPTER EIGHTEEN
WREN

Note to self: Sire honors his vows.

It's good news if I'm ever his wife; bad news every agonizing day I'm not.

For a month, he gives me orgasms and frustration.

The plus side to his ferocious tease?

We're becoming best friends.

He's teaching me how to play the guitar, using Dolly's songs, of course. I'm teaching him how to bake desserts, and we compromise on organic sugar. I completed my online classes to obtain my childcare worker license, and now I'm training with Ms. Davis.

Almost every day, Sire and I work at the church together, and every night, he'll hold me after we torture each other, and I love it.

I'm getting so good at teasing, touching, sucking, and tasting him; he seems as tormented as I am.

It's agony how much we want each other.

But Sire swears he has to kill my past before we begin our future.

So, I also spend the month working with Loch. We meet

online, scouring maps and satellite images to find where Waylon might be hiding.

Loch is a forest ranger with Alena in the Pisgah National Forest. That's over fifty miles from where I'm from. Yes, the terrain is similar, but the hiding places aren't.

It's late summer, and drone footage can't penetrate the deep canopy of the lush mountains. We could wait until after fall, but Sire's losing his patience, and I'm convinced that while the weather is good, Waylon will go back to familiar hunting grounds.

The point being, we either leave today, when we can spot Waylon on the move, or we risk losing him to a cabin where he'll hide this winter.

"Shotgun!" Jace opens the passenger door of our black crew-cab truck. It's parked outside an old Naval bunker where they store their gear.

"Really?" Sire deadpans him. "Shotgun?"

Jace shrugs like, *What? It's a game and I won.*

"Wren," Sire turns to me, "ride up front with Loch. I'm grounding Jace to the back row with me."

"What if I get carsick?" Jace gives me a little boost into the passenger seat.

"What if I kick your ass all the way to Tennessee?" Sire jumps into the back row.

We slam doors and buckle in.

"Why isn't Nick here?"

"It's the NFL preseason and his face is too famous," Loch answers me before Jace mutters, "Then why aren't we taking the jet?"

"Because our gear and seven asses weigh too much." Loch checks the rearview mirror.

Axel, Nash, and Grant are in the truck behind ours, waiting for us to take the lead.

"Then why can't we get a big SUV?"

"Jesus, Jesus," Sire huffs at Jace. "Want some wine with that cheese?"

"Fuck, you, bro," Jace grumbles.

I turn around, offering, "I really don't need to sit up front."

"Yes, you do, Angel." Sire winks. "Our little snowflake here needs to learn not to melt."

Jace growls, "This snowflake is six foot six and will turn this into a road *bitch*, not a road *trip*, if he fucking wants. Why didn't we bring the Tahoes?"

"Because," Loch clips, "then we'll be as obvious as a fart in church driving up those mountain roads. In the trucks, we look like hunters because we are."

To ease the tension, I play Dolly's songs and sing for them. Loch grins at my voice ... or is that a grimace? Then, Jace puts on his playlist, and the big, hot assholes start laughing at TLC's "Waterfalls."

"What?" I'm offended. "What's so funny? It's a serious song. A man dies."

Sire's wiping his crying eyes. "Angel, *what* do you think the chorus says?"

I glare at Loch, Jace, then Sire. They're pursing their lips like they're about to burst.

"What?" I'd stomp if I could. "They're saying, 'Don't go, Jason Waterfalls.' It's sad."

They explode, howling. Loch may just swerve off the road, and Jace can barely breathe, grabbing the back of my seat and huffing, "Little one, it's 'Don't go *chasing* waterfalls'."

"No, it isn't. It's about a man named Jason Waterfalls, who gets killed selling drugs."

Loch snorts so hard, a brain vessel just burst, while Sire tosses his head back. "Fuck, Angel. You're too damn cute."

I narrow my eyes. "I'm fixin' to show y'all *cute* if you don't quit laughing. Careful next time you sip your sweet tea. I may just put something extra in it for you."

Loch cuts me a glance. "What's that supposed to mean?"

"It means," Sire gazes at me, smiling, "don't fuck with my little woman."

I give them the silent treatment, refusing to sing anymore until we make our first pit stop at a Biscuitville.

Despite wearing worn-in tactical boots, faded jeans, T-shirts, and ball caps, my future kings have too many inches, muscles, menace, and ink. All six of them enter the diner like a mountain mafia invasion. Heads turn, eyes freeze, jaws drop, panties melt, and the other dicks in the room shrivel into shrimp.

The guys stand in line at the counter, while I glance around. It feels as if they're looking at me, too. With my color and curls, I rarely blend in, either. I'm used to it. But now I must look like a little brown beauty surrounded by six white country beasts.

"Yeah," I mutter behind my hand, "we blend in."

Sire grabs my other hand, lifting it to his lips. "Let them stare, Angel. All they see is a gorgeous queen and her court of killers."

Axel stands in front of me, glancing over his shoulder, clocking our audience. "Don't worry," he murmurs to me while Loch orders our lunches. "We'll use Grant as a human shield."

"Shield this." Grant punches his arm. "Don't worry, Wren. We'll stand behind Axel's giant ego and be fine."

Axel smirks, "Fucker, I got my giant ego in my pants."

Grant huffs, "Wanna get my giant fist in your face?"

"Shut up." Sire thumps their heads. "Goddamn, I can't take y'all anywhere."

But I love it.

We're like family.

They give each other shit over lunch, shit while we drive, shit when we park the trucks four hours later, shit as we sling our loaded backpacks on, and more shit until we hit a trailhead where Loch raises his right fist in the air.

They fall silent, and Loch turns to me, whispering, "You sure, Wren? There's no turning back now."

The familiar smells of home assault my mind with memories. Crisp mountain air. Damp, mossy earth. Clusters of mountain mint bloom to our right. The goldenrod flowers in the valley skunk the breeze while sweet pine needles crunch under our booted feet.

It's all too bittersweet. I swallow my emotions and focus, pointing up the ridge. "Yeah, let's hunt."

Standing behind me, with the rest of his brothers in line behind him, Sire whispers in my ear, "That's my Iron Angel."

Then, he swats my ass.

We changed into the proper gear before locking up the trucks: long pants and T-shirts. We grabbed our guns, and the guys let me pick first. I took the Browning X-bolt rifle with a scope; it's the closest to what I grew up with.

Loch made us wear camo baseball caps, too. I've tucked my hair inside mine, and I swear we look like a special ops force, because we are.

Silently, we hike for two hours, and I'm in my element. My pulse triples, but it's not from the effort.

I'm conditioned for this.

My heart responds to every footstep I take closer to Nannie's home, *my home*, and the haunting memories come back. All the sweet days with her, all the scary nights after she died.

I'm quiet while we set up our two four-person tents. Wisely, Loch insists that we leave a small footprint. Grant builds a fire circle, and Axel sets up the camping stove for boiling water. Jace finds a tree a hundred yards away and strings up our bear can full of MREs while Sire and I take axes and gather firewood.

"Hey." He gathers me into his arms once we're alone. "You okay?"

I rest my cheek on his chest. "It's all coming back."

We take a breath together before he says, "Well, then, let's confront it. What's your worst memory here?"

I close my eyes. "Waking up with a dirty hand over my mouth, and more hands, pinning my ankles down."

His lungs heave against my cheek, his arms squeezing me tighter. "I'm going to kill him."

"I'm beginning to be okay with that."

He cups my face, lifting my stare. "What's your favorite memory here?"

"Waking up to Nannie's wild blueberry muffins and feeding Banjo."

"Who's Banjo?"

"He was Nannie's old shepherd. So smart and sweet."

"What happened to him?"

I swipe a sudden tear. "Waylon shot him for trying to protect me."

The veil falling over Sire's indigo eyes turns them black. "I'm *really* going to kill him, Wren. You may hate me after. You may never want me to touch you again or—"

"I won't hate you. I'm not a snowflake, either. Nannie called it 'country justice' because judges and cops never give a shit for poor mountain people and '*colored*' people like they say, particularly if we're women. So, if you want safety, you gotta kill for it."

He nods, glancing away.

"You just thought of your father, didn't you?"

"Yeah," he mutters.

"Sire, when are you going to tell Axel? I mean, just being with you and your brothers today; you fight with so much love. Don't you think he'll understand? That he'll forgive you?"

"If I just hurt *him*? Probably. But if I hurt his kid? Never, because I don't deserve it."

"We all deserve forgiveness."

He swallows. "No, some of us don't."

"Hey, look at me," I say softly, and he meets my eyes. "Love keeps no record of wrongs. Did I read that in Corinthians, or was it on a cereal box?"

A grin plays on his lips. "Sounds like Lucky Charms to me."

"Do you want to get lucky with me?" I tease.

"Every fucking day of our lives."

"Okay, then. We're here, confronting my past, so let's confront yours. What can you do about your father and Axel?"

He inhales, staring into the forest, and lightning quick, a plan forms in his eyes. I marvel, watching it as he nods. "Every April, a megayacht anchors in Savannah, Georgia. Local rumor is it's a Russian oligarch's ship, and they're right. It's my father."

My heart starts racing. "And?"

"And next time, I'll pay him a bloody visit. I want intel and justice. I want to know if Axel has a child, and if so, I want my niece or nephew back. And..." he cups my cheek, "I want to make sure *our* kids will be safe, too."

My hands start to tremble like it's a sign. "How will you do that?"

"Make a new deal with him. Just me."

"No, Sire, don't do it alone. That's too dangerous. You need your brothers with you."

He shakes his head. "And risk them, too? No. I have some friends I can call."

"Friends? You don't need *friends*. You need your badass brothers or a SEAL team."

"Don't worry." He kisses my nose. "My friends are crazy. They're cousins and contract killers and—"

"Hey!" Loch calls out yards away. "Are y'all finding firewood or fucking?"

I roll my eyes, muttering, "I *wish*."

Sire chuckles. "Patience."

I point to my crotch, clad in camouflage. "I got your impatience right here."

He smirks, snaking his hand between my thighs, his thumb instantly teasing my exact spot. I gasp at his touch as he growls over my parted lips, "You're goddamn right this is *mine* tonight."

CHAPTER NINETEEN
SIRE

It takes forever for the sun to set and for me to get Wren into our tent.

"I need to take a quick bath first," she insists, so I stand guard at the edge of the nearby river with my rifle in hand ... and her engagement ring burning a hole in my pocket.

"Fuck, woman, you're killing me," I mutter, watching Wren strip naked before wading into the shallow water.

She teases, glancing over her shoulder, "Like what you see?"

"I'm going to fucking *own* what I see."

Damn, I know heaven and hell exist because I feel both with Wren.

Playing with her, pleasing her, the promise of having her: that's been my heaven. Not fully satisfying her, not seeing my ring on her finger while my cock is buried deep in her tight pussy while I come inside her: that's my hell.

But not for long.

Watching her naked in the dusk-lit river, her thick hair twisted in a messy bun with black tendrils weaving down her wet tawny skin to her narrow waist, water lapping at her full hips, her delicate hands obviously washing her pert breasts, then her sweet pussy...

Goddamn, I *am* lucky.

I *am* starting new.

Wren's right. We both need to confront our pasts because *that* soul-stunning woman, washing her sweaty neck, is my future.

She has no idea the plans I've been making. How I'm going to marry her when we get home.

When she's finally washed and ready for bed, it makes me spoon her tight under our summer-weight sleeping bag.

Nash and Jace settle into theirs beside us. We made the snorers—Loch, Axel, and Grant—sleep in the other tent.

Thankfully, the frogs by the night river are louder. So are the crickets, chirping in the woods around us.

It's peaceful.

But Wren, with her little silky sleeping shorts and shirt, and the hope she'll be my wife soon, has me firmly awake.

Quietly, I sneak my hand under her shirt, caressing her warm skin. Softly, she gasps while I pinch her taut nipple and suck her neck. I go back and forth, tugging on her firm peaks, and rutting my hard cock between her plump ass cheeks, until she's grinding back on me and we're both fighting to stifle our moans.

"Shh, little angel," I whisper in her ear. "Don't let them hear me make you come."

"Oh, we can hear you," Jace answers with a husky voice.

He's on the other side of Nash, who murmurs, "Like any of us will sleep until she comes."

The throb in my cock is instant. "You hear that, Angel?" I guide Wren to lie on her back. "They won't sleep until I make you come."

The firelight outside our tent is slowly dying out, but it's enough to see her face and the lust in her eyes.

"I want to make you come, too," she insists, tugging down my boxer briefs, my cock springing free. She wraps her fist around it, making me grunt. My tip drips when she turns to Nash and Jace, three feet away, and says, "And they can come with us if they want."

"Fuck," Jace sighs. He knows who the real threat is. "Brother, don't offer her if you don't mean it."

"Oh, I mean it. You can watch her." I unbutton Wren's soft top. "She's fucking beautiful when she comes. Her gorgeous eyes roll back. Her little nipples get so hard. Her pretty pussy gets so pink, it drips and—"

"Goddamn," Nash huffs, tossing his sleeping bag open. He's already fisting his thick cock under his boxers.

"Oh, Angel." I pull her shirt open, revealing her excited nipples. "Look, you're tempting Nash."

Wren glances over. Her hand squeezes my hard cock even tighter when she sees Nash, wedging his boxers down, exposing his soaring dick to her. "Oh my God," she sighs. "He's so hard."

"Fuck, so am I." Jace sounds like he's in pain.

Wren stares up at me, her gaze flooded with desire. I've been training and torturing her for a month. She can read the permission in my eyes, how I want this for her. I'm testing her.

She's not shy, tempting my brothers, "Both of you, watch my pastor make me come like a dirty girl, while I make your dicks come, too."

"Yes, my angel," I growl, kissing her mouth and finding her tongue.

It flips that switch inside me, and there's no going back. I cross over into my darkest desires, and I don't give a damn for decency, restraint, or shame. I have none. *We* have none.

"Spread your legs, Angel," I order her. "Open wide so your kings can see that pretty, virgin pussy that belongs to me."

That's their sign. We've shared too much in the past. Jace and Nash know to kneel, side by side, on the other side of Wren. They rip their boxers down to their thighs, while I kick free of mine.

I'm naked and kneeling on the other side of my breathtaking future bride, who spreads her legs for my brothers to see what belongs to me.

"Just let them stare, Angel," I demand. "Let them see how wet you get waiting for me to breed you. Aren't you?" I pinch her nipple. "You're so ready and waiting to take this hard cock and my cum?"

"Yes, Pastor, I'm all yours to fuck, to breed," she tempts me. She drives me insane with our taboo role play, because it's not.

I *am* her pastor, and this is my pussy to fill.

I press my swollen tip to her lips. I've taught her so well. She licks up my early drops. Fuck, I love it how she does it like my dick's a lollipop, and she's a naughty girl for my candy.

A hot shiver shoots down my spine, right to my groin, while I demand, "Spread your lips, Angel. Show my brothers how hard your clit gets for me."

Wren moans, holding her cunt open, her tongue hungrily lapping at my crown.

"Damn," Jace groans, staring at Wren, exposing her pussy to them while he slowly pumps his fist over his meaty length. "Fuck, man. You're so lucky. She's so beautiful. So pink and wet for you."

Wren moans at his praise, so I lightly tug at her nipples, thrilling her even more while I taunt Nash, "What do you think of my hot, future wife, brother? Do you see why I've lost my mind and heart to her?"

Nash cups his balls, pulling on them while milking his tip. I've watched him jerk off so many times, from juvie to kink clubs, I know when he likes what he sees.

"I'll fucking kill anyone else who touches her," he vows. "She's ours."

"But, please, touch *me*." Wren writhes, urgently lifting her hips while my cock bobs heavy over her hungry mouth.

"You want me to touch you, Angel?" I press my index and middle fingers to her lips, and she obeys. It gets me off how I'm the first to please Wren, to train her. Eagerly, she sucks my fingers until they're coated in her spit.

Lightly, I circle my slick fingertips over her clit, and she shudders, her lips gasping under my swollen tip.

"Suck my cock, Angel. That's it. Wrap that hand around it and suck me off while my brothers watch me play with your pretty clit."

As I circle her hard, wet nub, her choked moans don't stop. I know my brothers in the other tent can hear her, too, and that only arouses me more, my desires getting dirtier. I want the whole world to know, see, hear, smell, and bear witness to how Wren is mine.

I tease her clit until her pussy is weeping wet; she's practically crying in pain. Gazing down at her eyes, they look desperate with lust, my tip, thrusting into her flushed cheek; her nipples can't be any harder.

I pull out and demand, "Do you want more? Tell us, Wren. Tell your future kings what you want."

She pants, "Yes. Please, Sire. I want you. I want you *all* to touch me."

I feel the evil smirk emerge from my depths before she sees it. The fact that she moans when she does, imagining all the lecherous things I'm going to do to her, and she *wants* it, drives me fucking wild.

I even surprise myself at what I'm willing to do in moments like this.

"Get my queen off," I tell Nash. "Feel how hard and perfect her little nipples are."

Wren gasps, arching into Nash's touch. She makes him groan while he cups her breast and jerks off over it.

"Brother." I glance at Jace. He hides so much; I know. I love him for it, but he doesn't have to hide it from me. "Touch her, too, and show her how good it can feel."

Jace practically loses it. While I tease Wren's clit, he lavishes her pussy lips. Tickling over her folds, lingering over her inner thighs, returning to tease her with erotic torture, never taking what's mine, and she softly cries, "Oh God, it all feels so good."

"That's right, Angel." I rub my tip over her panting lips. She loves the filthy tease while I taunt, "Suck your pastor's cock. Come on. Show them what a dirty girl you like to be for me."

That always makes her moan, her eyes rolling back. With my cock over her lips, my fingers scissoring her clit, Nash pinching her nipple, and Jace teasing her inner thighs, Wren comes so hard, the whole mountain can hear her.

"Holy fuck, she wants it bad."

I hear Loch growl from the other tent, and he's not wrong. I'm in awe, too, and on my edge. "That's it, Angel. Keep coming for us, while you make me come, too."

Wren knows what to do. She gets that devilish look in her eyes, loving this part.

Reaching between my thighs, she knows where to massage me. How it makes my hips thrust my dick into her mouth. How it makes fire ignite my veins. How it makes my lips shake and my thighs quiver when she fingers my ass, teasing me, "Show them how you bless me with your cum, Pastor," before she wraps her lips around my cock, and I climax so hard.

I cup her head and grunt, over and over, watching her proudly swallow, before I shoot again across her cheek. I can't even be dignified about it in front of my brothers, huffing, "Fuck, Wren. Fuck."

This woman makes me lose my mind and surrender my soul.

She has my heart and needs my mouth between her thighs.

I crouch over her pussy while Jace holds her leg open, and I pin the other down. With a groan, I suck her clit and tongue her cunt until she's screaming and pouring into my mouth, until she comes again at the sound of Nash's grunt.

I glance up to see him shooting his cum over her tits. The sight must get Jace off because they're kneeling so close, almost touching tips while Jace does it, too. He splatters Wren's nipples, making her moan before I quickly suck her clit into another shaking orgasm.

I could come again to this debauchery, but that was enough for my angel. She needs to build up to this. I need to be careful with her.

She lies there, eyes closed and breath huffing, her gorgeous body a painting of our desire. I reach into my hiking backpack, next to our sleeping bag, for the personal wipes. Gently, I clean her while Nash and Jace lift their boxers. But I worry, "Wren? Angel, you okay?"

"Yeah." She grins.

"Want to open your eyes so I can be sure?"

Her cheeks blush. "I'm shy."

No, she's mine. Forever.

Softly, I kiss her lips. "You'll be my wife and our queen. You don't need to be shy about letting us pleasure you."

"Don't be ashamed," Nash assures. "We'll do anything for you."

"We're proud to be your kings." Jace sounds choked up. It makes Wren open her eyes, looking worried for him, and he swallows. "Wren, we all know what you survived, so don't be shy about letting us take care of you now."

I caress her hair. "Hear that, Angel? If I ever forget to take out the trash, my brothers will kill me for you."

She laughs, but it's true.

Wren has no idea how we'll kill for her tomorrow and always.

And how I'll die to make everything right for us, too.

CHAPTER TWENTY
WREN

"It doesn't look like he's there."

Sire searches through his binoculars while Loch does the same, confirming, "I don't see movement."

I use the scope on my rifle, scanning what's left of Nannie's house, but it's hard to talk. Charred rubble. Cinder blocks. A stone chimney. A burnt stove and debris. It's all that's left of my home.

But with Sire on my side and Loch on my other, we lie on our bellies and spy over the ridge. Grant, Jace, Axel, and Nash flank us, making sure we're not ambushed from behind, and…

This is my home now.

With Sire and his family.

When we work together like this, how can I be embarrassed about anything that happens between us? It only makes us closer.

Together, we're watching Nannie's barn. I never burned it down, so I guessed Waylon would return to it. My instinct kept telling me he would, and Loch listened to me, but now I feel foolish.

Did I lead us on a wild goose chase?

"Wren?" Sire asks. "Angel, it doesn't look like he's here. The barn is empty."

"I know. I just…" I keep scoping. I keep getting that instinct.

It's the same I felt when I met Sire.

You belong here.

Through the crosshairs of my rifle scope, I spot a monarch butterfly. It flutters out of the barn, to the thicket of my favorite red oleander bushes, and…

"Wait, y'all." I spot it, my pulse tripling. "Beside the barn, through the oleander grove, there's a fresh trail through it. It wasn't there before."

I lower my scope, nodding toward it. "I bet that trail leads over the next ridge and across the creek. There's an old farmhouse there—Mr. Grinzer's. He's a sweet older man, and Waylon's an evil piece of shit. He's probably forced his way in and moved his lab there."

We hike in a single formation, using the dense cover until we reach the next ridge. I lift my nose and immediately smell it on the breeze.

Grant does, too. "Fuck," he whispers. "Is that cat piss?"

"No." I raise my rifle scope, scanning the windows of Mr. Grinzer's tattered farmhouse, noting the new fan in the kitchen window. "It's ammonia and phosphorus."

"It's a meth lab," Loch agrees.

Quietly, we crouch into position and watch the property through our scopes and binoculars. After an hour or so, Sire whispers to me, "You okay?"

I lower my gun, grinning at him. "I'm hunting, city boy. I'm peachy. How 'bout you?"

He lowers his rifle, smirking back. "Woman, I've hunted, too. Just not for my dinner."

After two hours, a willowy figure opens the front door

and stands on the porch. He removes his respirator to light a smoke.

"That's Alan," I whisper to my men. "Hurt him and I'll shoot your ass."

"Noted," Axel chuckles.

A few minutes later, a larger figure emerges from the house, and rage crawls up my spine, one vertebra at a time. It puts pressure on my trigger finger. "That's Waylon," I hiss. "And he's mine."

"You can take a shot, Angel," Sire growls. "But his head is mine."

"Hold your fire." Loch sounds calm. "If that older man is in there, we need a new plan."

Waylon and Alan go back inside, and we watch the house while Loch and Jace circle the property. Thankfully, it's a sunny day, and the visibility is good.

When they get back, Jace sounds skeptical. "No one's out there. Where's the rest of his crew?"

I watch the front door through my scope, confessing, "Oh, I poisoned them."

Sire chuckles. Axel does, too. I lower my gun to see the rest of my men staring at me.

"What?" I shrug. "Let that be a lesson. Don't piss off a woman and then make her cook for you."

Nash nods, impressed. "What poison?"

I smile. "I brewed oleander into their sweet tea."

Loch laughs. "She's a genius."

"She's a *queen*," Jace admires.

But I stare at Sire, who's gazing at me with that look I love. It's the one that makes me feel like Joan of Arc, leading her army of ex-Bratva soldiers. He boasts, "And I need to marry her."

"Hurry up or I will." Axel winks at me.

To others, Axel's a dick. I guess with everything I know about him, I understand why he's that way. But to me, he's sweet. Deep down, like his brothers, he's protective of women, and I can sense it; Axel's heart belongs to one. I just don't know who.

And I know Nash is secretly in love with Vale. I just wish he'd tell her.

I cherish how they care for me, too. How they're doing this for me. It's like each king is fiercely devoted to his queen, but they're loyal to all of us. I guess that's how they got this far.

"Alright." Loch signals us to huddle. "Here's the plan..."

WITH MY BACK BRACED AGAINST A GIANT HEMLOCK TREE IN the woods behind the farmhouse, I hold my position. I have a clear shot across the grassy yard, with my rifle aimed, covering the back door.

Sire's at my three o'clock, on the edge of the clearing. Jace is at my nine, while the rest of my men storm the front door.

I'm calm. I know they'll be okay. They move like a tactical team.

They flush Alan out the back door first, and Jace booms, "Hands up! On the ground! Now!"

Alan's so stunned, he falls to the grass with his hands in the air.

Waylon runs out next, ripping his mask off with his left hand and lifting an AR to fire with his right...

But I'm too angry and accurate, remembering his threats and abuse. How he sold me into hell and how close he came to violating me, too.

I exhale—*Asshole*—firing a bullet through his right shoulder.

He spins, falling to the ground, and Sire's on him with his rifle raised. "How you like them apples, Waylon? My badass Wren just shot you."

Quickly, I chamber another round from the magazine. It's my training while Sire kicks the AR out of Waylon's hand.

He writhes on the ground in pain.

"Dad?" Alan's not sure what's going on, but Jace picks Alan up, one-handed, by the waist of his jeans, and pulls him away.

Grant helps Jace. He kneels on Alan's back, putting zip ties on his wrists before they help Alan stand and escort him toward the front of the house.

But Sire looms over Waylon in the backyard with his muzzle pressed to his skull.

"Did you hurt Wren?" Sire presses harder. "Did you hurt all those girls? Confess the truth."

"Hell, yes, I did." Waylon shows no remorse. "Virgin pussy is worth a lot these days."

I've never seen Sire like this, his face ferocious, his eyes slanting devilish and determined. That's all he needed to hear. "Then vengeance is mine," he seethes. "I will repay, says the Lord. And—"

"House is clear. We got him!"

There's more commotion at the back door. It's Loch, calling out, carrying Mr. Grinzer in his arms while Nash covers them from behind.

I watch it all in my scope as Axel emerges last, his shoulders dropping, relieved this is over, but...

A branch snaps behind me.

I'm crouched so small behind this giant tree; whoever it is can't see me.

Another branch snaps.

My men are too far away in the yard to hear the threat, but I do, approaching from my eight o'clock. Slowly, quietly, I turn, peering around the tree, using my scope.

It's a man in camo. He must be Waylon's backup, weaving through the trees, his rifle aimed at ... Sire.

Oh, hell no. Not my man.

WWWD? What Would *Wren* Do?

You have one in the chamber, three in your magazine.

Always count your shots.

I aim and fire at his thigh. He falls, turning my way. It's exactly what I want as I reload, lightning fast. He opens his body toward me, raising his rifle while I aim for his center mass, and fire again.

"Wren!" I hear Sire call for me while I keep my crosshairs on the body in case it moves.

"Here!" I shout out.

In a moment, I hear Sire by my side, huffing, worried, "Angel?"

"I'm fine." I keep my rifle aimed at the dead man. "He was going to shoot you. Check the woods. There may be more."

While Axel covers Waylon and Jace has Alan, the others swarm the perimeter, rifles raised, looking for more threats, but there are none.

We meet in the backyard, and Sire holds Waylon at gunpoint again, waiting for Jace and Grant to load Alan into a truck parked in the driveway.

Alan's in shock when I appear, standing by his open car window.

"Wren! Is that you?" He gulps. "Fuck, I hoped you were dead." He shakes, his brow, sweating. "I mean... I'm so sorry. I know what he sold you into, and I'm so sorry. I kept hoping you were dead instead of—"

"Are there others?" I demand, "Alan, tell me. Has he taken other girls?"

He nods toward the farmhouse. "Not here but check inside. Check his laptop. He's working for some evil shit. The Warden, and..." His bound hands twitch. His cheek tics. "I just need a little rush. Can you get me a—"

"We're getting you some help." I touch his clammy arm. "These guys are the good ones, okay? They'll pay for it. Don't worry. Just let us help you. You're safe now."

Tears well in my eyes, seeing the bruises on Alan, too. When he wasn't high, he always protected me from his father. And when he was high, I protected Alan. It's what Nannie would've wanted.

While Loch stays by the truck with him, I walk back to Sire, who's still got Waylon on his knees.

There's an eerie calmness to him.

Like that's Sire's body, but not his soul.

He passes his rifle to Jace, who takes it, covering Waylon while Sire unsheathes the machete strapped to his waist. I knew it wasn't for the thick brush on our hike.

Sire yanks Waylon's hair, exposing his neck before he places the blade to his open throat. "Look at my future wife," he snarls. "This is for my angel. She's the last one you'll see before you burn in hell."

"Fuck you," Waylon spits.

"Don't you dare get fucking blood on my Killshots." Sire seethes, preaching scripture into his ear, "Do it and I'll punish you according to your ways, while your abominations are in your midst. Then you will know that I am the LORD, who strikes." Sire punches his face with his empty fist.

"Aw, shit," Jace mutters, glancing at Axel. "Get two tarps out of my pack. He's about to make a holy, fucking mess."

"Wren," Sire ignores him. "What do you have to say to him in his final moment?"

I stand over Waylon and search his empty eyes. He's worse than the Devil. He believes in nothing, but I do.

I slap his face. "That's for Banjo." I pull back and spit in his eye. "And that's for Alan." With rage, I rear back and kick him in the balls, and he doubles over while I sneer, "And that's for me and the girls. Fuck you, you little dicked evil piece of shit."

But the urge is too strong. I kick his balls again because there will never be enough punishment for men like him.

Then, I gracefully make the sign of the cross. "And that's for Nannie. She's the only one who can save your soul now."

I look at Sire and find a glimmer of the man I love. "He's all yours, my Lord."

With a pivot, I turn away. I know what Sire will do after I leave, and it doesn't bother me.

I trust in God, Sire, and his vengeance.

I ride with Loch while we take Alan and Mr. Grinzer to the hospital. The sound of the gravel road and the silence of the victims in our backseat quiet me.

Loch reaches over, gently touching my hand. "Are you okay?"

"Yeah."

"You fight like a queen." He winks. "You know you're ours now, right?"

Through the passenger window, I watch the rolling green ridges of the peaceful mountains I love and shed my last tears. I say goodbye to my past.

"Yeah." I nod. "I know where I belong now."

CHAPTER TWENTY-ONE
SIRE

Jace rubs his abs, grumbling, "When are we stopping for lunch?"

I catch Loch, who's driving, rolling his eyes in the rearview mirror, so I kick Jace's boot. "Quit being fungry."

He scowls, "What's fungry?"

"Fucking hungry. We just ate breakfast."

"But that was two hours ago."

Wren blurts from the passenger seat, "I'm always down for hashbrowns: scattered, smothered, and covered."

My tiny woman is sitting tall. It's like a burden has been lifted off her shoulders.

Does the fact that I removed an evil man's head from his shoulders help?

Yeah, it may have a lot to do with it.

Feeling no regret, I tell her, "Then, it's a lunch date at The Waffle House. Don't say I don't spoil you, Angel."

She turns, giving me a heart attack of a smile, while I remember last night and how I only wanted to hold her.

After the day we had. After the blood we shed. After the

She beams through sweet tears. "But I'm so happy. Finally."

"You're home." I kiss her lips. "Finally."

Glancing to my left, I make sure Jace is recording this, and he is. So are Grant and Loch, who look like they've Face-Timed our mom so she can witness this, too.

God, they're such mama's boys. Fuck it. *We're all proud mama's boys.*

Axel and Nash stand, arms folded and side-by-side on the edge of the road. Even they're smiling.

I love my brothers. Soon, I hope they'll claim their queens, too. I hope they let me make everything right again, like this...

Lowering to one knee, I take Wren's hand in mine. It clenches my heart how her hand's so small and shaking. When I lift my eyes to hers and find them full of light and tears, mine fill, too.

My heart pounds, fast and true with my words.

"Wren Chapel, I prayed for you. I prayed to be a man worth having a woman like you, and I'm not sure I ever can be. You're brighter than any light I've seen. Wiser than every year I've lived. And so damn beautiful, I fall to my knees for you. You're my immaculate angel, and I belong to you: pinky, heart, and soul. I vow to live and die for you as my wife and queen."

She chews her lip, tears steaming down her smiling cheeks. I swallow, lifting the ring from my pocket, holding it over her trembling finger.

"Wren Chapel, will you save me, too? Will you marry me?"

I wait a heartbeat and a lifetime for her answer, panic and peace tumbling through me until...

"Yes." She nods, choking back a sob or laughter; I can't tell. "Yes, I'll marry you!"

Carefully, I place the ring on her finger, and she gasps at it, "Oh my God. A butterfly ring?"

I lift it to my lips. "Four karats of marquise cut diamonds, shaped into four butterflies. One for you, me, and the two souls we'll make together."

"Sire! It's so perfect!" She jumps on me, wrapping her arms around my neck, making me laugh as we fall back in the grass.

Butterflies erupt around us. Hoots, hollers, and whistles can be heard from my brothers on the side of the road. I suppose our mom is clapping, too.

But all I can see is the halo of the smiling woman above me.

Lacing my hands through her hair, I pull her lips to mine. "I'm still a fallen angel, Wren, but now I'm the one who's fallen so goddamn in love with you."

"I love you, too. So much." Her tears salt our kiss, her tongue a promising tease. Her body may be tiny, but her passion is as strong as mine. So is her will. "Please, don't make me wait any more, Sire Rutledge."

I grin. "Is someone getting impatient?"

"Someone's getting married. *Soon*."

"Soon? No, Angel." I brush a curl from her face. "We're getting married tomorrow."

CHAPTER TWENTY-TWO
WREN

I stare at Sire's front door with excitement bubbling under my skin and questions popping off like, "Shouldn't you carry me over the threshold?"

He chuckles. "That's tomorrow night."

Since he popped the big question, he's been smiling a lot, which is really rare and ruining my panties.

"And you're okay with it?" I ask, squeezing his hand. "That I don't want your entire congregation at our wedding?"

"Yeah."

"It's just that ... some still judge me. So, I just want us."

He kisses my hair. "Just me, you, and my family, I promise."

I tug his hand. "Are you sure you can't marry us, too?"

"I can't officiate my own wedding. But you'll like Evelyn. She's our Minister Emerita. She doesn't have a judgmental bone in her body."

"A woman minister? I'm impressed." He lets go of my hand to enter the door code, while my allergy to filters makes me blurt, "You know, for a year or so, I thought of being a nun."

He's focused on the door. "What thankfully changed your mind?"

"I got really horny and wanted to fuck and learned that the patriarchy is bullshit."

He laughs, "Shocker: you don't think men should be in charge of everything."

"Do you?" I laugh with him. "I mean, too many men are either perpetually thirteen or sociopathic dicks."

"A dick is not the measure of a man."

"Spoken like one with a very big one. Oh, and I saw your brothers' too. It's genetic. *No one* is over-compensating in your family."

He smirks, pushing the door open. "I'm well aware of what my bride saw. We clearly have a lot to talk about tonight."

I hike my backpack up and step inside, but halt, surprised when my boot crunches down on a manila envelope. "What's this?"

"Fuck." Sire grits his teeth. "He has to ruin everything."

"Who?"

"My sperm donor." He drops his backpack, and I lift my boot before he angrily swipes the envelope off the floor.

"Is it one of your father's clues?"

I pick his pack up and take it with mine to the laundry room. Turning back, I find him staring at the envelope like it's a ticking bomb.

"Probably," he scowls.

"Are you going to open it?"

"Why should I? I don't owe him anything but a bullet to the brain." I wince. It's as if he can sense it because Sire turns to me. "Sorry, Angel. I don't mean to ruin a night like this."

"Okay, then." I march toward our coffee maker. "Let's drink some java, open that damn letter, read it, talk about it, shower, try a sixty-nine tonight, get married tomorrow, finally fuck, and move on. Deal?"

Reluctantly, he chuckles. "You and your deals."

"Take it or leave it."

I fill the carafe at our kitchen sink, totally bluffing, of course. I'll do anything with Sire at any moment. Especially with these huge diamonds sparkling on my finger.

Every time I think about his perfect proposal, I get those happy tears.

He starts ripping the envelope open but stays devilishly focused on me. "I'll take your deal but with a modified sixty-nine."

"Modified?"

He smirks. "I'm six five and my beautiful wife will be five feet. So, yes, we'll always have to be *very* creative."

"You mean, I'll be your shorty and you're my zaddy?"

He draws up, standing even taller. "You're what and your what?"

"A shorty is a pretty young woman, and a zaddy is a hot, older man."

"As long as you're my hot-ass wife for life," he tsks, "call me whatever you want."

"Deal." I turn to fill the machine. "And when you say, 'very creative,' can it involve sex swings and benches? Oh, and vibrators, toys, and cute anal plugs like I saw at the club? Lucy, the bartender, highly recommended the store, Delta's. She said they have the best lube for my first time with you, and—"

I turn back, but he's not paying attention. His face is stone, his eyes fixed on the piece of paper.

I press the BREW button, giving him a minute before I softly probe, "Sire? What does it say?"

It makes him seethe, "He wants to know my blood type."

"What? Why?"

He tosses the letter on the counter. "The only reasons I can think of are for a blood donation, an organ transplant, or—"

"Or for pregnancy and paternity."

"How'd you know that?"

I shrug. "The only thing I know about my parents is that one probably had an *AB* blood type because I'm *AB* negative, and it's the rarest type. If I ever need blood, I'm screwed. It's hard to find my match."

He walks my way, pulling me into his arms. "I'm *O* negative, a universal donor. *I'm* your match."

"Just another sign I was right about us." I palm his chest. "Why does he want to know your blood type?"

"Knowing him? Probably for paternity. To see if I'm really his heir, or some shit like that." He lifts me, setting me on the countertop before him. "But fuck him right now. He's not ruining tonight, tomorrow, or our lives. Deal?"

I smile as his sexy lips near mine. "Deal."

Sire always opens me with his kiss. He starts soft and slow, but deepens his penetration, his tongue dancing with mine. His breath pulls me under with our moans, and I'm found, I'm unfurling. A heavy throb aches between my legs, opening my world and thighs to him.

I'm sitting tall enough to sink my hands into his hair, and pull hard, needing more of him, but he lifts his lips from mine, panting, "Birth control?"

"I'm on it." My eyes drift open to find his, surprised. "I had an IUD put in when I turned seventeen. It's not that I wanted to have sex then. I didn't. But I wanted protection in case I had no choices and a man ra—"

"God, Wren." He nuzzles my forehead. "God, I'm so thankful you're safe with me now."

"Me, too."

"But maybe you should keep the IUD in for a while." He winces like it's the last thing he wants. "Until I kill my father, I don't want him trying to take another grandchild. It'll be hard enough getting Axel's child back."

"What if you're wrong? What if Axel's wife wasn't pregnant when she left him?"

"I hope I'm wrong about Katya, but I don't think so. I've never had a woman beg me so many times to breed her, and that's saying a lot because I...uh...well..."

He shuts up, realizing the hole he's digging for himself.

I chuckle, amused. "Oh, please, tell me your body count, future husband, because we know mine is zero."

"Fuck." Gently, he pulls back. "This is a coffee conversation."

"No, let's have it now before boiling hot liquids are involved. Just tell me."

"You'll get mad."

"Maybe I won't. Maybe I'll get aroused."

He cocks his head with an unsure smirk. "Aroused? By who I've fucked in the past?"

Sire doesn't get it, and I understand. He thinks I'm a delicate flower while I feel like a feral lioness.

Maybe I'm like most women.

I'm both.

"You said it yourself." I wrap my legs around his, holding him close. "You have a past, and I don't. You've never been in love, but you've had dark needs. I don't care about anyone else. But I care about *you*. I want to know the dark stuff. The breeding stuff. You can't tell your future wife that you belong to a fetish club in Atlanta and not tell her about it." I pause. "*Before* our wedding."

He shakes his head. "You might run away, screaming."

"Or ... I might *come*, screaming." I beckon. "Come on. Spill the tea."

He throws his stare to the ceiling. "If I tell you this, you have to know I didn't love *any* of them."

"I believe you."

"Alright then." He looks at me, sighing, "Honestly, I don't know my body count or the names for most, and that's how I liked it."

"Liked what? What did you do with them?"

"Find a filter and let me tell you. Then, you can blurt questions. Deal?"

I shake his hand. "Deal."

He keeps mine, pressing it to his heart. I can feel it pounding in his chest.

"Wren..." He gets quiet, searching my eyes. "This is hard to tell you, and I don't know why."

"Because you fear I'll judge you about your bisexuality or your kink, but I won't. I promise." Softly, I shrug. "You'll have to be understanding with me tomorrow night, for my first time, so let me do it for you now. I understand you have a breeding kink, *and*..."

"*And,*" he breathes, "that can mean different things for people. A few really want to get pregnant, but most eroticize the role play, the risk, or the power of it. For me? I eroticize the domination of it. I'm known for it. I can fuck really long and hard, and I like to talk very dirty, almost degrading. But I never actually wanted to get a woman pregnant or have unprotected sex, so I'd wear a condom and come on them, never in them."

"Them?"

I'm not appalled; I'm aroused. My imagination is on fire. How could he think I'd judge him for this? I *want* this.

"Yes, *them*. Mostly, I fucked couples, husbands and wives,

or groups who wanted me. I had a liaison at the Atlanta club who'd contact me when someone asked about me."

My eyes widen. "Like a pimp?"

"No." He chuckles. "There was no money exchanged. But I insisted on consent, medical screenings, NDAs, rules, and such. So, there was some prep involved."

"When was the last time—"

"Last year," he rushes like he wants to get this over with. "I haven't been with anyone since."

"Why?"

"Because I realized I was trying to fuck my pain away, and it wasn't working."

I touch his cheek, suddenly worried. "Your pain?"

"Yeah." He swallows. "The rage I have for my dad. The worry I feel for my mom. The guilt I have for betraying Axel. The way I really want kids so much it hurts, but I don't deserve them. The way I've had this dark hole in my heart my whole life ... until I met *you*."

He cups my face. "I meant it today, Wren. I've been praying for you this year. Twice a day, I'd ask God to send me the love I never felt before, even if I didn't deserve it."

"You deserve love, Sire Rutledge." I seek his lips, wanting to make his pain go away. "And I promise I'll give it to you every day. I'll love every part of you, because they're not over when we get married."

"Wren," he vows, "I'll never fuck another woman again. I can't. I'm too in love with you."

"What about men? I can't fill that need for you."

And I can't find an insecure bone in my body about it.

Maybe I'm too sure we're meant to be together. Maybe I love him too much. Maybe I want to take all his pain away, like he killed mine, and I want him to be happy. I want Sire to be free of his guilt and shame.

He pauses, considering my offer. I can't tell if he's tempted or touched. Or maybe both.

"Just because I'm bisexual," he explains, "it doesn't mean I can't be with *one* person. In fact, it's all I want. I want to love and marry *you. Only* you. I told you, I'm a hypocritical patriarch that way." Softly, he smirks, caressing my waist. "I want to keep you as my badass, hot wife, all pregnant and barefoot with my babies."

I love his hypocrisy.

His honesty.

I love *him*.

I love him this much...

"But the other night in the tent with Nash and Jace, I sensed it; you liked the domination over me, and I liked it, too. You liked showing me off," I blush, "and I liked you sort of sharing me."

Pensively, he brushes his fingertips down my neck to my cleavage, letting me feel the jagged scar on his partial pinky; his proud sacrifice for me. Forever, I'm secure with him. Goosebumps bloom in the wake of his touch, desire tightening my nipples.

I stare at his menacing beauty and truly see Sire; he is a powerful contradiction.

But so am I.

Maybe we all are.

I know what I want, and how I want it with him. How we can talk about it, and we won't judge. We'll always love.

If this is marriage, this safety and seduction I feel with him, then ours will last beyond a lifetime. It'll be bigger than our hearts can contain, maybe our bodies, too.

His eyes lock on mine, letting me see God and the Devil reflected in their blue depths.

"As my wife..." gently, he fists my hair, "you're *mine*, Wren.

Only *mine*. You belong to me, and I'll behead anyone who tries to put our love asunder."

I believe him.

Evil heads roll around Sire.

He brushes our lips together. "But as my queen, I'll serve *you*. I'll share you with the kings, but *only* the kings. They care for you, too. They'll protect you and never hurt you. So, if you want to explore your fantasies, explore them with us."

"But what about *your* fantasies?"

"My only fantasy is to make you MY wife."

CHAPTER TWENTY-THREE
WREN

Walking down the aisle, I have to blink back tears.

Sire said he had everything planned, and as always, he keeps his vows.

Golden candelabras flicker on the stairs to the pulpit. The chapel lights are dimmed. Blue hydrangea petals blanket the aisle runner. Glass votives flicker beside empty pews. Large sprays of my favorite blue flowers bloom with white roses, spilling in arrangements behind my handsome groom, while my small bouquet shakes in my excited hands.

This is what Sire's mom can do on a moment's notice, and she honors me by giving me away, too.

"You go on and cry, because my mascara is already shot all to hell," Nadine side-whispers. With her arm hooked in mine, she escorts me down the aisle. "I swear, you, my son, and your love are sweeter than baby's breath."

"Thank you." I try not to choke up. "Thank you so much for everything."

This morning, Nadine met me at a wedding dress shop, where she had already chosen a dozen gowns in my size for me.

"We don't have time for major alterations," she said. "So, I hope you don't mind. I picked one in almost every style."

I didn't mind. I was touched. Delphine joined us. So did Zar. It was my first time meeting him. He's all tall, dark, and handsome with Texas swagger. And he really loved the simple, strapless white lace gown I chose.

"Darlin', Disney can go to sleep," Zar drawled. "Because you are a true princess."

"So chic. So elegant," Delphine agreed. "The tiny bodice with the long train, and the color against your glowing skin? *Oui, tu es belle.* You will wear a veil, no?"

Yes, I'm wearing my hair down and pinned back with a long, white lace cathedral veil sweeping behind me. I didn't want a judging audience of parishioners at our wedding, but I wanted to give Sire something traditional. Something to respect his calling.

Slowly, I march his way, and he must like it.

He stands at the altar in the dark grey suit I love, quickly swiping away a tear.

Don't. He makes my tears escape, too, streaming to my smile.

I don't recognize the beautiful song the acoustic guitar musician is playing. But I recognize Sire's brothers and their queens. I'm surprised they aren't sitting in his row, all on the groom's side.

Fighting a sob, I chew my trembling lip because...

Sire knew my side would be empty.

I have no one else.

So, Nash, Grant, Delphine, and Zar stand on my side like my honored attendants, while Axel, Jace, Loch, and that must be Nick—*God, he's cute*—stand with Sire.

The guitar fades when I stand before him, my heart fluttering like a leaf. The minister in her black suit and white shawl tenderly asks, "Who presents this bride?"

"We do." Nadine cups my hand. "We'll never give Wren away. She's our family forever."

Family.

Forever.

All the times I was given away and not wanted. All the school events when no one came to see me. Every time I saw a mother hug her child, and I had no one.

Finally, I belong.

More tears spill down my cheeks, and Sire reaches for me, but Loch rushes over, offering me his handkerchief.

"Thank you," I stammer, dabbing my eyes.

"Show off," Grant whispers, making us laugh.

I pass my bouquet to Nadine to hold before she joins my line, and the rest is a blur. All I do is hold Sire's hands so tight while mine shake. I stare into his indigo eyes. I vow to share my life with him before he promises me his soul.

Tears meander down my smiling cheeks, knowing our love is forever. But someone tell *my* soul.

Why do I have a deep fear I'll lose him?

Gently, he brushes my tears away. In my haze, I realize it's time for the ring exchange.

I panic. I've had no money, no time. I pat my dress like it has pockets and...

"Ahem." Nash clears his throat, gently touching my arm with his whisper, "He made this out of paperclips for you."

Paperclips? No, it's a man's platinum wedding ring.

"Read the inscription," Sire softly orders.

I guess he planned this, too? Glancing down, I'm barely able to focus through tears.

WREN CHAPEL

My name will be inside Sire's wedding band forever.

Sweetly, he smirks. "As my wife, you get two of my fingers."

Smiling, I gaze down, sliding the band over his wedding finger, my tears falling over the finger he sacrificed for me, too.

I don't know how I'm able to echo the minister's vows, but I do. "With this ring, I join my life with yours. I am yours, body, heart, and soul, from this moment forward."

I blink, staring up at him. This feels like a dream.

But it's not enough.

He's my best friend, too.

So, I blurt, "And I vow to sing all the lyrics to your favorite songs because it makes you happy, and I love you."

"With the way you sing, little one?" Jace mutters. "He's madly in love with you, too."

"He's right. I *am* madly in love with you, Wren Chapel." Sire gazes down at me, our ringed hands clasped. Love and warmth fill his eyes. Something heated stirs in them, too.

"Can I kiss her yet?"

He rushes the minister. With her final words, blessing us as husband and wife, I'm surrounded by applause and Sire's big hands, clasping my face.

This is a dream come true.

His kiss starts tender, like he's worshipping at my feet, reverent and restrained for the ceremony. Then it climbs, hotter, harder, and hungrier.

His lips. His tongue. His heat. I'm throbbing between my thighs. I shouldn't be this aroused in my wedding dress.

He grabs a breath. "I love you, Wren, my wife." He nips my bottom lip before passion seals his to mine again, his next kiss flipping my world.

I clutch his jacket, needing him, demanding him. The low, aroused groan he emits makes me forget where we are; I don't care.

I belong with Sire.

My husband.

With panting breath, he pulls away, his burning eyes locked to mine while he tells everyone, "Leave."

CHAPTER TWENTY-FOUR
SIRE

I'M A VERY DARK AND TWISTED MAN FOR WHAT I'M ABOUT to do.

I'm not even embarrassed when the minister excuses herself. With all my years of service here, I've earned this sacred sin.

The guitar player packs up while the photographer takes a few photos, and I fight for patience. Holding Wren's hand, my *wife's* hand, has my instincts raging to have her.

Now.

My mother protests, wanting us to join her for the dinner she's planned, but my brothers smirk at me, understanding.

"Let's take a raincheck, our queen." Axel appeases Mom. "We have the rest of our lives to celebrate their union."

He cuts me an evil grin before leaning down to peck Wren's cheek. "Welcome to the family, our little poisonous princess. We're honored to have you."

Wren beams, blushing at my brother's kiss. One by one, they press their lips to her cheek and offer praise, admiring my wife.

It really stirs my cock when it shouldn't.

Delphine pulls Wren into a hug. "Call me tomorrow. You will have woman questions and I will help. *Oui?*"

"Yes." Wren nods, and my dick swells more, knowing that after tonight, I'll leave Wren with no question about who she belongs to.

Adding to the fire in my veins, Delphine nods to me. "I left your bag under the second pew, my king."

"Your bag?" Wren wonders.

"Don't question your husband," I joke.

"I'm Nick, and congratulations." My sweetest brother introduces himself with a kiss to Wren's forehead. "Sire's praise didn't do you justice. You're breathtaking." He punches my arm. "And a saint for loving this devil."

"Ouch." The fucker's so strong that actually hurt. I rub it, laughing. "Don't you have a quarterback to sack somewhere?"

"I got his sack right here."

Zar teases, proudly holding Nick's hand as he kisses my cheek. "My second king," his bearded lips linger over my flesh, "always a pleasure to see you."

He pulls back, and I catch Nick, amused by his man before Zar adds, "Your stunning wife is as hot as a two-dollar pistol. Hurry up and make her a queen, so we can play."

"Play?" Wren questions again.

Zar turns to her, gently cupping her bare shoulders. "You have questions for me, I know. Let me take you to a queen's lunch this week, and I'll tell you everything."

"It's a date." Wren beams.

And it's a loving, lecherous jolt I get, recalling Zar's initiation and how he'll tell Wren about it.

How he'll tell her that I took him hard and from behind. How I stood, bending him over and grabbing his shoulders. How he begged me to breed him and pound him until he came on the table. But how I didn't come. I refused to, knowing Wren was waiting in bed for me.

Lastly, and in the opposite of least, is my mother, pulling me into a hug. "Please, Sergei," tears choke her voice, "no more sacrifices, my sweet son. You're finally in love, and you deserve it."

"Thanks, Mom." I peck her cheek with love and guilt warring inside me.

Yes, I'll give Wren all the love she deserves, but I'm not done sacrificing until I make everything right.

Lovingly, Mom grabs my chin. "Be *gentle* with her."

"I'll die before I hurt her."

Her voice softens, worried, "Please use lube and go slow."

I can't believe my mom is giving me advice on how to take my wife's virginity tonight.

Then again, I'm making it damn obvious I'm about to do it. Right here. In my church. The visions won't stop until I do.

"Wren, dear." Mom pulls her into a hug. "I owe you a big reception. You just say when."

"Yes, ma'am."

"Yes, *Mom*." She gently corrects her, and Wren's dark lashes flutter, blinking back tears.

"Yes, *Mom*. Thank you."

Damn, I don't think my heart can take much more.

I cried at the stunning sight of Wren in that dress and veil. I didn't care if my brothers saw me do it; Wren is so goddamn beautiful and all mine.

Then, I choked back tears when she cried at my family, becoming hers. She'll never be alone again.

I don't know how I made it through our wedding when my soul ached to seize every moment with Wren, right then, all at once, and forever.

God, this is love.

And goddamn, I need her. "Everyone, leave. *Now*."

Silently, I hold Wren's hands at the altar until we're alone.

Once the door slams behind Axel, she gazes up at me. "Are we really going to—"

"Yes." I cup her jaw. "I can't stop the vision. I've had it since I met you. How I'm supposed to make you my wife right here."

She glances at my pulpit, the altar, then the cross. "Isn't it a sacrilege?"

"To consummate my marriage with my wife? To let God witness our union?"

She lowers her voice, grinning. "To fuck? In a church?"

I chuckle. *May her mouth never find a filter.*

"If we were standing outside, in God's true church, and I laid you on the grass, right there after our wedding, and made you my wife, would it be sacrilegious?"

"No," she sighs. "It would be beautiful."

"Well, then." I seek her lips. "I owe you fucking in a field of flowers, too."

I'm doing this. I have to. When I get these visions, they don't stop until I fulfill them.

Once again. Is it God or the Devil telling me to do this?

Once again. *I don't care.*

Softly, I kiss her. "Wait here."

"Where are you going?"

"To turn off the lights and security cameras."

The candelabras still flicker from our ceremony as I aim for the sacristy room beside the sanctuary. Here, we store our vestments and get ready for service. We also control the lights and cameras. I turn them off and return to find Wren, with her hands clasped and her head bowed toward the cross.

I gulp with a lump in my throat.

God, I know you exist because...

My angel is praying.

And she truly looks like one.

White, virginal lace shrouds her. Her dress. Her veil. Her pure face. Her immaculate body.

My soul is not mine. Neither is my heart nor body. It's all hers and aching at the sight of my new wife.

Longingly, I approach her. "What are you praying for?"

With her eyes closed, she sighs, "For it not to hurt."

"Come here." I pull her into my arms. Holding her, I'm a storm of hard urges and soft emotions. "I'll go slow. I can't promise it won't hurt, but I swear I'll make it feel good, too."

"How?" She's sounding worried.

"Your fellow queen, Delphine, left us a few things."

In quick steps, I grab the white, quilted satin bag that Delphine left hidden under the pew. I show Wren the heart tag with *BRIDE* scripted in gold.

It makes her smile. "What's in it?"

"Some items I asked another queen to get for us."

Her eyes light up. "Like?"

"Like toys, lube..." I drop the bag beside us and lean down, hungrily kissing her neck. "Like I'm about to fuck you for the first time, my wife, and like hell if I won't make you enjoy it, too."

I gather her into my arms and carefully guide our bodies to the floor.

Evil and erotic sensations burst through my body at the sight of Wren veiled in white against the blood red carpet. The candles flicker. The cross looms. The welcome weight of my new wedding band catches the light with my arms braced over her. Her eyes glow, her gaze unknowing and trusting and ... *mine.*

Mine.

Mine.

It flips the switch, and I kiss her. I kiss my wife, my Wren, my whole world is contained in this perfect woman.

In three breaths, she's taking my kiss, too. She's making

my ears ring, my skin sweat, my erection is painful. She's grabbing my tie and hair and wanting more. *More.*

Biting and kissing her neck, she cranes it open for me before I steam over her ear. "I'm going to fuck you in your wedding dress. I want my bride's blood on my cock and soul. You're going to take every inch of me into your tight virgin cunt until you're my wife. Say *I do.*"

"Yes, Sire, I do. I will," she sighs with new submission.

It's the rush of blood I need. Lust slams through my bones, and I rip her tiny bodice down, threads and boning snapping in my grasp.

She gasps as I expose her. She moans when I circle my tongue around her hard nipple.

"Fuck, Wren. Your perfect little tits." I tongue one and nip at it, too. "I'm going to suck them until I die."

She rasps, "What about when I get preg—"

"Even better, Angel. Every inch and drop of you is mine now."

The thought of tasting her blood, her milk, her cum; I'm addicted. I'm abhorrent.

I'm hers.

I tongue and suck her nipples, kissing the butterfly tattoo over her heart, too, until she's bowing her back. "Sire, *please.*"

"You want to come while I suck your pretty nipples, my angel?" I latch on, hard, making her cry out. Plopping my lips off, I boast, "I've made you come like this before. You're such a dirty girl when I suck your tits."

"Please." She yanks at my jacket. "Please, I want to feel you, too."

"You want to feel your husband?"

Bracing on one hand, I grab hers with my other and cup it over my soaring erection. "*This* is what you do to your husband, Wren. You make me so hard, I can come in my pants for you."

Rising on my knees, I loosen my tie until I can yank it off. Shrugging off my jacket, I toss it aside before I do the same to my vest.

Unbuttoning my shirt, I gaze down at her, wanting me, and my nostrils flare, fighting for restraint.

She looks so pure, but she's giving me that fuck-me expression. Her exposed breasts heave with wanton breath. Dark curls, framed by white lace, spill around her. She's ready and waiting for my cock, and my heart clenches.

"Fuck, Wren." I leave my shirt hanging open. "I need to see *all* that's mine."

She chose a dress that's perfect for her, *for us*. It's simple, sacred, and soft white lace. It lets me lift the gossamer layers to her waist and salivate at what I see. "Damn, Angel. What are these?"

"Untie them," she teases about the white lace panties I'm touching. They're barely held in place with tiny strings tied in blue bows.

"Untie them? Fuck that." I fist the lace, ripping them off.

Gazing at her virgin pussy about to be mine, two men wage a war inside me, and both want to fuck her in front of his pulpit.

One man lies down, sinking his face between her thighs, and gently kissing her hard clit, needing to taste her sweet cum on his tongue.

The other man ruthlessly holds her legs open, the raging, hard dick in his pants aching to plunge inside her and make her bleed.

"Oh God, Sire, yes." She seems to love both.

Fisting my hair, she lifts her hips, smearing her wet pussy over my mouth. I've taught her this, how to seek her orgasm proudly.

"Do it," she demands. "I'm your wife now. Put your fingers inside me. Please."

Jesus, Jesus. I need help.

One man wants to carefully open her with his fingers first, but the other craves her first blood on his cock.

All I can do is answer this hunger inside me. It's ruthless and right.

"You don't get anything inside you until you come on my tongue, Angel. Do it." I reach up, tugging at her taut nipple. "Be a good girl and make your virgin pussy come on your pastor's face, right in front of his pulpit."

"Oh, God." Wren shivers, spreading her thighs wider as I suck her clit.

Fuck, yes, she's getting off on this taboo, but it's not wrong. It's right. It's us. We're married before God.

For the first time, I touch her slick hole with my fingertip, and I groan. I forbade myself from touching her virgin cunt until now, and this is why.

This is mine.

I can't hold back anymore.

Circling her waiting entrance—it's pure, tight, wet silk—I flutter my tongue over her hard clit, and she gasps, responding to my new touch. Her thighs shake, and she comes with a sudden shudder. "Sire, please."

"Good girl," I praise, licking my lips. "Say it. Say you're my good girl who wants me to fuck you now."

"Please," she pants, tugging on my shirt. "Please fuck me. *Now.*"

I can't resist. I crawl up her body and kiss her with her cum on my tongue. She moans at the taste, gliding her hands over my exposed chest, caressing my hidden scars, and teasing my abs.

"I don't feel good; I feel bad," she growls into our kiss. "I feel like a naughty girl who wants you to fuck her right now." She unzips my pants.

I'm a heavenly, horrible man for craving this sight...

My bride, in her ripped wedding gown, her tits exposed, her dress hiked up, her legs open, and her pussy so wet and waiting for me. All as she lies before my pulpit and expertly frees my hard dick from my boxer briefs. She wants to get fucked in my church, and I'm ready to answer her prayer.

Leaning over, I open the bag Delphine left for us. From it, I take the bottle of lube and the toy I told Delphine to buy.

I show it to Wren. "I'm going to use this vibrating cock ring. I'll rub it against your clit and go slow, inch by inch. I'll use lube, too."

"Okay," she whispers, wide-eyed.

"You say *No* or *Stop*, and I'll listen. We can play kinky consent games months from now."

"*Weeks* from now," she insists, smiling.

"Such a naughty girl," I smirk, drizzling a ribbon of lube over her pussy before covering my cock next. I slide the ring in place, just under my crown, in case that's all she can take. I spared no expense for her pleasure. This is the best cock ring on the market.

I click it on and position myself at her entrance. Braced over her, my tip drips, sensing her wet heat, anticipating her tightest cunt. I want to kiss Wren while I do this, but her lips meet my chest.

"Look up at me, Angel. Let me watch your eyes while I make you mine."

Like she can read my soul, she stares up at me and lifts her arms overhead like a sacrifice, bracing her wrists like they're bound with her stigmata tattoos, confronting me.

"I'm yours, Sire," Wren offers herself to me exactly like my vision.

My birth.

My death.

My salvation.

My wife.

An overwhelming urge seizes my body as her mouth parts, gasping as I hold her sacred wrists down and press my swollen tip inside her, shivers shooting down my spine to feel her finally. It forces a deep groan up my throat, feeling our first penetration, at how her pussy's so fucking tight and wet for me.

I tilt my hips, making the toy tease her clit. I need her to open for me because, *goddamnitholyshit,* her virgin cunt is resisting my cock, and it feels too good.

"Oh, God," she sighs like she likes it. "Is that you or the toy?"

"It's both," I grunt, pressing my tip in more, watching her gorgeous face.

But she winces.

Fuck. I grit my teeth, making myself stop. "Breathe, Angel. Relax and let me in."

With an exhale, she softens.

"That's it. Now play with your nipples. I can't reach them with my mouth, so pinch them for me. Be a good girl and stay wet for this cock. You're going to take every inch of it, even if it takes us all night."

I let go of her wrists and wait and watch, loving the sight of my bride playing with her hard nipples right in front of the altar, until she's writhing for more of my cock. "Sire." With a brutal, tugging pinch to both, she begs, "More! Fuck me more."

Reaching down, I slide the ring lower on my shaft. Clicking it to vibrate at a higher speed, I suspect this next inch will make her bleed if she does.

I try to find the man in me, not the monster, while I brace on one hand, and use my other to rub her clit until the toy can reach it. "Breathe with me, Wren. Exhale." She watches my eyes, trusting as I clench my molars and slowly push another inch inside her.

"Oh!" She cries out.

Fuck, she's clenching around me. She's tight. So, fucking tight.

"Wren?" I grunt, "Angel, are you okay? Open your eyes."

She nods, fluttering her lashes open, her lungs huffing for air. "I'm... I'm okay."

"Am I hurting you?"

She shakes her head. "It did. It burned and now," she pauses, "it's just a lot of pressure."

"Breathe with me, that's how we'll do this."

Actually ... I don't know how we'll do this.

I'm so fucking hard and huge for her, and she's the tightest heaven I've ever felt. I know in time, she'll stretch for me, and I'm a sick devil because part of me doesn't want it. I want this taboo first forever.

But most of me, her husband, wants her to expand and explore. I want Wren to be open and taking every damn thing she wants.

Her fingertips caress my abs. They're flexing to hold back. "I'm okay," she assures. "I want it, Sire. Keep going."

I glance down at where we're joined to be sure ... and delicious, evil shudders whip down my spine.

Wren's blood.

My wife's virgin blood.

Drops bloom on the white lace of her wedding dress. Slowly, I pull out an inch and see my salvation on my glistening shaft. I shouldn't want this, but I do. I crave it. I need it.

Carefully, I pull all the way out.

"What are you doing?" She grabs for me.

"You're pussy's bleeding for me. I just opened you, and I need to taste it."

This is the man with the breeding kink. This one loves that we're still animals, ruled by raw urges and ruthless instincts. This man takes what he wants.

When I put my mouth on Wren's swollen pussy, tasting her blood, desire, and the edible lube, I'm home. I slowly glide two fingers into her for the first time, inside where I belong.

Gently hooking them, I rub her most sensitive spot, and she moans, writhing her hips and fucking my fingers back. I suck her clit, then her blood off my digits before sliding them back inside her, slowly pumping them and stretching her open.

In minutes, my bloody bride is screaming and coming again.

Good God, I want her.

Nothing but her.

Rising up her body, I slide the cock ring to my base before guiding my hard tip back inside her. A groan chokes me. *Fuck, her pussy's the sweetest strangulation.*

This time, she lifts her hips for me. This time, she takes me, slowly and inch by inch. She exhales, wrapping around me and begging for more.

My eyes roll, my molars clench, my pulse has tripled at how fucking tight, wet, and perfect she feels. I could die in ecstasy inside my wife's pussy.

Sweat glistens on my body and hers.

The candles burn low.

My muscles ache with the restraint I'm using until finally, I'm buried all the way inside her, and gaze down, grieving for the first time our height difference.

I love how tiny Wren is. How mighty she is, too. How she makes me feel like a God, but I need to kiss her. I need to come. I need to fuck her with her lips on mine.

"Sire," she gasps. "Can we... Can I..." She pushes against my chest. "Can I be on top?"

"Angel, that's too much of me to take for your first time."

"I can do it."

And I can't say no to her.

Not right now.

Scooping my arm under her waist, I shock her at how easily I can lift her like a doll. Flipping our bodies over, a swirl of white lace surrounds us, but I don't lie back.

I sit with Wren straddling me, with my cock buried halfway inside her. Rustling with her lace, I lift her dress so we can see it.

"Fuck, Angel," I grunt. "Look at your swollen pink cunt impaled on my thick cock."

I rub her slick pink clit. She grabs my shoulders, rolling her eyes with a shudder, and I lick my lips.

I'm not feeling so godly anymore.

I'm immoral.

Lecherous.

Violently in love and lewd.

I rip the rest of her bodice open. It's hanging on by threads like me. "Now, be a good bride in her wedding dress and ride your husband's hard dick. Fuck him and prove your vows."

Leaning forward, I shamelessly tongue her nipple, and she moans, lowering to take more of my shaft. Cupping my head, she makes me suck her sweet tits, while I grab handfuls of her lace, guiding her hips.

"That's it, Angel," I steam over her wet nipple, "you're not a virgin anymore. You're my dirty wife who's going to ride my cock with this tight wet cunt until I come inside you."

"Yes, Sire," she sighs, gliding up and down my throbbing shaft, taking what she can until her slick cunt is full.

"You like that?" I brush my lips over hers. "Do you like being my good bride and fucking your husband's thick cock until you make him pump his cum inside you?"

"Yes," she gasps, and I squeeze her hips.

"Do you like being my bad girl and fucking your pastor in

his church, and driving him fucking crazy with this tight, wet pussy choking his hard cock?" My eyes roll. "Fuck, I'm so hard for you, Wren."

"Yes, Sire." She shakes, grinding hard over the vibrating ring at my base. "Yes, I love being so bad for you."

She's molding to me, melding with me. We're becoming one, and it's potent. Her eyes lock on mine and...

We match.

We burn.

We belong.

I nip at her trembling lips. I need to know. "Do you want to be a good girl for me, Wren? Do you want all the dirty things I crave with you? Do you want all the dark things I need to do to my wife?"

"Yes. Yes, I want it. Sire..." She pants, "Please..."

She circles her hips faster, raising the heat in my spine. The fire in my blood. The craving in my cock. She's fucking the man and the monster.

I'm not done with her.

I fist her hair and veil. "Do you want me to breed you, Wren? Do you want me to tie you up and fill you with my cum for days?"

"Oh, fuck yes." She shakes, her lips huffing over mine. Her fingers dig into my neck.

Lightning starts shaking my thighs. The urge builds, drawing tight, fire cracking through my bones for her.

Only her.

I growl over her panting lips, "Do you want me to breed you, Wren? Naked and hard and in front of my brothers? Do you want me to let them suck your pretty tits and come on your lips and lick your sweet pussy before I fill you with my cum?"

"Ugh... fuck. Yes, Sire... Yes—" Wren bucks so hard, her eyes roll back, her body convulsing over mine. She can't even scream at the new sensation seizing her body; her first orgasm with her tight, pussy clenching around my thick, pulsing cock.

God.

She's breaking.

She's beautiful.

She's mine now.

"Fuck, Wren." I can't wait any longer. "Oh fuck, I feel your pussy coming for me." I have to thrust hard into her, and I do.

Falling back on the carpet, I trap her hips, holding her still while I hammer my cock so fucking brutally hard inside her tight cunt. I watch her, crying out, but the instinct is too powerful, the vision too strong.

I'm possessed, gazing up at her, then the cross, then back at my salvation, my Wren, and the spirit makes me roar—my back bows. I strain. I can't breathe until I rise, grabbing her into a kiss as I groan, releasing and coming so hard inside her, I see heaven.

My heaven.

My wife.

Will I fulfill every vow I made to her tonight? Dirty and divine?

God and the Devil help me, I will.

CHAPTER TWENTY-FIVE
WREN

FOUR MONTHS LATER

IT'S A STRUGGLE, BUT I MAKE MYSELF SMILE, SINGING WHILE I decorate Christmas cookies. It's my annual duet with Bruce Springsteen. We're crushing "Santa Claus Is Comin' to Town."

The speakers thump so loud, I almost don't hear Sire and his merry band of menacing brothers, bounding through our door.

He's the first inside, all sweaty and charging my way. "Come here, Angel." It's how Sire always greets me before his lips are on mine.

In three seconds, he's pressed against me. I feel him getting hard under his running shorts as I sigh into our kiss. "You smell like a wet dog."

He laughs, pulling away to yank off his soaked sweatshirt. "Better?"

I gaze at him, all glistening ink and muscles. "Yummy."

"Speaking of..." Axel constantly interrogates, "What's for lunch?"

I peek past Sire and answer him, "Cheesy sausage balls and buttery biscuits."

Nash elbows past Axel, aiming for my oven. "That'll be my *Yes* to your lunch invitation."

Sire turns to them, frustrated with the cock-block. "I didn't invite you to stay for lunch, fuckers."

"But I did." I put a biscuit on a napkin and hand it to Nash. He winks, shoving the entire thing in his mouth.

Manners? Who needs them when you look that hot?

All three of them do, though I scrunch my nose. "*Ew.* Shower before we eat."

"Yes, ma'am." Axel pops a Snickerdoodle in his mouth. "Sire, go first."

"Fuck you." He grabs two frosted Christmas trees, chomping with his mouth open. "I'm not leaving you alone with my hot wife and her warm cookies."

Axel bounces his brows at Sire, who smirks, but Nash rolls his eyes.

"Speaking of not leaving me alone..." With my wooden spoon, I point to the large windows in our living room, over-looking the bustling street below. "Wanna tell me who's that crazy man on the hog outside? The one you told to stalk me while you three went on your Saturday run?"

This is my struggle.

It's what I'm not happy about.

Nash glances at the floor. Axel looks at the ceiling. They're guilty as fuck, but my happy husband of four months?

He looks me in the eye. "Wilder or Remi. I haven't checked who's on watch today."

My voice shoots up three octaves. "You told a crazy motorcycle gang to *watch* me when you're not here?"

Sire grins. "They're not crazy."

"*Bullshit.*" Axel coughs on cookie crumbs.

"Not crazy?" I storm toward the window, pulling back the white sheer, giving Mr. Motorcycle my middle finger. "Look at him!"

The hulking guy with shaggy blond hair and gold aviators leans against his massive Harley. Smiling up at me, he twiddles his fingers under his chin like he's lost his goddamn mind.

The other guy I noticed "watching me" earlier is equally as big as him, but he has darker hair. He doesn't smile when I wave, aka, flip him off. He chews a toothpick and scowls.

"They're crazy." I turn away from the window. "And I know MCs when I see them."

"They're not in an MC. They're *cousins.*" Sire gives me a guarded look, one he doesn't let his brothers see.

That's right! He told me months ago about the crazy contract killer cousins who'll help him kill his father this spring.

But what is he up to now?

I'm used to the kings, his brothers, guarding me when he's not around. Not someone else. It makes my pulse race. "How do you know we can trust them?"

"You *can't.*" Axel fumes like me, then snarls at Sire, "I don't know why you hired them to watch one of our queens when we have other men to do it."

Coldly, Sire arches a brow. "None are as bloodthirsty as them."

"But why do I need watching?" *Something's going on.* "After you went all Sleepy Hollow and the Headless Horseman on Waylon, I'm safe. I'm fine. Besides..." I point to the Glock on the coffee table. "I can make heads roll, too."

Nash tongues his teeth, slowly peeling off his soaked Henley. Axel tugs off his running shirt, too. Silently, Sire gathers their sweaty garments and strolls toward our laundry room.

Yes, it's December, but it's Charleston. It's mild, they're hot, and I'm fuming.

I flit my hand at them. "I'm not falling for all your mafia muscles and ink." *Okay, I am,* but... "Quit stripping and start talking, now, or no biscuits for you."

"Tell her." Nash doesn't like my ultimatum.

"We don't know the facts yet," Axel seethes.

"We should just take her with us." Sire strolls back into the kitchen. "Or I'll never get to eat my wife's cookies again."

"Tell me *what* and take me *where?*"

Again, they do their brotherly bond shit and don't say a word. Ice would be impressed with their performance.

"Great." I throw up my hands. "The silent ex-Bratva treatment. That makes me feel *so* much better."

Marching toward the kitchen, I shove past them. Plucking a warm biscuit from the tray, I wrap it in a napkin before charging toward the door.

Sire barks, "Where do you think you're going?"

"To buy an insurance policy."

I'm too small and fast. Bounding down the stairs, I burst out of the door, emerging on the sidewalk before they can stop me. Quickly, I glance both ways before charging across the street.

Blond motorcycle dude crows at my fearless approach, "Well, hey there, little cub. Did you lose your lion?"

"Nope." I walk right up to his black leather and chrome everything. "I'm sure he's watching. Isn't he?"

Blond guy leans, looking over my shoulder, and twiddles his fingers again. "Sure is. Your husband's standing at his window, and I've got about one minute alone with you and at a safe distance before he shanks me. *Again.*"

"Well then, tell me fast. Why does he want *you* watching me?"

I can't see his eyes. His gold aviators reflect the sun, but by his smirk, I can tell he's liking this. "What do I get for telling ya?"

"My buttery biscuit."

He cocks his lips. "Darlin', while I'm sure your buttery biscuit is worth dying for, your lion will kill me, all slow and shit, and I ain't got the patience for that."

"Then quickly enjoy this." I lift my hand, offering my biscuit. "And tell me what you can."

"Nothin'. He just said to watch his princess."

"His *princess*?"

"Yeah. Shocked me, too, but he said, 'You can't miss her. She looks like a little Jasmine from Aladdin,' and I'm a sucker for Disney and not dying today. You know your husband's an apex predator, right?"

"That's it? That's all he said?"

"Kill anyone who touches you. Need he say more?"

"Who's the other guy watching me?"

"A sucker for banana nut muffins. But he ain't a nut like me. He won't crack."

He snags my biscuit and, like Nash, pops the entire thing in his mouth.

"My name is Wren. I'm Sire's wife, and no one's goddamn princess. I'll poison your next biscuit with yew berry jam if you piss me off, and ... thanks for watching me."

"Wilder." He salutes with his mouth full. "The Pastor's wife is pretty and poisonous. Copy that."

When I return, Sire's silhouette looms at the top of our penthouse stairs. "How'd *that* go?"

"As you knew it would." I stomp up the stairs. "Wilder is bat shit crazy, but I trust him now."

He steps back. "You going to feed every man I hire to guard you?"

"Feed them." I swish past him. "Or poison them. Instinct: every woman should listen to it."

"Poison them?" Sire smiles, impressed. "With what? There's no oleander outside."

I shrug. "Poisonous yew berries grow in the graveyard. They make great jam."

Nash pauses with his mouth open. He's about to eat another biscuit, but this time, he found my cranberry jam. It's touching his shocked lips, but I wink. "You're safe."

Then I turn to Sire, using air quotes, "And since when am I your *princess*?"

"Since we haven't officially made you a queen yet."

Sire's still shirtless and unshowered. His amber cologne mixes with his masculine musk and the pussy-purring sight of his sexy face with that devilish body and the animal in his shorts, and ... it's done.

I'm horny.

His.

And unafraid.

"Well then," I linger my fingertip down his naked abs, "why don't *you* and *all* the kings make a queen tonight?"

"Ahem." Nash chokes on his biscuit.

I glance at Axel, and he's devouring my cookies, grinning. "We're ready when you are, princess."

"Fuck you," Sire snaps at him. "*I'm* not ready, and neither is she. We don't initiate her until her body is ready."

I stand toe-to-toe with my deadly, devoted husband. It puts my button nose to his inked pecs. I'm so in love with him and pissed off ... I'm the threat.

I poke his chest. "While I admire the patriarchal bullshit you're shoveling, it's my body, not yours. My virgin ship has sailed. And with the way we've been going at it for months? The Titanic has less fucked holes than I do. I'm ready."

Nash snorts. "Should we excuse ourselves?"

"No." I turn to him. "Because I want you to be my second king. You'll initiate me, too."

"You're *not* ready for all of us." Sire flares his nostrils. "I know it's your fantasy, Wren, but this is a fact: your body isn't ready."

That's not it. Not all of it. I can see it in his eyes.

"My body?" I touch his chest. "Or your heart?"

His face softens. "Both, Angel."

These have been the best months of my life. Being married to Sire is heaven, in life and in bed. We share everything. We talk for hours. He holds me all night.

He said he wanted me all to himself for a while, and I understood.

All those virgin flower metaphors have some merit. I have bloomed. I've blossomed into a grown woman—a very grown woman who's very sure of our love.

"You know you have all of me," I assure him. "But I feel left out. It reminds me of years ago, when I didn't belong, but I do now. I belong to you, and I'm ready to be a queen."

He shakes his head. "Wren, you have no idea what it'll be like. An initiation is intense. It's physical and passionate, but it can get extreme."

"I know. Delphine and Zar already told me."

"Did they?" Axel sounds skeptical.

"Yes." I turn to him. "You and the kings have your code, and the queens have ours. I know exactly what happened when Zar was initiated, and Delphine, too."

Axel cocks his head. I swear, when he uses his ice-blue eyes like that, as if he's testing me, I freeze, while other parts of me smolder.

"So," he challenges, "you know about Delphine and Loch, too?"

"Uh..." I've stepped in a cow paddy now. "Delphine's married to Grant. *He's* her king."

"Yes, Grant's *very* much her king. He worships her." Axel crosses his beefy, naked arms. He has more ink than all of the brothers, and right now, it's distracting. It's hot, though he lectures, "Grant will do anything for Delphine, like let her train Loch to be her second king. There's a story there you don't know. In fact, there's a lot you don't know."

"Then tell me. Problem solved."

"She's right. We need to tell her." Nash looks resolved. "All the queens need to know, because this Turner fuck is no joke. He's why you have the killer cousins watching her."

"Turner?" I glance between them. "Who's that?"

"Fuck," Sire mutters, stepping back. "Why tell her until we know more ourselves?"

"We're about to find out more," Nash says. "And Wren can help. It'll be a hostile meeting, but with Wren there, being all..." he gestures to me, "all Wren and rainbows and a helluva shot, she's an asset."

"No, she's my *wife*." Sire's lip curls. "She's more than an asset. Besides, they're my friends. It won't be hostile. They come to my service sometimes, and I've been on their yacht. I married Silas and Eily, for God's sake."

"Yeah," Axel huffs. "They worship *you*, but I've haunted *them*, and they have no idea you're my brother. They don't know who we really are, and they hate me." Axel smirks. "Except Eily, of course, so yeah," he considers me, "she'll love Wren. Bring her."

I seethe, "If y'all don't quit talking about me like I'm an asset or an accessory, I'll shoot your asses."

Sire teases, "Thought you preferred poison."

"What I prefer are some answers." My fists land on my

waist. "*Who* are Silas and Eily? *What* are you talking about? Haunting and yachts? Is that where we're going? On a haunted yacht?"

"More like a *super*yacht." Nash munches on my sausage balls. "Silas and Eily Van de May are two of the six poly lovers with the hottest actors in the world."

"Poly?" My pulse quickens. "Like six people? Fucking? Together?"

Sire chuckles. "While I'll admit, we get extreme with our initiations, those six…?" He shoots me a devilish smile. "You want to go on a kinky cruise, Angel?"

When my hot husband looks at me like that? "Always."

"Then get ready." He snares his arms around my waist, tugging me near. "My innocent wife is about to see a naughty new world."

CHAPTER TWENTY-SIX
SIRE

On our drive to Hilton Head Island, I twist my neck, popping out the tension while Wren blurts questions and murders songs.

When Queen's "We Will Rock You" thunders through the speakers, I don't have the heart to tell my beautiful wife that Freddie Mercury is not singing, "Kickin' your *cat* all over the place."

No, Wren's the dose of levity we need because this is some serious shit.

Axel and Nash have been following the lead I gave them. The clue my father left me. It's pointing us to this popular vacation island with a dark world most don't want to know about.

The problem is, we need more intel on the human traffickers we're hunting, and the former cop who has that intel is Cade Bryant.

She's one of The Six.

"So," Wren marvels once she's done kicking cats, "Silas and Eily Van de May are partnered with Daniel Pierce and

Redix Dean? Hollywood's hottest men who have that hit show together?"

I hold her hand in the backseat. Axel drives. Nash searches on his laptop, and I get to explain way too much to my wife.

"Yes, Daniel and Redix are married to their wives, Charlie and Cade, and they're in a secret polycule with Silas and Eily. They're three married couples who love each other."

"But," Wren blinks, "they're high key *famous*."

"But," I cock a brow, "they're not *out*. Only a few know."

"So, how do *you* know them?" Wren asks Axel. "Sire married them. They worship him, of course, so why do they hate you? Shocker."

I laugh.

I love how Wren gives Axel shit.

"Because," Axel grumbles, "Eily Van de May hosts an epic, erotic Halloween party, and she asked me to scare the shit out of the guests these past two years, and it worked. The husbands hate me."

"How do you know Eily?"

Axel lauds, amused, "She walked right up to me on Meeting Street and asked for my help. Guess I look sinister, and she's like *you*: a little rabid dog with a bow and bone when she's hungry."

Wren narrows her eyes. "Is that a compliment?"

"Yes," Nash answers her. "And they don't like me, either. I had a run-in with Cade Bryant at Delta's, the sex shop, and let's just say I left a bad impression. Now, we need you to ease the tension."

"Who's Cade Bryant?"

Nash lowers his Clark Kent glasses. He doesn't need them. He just looks like a mean motherfucker without them, which he can be, thankfully.

"Cade Bryant," he explains, "is a former cop who busted a

major trafficking ring. The same ring where we found you, and we need to ask her how they operate."

Axel pulls our Tahoe into the parking lot of a private marina with yachts in every slip.

I reached out to Silas Van de May and secured our guarded invitation.

We have one night on his ship, one meeting with The Six, and I have one chance to figure out how this is all connected to my evil father.

"I gotta say, Pastor. I didn't know you kept such criminal company."

Silas Van de May sits on his ivory sofa across from ours. We've been friends ... until now.

"He's not a criminal." Eily, Silas's wife, sits on his lap, playfully slapping his naked chest. "I *asked* Axel to scare us. Remember? Quit being a boner killer about it."

A famine would be more welcome in this room than Axel and Nash.

While me? I'm getting a different vibe from them.

"Wren..." Eily leans forward, all tiny and mighty like my wife. "Please excuse my husband and partners. Normally, they're sweet, but they got kids and haven't been laid in a while, so they'll be uptight until we do."

"I understand." Wren curls beside me on the onyx sofa. Nash sits beside her, and Axel's beside him. "I was frustrated until Sire finally fucked me, too."

They laugh while our other hot hosts, sitting with Eily, glare at my brothers.

But each time the men look at me, *I* feel like the famous one, the one their eyes devour.

It's odd.

And obvious.

The intercoastal sparkles outside the yacht's windows. It's a mild day on our cruise toward the Florida Keys. Our hosts are six of the finest people I've ever seen—three buxom women and three beefy men—doubling down on their allure by wearing swim trunks and bikinis.

Call me starstruck, but Redix Dean looks like a golden surf God with his arm draped over his wife, Cade, and his other arm slung over his co-star, Daniel Pierce, who's a British superhunk and hero. All while Charlie, Daniel's badass wife, proudly reclines in Redix's lap.

Or call me aroused because I clock how Redix strokes Daniel's shoulder. How Cade caresses Charlie's thigh. How Silas has one hand possessively on his wife, Eily, with his other, comfortably touching Cade's neck, all while his bare leg is snared over Redix's.

"Have we met before?" Redix aims his famous Romeo eyes at mine. They're heated and intense.

"Not that I'm aware."

"I wouldn't call it a *meeting*," Daniel adds with a smirk. "It was more like a performance, and you were the very big star."

I cock an eyebrow, confused.

"In Atlanta," Daniel reveals, and my pulse skyrockets. "Redix and I film there, and thoroughly enjoyed watching your show from a VIP room in a club one night."

"Dear Lord, my pastor." Silas grins, groping me with a curious look. "They told me about it the next night, and I got a very *hard* impression of how much they liked what they saw."

Jesus, Jesus.

My heart would explode if I hadn't already told Wren about my past at the fetish club in Atlanta. Of course, my brothers are also aware of it. They've indulged their kinks there, too.

Back in the day, this would be my kind of party. I know The Six are bisexual. Anyone with a pulse would find them attractive.

But today? It threatens to be a bloodbath.

Most of them despise Axel and Nash, while I feel like a visual buffet for ravenous men. My dick would soar if I didn't have an even bigger problem.

"Look…" I squeeze Wren, and she palms my chest. That's her signal; she's not mad about the Atlanta comment. "Clearly, we have a lot in common. But we're here today because my associates and I are after the same people you were, and we need your help. We're missing puzzle pieces, and you have them."

"Why should we give them to you?" Cade asks. She's the former cop and the one who needs to trust us.

"Because you busted Senator Evans and Claude Olan Turner the third," Nash answers her. "They're in jail, and now Turner's son has taken over. He's young, ruthless, and ambitious. He's expanding his trade."

Redix lifts his chiseled chin. "Why do you care?"

"My parishioners come to me for help," I explain. "They tell me about people in trouble, and Axel, Nash, and I are part of a secret group that gets justice when the cops don't."

"Why do men like you want justice?"

Charlie challenges us. She's almost as famous as her husband, Daniel, but for heroic reasons. She's a former Marine with a scar on her stunning face to prove it.

"Because it's wrong," Axel fumes. "Isn't that reason enough?"

"Because I'm a father," Nash adds. "I have a daughter, and I give a shit about those girls. We want to help them."

Eyes read eyes.

Muscles tense.

There's not a smile in the room, while the tension is so heavy, it could sink this vessel.

"Because," Wren calmly explains, "I was one of the women they rescued from those traffickers. Sire even let them cut off his finger for me. My men work for a woman who survived trafficking, too. They're good men, doing dangerous work, and we need your help. Please."

Sweetly, Nash touches Wren's thigh. It's not sexual. It's protective. It makes me agree with Wren; Nash is meant to be her second king.

Cade nods at Wren, and it makes me agree with Nash, too.

We needed Wren here. We need women to make us put our swords, egos, and dicks down and focus on the real problems.

"Okay." Cade opens her hands. "What do you need to know?"

"How did they move the money?" That's Nash's department.

"They inflated the price of the golf tours," Cade explains. "They offered VIP access, luxury accommodations, and bullshit to cover the trade. Then, they laundered it through high-end real estate sales."

"How did they move the victims?" That's Axel's area.

"Boats on the intercoastal and trucks on the interstate," Silas answers. "They wait for high season and use rental properties to blend in with the tourists. They're damn hard to catch."

I know all six but Daniel, who's British, grew up here in the Lowcountry. They know these waters and islands better than we do.

"How would you do it?" I ask Silas. "Where should we focus?"

Silas tousles his long, bronze hair. Damn, I must admit, he's a beautiful man.

He tsks, "If I had to guess? Myrtle Beach for its crowds. Savannah for their port and trucks. Then again, maybe I'd go small, rural, so they wouldn't find me."

"How is this coastal ring connected to Tennessee? The mountains?" I press, and Cade narrows her violet eyes.

"Tennessee?" She shakes her head. "I'm not sure."

"What about Russia?"

Wren blurts it, and I suddenly tense. Without looking, I can sense Axel instantly seething and Nash sitting on a razor's edge.

My angel just fucked up.

Damn, Wren's wicked smart, but we all make mistakes. Fatal mistakes.

"Russia?" Daniel, with his proper English accent, asks, "Why do you think Russians are involved?"

I open my mouth, but Wren blurts again, "Because when I was blindfolded with the other girls, I heard a man speaking it. Maybe it was another country or someplace—"

"Slavic?" Daniel offers. He's warming to Wren.

"Yeah." Wren nods. "Some place like that. But of course, it stood out, so I was curious."

"Maybe it's nothing." Axel tries to cover for us.

"Actually..." Cade snaps her fingers. "Maybe you're on to something. One of the men we busted with Senator Evans was a top-level Russian diplomat. The asshole was immune. We had to let him go."

Bomb.

Drop.

"Who?" Nash sounds nonchalant.

But our world just exploded.

Cade confides, "Valentin. I remember the first name, but the last name was something like Sheremet-something."

Sheremetev.

Valentin Sheremetev.

I know who he is. So does Axel, who's probably hiding his conniption right now. Fuck knows, I'm hiding mine.

Valentin Sheremetev is our father's sworn enemy. They've been warring over territory for decades.

"So, what are you gonna do?" Silas asks us, oblivious that our secret world just flipped.

"Follow the money trail," Nash assures. "Intercept shipments, eliminate the demand and the suppliers."

Murder the fuckers.

That's what he means.

The Six nod. They seem appeased. The tension in the room evaporates while I hide the war inside me, making me rage.

Is this the connection?

My father wants me to think he's sending me on missions to save victims when really ... I'm destroying his enemy's operations here?

Fuck, I'm going to kill him.

But I can't.

If I kill him, his soldiers will kill us. All this, while my father has Axel's child.

It's like any war. No one really wins.

Except there is one thing I *will* do.

I will die getting Axel's child back.

CHAPTER TWENTY-SEVEN
WREN

The minute I'm alone with my men, I expect Axel to go Bratva on me for blurting the Russian thing.

But instead, he picks me up, swinging me around. "Like a fucking queen!"

"What did I do?"

He passes me to Sire, who greedily takes me draped over his arms. Sire's been quiet all afternoon, but Axel's had a personality transplant. He's happy and shit.

"Sheremetev," Axel boasts with icy revenge in his eyes. "Our father's enemy. We never would've gotten that intel without you."

Nash plops down on an ivory settee. "We wouldn't have anything without her. Thanks to Wren, they no longer hate us. And thanks to Sire, they're big fans of his dick."

This whole ship is decked out in black, ivory, and gold. We're on the private guest level, having a secret meeting in Axel's stateroom, while our hosts are having an afternoon orgy upstairs.

Thankfully, we've been invited to join them for dinner at eight.

Do I want food? No.

Am I hungry? Yes.

I haven't forgotten that whole exchange about Daniel and Redix watching Sire in the Atlanta fetish club, and how much they enjoyed it with Silas. It's boiling on a back burner in my mind.

But right now?

This is the burning issue.

"But what does it all mean?" Nash talks to the ceiling. "Does this mean that Ruslan's found us?"

The tension in Sire's body, holding mine, is instant. I feel it, but this time I find a filter. I blurted the Russian thing on purpose, to get intel, but I'd never betray Sire's secret about his father.

"It means," Axel reclines in the velvet chair beside Nash, "the enemy of my enemy is my friend. We won't let Sheremetev know we're here, but we know *he's* here. And now, we figure out the connection."

I've figured it out.

So has Sire.

It's his father and the notes.

I get the feeling I opened a can of worms, but we can't talk about it until we're alone.

"Did I do okay?" I wrap my arms around Sire's neck.

He kisses my cheek. "You did great, Angel. Thanks for your help."

Nash looks around. "Now that we have the intel we need, what do we do? We're stuck here."

"We wait until we dock in Key West tomorrow and fly back," Axel grumbles.

Nash groans, "That's twenty-four hours from now."

"Oh, suck it up, Buttercups." I kick my legs so Sire will put me down. He does while I boss them, "We're on a sexy superyacht, sailing toward warmer weather with six of the hottest people alive. We're gonna have fun."

"Fun?" It's a foreign word to Axel.

"Yeah," I chirp. "You know, it's that word between your favorites, *fuck* and *fury*. Try it. You may like it, too."

"True that." Nash chuckles. "Furious fucks are fun."

Axel mocks, "Says the man who's taken a vow of chastity for Vale Monroe."

Playfully, I kick Axel's shiny black shoe. "Leave him alone. He's in love with Vale. Now, come on." I circle my finger. "Let's put on our bathing suits and go up to the pool deck."

"Sorry, princess." Nash smiles, relieved. "I didn't pack one."

Axel brags, "Me neither. And you don't want *me* naked. The Six aren't ready for my nine inches."

Whatever. They're being big, bratty Bratva boys.

"It's okay." I aim for the door. "I knew y'all would do this: be sticks in the mafia mud. So, I packed Sire's suit and two extras. I'll go get 'em."

"Fuck!" Axel puffs, annoyed. "You had to go and marry a *smart* wife."

"Shut up." Sire laughs, following me to our stateroom. "Your future wives will be smart enough to murder you in your sleep."

The moment we're across the hall, alone in our room, I can't hold it in. I whip around, hugging Sire. "Are you okay?"

"No." He nuzzles his forehead to mine. "Valentin Sheremetev is my father's rival. How he's connected to all of this shit, I have no idea."

"Your brothers don't know your father's found you, but you do. So, what's the risk in contacting Sheremetev? Maybe he can help."

Because *I* want to help. Sire's cursed with guilt over this. He won't let us start a family until he fixes Axel's.

"Men like Sheremetev don't help; they hurt." He's tense and reeling with the news. "And it would put you in more danger. No, my father's up to something and I'm going to find out what."

"You never answered him about your blood type."

"Because I'm not his bitch," Sire seethes. "I don't owe him answers or my blood. I only want his."

"What if you tell Axel now? About Katya and his kid?"

"No." Sire gets that look, the one that takes heads. "That's my father *and* Sheremetev on our shores. But they're not touching us? It's off, and I'm not risking anyone until I know why."

I rest my head on his pounding chest. I can't make this go away right now, so I hold him until his breath calms.

"Alright, then," I sigh. "There's no one to poison or shoot today, so I meant it—let's have some fun."

I seek his kiss, and he gives it, slowly, softly, deeply, until it's heating and his hands cup my ass.

"Let's have a *fuck*." He presses into me. "My wife was a badass today. Damn, woman. Quit stealing my breath. I won't have any left."

"Mmm," I hum into our kiss. "Wanna tell me what Redix and Daniel saw in Atlanta?"

"Jesus, Jesus." He kisses my neck.

"*Tell* me."

His lips steam over my shoulder. "Seems they saw me with others."

"You mean, they saw you *breeding*?"

"Yes. Sometimes I'd breed people in the middle of the club. They'd ask me to."

He's getting hard for me, I'm getting wet, and I know what we need.

"Sounds like the men liked watching you, and Silas *really* enjoyed hearing about it."

He unbuttons my jeans, focused on me. "Lots of people liked watching me fuck."

I cup his erection, biting his lip. "*I* want to watch you fuck."

He chases my kiss. "Then find us a mirror."

"No, we find ourselves on a superyacht with three men who want you to fuck them." Sire's breath deepens. He's not denying my observation. "They made it obvious, and I want you to do it."

"Fuck, Wren. Don't tease me." He plunges his hand into my panties, but I grab his wrist.

"I'm not teasing. I mean it." I search his eyes. "You're giving me my fantasies. You're making me go slow with the kings, and I'll be initiated soon, so let me give *my* king what he needs, too."

His gaze deepens. "I need *you*. I need my wife."

I touch his cheek. "And I need you, too. But they want you, and it's okay if you want them. I know you love me, and this is how much I love you. I'm not threatened by you being with men. In fact..." My teeth grab my bottom lip, "I want to share it with you."

I've thought about this for months. Sire knows it's my fantasy, for me, for him, *for us*.

When I married him, vowing to love him, I meant *all* of him.

Sire loves me; he craves me. I feel it. But he shouldn't have to deny his other desires. I know he has them. Sometimes, when he's inside me, fucking me into oblivion and multiple orgasms, if I whisper our fantasy in his ear, he comes.

We come.

I love embracing every part of him, even if he's willing to give it up for me; I don't want him to.

With panting breath, he shakes his head. "We're not even sure if it's what they want."

"Is it what *you* want?"

"Fuck," he mutters. "This is why I fell in love with you, Wren. You met the worst side of me first. I told you my darkest secrets, and you said we'd fall in love ... and we did. I love *you*."

"We love each other." *How can I make him understand?* "But you suffer over this deal with your father. You have so much guilt and shame about it, and I don't want you to hide anything else."

He blinks, chest heaving, truth told.

I urge, "You told me the night we met that you lie with men, too, and I'm saying I want to see it. *All* of you. Your sexuality isn't the darkest part of you, Sire; it's one of your deepest, most beautiful sides. And you've shown me ... it's mine, too."

He looks at me, disbelieving, then relieved. "You don't just want the fantasy? You want the real thing?"

"Yes." I chew my lip. "Is it what you want?"

Say yes. Say yes.

"I can't lie." Neither can his dick. He's hard and pressed against me. "You want it, and they hinted they want it, too. The thought of pleasing you, of sharing it with you; yeah, it gets me off. And the only way I'll ever be *that* man again, like I was in the club, is if I'm with you."

"Okay. Then let me find out what they want."

"How?" He worries, "Silas is my parishioner. So is Eily. I married them. I don't want to fuck up what we have."

"Do you find Silas attractive?"

He huffs, "Silas Van de May would arouse a corpse."

That's true.

I tease, "Could he fulfill our fantasy?"

His lips brush over mine. "Only if he's yours, too."

"What about Redix and Daniel?"

He nips my bottom lip. "Angel, that's like giving me three hot bulls. You sure about this?"

I smooth his thin white T-shirt. "Let me talk to Eily. We instantly connected. You felt it. So, let me find out what they want."

He doesn't argue. He laces his hand through my curls, tugging tight. "Whatever happens, Wren, you're mine and I'm yours. You're the love of my life; promise me that never changes."

"I promise." I take our vow, and our deep, devoted kiss.

Palming his pecs, I catch my breath. "Put on your swimsuit, I'll put on mine, and I'll make Tweedle Dick and Dong do the same."

He grins. "You're hot when you think you're the boss of us."

I grin back. "You're lucky, because I am."

CHAPTER TWENTY-EIGHT
WREN

In minutes, I'm changed and knocking on Axel's door.

"Yes, Princess?" He opens it, naked and wet, like he just took a shower.

I glance down at Axel's body, covered in muscles and ink. *That's why he's not shy.*

He scans my curves in a white string bikini, and swallows. His body reacts to mine, but his face doesn't. He's stoic, and I like it.

"Who is she?" I ask, handing him a pair of black swim trunks.

"She?" He takes them, standing there.

Still naked. Still getting hard. Still looking at me like he's seeing someone else.

"Yes, the woman you're in love with. It's sweet. I can see her in your icy eyes. Not your *dick*. But your eyes."

Axel lowers his husky voice. "I'm working on her. Okay? She'll be my queen, I know it, but I need time. She won't be easy."

I tilt my head. "Can I help?"

I've shocked him. Suddenly, he looks like he'd kill for me, too.

"Yeah, you can help me. Don't tell anyone. Okay? I don't need shit for this." He swallows. "I don't want to lose her."

"I won't tell."

"Thanks." He leans over, stepping into the trunks.

"But can I ask you something?"

He chuckles. "Can anyone stop you?"

"No, so tell me. I love how you love your brothers. Y'all have no idea how special it is. A family is all I ever wanted. So, tell me, even when secrets are revealed and they hurt, can you forgive them? Isn't that what a family does?"

Silently, he tugs the trunks up. Respectfully, I don't watch him wrangle his long snake while doing it.

I search his glacial eyes and see ... *Axel's hiding more than his future queen.* It's obvious by the way his eyes melt.

"Yes, I'll always forgive my family." Sweetly, he leans forward, pecking my forehead. "I just pray they'll forgive me, too."

He leaves me wondering what the hell he meant, while I aim for Nash's door next.

I knock, and he doesn't answer naked. No, he answers with a white towel wrapped around his waist, his snake obvious and hanging long, too; my libido can't take much more.

It's a pressure cooker about to blow.

Them.

I flit my hand. "Is this a mafia thing? Lion tattoos, lethal muscles, and long dicks?"

He smirks. "Don't forget all the blood, too."

I roll my eyes, handing him the navy trunks. "Here."

He takes them, trying to focus his eyes on mine, and not my body. "Wren, we need to talk."

"Okay. Should I come in?"

"And have Sire behead me? No. Just..." He glances down the hallway. All doors are shut. "Listen, I'm honored that you want me to be your second king, but I can't."

My chest falls. "Why not? After Sire, I feel closest to you."

"Because I've always loved Vale. Still, I used to be able to fuck others and not care, but now, I care too much." He stresses. "I see her every day, but I can't have her, and I can't be with anyone else, and I'm losing my fucking mind."

I nod, warmth flooding my heart for Axel and Nash. They're just like Sire: deadly beasts with big, beating hearts.

They'll protect me, and I'll defend them, too.

"But," I plead my case, "doesn't every king have to claim a queen *and* a second queen? I mean, once everyone's found their love?"

"Yeah," he sighs, resigned.

"Vale will be your queen one day. I believe it. But who will be your *second* queen? Sire has Zar. Loch has Delphine. Axel will claim a second queen, too. So, who will be yours?"

He can't answer me.

That's how much Nash loves Vale.

"Let me be your second queen, and I'll help you." I touch his hand. "I respect your love for Vale. We don't have to do everything together, but I want to be initiated. I want to be *Sire's* queen, but he's too protective of me. He thinks I'm not ready. Like I'll break, when I won't. Help me make him see it."

"See it?"

"Yes," I insist. "Every queen has tests, right? To make sure she wants to be initiated?"

He nods.

"Then help me. Test me tonight."

CHAPTER TWENTY-NINE
WREN

"See…" Eily swishes her hand toward the others, mixing piña coladas at the poolside bar. "Told you, once they got their rocks off, they'd relax."

She reclines on a giant pink penis pool float. I'm riding an eggplant emoji float beside her.

The sunset flames up the sky while Sire and Silas stand closely in a deep conversation. Is it about us? About them?

I sense a reserved vibe toward Axel and Nash, but at least they're being offered drinks, and Cade is talking to them.

Our worlds are too interconnected for us to be rivals. In fact, we share common enemies, so we should work together.

While some of us?

Maybe we should do *more* than work together.

I watch, fascinated, as Daniel kisses his wife, Charlie, then he kisses Redix, making him laugh about something.

I blurt, "I'm sorry, but I'm dying to ask if—"

"If we all fuck each other?" Eily trails her fingertips over the water. "The answer is yes. But even more? We love each other, too. Though Silas is possessive over me right now." She whispers, "We just found out I'm pregnant."

"Congratulations!"

"Thanks," she beams. "It took me and Silas a while, and I almost gave up hope, but now we're busy drawing up house plans, picking nursery paint, and bathroom tile. Charlie, Daniel, Cade, and Redix are moving to our island. We'll each have a house and raise our kids together."

"So, you share a lot more than sex."

With pride, she nods. "Way more. There's a lot of love, history, and commitment, too."

I purse my lips, trying on a filter for size. It doesn't sound like The Six are open to other... Lovers? Is that what they're called?

I don't know their world, but I feel its warmth. Its depth.

Maybe my impression was wrong. And I won't blurt something that messes up Sire's friendship with Silas because I have a case of the curious kinks.

"So, usually, we're a closed polycule," Eily whispers.

Why is she whispering?

"We're only open to others for Halloween and holidays," she shares.

I nod, imagining their world, realizing ours is similar, yet not.

The kings and queens are open for initiations and tests. It's our bond. We'll need it to survive. Otherwise, each couple is different.

I can't imagine Nash or Axel will ever share their women. Only for initiations. Only if they get to punch their brothers afterward.

Loch has fulfilled his duty as a second king to Delphine. Now, he said he's vowed to Alena—no one else. And Alena doesn't need to be initiated. She's the daughter of a king and part of the family.

Jace? He breaks my heart. He's like one of Dolly's sad

country songs. He will always love someone, but who is she? I sense he's lonely without her.

Nick and Zar apparently serve a Dom and his wife. Sire said there's a whole hot story there.

While Delphine told me that Grant's okay with her being with other women at Nadine's club. Often, Delphine shares him. After she was bought and sold in a French brothel, Delphine insists on her freedom, and I've never heard Grant complain.

But me and Sire?

What will we be?

Always together, yes. But what about...

"*Buuttt,*" Eily coos. "This is Redix and Cade's birthday weekend, and Silas has always found our pastor to be very hot and..."

With her big, jade eyes, she pauses, searching mine.

I blurt, "And?"

"And," she laughs, "we don't want to make it weird and freak anyone out."

If she only knew.

"You can't freak me out. I've been through hell and back. Nothing shocks me."

"Shocks? I believe you. But shook?" She drifts closer. "How shook would you be if I told you that Redix, Daniel, *and* Silas want your husband tonight?"

No one should be allowed to feel this excited.

And horny.

I wink. "I wouldn't be shook; I'd be right. I knew it."

"Really?" Eily's cute face lights up. "They want the breeding kink. Let's be clear."

"It's crystal clear," I chuckle. "And I want it for Sire. But what about you? What do you want?"

Eily lowers her brows. "Honestly? So many times, I feared Silas and I would burst into flames in Pastor Rutledge's church because, my dear Lord, look at the man. God ate and left no crumbs with him."

I just made a best friend for life.

I went from having no one to having so many people, so much love. I want to pinch myself.

"Let *me* be clear." I smile. "My husband wants to share his crumbs with the men. But with women? No, he's all mine. And unprotected sex? Never. He likes the breeding power and role-play, but not the risk."

Eily nods, impressed. "I get it. We all have boundaries. Like, I'm not open right now. I don't feel like it. Hell, I might barf any second. But I want Silas to have fun. He's always had a thing for Pastor Rutledge."

Heat blooms between my wet thighs. "And I have a fantasy…"

"Which is?"

I feel like I can tell Eily anything. "I'm a hypocrite, I know. I'm too jealous to share my husband with women, but I want to share a man with him. I want to share Silas with him. Not fuck him. Just, you know—"

"I know." Eily reaches for my hand. "You were a virgin with Pastor Rutledge … I mean, with *Sire* … weren't you?"

"How can you tell?"

"Takes one to know one. Silas was my first, too—my first, my soulmate, my always. We've shared a lot. Me and him. Us and our partners. I've lived and loved a lot, and you deserve it, too." She squeezes my hand. "Have Silas tonight. I trust him. He knows our boundaries." Eily turns her generous gaze toward Axel and Nash. "Are they with Sire, too?"

I roll my lips over my teeth, fighting not to laugh. "Uh… no. Axel and Nash aren't bi."

They're his brothers.

"Are *you* with them?" she asks. "Because damn, they're a whole meal, you lucky bitch. You four seem very close."

Am I very close with them?

I think of Axel swinging me around. Nash, being protective. Jace is so friendly. Grant's always so funny. Nick is sweet. And Loch? He treats me like his equal.

"Yeah," I answer with warmth. "We're getting close."

"Like... *close* close?"

I bite my lip. "We're still exploring that." It's the truth.

Do I adore my future kings? With all my heart.

Do I trust them? With my life.

Do I want to fuck them? Well...

Nannie used to say the patriarchy shames a woman's desire, and it's on purpose. Because your desire is your power. She said you have to know what you *want*, to know what you won't tolerate.

What I love is how Sire knows what I want, and he doesn't shame me. He just wants me to go slow. He doesn't want me to get hurt. That's why we're waiting for my initiation.

Until then?

I edge my float up to Eily's, asking, "So, how do we do this? This will be our first time, uh... you know..."

I trail off, and Eily winks. "Girl, I got ya. If I can plan six sinful nights for New Year's and a hot and horny weekend for seventeen for Halloween, then—"

"Seventeen!" I whisper my shout.

"Yes." She nods, impressed with herself, and she should be. "They call me the pornified party planner."

I laugh so hard, I almost fall off my float.

"Babygirl!" Silas shouts to Eily. "What are y'all laughing about?"

"Nothing." Eily twirls on her penis float, calling out, "Wren and I are just breeding plans for the night."

CHAPTER THIRTY
SIRE

I'VE ALWAYS PRIDED MYSELF ON BEING A DETERMINED MAN. I know what I want.

Do I want the three men, standing naked together with their rock-hard dicks, waiting for me? Sure.

When I'm at the pulpit, I want to save souls. When I'm with my family, I want to save their lives. When I die, I want to be condemned. I deserve it.

But when I'm with my wife? I want redemption. I want heaven, and I find it inside Wren.

You think you love someone, then they accept you even more, and you fall deeper, harder, and forever.

All the times I've done this before, with dozens watching me, I've never had the eyes of the one I love wanting to see me.

All of me.

Accepting me.

That's me with Wren. She asked Eily to arrange this.

We're in a lavish room, the ship's parlor, with a wall of windows to the night ocean outside. Crescent-shaped ivory and onyx sofas circle the space. A tufted leather platform stands at its center. Lights glow. Music lulls. Sex toys, lubes, condoms, and more are on every table.

This is obviously where The Six play their games, and tonight, I'm the winner.

And my prize is my stunning wife.

She kneels, naked, near the edge of the low platform, her cheek pressed to the leather, her luscious ass in the air.

I lick my lips, my dick jutting hard at the sight presented to me. "You're such a bad girl, wanting to watch me breed tonight, aren't you?"

I sit behind her, lingering my fingers over her pussy lips, spreading them to see what's glistening and mine, and she gasps, "Yes, Pastor."

I smear her slick arousal up to her little puckered ass. "Is this what my wife wants? To watch her pastor breed men before I breed her?"

"Yes." Wren trembles. "Please, my lord."

We talked about this an hour ago. Wren's boundaries and mine. The men's desires and their wives' demands.

Granted, it wasn't the usual dinner-table chat, but I don't fuck around when I fuck. Because once I'm possessed, lust owns me, and it's like stopping gravity.

You can't.

I even had a conversation with Nash and Axel in Axel's stateroom. They know the limits tonight—mine and theirs. But they want Wren to be my queen. They know how long I've been waiting for a love like ours.

Maybe I'm too protective of her.

I'm definitely too possessive.

Because one day, this will be real. Choking back tears, I'll come inside Wren, unprotected. Praying to get her pregnant.

The reason why I won't start a family with her yet ... is why I'm determined to fuck so hard now.

It's my kink. My wiring. My rage and dominance. My

urges and anger. I need to put this fury I feel into something else until I'm free of this hell with my father.

I want the peaceful family with Wren that I never had. None of my brothers had it, and that's why we fight so hard for it now. That's why we bond.

And it's definitely why I need to breed.

Grabbing a bottle of lube, I prepare the anal plug for Wren. I packed this toy, hoping I'd use it in our bed tonight. Circling it over her tightest hole, I relish how all get to see it now. "You want this, Angel?"

"Yes," she sighs.

"Hold your cheeks open and show everyone how I've trained my virgin. How my sweet bride has learned to love a naughty pony plug in her ass so she'll be ready to take my hard dick."

Moans lift my glance from Wren to the naked women sprawled over the ivory sofa.

They're clearly enjoying this already. Cade kneels, moaning and eating Charlie's pussy. With one hand, Charlie's pinching her own nipple, while her other reaches, slowly fingering Eily's pussy beside her. Their lust-filled eyes are watching me prepare my wife's ass before I fuck their husbands' asses, too.

My gaze shifts to Axel and Nash, sitting on the onyx sofa opposite them. They have secret loves, I know, but they have eyes, too. The sight of hot, naked women eating pussy and getting each other off makes them very hard.

Can't blame them.

We're all stripped naked.

I insisted.

Wren swears she can handle an initiation, so I want her to experience a sex party first. This is a one-night-only role-play event.

But our initiations?

They're real, raw, and forever.

Teasing my fingers over Wren's slick clit, I make her wet and whimper as I ease the anal plug in, smacking her clit once it's seated.

"Oh, God," she gasps. "I'm gonna come."

"Wait, Angel." I remove my touch, watching the edge of her orgasm, shiver away. "You'll come when I tell you to." I stand. "Now, get in your breeding position."

Moans keen across the room. It's Charlie, coming to my kink and on Cade's tongue.

"Goddamn," Redix, Cade's husband, groans, admiring the sight of his wife.

But my cock firms, hard as stone, watching *my* wife do as I've trained her.

Rising on all fours, Wren presses her legs and feet together, a pose that makes her pussy feel even tighter. Proudly, she looks straight ahead at Axel and Nash, admiring how shamelessly she sways her back, presenting her waiting sex to me with her pink ponytail swishing between her legs.

"Good girl." I stand, stroking my cock, walking around, and crouching before her. Clasping her chin, I vow, "I'm going to breed the men, but I'll save my cum for you." I kiss her lips. "Why?"

There's so much desire swimming in her eyes. So much love flooding my heart. "Because I'm yours, my lord," she sighs. "Because I love feeling my pussy drip with your cum. Your seed belongs inside *me*."

"That's right, Angel." I kiss her again. "Wait right here, and I'll breed you." Reaching between her arms, I palm her pert, tempting breast. "And tonight..." I pinch her nipple. "I'll let my kings help me."

Wren gasps, lust igniting in her eyes.

Yes, I'm ready to explore her fantasies. I could almost start now. Axel and Nash know what to do, but not yet.

Wren wants this first, and so do I.

I rise, approaching the naked men patiently waiting for me. My cock soars even harder, knowing Wren is about to see this side of me.

Kissing is off the table; we discussed it. So is talking this to death. There's trust, consent, and lust. Done.

"Kneel," I demand, and they do. "Good boys. Now, tell me what you saw that night."

Fuck, Redix looks up at me like I'm a God. "We watched you breed two men," he says. "They looked like bodybuilders —big men—but you broke them."

Oh, I remember that night. They were Australian. Their asses and accents got me off.

I press my fingers to Redix's lips. He sucks them while I coax, "Did you watch me fuck them while you fucked Daniel?"

Redix nods, sucking, smirking.

None of these men are small or submissive. It's the opposite, and what's making this so goddamn hot. For them. For me.

"Is that right, Daniel? You got your ass fucked, watching *me* fuck?"

Daniel nods, his ocean eyes gleaming with proud guilt. I sink my hand into his coal waves. "Well then, suck my cock and make me want to fuck your ass, too."

Urgently, Daniel plunges his mouth down my shaft, and I grunt, pleasure shocking my system. I look at Wren and boast, "Oh, he's good at this, Angel. He *really* likes sucking my hard cock."

Daniel moans with my dick in his mouth, and Wren's lips part. She's enraptured by what she sees, so I fist Redix's long hair, yanking his neck open. "Do you want daddy's big dick, too?"

"Oh, fuck yeah." Redix is as eager as Daniel.

They told me earlier they're vers, they're versatile. In their polycule, the men top and bottom. But with me, after what they saw, they want to bottom.

They want it hard like I like it.

Together, Daniel and Redix suck my cock, one focused on my tip, the other lavishing my shaft. It ignites my blood as Silas kneels between them, stroking his dick.

I can't believe I'm doing this with him. So many times, I've watched Silas sitting on a pew and praying.

Then again, he's hot as fuck, naked, and on his knees, taunting, "Damn, Pastor. I've always wanted to suck your heavenly cock."

I smirk, cupping his head. "Then be a good boy and fucking choke on it."

Redix and Daniel lift away so I can palm Silas's skull while he takes my inches, moaning with his desire fulfilled.

"That's it. You fucking love it," I brag. "Good boy. Suck my cock. All the way. Take it." Silas is hungry, drooling, and gagging on it. "Mmm... Someone's being a bad boy, wanting to suck his pastor's cock, aren't you?"

Silas moans again, and Daniel mutters, "Bloody hell, this is hot." He starts sucking my balls while Redix moves behind me, pulling my cheeks apart.

When I feel Redix's tongue lick my ass while Silas sucks my cock and Daniel fondles my sack, I fucking lose it. My eyes roll. "Oh fuck, Angel." In a lustful haze, I look at her. "Is this what you want? To watch men sucking me off and tonguing my ass?"

"Yes," she sighs. Her nipples are diamond hard.

Fuck. With Wren here? Watching me? With all the love in my heart? Bursting for her? Looking at her.

This feels different.

I feel different.

I'm not so full of pain. I'm not so lonely and trying to

fuck it away. This is pleasure, too. But it's my kind of pleasure.

The dark kind.

"Angel," I pant. "Sit back and spread your legs. Show me the pussy that belongs to me. I need to watch you get so fucking wet for this."

Wren obeys. Turning, she sits, facing me. Desire hoods her eyelids as she leans back, propped up on her hands, jutting her tits and letting her thighs fall open.

"*Fuuucckk.*" I reach around, grabbing Redix's hair. "Get up, Birthday Boy, and put your ass in the air. Go on. Show me what you want me to breed."

Redix said he wanted it rough. So tonight, ask, and he shall receive. The platform where Wren sits is big enough for him, too.

"Face my wife," I order him. "Let her see how hard your cock gets for my fuck."

More moans fill the room. I glance over, and it's Cade, Redix's wife. Charlie's between her legs now. She's eating Cade's pussy while Eily sucks Cade's tits and Cade watches me, getting ready to fuck her husband.

Grabbing a condom, I smirk, rolling it on. Rudely, I pour lube into Redix's crack.

Damn, he has a fine ass for a man.

"You want it rough?" I make sure.

"Fuck, yeah." He reaches back, pulling his cheeks open, spreading them wide apart. "Breed me, Daddy. Fuck this ass and make it rough."

Fisting my shaft, I press my sheathed tip to his slick entrance. I glance over his shoulder to Wren, sitting before us.

One last time, I demand, "Say it, Angel. Say what you want."

"Fuck him," she sighs, fingering her hard clit. "Fuck him and enjoy it, and then fuck me, too."

Quickly, I glance at my brothers. It's not like we haven't seen each other fuck. But I've never been the center of their attention.

Thankfully, I'm not.

They're eyes are glued on Charlie eating Cade's pussy and Eily sucking Cade's luscious, huge tits.

"You want it rough, boy?" I snake my arm around Redix's neck and yank him up, pressing my chest to his back as I drive my cock inside his ass with one brutal thrust.

"Oh fuck, yeah," Redix grunts, pain and pleasure straining his voice.

Redix is as big as me. All three men are, but they want my domination, my brutality, and I give it, hammering his ass, invading his body, skin slapping skin.

I choke him hard, not enough for him to pass out, but enough for him to submit while my hips don't relent. I take his ass, hard. *Fuck, it feels good.* No tender feelings. Only savage fucking.

"Oh, fuck yeah," Redix groans. "Give me that big dick, Daddy. Fuck yeah. Breed me. Hard, like you do it." I reach around and fist his hard cock, pumping it. "Yeah. Yeah. Milk me," he begs. "Make me your bitch."

Silas strokes off, urging me, "Goddamn, give it to him, Pastor. He's been wanting you."

Daniel claims, "We all want you."

They kneel on the edge of the platform, and I glare at Daniel, feeling evil and erotic. Pounding Redix's ass and pumping his cock, I snarl, "You want me to breed you next?"

"Umph...fuck yeah, you do," Redix grunts, answering for Daniel. "You want his big dick. Fuck. *Fuck,* it feels good."

"Yes," Daniel rumbles, agreeing.

This is my possession. I have no shame. "Then eat my ass while I fuck your man."

Daniel obeys, squatting behind me, and for minutes, I take it out on Redix. All the rage I've felt, he takes it. He wants it. He cries out for it.

And all the pleasure I feel, I see it reflected in Wren's eyes.

I lock my gaze on my angel and almost lose it. She's touching herself, her middle finger, strumming her hard clit. She doesn't look jealous. She looks erotically enthralled, impressed ... and fuck ... in love with me.

"Say it, Angel," I grunt. "Tell me what you see."

She pants, her eyelids drooping. "I see you breeding him brutally, and he loves it. I see how you make his big cock so hard, it's bouncing and dripping with your thrusts. And I love it. I love you because it gets you off, too. Doesn't it, Pastor?"

Goddamnit. It's almost too much. *Wren, seeing me like this. Still loving me like this. Only wanting more of me. Like this...*

There IS *salvation, and it's her.*

"Come for me, Angel. Come, and show them you love being my dirty girl. You like watching me fuck men for you."

"Mmm... fuck." Redix grunts. He's close. So is Wren. I know my angel's eyes.

With my arm around his neck, I choke him tighter, biting his shoulder. Darkness and desire, a storm in my veins. My cock swells, my hips pummeling his ass. He arches his back, meeting my thrusts.

"Oh, fuck," Redix groans. "Oh, fuck, breed me, Daddy. Fuck yes. I'm coming."

"Show my wife," I growl. "Don't touch your hard, bouncing dick. Let her see how much it wants my cum in your ass."

He won't have it. No one gets my seed but Wren. I'm wearing a condom, but the thought gets us off.

Wren moans, shuddering with her orgasm at the sight of me, making Redix's curving cock, untouched, shoot cum, over and over, painting the black ottoman.

Panting, Redix rolls aside after I pull out and let him go. Dragging in a long inhale, I control my urges. I've earned my stamina.

Daniel's next. He changes places with Redix while I snap off the condom and roll a fresh one on.

Silas stands to the side, waiting, but Daniel's such a hulk of a man, I make him kneel and put his ass up while I rise, crouching over him.

After crudely pouring a little lube in his crack, I slowly plunge my dick in his ass, and he grunts, "Bloody hell. Oh fuck. Oh fuck, yes. Breed me with that big dick."

"You like this?" I grab his shoulders and pump my hips. It's a primal, animalistic breeding position, and he arches open for it. Taking it. "You like me breeding you? You're such a big boy, taking my dick in your ass."

"Fuck, yeah. Do it," Daniel growls. He's so big, so muscular, he loves the submission. So many men like him secretly do. "Fucking breed me, Daddy. Pound that arse. Pound me hard. Goddamn, Sire, breed me."

I fist his black hair. I pump into his gaping ass. "You want my condom to break, boy? You want me to fill your ass with my cum?"

"Fuck, yes. Fill me with your cum," Daniel grunts, reaching between his legs to jerk off his hard dick. "Breed my arse, Daddy. Hard. Real fucking hard."

"God, he wants you," Wren sighs, pumping her fingers into her glistening cunt. I look up and grunt at her desire. It matches mine. "You're such a sire. A stallion. He's opening his ass so you can breed him. It's like he's in heat and needs you. Just like me."

Oh, fuck. Hang on. Wait for her.

I yank Daniel up. With my arm around his neck, I snarl, "Want me to go even harder in your ass?"

"Harder?" he huffs, shocked, like it's not possible.

"Fuck yeah, I can go harder. Like this..." I growl, pumping my hips. "You want it rough, boy?" I choke him tighter, my chest pressed to his back. "You need some dirty breeding?"

"Yes, Daddy." Daniel touches my hip. "Please. Please."

Pounding his eager ass, I taunt his ear, "You want me to breed you like a bitch? You like this? You're such a big boy, taking my dick in your ass."

"Umph...fuck yeah. Do it," Daniel pants, jerking his hard dick. "I want that big dick. Give it to me. Fuck. Fuck, Pastor. You fuck my arse so hard. So good. Fuck, fuck, I'm coming."

He groans, releasing like an animal in ecstasy.

It makes Wren moan, shuddering with her orgasm at the sight of Daniel's cock spurting white ropes of cum. He cries out, his cum splattering her thigh, and I fucking lose it.

CHAPTER THIRTY-ONE
WREN

Good God, I could never deny Sire this pleasure.

Hell, I won't deny it myself.

The way he's so dominant, so natural. He fucks like an animal, breeding his willing recipient. He lets me see. He's everything.

He *is* a sire.

And he's mine.

I finger my aching pussy, watching him fuck men. It's so primal and taboo, I can edge and come all night.

I feel the same desire as Redix and Daniel, getting fucked.

As my first, Sire has been tender with me, each time going a little harder. But he hasn't fucked me like his instincts are more important than intimacy. Like he's an animal, not my adoring husband. Like he needs to fuck me, not love me.

Is it crazy to want both?

"God, he wants you," I sigh, pumping my fingers into my aching cunt, matching Sire's tempo. "You're such a sire. A stallion. He's opening his ass so you can breed him. It's like he's in heat and needs you. Just like me."

Sire locks his glare on me. He sees my fingers, banging my

cunt, where he belongs, and he twists his neck, fighting his urge to come.

I know my husband's body, and I know mine.

I need him to fuck me like *that*.

He yanks Daniel up, wrapping his inked arm around his neck. "Want me to go even harder in your ass?"

"Harder?" Daniel doesn't believe him.

"Fuck yeah, I can go harder. Like this..." Sire pumps his hips, and my jaw drops in awe, in lust, in love. "You want it rough, boy?" He chokes Daniel, pressing his back against Daniel's chest. "You need some dirty breeding?"

"Yes, Daddy." I shake, watching Daniel touch Sire's hip. "Please. Please."

"You want me to breed you like a bitch? You like it?" Sire's a beast. A beast I love. "You're such a big boy, taking my dick in your ass."

"Umph...fuck yeah. Do it," Daniel begs, jerking off his hard dick. "I want that big dick. Give it to me. Fuck. Fuck, Pastor. You fuck my arse so hard. So good. Fuck, fuck, I'm coming."

Sire grunts, his neck straining, fighting his orgasm while he fucks a man's ass and makes his thick, veiny cock, shoot his cum so far that it splatters my thigh.

"Oh fuck," I moan, waves of an orgasm crashing through me.

My eyes slam shut while I shake, hearing Sire seethe, "Lick it up." He orders Daniel, "Lick your cum off my wife. Now, you dirty fucking boy."

Fluttering my lashes open, I moan at the sight of Sire's dominance and Daniel's submission.

With Sire fisting his hair, Daniel, the man of steel, smirks up at me, licking his cum off my thigh. I try to hide my pleasure at his tongue on my flesh, but my husband must sense it.

"Get off her. Right. Fucking. Now," he snarls at Daniel,

who rolls aside, retreating to the sofa to join his sated wife, Charlie, cuddled with Redix, Cade, and Eily, who chews her lip, wanting this next part for her husband, Silas.

Snapping off the condom, Sire wraps it in a tissue before grabbing a packet from the side table. With his teeth, he opens the personal wipe and cleans himself.

God, he looks so primal, powerful, and brimming with pride.

"Such a beautiful, dirty girl for me, aren't you, Wren?" He wipes his swollen tip, then his thick, jutting shaft, his eyes devilish and on me. "You can't stop touching your pussy while you watch me fuck men for you. Is that what you want? To be bred like I bred them?"

He smirks, challenging me, "You want me to fuck you hard and in the ass?"

"I... I..." My libido screams, *Yes!* My pride insists, *I'm equal.* But my logic scoffs, *Hell no!*

He sees it in my eyes.

Wisely, Sire grins. "You're not ready for that, Angel."

"Yes, I am." I blink up at Sire while proudly splaying my pussy for the room, cool air kissing my tingling clit. "Please, fuck me."

I fall back, willing, as Sire climbs over me, pressing his clean, bare cock to my waiting entrance, the one he opened.

"First and always, Wren, you're mine," he sighs, slowly urging inside me, inch by inch, not stopping and rolling his eyes. "*Fuucckk, Angel.*" I moan as he shudders, "This wet pussy is what I need. Goddamn, woman, you're mine. You're all I want."

I want *him.*

Lifting my hips, I grab Sire's hulking, inked shoulders, and I take him so deep inside. For minutes, it's us, it's only him, passionately fucking me, my lips, kissing and biting his chest, but then I remember...

Nash and Axel.

I glance over, and they're watching him fuck me. It makes me moan. I turn my head slightly and see the hot group on the sofa, and Silas standing, waiting, stroking off to me, getting fucked.

I suspect Eily told him my fantasy.

My husband gazes down, reading my mind. With a slow thrust into my pussy, he smirks, "My dirty little girl, I know what you want now."

Shifting our bodies, Sire whips me around like a doll. He flips us, sitting up, and making me ride him while I wrap my legs around his waist.

We love this position. He can kiss me while he fucks me like this. It almost makes our heights even.

Our lips touch as he taunts, "What's our fantasy, Angel? Say it."

"I..." I glance at Silas, hard and waiting for us. "I... I... I want... Uh..."

Seriously? I find a filter now?

Now that it's right there and hot and hard, and I can't even blurt?

Sire grins, nipping at my stammering lips. "You want to watch me suck a hard dick for you, Angel? Is that what you want while I fuck you, too? You want to see a cock in my mouth while you come on mine, don't you, dirty girl?"

There's erotic...

And then there's ecstasy.

That's what this is.

Ecstasy ... with my lips so close to my husband's sexy face, his breath steaming with mine.

"Silas," he beckons him, and Silas joins us, kneeling beside us.

Turning his head, I moan at the sight of my hot husband, at Sire's menacing facial ink, those gorgeous eyes, and those luscious, devilish lips with tickling whiskers, parting to suck a huge dick. It's the hottest I've ever seen as a man's hard cock slides into my husband's open, moaning mouth.

"Fuuucckk, Pastor." Silas throws his head back. "Fuck yeah, your mouth is heaven. Goddamn, you can suck dick. So good. So fucking good."

"Mmm," Sire moans with a cock pumping into his mouth, making my pussy clench around his.

I tremble, watching, marveling at how he relaxes his chiseled jaw, taking as much dick as he can into his throat, his gag, not stopping him.

No, he pulls away, only to throat the cock again, but this time his gag turns into a skilled *gluck*. His throat opens. His eyelids flutter. He wants a dick, deep in his throat. I can see it.

"Oh my God." Lust explodes through me. I circle my hips, grinding my excited clit around Sire's thick base. "Yes, Pastor, that's so hot. Suck his cock. Let me help you."

He lifts off Silas's dick.

Sire kisses me before our tongues meet, licking and lapping together over the swollen cock between our lips.

We kiss and touch our tongues over the dripping slit, salty precum filling our mouths, our aroused breaths merged, our bodies fused. It's so erotic. Intimate. Trusting and honest.

Sire is showing me everything. Sharing everything. Giving me everything.

"Put it in your mouth, Angel," Sire commands. "Let's suck his cock together while you come on mine."

I am.

I will.

Tentatively, I open my mouth for another man's cock. With my husband watching. With his permission. With his lips steaming by mine, stretched over a swollen shaft. *Oh my God.*

"Such a good girl," Sire praises. "That's it. Suck his cock for me. Let's make him come together because my men get you next."

The pleasure overwhelms. Flooding my senses. I don't even need to rub my clit, my lust takes over. Sire pinches my nipples. "That's it, Angel. Such a good girl taking all the cocks you want. Come on. Do it."

With another man's dick in my mouth and my husband's cock, stretching my wet pussy, I come. I scream, shaking, my cunt clenching hard with my orgasm muffled by the mass in my mouth.

"That's it." Sire kisses my neck, pulse after pulse, shaking my body. "Keep coming on my dick while you watch me make him come in my mouth."

I moan, my eyes fluttering open. I'm in a haze, an orgasm resonating through my flesh. Like a symphony of pleasure that won't stop. I watch Sire cup another man's balls, his mouth, moaning and full with a huge cock.

"Fuck, yes, Pastor, I'm coming." Silas's thighs shake. "Fuck, you're hot. I'm coming down your throat. Oh, God." He cups my husband's head. "Oh fuck. Fuck yeah, Pastor, swallow my cum."

Sire swallows with a groan, his cock raging hard inside me, his hands grabbing my hips.

With another man's cum dripping from his sexy lips, he turns to me, smirking, "Like what you see, Angel? I told you... I'm the Devil in bed."

So am I.

"Please," I pant, my sex pulsing and clenching. "Please, I want more."

I don't know what I want. I just feel it, I need it, and I don't get a chance to ask.

Sire falls back, lying flat on the bed. That must be his

signal for Axel and Nash, because suddenly, they're nude, hard, and by our side.

Silas retreats from my periphery while three of my seven kings surround me.

I guess this is my first test.

Sire clutches my hips, urging me to ride him.

"Show her what our next test will be like. Right, Wren?" Sire grabs my throat. "You said you want all of us?"

Axel clasps his hand over his brother's, wrapped around my neck. Their blood, their double grasp, beyond hot. Together, they squeeze just enough while Axel taunts my ear, "You want all of us to fuck you, princess?"

A sudden, thrilling pressure teases my ass. Axel's pulling on my pony plug, praising me, "Such a dirty girl, getting your body ready to take so many cocks in this tight ass."

"Oh, God." I tremble, watching as Nash lifts my empty hand, guiding me to fist his hard cock.

"You want all this?" Nash steams over my other ear. "You want five big cocks to take turns with you, Wren? Are you sure?"

Ruthlessly, Sire thumbs my clit. Reaching up with his other hand, he pinches my excited nipple while Nash pinches the other.

"Yes!" I throw my chin up. My pussy. My ass. My tits. They're taking them, and I don't own my body; Desire does. "Yes, I want all of you."

"You sure, princess?" With a slow tug, Axel pulls out my anal plug.

I gasp. I shake. I don't get a chance to breathe before Axel's fingers are plunged inside me.

"You want him in your ass, Angel?" Sire challenges, "While I fuck your tight pussy? Or do you want me to breed your ass, while they take turns with your cunt?"

I open my eyes. Looking down, I pant, barely focusing on Sire beneath me. *I love him so much.*

They're overwhelming me with pleasure; he knows it. Sire is making sure of it. He's testing me. He needs to know I want this. It doesn't hurt.

"Yes, my king," I groan, leaning forward.

I jerk off Nash's hard cock with one hand while I brace my other on Sire's hard abs. Arching my back, I open my ass to Axel's fingers and jut my breasts out, wanting them to be pinched, too.

Let our friends watch, too. I love it.

"Fuck me," I growl. "Fuck me, all of you."

I don't know where the voice comes from, but it's mine.

Mine.

Mine.

My desire.

My power.

"Show her," Sire growls. "Show her how we'll make her ours."

Nash rises beside me, his hard cock hovering over my panting lips. I lick at his early drops, but I keep our secret promise. I don't put Nash in my mouth. I take him just enough to show Sire how much I want this.

Tonguing Nash's swollen tip, I feel Axel slide, two... then...

"Oh my God," I cry out, feeling Axel pump three fingers into my ass. I'm so overwhelmed by Sire's size stretching my pussy, too; I don't know where the pleasure comes from, but it's everywhere.

It's here.

It's now.

"Yes, Angel." I hear Sire. *I love Sire.* There's one being made for our soul, and he's mine. Always mine and forever.

"Yes, Angel," he calls me. "Come for us. Show us you're ready to be ours."

His hips lift. Brutally hammering his cock into my pussy, his hands hold my hips prisoner, and I'm forced to take this pleasure.

Indulging my mouth. Teasing my tongue. Stretching my ass. Pinching my nipple. Filling my pussy. Thrilling my clit. I come so hard, I convulse, crying. I sob, laughing, and shaking.

It lasts forever and never long enough.

In a sudden grab, Sire pulls me to him, wrapping his strong arms around me and holding me so tight while he groans, coming inside me, "Christ, Wren."

Through his grunts, his release, he vows, "Damn, Angel, I love you. I swear, I'm gonna fucking die for you."

Why?

Why do I suddenly believe it's true?

CHAPTER THIRTY-TWO
SIRE

Four months later

A sea of pastel Easter hats stretches from the first pew to the last. It fills me with peace. Pride. Joy.

Strumming my guitar, I sing, casting my smile at Wren in the front pew.

My angel always dresses elegantly for church. Her simple white sundress matches her wide-brimmed hat. But her smile? Her perfect face is twisted, trying not to laugh, and when I follow her stare, I see why.

Little Annabelle May sits with the other kids on the altar steps. Proudly, they sing with me, "Jesus Loves Me," but Annabelle loves picking her nose more. Her little finger is digging for gold in front of the whole congregation.

I glance at her parents in the fourth pew. They look mortified, so I stand, strumming and singing into my headset as I work my way to Annabelle. When she sees me, she proudly hugs my leg, wiping her golden treasure on my dark suit pants.

I laugh. So do my parishioners while I finish the song.

Sitting with the kids for a final round of "Here Comes Peter Cotton Tail," I encourage them to hop for their laughing parents, and they do.

It's a simple joy, and all I want with Wren one day.

Damn, she's beautiful, smiling at the kids, too.

Love almost chokes my breath away.

The instinct that Wren is mine. The one I'm meant to be with. The mother of my babies. The woman I need to breed. It's primal. Overwhelming. Highly inappropriate at this moment, and I don't care.

Spring is the symbolic season of fertility. A time for new life and new beginnings. It's the perfect day and Easter service ... until an old, sinister spirit crawls up my spine, raising the hairs on my neck.

Searching over the pastel hats, this evil presence feels familiar. I spot the shadowy figure looming in the back.

The Devil's advisor.

My father's Sovietnik.

He's here.

In his black suit, he blends in. His hair is silver now, but I'd recognize his vicious eyes anywhere.

They're aimed at me.

I glance at Grant, sitting with Delphine in their usual pew. Praying Grant was too young to remember Viktor Aminoff from our tragic childhood, I finish the service.

Viktor would never cause a public scene. He lives in the shadows. He wants *me*; I know.

It takes an hour for all to leave, including Grant and Delphine, but Wren stays, hugging the kids and their parents.

Sure, Mrs. Cabot leads a group of parishioners who hate Wren. They cut mean eyes. Whisper behind hands. They shame my age-gap marriage like I'm going to hell.

No fucking shit, I am.

And I'll meet them there with their hypocrisy.

Wren is my salvation, and my only sin is everything I'll do to keep her safe.

Like now.

I peck her cheek. "Why don't you go with Ms. Davis and make sure the kids take their crafts home?"

She blinks. "But we didn't have bible school today. It was a kids' service."

Fuck. Think.

"Then, wait for me in my office." I kiss her, nipping her lip. "I want to play with *your* bunny tail."

"Yes, my lord." Happily, she grabs her purse, swinging it over her shoulder.

I watch her disappear through a side door, towards my office, before Viktor rises from the shadows of the vestibule.

Yes, I'm a man of God, but I was born into evil. I expect the worst in most, so I prepare. From under the first pew, where Wren sits, I reach, pulling out the Glock I keep hidden there. There's one hiding under my pulpit, too.

"What the fuck do you want?" I aim at Viktor, slowly stalking my way.

He smiles. "*Dobryy den'*."

I sneer, "English. I won't speak *his* language."

Thanks to my father, Russian is acid on my tongue.

"Good afternoon." Viktor clasps his hands. His Russian accent thick, his English impeccable. "Impressive service. Impressive wife. She will make beautiful heirs."

"Touch her and I'll kill *your* heir. I'll kill Katya."

Katya, Axel's first wife, is Viktor's daughter. She always looked familiar, just like her father. She was the perfect succubus to seduce Axel: a female demon requiring semen to survive.

"Easy." Viktor surrenders his hands. "I'm not here to rouse our proudest lion."

"Fuck you, I'm not his lion, and I'm not his heir."

Lions are the supporters of our family shield, but I never saw them as representing our father.

No, I have them inked on my skin, all my brothers do, to honor our mother.

She's the lioness, the reason we survived.

"You've been playing games again, Sergei." He halts, steps away, admonishing me like a child. "You make deals with your father and don't honor them."

"He's a wife-beater and child abuser; I'll never honor him. But I *will* kill him."

"That's not necessary." He nods toward the cross. "We all meet our maker one day."

"Ready to meet yours now?"

My pulse doesn't race. I'm numb. Stone. Cold. Possessed by the spirit who remembers being burned.

"No, I'm here to discuss a new deal."

I huff a laugh. "Dead men make no deals."

Calmly, Viktor sits in the second pew, crossing his leg over the other like a vile gentleman. "Perhaps you are willing to die in lieu of a deal, but what about your breathtaking wife? You've chosen well. Your father is impressed. She's nice, strong stock."

Rage fills my exhale, logic firing across my brain. *Wren's safe in my office.* She knows I keep a gun hidden under my desk, too.

"No," I counter, "I've chosen never to have a child until I get Axel's back." His eyes widen. *Fuck, I'm right, and it makes me sick.* It makes me seethe, "Who did you take from him? His daughter or his son?"

Viktor gloats, "My grandson thrives. He adores his mother and father."

I reel. *Axel has a son. Taken from him. This will kill him.*

Choking on guilt and grief, I rage, "Ruslan is *not* my

nephew's father, and Ruslan knows it. Why would he take Axel's son when he only wants mine?"

Evilly, Viktor shrugs. "You left us no choice. We have a spare, now we want an heir."

"Never," I snarl.

"Well then, perhaps we can make an alternate exchange. There is another piece of you we want."

"Piece of me?" Bitterly, I huff, bearing burns from my father. They may hide under my ink, but not from my soul. "No, he's taken enough from us."

"Then we won't *take* this time. We'll accept a donation."

My blood? Is that why my father asked about it?

Viktor lowers his voice. "Your father has a genetic condition that causes kidney disease. He needs a transplant. He—"

"He needs *my* kidney?"

Of course, he does.

Karma never fails.

"Or, one from your brothers." Viktor raises his bushy eyebrow. "But you don't want that, do you, Sergei? Then they'll know what you did."

"I did nothing but keep my family safe."

"No, you thought you could deny your father, your role, your responsibility, as you always have, and now we have your nephew. What would your brother, Aleksi, say if he found out you sacrificed *his* son and not *yours*?"

I can imagine Axel's pain.

He's my blood, my little brother who'd sleep with me when we were afraid. I can feel his rage. His suffocating ache. The painful instinct and urge for his child. I want to fall to my knees, dying for him. I love my brother. I love my—

"What's his name? My nephew?"

Viktor brags, "Lev, our little lion."

"So help you God if you or Ruslan hurt him. I will behead—"

He flicks his hand. "We would never harm an heir. We may need him. But he's too small. We can't take his kidney yet, so we'll take yours."

This is barbaric, savage, and my father's hallmark. He doesn't care *who* we are; it's *what* we are to him. His blood. It's all he cares about.

But I care about everyone else but myself. My blood is my grace, my redemption.

"I will give him my kidney in exchange for my nephew."

Viktor scoffs, "It won't be that simple."

All the days I had to sit at my father's feet, witnessing his wrath, I know...

"Oh, Viktor, death is very simple. But for my father? Finding a kidney isn't. I know him. He won't accept anything in his body that's not his blood, and good fucking luck getting my brothers to give him a goddamn thing once they find out what's at stake: their nephew."

Viktor tapers his eyes. "Oh, but you won't do that, Sergei. You know better. What about your beautiful mother, Queen Nadia? What about your other queens? Your nieces, nephews, and children one day? Kill us, and we will have them killed. You know this."

My logic revolts. "You'd kill your own grandson?"

Viciously, he snarls, "We *all* meet our maker."

This man is vile. Viktor used his daughter, raising her to be as ruthless as he is, sending her to seduce my brother. Only a heartless woman would take a child from a loving father. And now, he's willing to sacrifice that child, all for money.

But I have the power—the blood.

"If my father wants a piece of me, let him kneel before me and fucking beg for it."

"He is not well enough to travel."

"Not my problem, Viktor. It's yours. That's why he pays

you the big bucks. You're his little bitch-boy who cleans his mess."

"Careful, Sergei." Viktor rises. "You forget who you're dealing with."

"Yeah, you're dealing with me."

An angel's voice calls across the sanctuary.

I whip my focus on him, to Wren, standing with the gun from her purse, pointed at Viktor.

"Lay a hand on my husband or my family, and I'll put a bullet in your skull." Wren squints one eye, her aim locked and loaded. "Or watch what you drink. Y'all like tea in Russia, right?"

"You would not be so foolish, young lady," Viktor chides her.

But Wren laughs. "Time's up, old White man. Only ladies follow *men's* rules, and I ain't feeling lady-like."

Jesus, Jesus. I'm so in love.

"Angel," I beam with my gun drawn, too, "I know he's standing on a blood red carpet, and your aim is true, but I don't feel like cleaning brains off of bibles today."

I focus on Viktor. "You heard my deal. If my father wants another piece of me, he can get on his knees for it. Otherwise, it's like you said; I know better. He lives or we all die."

I wave my gun. "Now, hurry along, and enjoy some shrimp and grits before you leave our fine city."

CHAPTER THIRTY-THREE
WREN

"Tell me how you knew." Sire aims his car south on the interstate, but he keeps glancing at me, grinning.

It's not fair. He's so hella hot, love dances in my veins.

But I know he feels this, too—this ominous fear. Sometimes, we're so in love, so wrapped up in each other's arms, we forget the danger we're in.

Until it comes slithering into our lives.

Still, Sire distracts me. I guess it's to protect me, and it works. For a minute. He won't stop luring me with that pussy-purring smirk.

"What?" I huff brightly. "I'm not telling you how I know when you're lying. I'm not playing all my cards mere months into our marriage."

"You overheard us?"

"No."

"You spotted Viktor before you left?"

"Nope."

The coral sunset ignites the sky outside my passenger window. Sire takes the next exit, turning onto a remote Georgia highway. All I see is rolling farmland.

"Where are we going?"

"Tell me how you knew first." His warm hand caresses my bare thigh. This sundress is demure; that's desirable to him. "Deal or no deal."

Keenly, I study him. Drawn to his visage: my charismatic, consecrated, chameleon killer.

Sire has changed out of his dark grey pastor's suit, and no one should also look that potent in a plain white T-shirt ... but he does.

I want to lick the ink off his neck, kiss the tattoos on his face, unzip his faded jeans, and suck his beautiful, big cock while he drives. He smirks behind his sunglasses, knowing it.

"Okay, fine," I sigh lovingly. "You smile when you lie."

"No, I don't."

I laugh. "You're smiling *right* now."

"Fuck." It falls from his face. "I'm that obvious?"

"Only to me, and that's how I knew shit was up. And I heard what Viktor said, so tell me. Where are we going, and will you do it? Save your father's life in exchange for Axel's son?"

His nostrils flare with murder on his mind. "We're visiting some friends who'll eliminate the first threat to my nephew."

"Who and who?"

"The killer cousins I told you about, and Viktor. Any man who threatens to kill his own grandson needs to die."

I turn in my seat, my pulse racing. "Yes to the last part, but no to you doing it with the killer cousins. Wilder's a few pickles short of a barrel; he's nuts. And the other one?"

"Remi," he supplies.

"Yeah, Remi. He looks like he'd steal the nickels off a dead man's eyes."

"If the man pissed him off."

"And you *trust* them?"

He takes a left turn. "I trust if I pay them to do something, they will. And I'll help them. Besides, Wilder and I go way back. We were in juvie together."

"Yeah, he said you *shanked* him."

"Just a little." Sire grins. "And he never stole my cherry cobbler again."

I shake my head. Sometimes, Sire's so godly, and other times, he's so street. It's sexy, but not now.

It's dangerous. Fatally dangerous. My instinct keeps telling me. Dolly Parton. Butterflies. God. The sky. I don't know where it comes from, but I trust this inner voice.

Sire will die. Stop him.

I try to use reason. "So, where are we going? Wilder's halfway house?"

"No." He looks dead serious. "We're going to the cousins' brewery. The clock's ticking. Viktor's here, on my father's yacht in Savannah, but we'll make sure he doesn't make it back to Moscow."

Sire's so calm when all hell breaks loose. I bet he's as calculated as his father; he's his worst threat. He knows his father's next move.

But what breaks my heart is ... *Sire's soul is dying because his father is winning.* He has Sire's nephew, Axel's son.

I heard Viktor confirm it today. He said it was a choice: Sire's son or Axel's.

Though it broke their hearts, I believe my birth parents gave me away for a loving reason. They couldn't take care of me, so they left me in God's safe hands.

But Sire or Axel would never give their child away. No, it's the opposite. They'd kill to keep their child.

How was it ever a choice for Sire?

It wasn't.

"So, you're going to kill Viktor? Won't your father retaliate?"

"Viktor's replaceable. I'm not. It sends a message to my

father and Katya. Vengeance for what they did to Axel. They took his son, so I'll take Viktor."

"That's brutal."

He glances at me. "*That's* our family."

It leaves me silent until we step out of the car in the parking lot outside the brewery. String lights glow. The warm, wooden barn with its large windows and red metal roof beckons you inside. Even the black iron sign, lit by flickering gas lamps, reading "DEAD GOOD BREW," doesn't scare me.

But this does...

"Sire, don't." I grab his hand, sudden tears spilling down my cheeks. "Don't do this. God. Dolly. I don't know, but something is telling me to stop you. Like something bad's going to happen, and I always trust my instinct."

"Angel," he cups my wet cheek, "I'll never lie to you. Yes, something bad will happen, and I'm sorry it upsets you, but that's the life I was born into. Just know, I'm trying to get us out."

"But don't do *this*. Don't go on that boat."

"Viktor needs to die. Axel's son isn't safe with him around."

"Okay. I want to protect the child, too, but let the cousins do it. You stay here." I plead to his indigo eyes, this fear suffocating my cry, "Don't *leave* me."

He softens. He only does it with me. Pulling me closer, he nuzzles his forehead to mine. "I'm never leaving you, Angel."

"But you *will*," I swear. I feel. I know. "I can sense it. I'm going to lose you."

Gently, he kisses me, our lips salted by my tears. "It's your childhood wound, Angel." He murmurs, "You were abandoned so many times, and now you fear you'll lose me. It's normal and *never* going to happen. I'm yours forever. My family is yours, too."

I shake my head. It doesn't feel true. "You can't promise that. Things change. People change. What if I lose you? I'll want to die, and I will. They'll kill me when they find out that I knew about Axel's son and didn't tell them. Axel will hate me. Your *mom* will hate me."

He searches my eyes. Sire can see your soul, and he softly smiles. "They'll never hurt you or hate you. Hate resides in an evil heart, like in my father, but not in my family. They love my wife almost as much as I do."

I blink back tears. "But your brothers? You said you're all brutal."

"We are. We kill for a cause, but we *don't* hate. We won't be like our father."

"So, they'll forgive you? About Axel's son?"

His eyes glance to the night sky, to heaven above. "I'll die trying for their forgiveness."

I grab his shirt. "Sire, don't *say* that."

"It's a figure of speech." He cradles my head to his chest, kissing my hair. With a deep, resigned sigh, he vows, "Okay. I'll hire the cousins to get rid of Viktor, but I won't go. I'll stay here with you."

"Promise?" I exhale, snotting his shirt.

"Yeah, because it feels like it's time."

"Time for what?"

He pulls back, lifting my chin with his half-pinky. "You don't trust that my brothers will always love you. That you're ours forever, no matter what. So, it's time we initiate you. I want you to feel it. To believe it. I think you're ready."

The flip in my heart is instant. This feels true. Right. Destined. Dolly-approved and written in the twinkling stars above. I'm suddenly safe ... and seduced.

"You'll really let them, uh ... *initiate* me?"

He lowers his brow. "I'll let them *bond* with you."

"Bond? But, I thought we fu—"

Knowingly, he grins. "You have to feel our bond to believe it."

"When?" Me and my blurts. They can really fuck up my fucking plans. I shrug, blasé. "I mean...whenever."

Laughing, he tucks me under his arm, leading me toward the brewery. "Let me take care of business first before I take care of my eager little queen."

If I could skip jubilantly to the brewery door, I would.

"WHAT'LL YOU HAVE? I GOT A ZERO-CARB SELTZER THE ladies like."

"Well..." I tap my lips, asking the bartender, "I ain't a lady, so what would a Glock-carrying wife drink? One who's underage?"

He winks, impressed. "You'll like our Dead Russian Stout."

Sire mutters in his brew, "I heard that."

The bartender's name is Bishop. He's one of the crazy, killer cousins who turns around ... and with those broad shoulders and those jeans and that ass? I watch him pull pints and pussy. Holy beer hops, he's hot. Every woman at the bar is drooling.

For Bishop. For Wilder. For Remi.

Catnip must be in their brew.

"Yeah, give her the high-test stuff." Wilder sits beside me on a barstool, crowing, "Let's put some hair on her pretty little chest."

"Say another word about my wife's pretty little chest." Sire, perched beside me, doesn't even need to look at Wilder. His sarcastic tone tolls with a lethal threat.

"Damn, little Disney princess." Wilder elbows me, muttering his drawl, "Someone's sounding all shanky again."

Does the young Brad Pitt know he has a redneck twin? Wilder Pitt. Is that his full name?

"Just take the job," Sire insists, wrapping his arm around me. "You got twenty-four hours before he sets sail."

Bishop sets a full glass in front of me. I glance at his big hands. *You know what they say about men with long fingers.*

"And if someone asks?" Big Bishop probes, "Like your brothers? Like Jace? He's in here all the time."

Sire shrugs. "It was anonymous. As usual."

"How many?" Remi, a man of few words, hovers behind us. He makes me anxious. And aroused. Remi glares like he just got sprung from prison, where he served time for the illegal distribution of female orgasms.

"Have fun." Sire takes another sip. "Get as many as you want. I'm only after one."

"I don't know." Wilder spins a cardboard coaster. "Lately, I'm bored. I need motive, not money for murder."

Bishop cuts him a look, venting low, "Hey, dumbass. Karaoke starts in thirty minutes. Turn off the microphone in front of your fucking teeth until then."

I perk up. "Karaoke?"

"Oh shit," Sire mutters.

Bishop grins at my excitement. "You a fan?"

"Yeah," Sire answers for me. "But you won't be. Not once she's done."

"Uh!" I backhand his arm. "I'm a karaoke champ. I don't even need the words on the screen."

Sire pulls me in for a kiss. "Yeah, Angel. Lyrics? Who needs 'em?"

I mutter over his luscious lips. "When will you initiate me?"

His lips find my ear. "We'll *bond* with you, and I'm thinking in Atlanta. Tomorrow night."

I'm not thinking at all.

Shivering with delight, I tune out his conversation with the cousins. How can I pick a song from the karaoke menu when I can only imagine what my test will be?

After our night on the superyacht with The Six and Nash and Axel, it's like Sire wanted me to himself again, and honestly, I liked it.

I'll always cherish it.

It's our normal: me and Sire, cuddling in bed after hot sex. I rest my head on his inked chest while he plays with my curls, and we muse about our kids' names one day.

I love our quaint life. It's all baking, music, church, and tactical training.

Sire hides guns everywhere and takes me target shooting once a week. Every Tuesday night, Jace and Grant teach me and Delphine Krav Maga. Sire says he can't hurt me, so he lets his brothers try.

Poor Jace, I really kicked him in the dick last week. Jokingly, I offered to kiss it and make it better. I thought Jace was joking when he replied, "Next time."

I guess he wasn't joking.

Finally, the karaoke begins, and I'm third to go. Belting Madonna's "Like A Virgin," I'm seducing my husband.

He sits at the bar, a proud lion hungrily grinning at his intended mate. My lure, irresistible. My voice, a siren's song. Or so I assume, until I'm done and Sire's pulling me into his lap with a laughing kiss.

Wilder sits beside us, looking bewildered at our mating ritual. "Hey, uh, Princess Jasmine?" An unlit cigarette hangs from Wilder's lips. "You know what a virgin is, right?"

"Sure do. I was a horny virgin until an hour after I married

Sire; right there, in front of his church's altar." I toast my beer. "Bye-bye, hymen."

Behind me, Remi snorts into his mug. Sire laughs into my hair, squeezing me tighter.

But Wilder continues, "Yeah, well, you know, virgins aren't touched for the *thirty-first time* in that song. They're touched for the *very first time*, in fucking *and* that song."

My blush is instant. I hear my mistaken lyrics and how I crooned them to the entire crowd, probably thirty-one times.

In a huff, I turn to Sire. "Why didn't you tell me?"

His brows shoot up. "Because you're packin' heat, and no one comes between you and Dolly and your songs."

Wilder laughs, jumping off his stool. "I'll take the damn job for free if she gets up there and sings again."

Do I like the crazy hot cousins? Yes. I like their beer and karaoke, too.

Do I trust them to take care of a deadly threat to our family? Okay, I know when I'm in the presence of killers.

But still.

If they eliminate Viktor, it means an even greater threat will come for us.

It'll summon the Devil.

Sire's father.

CHAPTER THIRTY-FOUR
SIRE

"You sure about this?" Grant asks before hissing a sip of whisky over his teeth.

"You saw where we found her." I'm drinking water. I want to be fully sober for this. "You saw where she came from, too, and the hell she went through."

Axel solemnly adds, "And then her childhood? Man, I can't stop thinking about how cruel some were to her."

I swallow the lump in my throat. "Exactly. Wren went from having no one to being my wife. She'll have me forever, but I need her to trust you all, too. She's afraid she'll lose us."

Thoughtfully, Jace nods. "You want us to make her feel it. How we care for her."

"Yeah." I turn to Nash. He's oddly quiet. "You okay with this, bro? This is what she wants. You'll be her second king, and it starts tonight. This is her test. Next week, we initiate her."

"I'll always be here for her." Nash leans forward, opening his hands. "You know I will."

"I'm loyal to Alena," Loch explains. "But you know I'll always serve our queens."

My eyes slice to Grant, stifling a brotherly grin.

Grant let Delphine transform Loch from a closeted virgin into a skilled pleasure Dom. All so Loch could become Delphine's second king, and long before Loch professed his love for Alena.

Nick and Zar share a chair. Cheekily, Zar adds, "We're here for *immoral* support, of course."

I raise my water glass to my second queen. Zar always lifts the mood.

Reclining on black leather sofas and chairs, we're illuminated by two red neon bunny lights in a private VIP room of The Rabbit Hole. A white faux rabbit fur blanket covers a low platform. Mirrors line two walls. A black sex swing dangles from gold chains, swaying from the center ceiling. Low acrylic tables supply condoms, lube, toys, and more.

I called ahead with special requests. Given my history in this Atlanta fetish club, they go to great lengths to please me.

Delphine is with Wren, getting her ready at the hotel. They're on their way while my emotions threaten to end this night.

Possession. Passion. Protection. Perversion. Desire and the divine. It's a war inside me.

I'm not sure I can fully share Wren, but I'm sure she needs this.

Outside the cousins' brewery, I've never seen her so afraid. Tragically, she wasn't as scared when I rescued her from a sex trafficking ring, or when we hunted down her captor, and she shot him.

No, Wren was fearless then.

But she's terrified she'll lose me now. That something will happen to me, and my family will abandon her. I understand. As a child, almost every night, I feared I'd lose my mom.

So, tonight is more than an erotic test for Wren. A prelude to her initiation. A taste of our carnal tradition.

This is proof. Vows made with flesh. Penetrating promises. A covenant of carnal bonds. Sacred sin.

Forever, Wren is mine.

Always, my brothers will care for her.

Some bonds last a lifetime.

She'll feel it tonight.

"So, we go slow with her and take turns." I pop my neck. Goddamn, this is true love because murder itches through my veins, even as I demand on Wren's behalf, "Whatever she wants, we do it. And if you hurt her—"

"Off with our heads." Grant stretches. "Got it."

"Condoms," I bark.

"Check," they reply.

"Consent."

They nod.

I slice my eyes over the soaring landscape of black-suited kings, my beastly brothers. I trust them, but still... "Do not *come* in *MY* wife."

"What about *on* her?" Jace smirks. He's a hidden devil. "She really liked it last time."

"Fine," I hiss. "But don't do it in her eyes. Cum stings."

Nick and Zar chuckle while Axel jokes, "Why yes, our proud bi brother, we'll take your word for it."

I smirk. "Like I didn't impress you at our party with The Six."

"Like you wouldn't impress a group of silver-backed gorillas." Nash's eyes glimmer, amused. "Goddamn, man. You're a National Geographic documentary on breeding in captivity."

Our laughter almost drowns out the knock on the door before Delphine enters, holding Wren's hand.

Lightning jolts my heart at the sight of my stunning wife, wearing a white silk robe and matching heels. She's biting her plump, glossy lip. I know her body. I was her first. I'll be her last. I know when Wren's aroused. Curious. Nervous. Her long lashes blink, adjusting to the red-lit room until they find my eyes.

Proudly, she gives me her smile, and love has a heartbeat. It's living, breathing, changing, and growing even stronger inside me. How is it possible to love Wren even more, because I do?

My Iron Angel.

My, how your wings have grown.

Delphine leads her to the center of the room. Gently sliding Wren's robe off her shoulders, she demands, "Be *great* for her, my kings."

I'm an animal.

Unleashed.

Untamed.

Unworthy.

I shouldn't be allowed to have a wife *that* glowing and so goddamn beautiful.

My swelling, possessive dick strongly agrees.

Wren's ripe breasts perch over a white silk underbust corset. They're not covered. Her dark, rouge nipples pointing proud and high.

I swallow down a growl at the naughty spot on her white silk panties. She's ready and swollen. Wren's pussy is already wet.

Fuucckk.

No.

I pounce to my feet, roaring, "We're done! She passed the test."

Suddenly, I'm not into the initiation thing, test thing, group thing, public thing, breeding thing, or anything with any human but Wren.

That convent on a cliff in Italy is our next stop.

"*Oh, non!*" Delphine wags her finger at me. "Your queen

knows what she wants." Smiling with Wren, she turns her around, presenting her backside.

Goosebumps bloom over Wren's sweet ass. Her tawny skin a beacon with that white bunny tail anal plug begging for my mount.

Dear God, I'll pay my penance and *answer my prayers in that pussy. That ass. That body.*

That woman who saved my soul.

Looking over her shoulder, Wren smiles, shaking her bunny tail at me. "Pastor Rutledge, I'm ready for you."

She's playing a game.

I'm not.

In four feral steps, I whip her around, grab her throat, and slam my lips to hers, swallowing her gasp. Her lips are soft and pliant, but Wren's will is unbreakable.

Demanding her tongue, I can't tame hers with mine. Her desire is too strong. She knows what she wants. Fisting my white starched shirt, she grinds into me, rubbing her soaked pussy over my fine dress pants.

We never wear boxers under our dark suits for tests and initiations. It's to be ready, to show respect for our queens.

I do. I'm ready. I respect my queen.

But I'm about to fuck the living hell out of my wife.

"You're ready to breed, Angel?" I reach down, ripping her delicate panties off. Silk threads don't stand a chance against my animal urges. "You want everyone to see what a hungry little pussy you have for my cock? For my cum?"

She pants, "Yes, my sire."

I slide a finger through her slick lips. "Fucking right, this pussy is mine to fill. Only *mine*."

I whip my glare to Nash. "Help me with her."

He rises, licking his lips. There's not an erection that can hide in this erotic room, including his.

"Help me lift her and put her in the swing," I demand.

The swing has three thick, padded straps. One to support Wren's back. The other for her to sit on. The third strap has two stirrups that can be used for her feet or hands. Either way, the swing lifts her to our height.

Suspended for my use.

Dangling for her pleasure.

Presented for public viewing.

Fuck yes, I planned it this way.

Proudly, Wren lets us situate her, swinging before me. Her long hair, swaying. Her open pussy, glistening. Her bunny tail, maddening.

Falling to my knees, I growl at Nash, "Take a seat and watch me make my wife's pussy drip for our cocks."

My angel is so ready.

I press my nose to her clit, inhaling her feminine scent. When I lick, her tangy flavor floods my mouth. Her proud lips swell while I worship her, kissing, laving, fluttering my tongue. Hungrily, I eat her pussy while all watch, and I get to taste how aroused she is.

How open.

How hungry.

This has been her taboo fantasy for months. Confirming it, she grabs my hair, moaning.

"Good girl," I praise. "Make your pastor taste the heaven in your cunt."

It's palpable after minutes of lavishing her hard clit, and curling my fingers inside her tight, slick walls.

It's audible in the heavy breaths of others, watching as Wren shamelessly gazes down, fisting my hair and panting at the sight of me devouring her pussy.

It's visible when I tell her, "Now, be a good girl and show them how your pussy loves to squirt on your pastor's face."

Brutally, I pound my fingers inside her clenching cunt.

Together, we've taught her pussy how to do this. Her thighs shake as she screams, throwing her head back, rattling the swing's chains with her first orgasm.

Her gushing desire leaves no doubt, her juices flooding my mouth. Proudly, I swallow her cum, letting some drip down my chin before I slowly rise, lowering my zipper.

No warning. No tender nothings. I growl, "Now, let's make this tight, squirting pussy come on your pastor's cock."

I drive my aching dick inside her, and she cries out, "Yes, Sire!"

"You want it rough, Angel?" Grabbing the gold chains holding the swing, I lean over her, crudely gliding my cum-slick lips over hers. "You want me to breed you, hard?"

"Yes," she pants. "Yes, fuck me. Fill me with your cum."

"If you can survive *my* fuck..." Savagely, I thrust into her cunt, and she moans. "Then you can take all *five* of us, can't you, Angel?"

"Yes," she rasps, her eyes rolling back with pleasure.

It's a true test. Grabbing Wren's hips—satin, silk, and soft flesh filling my grasp—I unleash, relishing her pulsing, wet heat. I'm an animal fucking her harder than I ever have. I may even bruise her, but I'll never break her.

I believe her now.

Wren loves me. Accepts me. Wants me. Needs me to love her, and with all my soul, I do. I'm hers. She's mine. I'll never leave her, and I will make sure she'll never be alone again.

A testament to her need, she pulls on the straps, lifting to kiss me while I hammer my hips, driving deep inside her. Our lips meet with her heavenly gasps rising higher and taking me with her. We're climbing to the edge together.

White heat coils tight at my spine. Blood builds, swelling my heart, my cock. *I could die right now, a complete man inside her.*

"You're such a good girl." I press my forehead to hers. "You like this, don't you? Wanting me to fuck you so hard."

Her lips shake. "Yes, Sire."

"Show my brothers how you love my fuck. How you play with your pussy for me every morning, driving me crazy to fuck you, don't you? How you're a naughty girl, fucking a dildo while you suck my dick. How you love my cock in your ass now."

"Yes." Her eyes roll. "Yes, I'm such a slut for you. Please, Sire, show them."

Damn me to hell; you'll find me fucking her there.

My thighs shake. So do my lips. I'm right here with her. *Always with Wren.* She's every reason I breathe. Why I live. Why I can't stop. I won't stop. She's my life and death.

"You're going to take my cum, all of it. You're such a good girl, letting me breed you." *This instinct, I need to fulfill it. Like my life depends on it. Why?* "I want to see you swollen with me."

"Yes." She grabs the base of my throbbing cock, squeezing. "Don't you dare pull out. Give me all your babies." It's the point of no return. She knows how to make my fall from grace so devilish and divine. "Yes, Pastor. Fill my pussy with your warm cum. Do it."

"*Fuucckk*, Wren." She grabs me, owns me, yanking me over the edge.

I grunt, pressing my huffing lips to hers, my fists holding the straps, afraid my body will fall as hard as my heart has for her. My dick comes so fucking hard inside her. With another pulse, I spurt again. "Fuck, I love you." And again, grunting, spurting, I open my eyes to watch.

To pull out.

To worship.

My pearly cum drips from her pink pussy. Her ripe cream coats my swollen cock. Proudly, I want all to see it.

I leave my dick out, exposed, as I walk around the swing

and grab her from behind, kneading her nipple while I reach down, strumming her clit.

"Open your eyes, Angel." I taunt her ear. "Look at my brothers and show them how you come when you feel *my* cum dripping from your pussy."

CHAPTER THIRTY-FIVE
WREN

Loved and lewd. Pure and pornographic. Divine and dirty. I feel every powerful emotion, every beautiful sensation with Sire.

The world divides women into virgins or whores, when we're both. We're neither. We don't believe in your goddamn rules. We know the truth.

This is my power. My desire. Yes, I feel it.

"Open your eyes, my angel." Sire's warm lips steam over my ear. His touch, everywhere I need him to be. His love blankets me with his praise, "Look at my brothers and show them how you come when you feel *my* cum dripping from your pussy."

I do.

Every time.

I belong with Sire.

I bond with his brothers, anchoring to their lustful eyes on my splayed sex. On Sire's fingertip, strumming my excited clit for them. On my pussy, pulsing after his brutal fuck.

"Good girl," Sire praises. "That's it. Drip with my cum. Show them you're mine."

The truth floods me. "Yes, Sire." I clench my sex, feeling a drop fall to the wooden floor. It makes me scream through the orgasm suddenly rushing through me, my eyes locked on Nash, Axel, Jace, Loch, Grant, then Nick watching my claimed pussy come. Pulse. Drip.

I belong to their brother.

Will they care for me, too?

It takes a minute for my breath to return as Sire moves to my side, turning my head for his tender kiss. "Angel, do you need a break?"

"No," I sigh over our lips. "I need more."

"More?"

"Much more."

I'm not holding back. Why should I? I can't be any more aroused, any more vulnerable, any more trusting.

Coaxingly, Sire gazes into my eyes. "Then let's get you ready for much more."

He caresses my breast, and I moan, loving how handsome he looks, how dominant. All the men do, wearing suits and adding to the kink.

I'm naked except for a bustless corset and heels. Delphine dropped her robe. She's nude. Zar is dressed in a suit, too, but as a queen, he's proudly unzipped, displaying his double cock ring harness for Nick.

There's something powerful about being exposed. Something royal about being watched. Yes, all queens should be worshipped like this.

"Loch," Sire calls him, and I gasp. *Loch's allowed to test me?* "Make sure my queen is ready for more."

Loch cocks a grin, rising to his feet. Shrugging off his dark jacket, he loosens his tie before unbuttoning his starched shirt, revealing the devil tattooed on his hulking chest.

All I've known with Loch is partnership and respect. He

always trusted my opinion when we met online, looking over mountain maps.

But he's the kind of man, if you met him alone on a dark, wooded trail, you'd be overcome by an animal attraction. His face, primal perfection. His body, beastly beautiful.

Reaching for a bottle of lube and a Hitachi wand vibrator on the table, Loch tells Nash, "You know I love Alena. I'll never touch another woman again, but I've been trained to serve our queens."

Nash nods, his eyes narrowed. He's not happy about this, but Delphine is.

Proudly, she's smiling at Loch while Grant kisses her neck. The taboo undercurrent between them makes my legs, suspended in the air, start to subtly shake.

"You okay, Angel?" Sire won't leave my side. He stands on my left, holding my hand wearing his wedding ring, while Loch joins us.

"Yes. I'm more than okay."

Loch grins, looming on my right. When he pours a generous amount of cool lube over my warm pussy, my gasp is drowned out by his thumb clicking the wand, its buzz filling the room.

Loch stares down at me, his command intense, "You're going to love how this feels, won't you?"

I nod.

"That's our good girl." Loch licks his lips, gazing at my glistening pussy. "Now, relax and focus on your pleasure."

"Oh God," I cry out as he whispers the vibrator over my clitoral hood. Over and over, he barely lets it tease my hard nub. It's excruciating ecstasy, making me writhe, the swing's chains rattling.

"No, no. Hold still for us, Wren." Power weighs Loch's heavy tone, but his touch is featherlight. "We'll always take care of you. You know that, right?"

I nod. I moan. I feel.

"Just like this," Loch coaxes, his toying touch perfection over my pussy. "We'll watch you get so swollen again. We want you ready to take us. Is that what you want? To feel how we'll take care of you?"

"Yes... Yes..." I stammer through lust, through tears, feeling overwhelmed by Sire caressing my breasts, too. Everything is warm, wet, and welcome.

Circling the humming vibrations over my mound, Loch trails it down my inner thighs, up towards my pussy lips, down to my anus, before teasing toward my aching clit. "Good girl," he praises, barely touching it, and making me tremble.

Loch knows what he's doing. Like an erotic god, he'll master your erogenous zones, pleasing way more than your pussy.

Thank you, Delphine.

And *Congratulations, Alena.*

I roll my eyes, moaning aloud, "This feels so good."

"Mmm," Loch admires my pleasure. "Brother, your wife likes it when her kings please her pussy."

Loch taunts Sire, who taunts right back, "All the reason why I'll please your queen one day, too."

Nash barks, "The fuck you will."

"Alena's off limits," Axel angrily agrees.

Why? What is it between Axel and Alena? I know he's not in love with her.

But I catch the knowing smirk between Sire and Loch. Like, *no one has to know.* Like they're making plans. For what?

I'd blurt my questions, but pleasure renders me speechless.

"You're doing such a good job, Wren." Loch's deep blue eyes bore into mine, holding me, trapped on the edge of another orgasm. "Be a good girl and wait to come. We're not done. Look." He nods toward Sire. "Your husband really wants to please you, too."

With panting breath, I glance at Sire. He's hard again. Watching his brother torture me with a vibrator, he strokes off, gloating, "Ready for more, Angel?"

"I... I... I need to come," I huff, desperately.

"Not yet," Sire orders, and Loch withdraws his touch. Leaning forward, Sire cups my face, nuzzling his nose to mine. "Say what you *really* need from us, Wren. Don't be shy with us. We're here to take care of you, remember?"

Closing my eyes, all I can feel is the warmth in my heart, the deep ache in my cunt, the well of lust in my body. I don't know where it ends, but I want to find out. I grew up, so starved for touch, for love, for happiness, for pleasure, and now...

I want to feel it.

Sire's offering it all to me. He loves me. He wants me to have this.

"Both," I sigh, opening my eyes. "I mean... two. I want two."

Before my eyes, Sire crosses over.

The fallen angel rising as a wild, feral animal: I crave the savage look in his indigo eyes. It's the one who leaves my loving husband behind and becomes the arch brute inside. I trust that later, my man will return. But now...

I want this beast.

"Play with her pussy." Sire rips off his tie, unbuttoning his shirt while commanding Loch, "Don't let her come until my dick is deep in her ass."

I shiver as Sire steps behind me. Like they've done this before, Loch hands him the bottle of lube.

Standing in front of me with the wand poised over my pussy, Loch waits while I feel Sire crudely spreading my cheeks, circling lube over my tightest hole.

"Such a dirty girl." Sire nibbles my neck, goosebumps erupting over my skin. "You want my dick in your ass tonight, don't you? That's why you're tempting me with this naughty tail."

Tugging on my bunny anal plug, Sire reaches around, plucking my pearled nipple, too. It traps my aroused gaze on Loch. Staring up at him, I gasp, feeling his brother, my husband, slowly pull my anal plug out.

"Yes, my lord," I pant at the taboo, the pleasure, moaning when I feel Sire quickly press the fat head of his dick into my little gaping hole.

"I'll go slow, Angel," Sire coaxes with his whiskered lips to my ear. "I'll make it feel good. Right? I've trained you. Tell my brothers what you beg for now."

"You," I rasp, feeling Sire pushing an inch inside me, stretching me while I stare at Loch and confess, "You, Pastor Rutledge. I love it when you fuck my ass like a dirty girl."

"*Fuucckk*." Loch's eyelids drop with lust.

"Make her come for this." Sire snaps him back.

Hooking his arms under my legs, Sire holds me with my back to his exposed chest, my legs dangling over his hulking arms. The swing supports half of my weight, the other half held by my husband, tilting me, exposed, and about to take his dick in my ass while presenting my empty pussy to his brother.

Oh. My. God.

I'm doing this.

And it feels so good.

"Do it. Make her feel good," Sire demands. "Make her come while I fuck her ass."

Loch licks his lips, focused on where I'm receiving, waiting, taking, trusting.

He circles the vibrating wand over my clit, making me cry

out, lust exploding through my veins as Sire grunts, driving his thick cock all the way inside my ass.

It's all white light and no noise except my scream while my orgasm is sweet destruction. I convulse with every sensation and none but the overwhelming pressure, the pleasure ripping my breath and vision away.

"Remember, Wren..." Loch's throaty, aroused voice nears, his lips tenderly pecking my hot cheek. "You're one of my queens, too. Always."

His warm lips retreat, leaving his deep vow on my skin. My heart beats, happy. *I believe Loch. I trust him.*

In a pleasure haze, I watch Loch take a seat, close his eyes, and toss his chin back. He plunges his fist into his pants, stroking his hard cock. *Alena. He needs her right now.* It's so sweet. So hot.

"More, Angel?" Sire holds me, his lips pressed to my ear. "Tell me. Tell us what you want."

"More," I beg, aching for this. "Double penetration. Please."

There.

I said it.

I want it.

Now.

"Jace," Sire calls another brother, and I moan, loving my husband even more. Trying to believe this is my life. My pleasure. My world, where so many men are devoted to me. Where so many women adore and support me.

I went from nothing and no one—last Christmas, I cried, shivering alone in a tent—to everything shared with so many. To a love with Sire I never knew was possible.

Joyful tears well in my eyes. I can barely focus on the sight of Jace standing before me.

Good God, he's so brutally beautiful, too.

With a tender, gruff voice, Jace asks, "You sure you want this, little one?"

What's little? Not Jace's body. Not his colossal inked hand, stroking his swollen dick. Like his brothers, he's wearing a sexy dark suit, so there's nothing little about my desire either.

"I... I..."

This sudden feeling in my chest. What is it? It's not fear. I know what love is, too. I feel it everywhere in Sire's warm touch, holding me, claiming half of me.

So what is this new light, beaming inside my soul?

Is it trust? Belief? Lust? Power? Some unnamed bond? They tumble together while I'm silenced by emotions, staring up at Jace.

"I'll go slow." He thumbs my cheek. "Just say what you want."

"Double penetration," I say it again, confidence finding my voice. "With my husband. With you. That's what I want."

Desire flashes across Jace's eyes. Snatching a condom from the nearby table, he rolls one on. I'm so stretched by Sire. So overwhelmed by his thick dick, filling my ass, I have no idea how Jace will fit.

But I want to try. I scan our audience, their eyes hooded with desire, wanting to watch us try, too.

This is the belief Sire mentioned. The erotic bond. We don't need to share blood when we share our flesh. When these men prove if I trust them to be inside me, they'll never leave.

They'll be mine, too.

"Be gentle," Sire growls, warning his brother.

I can feel Sire's sweat on his pecs, his concern, his heart pounding against my back. "I want this," I assure him.

Reading Jace's sapphire eyes, they're not sure, but his hard dick is, so I urge, "Please, try. I want to feel it."

Pouring more cool lube over my waiting pussy, Jace promises, "Say stop, and I will." He touches my chin, lifting my stare to his. "We'll never hurt you, Wren. We'll always take care of you. You understand?"

I nod, getting teary. Not from terror. It's how tender Jace is. How loving Sire is, too.

"We got you, Angel," Sire sighs over my ear, holding me against his chest. "If you like it, say so, and we'll make sure you *love* it."

While Jace slowly teases my entrance, Sire turns my chin. Deeply, he kisses me with every ounce of love and trust between us. I'm flooded by his protection, his possession. Sharing is not something Sire will usually allow. No, he'd fucking kill someone. But he needs me to trust his brothers. To bond. To believe...

I'll never be alone again.

Is that this feeling? This potent heat between him, me, and his brother?

Slowly laving his tongue over mine, Sire reaches down, teasing my slick clit with his fingers, while Jace breaches my entrance, pressing an inch inside me.

My gasp, instant.

"Angel." Sire pulls back, searching my eyes. "You okay?"

"Yes," I pant, anchored to his stare. "Yes, keep going." I talk to my husband while his brother listens, slowly urging another inch inside me.

"God," I groan, seeking Sire's lips. I need the anchor of his kiss, whimpering when I feel Jace pull out, before barely pressing a few inches inside me again.

Grunting, Jace worries, "*Fuuck,* Wren. Fuck, you're so damn tight. Tell me this feels good for you, too."

Jace's fingers start to tease my clit, too, like it's his instinct, giving me pleasure. His fingers flutter over my clit, alternating with Sire's, and it's so erotic. So intimate. So goddamn ... *full*.

That's how this feels. Full of them. Full of their care. Full of pleasure. What are the words for this?

"Yes," I rasp, turning my stare to Jace. "It feels so good. Give me a little more."

Gazing down at where we're joined, Jace clenches his granite jaw. Slowly, he drives another swollen inch inside me, the pressure and pleasure between our bodies increasing, swelling.

Clearly, Jace is aroused. He's rock hard. But he's holding back.

Is he worried about me? Is his heart somewhere else and in love? Is this his kink, a double penetration? Is he so alone and needing a warm connection? Some kind of sex?

Yes to all of it. I can see it flooding his bedroom eyes.

"Fuck me." I want to take care of him, too. I can't feel pleasure unless we all do. "Fuck me, both of you, and stretch my tiny holes. Use me. Tell me I'm a good girl, taking all this dick."

"Fuck, Angel." Sire's been motionless inside me, not wanting to hurt me. Slowly, he starts thrusting. "You like this? You like being a good girl, taking two big dicks in these tight little holes?"

"Oh fuck." Jace rolls his eyes. He starts thrusting, too. "Fuck, this feels so fucking good. You're so fucking warm, so goddamn tight and wet."

Jace hasn't fucked in a long time. I can tell. All his tension, over who I don't know, melts from his body. I touch his starched shirt, feeling his huge pecs, lax at my touch. I'm right.

"Yes," I rasp, their dicks like shallow, slick pistons taking my body; tender in my cunt, taboo in my ass. Two men hold me, pressing their lips to my ears, their aroused breath making me confess, "I feel so tiny in your arms. Harder. Please. I love it."

Sire moans, needing this too. He gets off on my pleasure. Sometimes, I think it's all he cares about, but I care about him, too.

"Yes, Pastor." I get off on his pleasure. "Forgive me for being such a greedy little slut for you." That makes Sire grunt, driving into my ass, his fingers pinching my clit. "Oh, God, yes. Breed me like one."

"Fuck, yes, Wren." The tenderness leaves Jace's voice. "We'll kill for you." He pulls out, driving back inside my aching pussy with a snarl, "But goddamn, I'm gonna fuck you like our little slut now."

Heat flashes over me. Stars dot my vision. My thighs start shaking. My clit ignites with Sire strumming it.

"Yes, Angel." Sire turns my head, taking my kiss again. His lips. His love. His words, taking me, too. "Come so fucking hard for us. My sweet, slut. We'll fuck you all night."

"Mmm." I anchor to Sire's kiss so I can fall into an ocean of pleasure, so I can come back to him. But not before dark, tumbling, wet waves make me thrash with pleasure. There's no land. No time. No sight. No one but Sire, while a giant wave eclipses my world, destroying it with an orgasm so strong, I'll never be the same.

Virgin. *Gone.*

Alone. *Gone.*

Pain. *Gone.*

It's Sire and me and this new shore. My new home.

"More," I groan, feeling Jace pull out before warm spurts splash across my tits. My eyelids flutter, seeing Jace. He's so fucking hot, coming on my nipples. He looks so relieved, while I feel so powerful. I shudder with another climax. "Oh, fuck, yes, give me more."

"Grant," Sire calls out, and I tremble, thrilled, needy, and open.

Grant's different because Delphine joins him. Loch hands her the Hitachi wand while Grant rolls on a condom.

"Say it, Angel." Sire won't leave me. He's still inside me. *He always will be.* "Tell me you want this."

"More," I sigh over his lips. "I want to feel more."

I was never held. Never loved. Never treasured. Still, I tried so hard to be happy. And now ... I am. I'm loved.

Sire holds me every night. He worships me every day. He loves me forever. He's more than what I need.

But sometimes, a woman should finally get what she desires, too.

"Careful with her." Sire gently thrusts, contrasting his concern for me with his carnal need to fuck my ass. *I love him.*

Grant is careful, and Delphine, generous. I can tell she trained Loch. Lusciously, she teases my clit with the wand while Grant matches Jace's inches. They could be twins. But while Jace seems tortured by love, Grant acts freed by it. He's perfect for Delphine.

Carefully, Grant slides half of his cock inside, waiting for my exhale. I can't stop moaning at the sensation returning. The stretching. Fullness. Burning. Pleasure.

"Fuck, brother," Grant huffs. "She's clenching my cock. Match my tempo. Slowly..."

They've done this before with Delphine. She told me about her initiation, and I'm thankful.

While Sire drives into my ass, Grant drags out of my pussy. When Grant pushes back into my channel, Sire kneads my excited nipples, pulling out of my ass. All while Delphine lavishes my clit with the vibrating wand.

Erotic euphoria. Lewd light. Fucking frenzy. Every word and sensation is not enough, and claiming every inch of my flesh.

"Oh my God." I fall into my ocean again, Sire's lips returning to mine. He's my oxygen. My rescue. My world, while I dive into pleasure for so long, I don't care how long it takes, I just float until I come so hard again, screaming into Sire's kiss.

"Fuck, Angel. Do you want more?" He sounds worried. Or, exhausted? I open my eyes and find his, searching mine while Grant and Delphine retreat to a sofa.

"Are you okay?" I ask him.

He grins. "You're worried about me? While my hard dick is in your ass?"

"Yes."

"My angel," he brushes his lips over mine, "your body is where I belong. I can stay here forever."

I giggle. "No, you can't. I know how to make you come."

"Don't." He hoists me higher. "Don't until you're done. This is for you. What do you want?"

"You."

He smirks, licking his lips. "Naughty girl." He thrusts his generous cock. The man could be a porn star, I swear. "You got me in your ass, so who else do you want in this pussy? Enjoy it now, because no fucking way do they get you after your initiation."

My initiation.

This already feels like it. But it's not. There will be a ceremony. I'll receive my...

My second king?

CHAPTER THIRTY-SIX
WREN

I kiss Sire before answering him because it's not *who* I want, but *what* I want. I want to make this work for everyone.

"Nash?"

I search for him in the red-lit room, finding him sitting beside Axel on the leather sofa. Their suits, black. Their legs, spread. Their dicks, hard. I can't blame them.

Grant is fucking Delphine on a sofa right beside them. Zar's face is buried in Nick's lap. He's sucking Nick's cock. Their brother looks lost in ecstasy.

So does Loch. His hard cock is out, along with his phone. He's jerking off and making a video for Alena. Is that their kink? OnlyFans would be so proud.

Maybe.

But I was right.

It's an orgy. Though Nash looks worried, his brows bend while his dick soars under his pants.

"Nash," I beckon him again, hoping he can read my eyes in the red room.

Trust me. Please. Because I trust you.

No one else notices Nash hesitate. No one else knows he's torn between duty and love. But I do. I feel it, what Sire said I would...

The bonds.

The vows.

The love.

The way Loch honored me *and* Alena. The way Jace needed me, because he can't be with who he wants. The way Grant knew what to do for me, and Delphine helped.

Commitment. Love. Lives. It's like what Eily said about her life with The Six. It's way more than sex.

Nash stands between my open legs. He's a man with a pulse and a desire for pussy. Of course, his cock is hard ... and huge.

But he's in love with someone else.

Like me, Nash was a foster kid. He had no family until he met Sire's. He knows how I feel. Family, love, and loyalty mean everything to us.

Maybe I'll always fear I'll lose Sire. Maybe my premonition is wrong. It's a childhood wound, not a warning.

But if I lose Sire, my soul, Nash will be there, guarding my shattered pieces.

"Hey." I grin.

"Hey." Nash grins back.

"Feel like a fuck?"

I want him to relax. Nash knows we need to do this. His brothers guard Alena, so Nash needs to make his bond with me, too.

"Uh..." he hesitates. I've never seen a menacing man look so hot, horny, and torn.

Okay ... Sire was during our first few days. But now Nash is the conflicted one.

"Man." Sire tenses, holding me. "Yes, she's my wife. I'll kill you anytime but now. Give her what she wants."

"Just the tip." I join Sire's fingers, teasing my clit. "Just tease me with your bare tip. That's all I want to feel."

Relief floods Nash's eyes, reading mine. *This is our secret. Our way to make this work.*

Licking his lips, Nash drags his zipper down. With a stifled moan, he frees his hefty cock, fisting his swollen shaft.

Good God, Vale Monroe. You're going to want this man's crown for sure.

I know Nash will be with her one day. They'll marry, and Vale will be a queen with me. They'll be so in love. They just have to get over the best-friend's-dad thing.

Or maybe ... they just need to revel in it.

There's so much lust glossing my pussy, I don't need lube. I'm so sensitive, gasping when Nash glides his crown over my clitoral hood. He teases, lightly touching and tapping my excited nub, his lips parting, his breath changing, watching how I'm open and taken.

How Sire is slowly thrusting into my ass, his chest soaked and pressed to my back. I don't know how much longer my husband can last, but I don't want another man if Sire's not with me. I could never do this if I didn't feel him inside me, too.

"You're being such a good girl," Sire sighs, pulling out all the way. I gape. I groan, hearing him taunt, "You're letting my best friend get off on your pretty pussy while I fuck your ass."

He thrusts back inside me while Nash rubs his tip, harder over my clit. *Fuck, it feels good.* I cry out, "Yes, Pastor, fuck my ass. Show your friend what a good girl I am for you."

"Goddamn," Nash huffs, rubbing his cock over my clit, faster.

Sire can't talk. He's barely hanging on. He needs to come, and so does Nash. Not just for his release or relief. It's for our bond. Everyone needs to witness it.

But Nash will fight it. He's committed to Vale; I want him to be, but I know how to finish him fast.

"See this pretty pussy?" I spread my lips for Nash while I reach over my head, holding on to Sire, too. His neck is sweating, and I love it.

"Yes," Nash snarls, precum pearling on his tip. He's fighting his lust.

"Now close your eyes," I tell him. "Close your eyes while my pastor fucks my ass and you get off on it, Daddy. Don't you? Don't you get off on good girl pussy?"

"Oh fuck, yes." Nash throws his chin up. Slamming his eyes closed, he shakes. He sweats. I can see the ink on his chest and abs, through his soaked white shirt.

"Fuck, Wren," Sire groans. "Fuck, Angel. What are you doing to me?"

It's not our kink. It's Nash's. But it's getting Sire off. The bond is getting all of us off.

"Yes, Daddy. My pastor's cock feels so good in my ass, I'm going to come for you both." I am. So is Sire. So is Nash, feverishly rubbing my clit.

He just needs to let go. He's imagining Vale. I know it. I want him to.

"Yes, Daddy," I coax him. "Please, let your big dick come on this pussy while he fucks my ass."

"Yes, you're such a good girl. Oh, fuck," Nash rasps, yearning for Vale, his body shaking, his eyes closed. His hard dick shoots his cum over my belly, my tits. He desperately whispers to himself, but I hear it. "Vale. *Please.*"

Nash can't hide it. I don't want him to, and Sire can't take any more. Neither can I.

Sire grabs my face, turning my chin. "Angel. My angel, I swear." With primal grunts, he kisses me, grunting over our lips before he spills inside me, his fingers not forgetting my clit. He knows how to take me; he owns me.

When I come this time, I let every tender tear fall, every moan go, every flutter release. I fall into my ocean, and Sire dives in, breathless, with me. His touch and kiss, everywhere. Always holding me. Always with me. I convulse, then tremble. I cry, then laugh. I'm blinded, but then I open my eyes and all I see is Sire.

My soulmate.

My soul.

Mine.

My body shakes with emotion. We all know there's one left.

Axel.

He makes me cry tender tears even harder as Nash falls away and Axel approaches me, naked and in my husband's arms.

Tenderly, Axel enters me. His cock covered by a condom, he goes slow. He makes it feel good while Sire holds me. Closing his eyes, Axel honors me and the secret woman in his heart.

While he's barely thrusting inside me, I gaze down at his new piercing. He didn't have it before. *Axel got it for her.* He's saving it for her.

I know.

Under all of Axel's darkness, I can feel his love. All this love.

The kings love their queens. They'll never abandon them. And more so, my husband loves me. Ours is the kind of love that will never leave. It's written on my soul.

Forever.

It feels the same a week later, during my initiation in Axel's office, in his boardroom. All of the kings are there except Loch. Loch's life with Alena begins tonight. It's their engagement party.

But not before Sire makes me his queen. He slides a gold

Fabergé pink sapphire ring on my right wedding finger, a Russian tradition. He vows to be my king, and all witness our love. Our tears and smiles. Our bodies joined, too.

They witness Nash becoming my second king. Only he and I know how he keeps his vow to Vale, how he's waiting for her.

Jace and Grant want me to be sure. They let me feel our bond once more. So does Axel. With Sire inside me, too, each king gives me a piece of his heart. The rest belongs to their queen.

As it should. It's what I love about them.

And that's how we live and love.

It's how we survive.

I finally trust that I'll never lose my kings.

Until the Devil returns to take my husband.

CHAPTER THIRTY-SEVEN
WREN

"This won't fit in our bedroom." I straddle a black padded sex bench, pondering aloud, "And it'll barely fit in our guest bedroom."

"Do like me and Nash..." Vale lingers her fingertips over the kinky furniture like a game show hostess. "Move to a new house with an extra bedroom you can turn into a sex room."

It's been three months since my initiation and over a month since Vale's.

In that time, to say heaven and hell have broken loose is an understatement. It's been more like *John Wick* meets *The Notebook* with nights of *Fifty Shades*.

But I'm not complaining.

"Hmm." I twist my lips, surveying the options in the third-floor demonstration room at Delta's, my favorite sex store. Vale is their manager and my co-conspirator. "I'll never convince Sire to move. We're too close to his church, but..."

I reach for the phone in my back pocket.

Laughing, Vale flops down on a red sex chaise. "That's my girl; bribe him with kinky sex for a house near ours."

"Been there; do it almost every night. I have no leverage." I type my text. "But I have a king in my back pocket."

Like a cat, she stretches. "Which one?"

"Loch. I'll get him to squeeze this bench into our guest room, where he stays half the time. It'll cramp the space and our sex life."

I send the text.

On the heaven side, we have a new queen: Vale Monroe. She and Nash are making that best-friend's-dad taboo really work for them. They're in love, engaged, and Alena knows.

I'm so happy for my second king.

And ... *I told him so.*

On the hell side, when Alena found out that her best friend was in love with her father, she also found out about Loch.

The whole who-Nash-and-Loch-really-are thing. The ex-Bratva thing. The we-have-sex-trafficking-enemies thing. And the whole Loch-was-guarding-Alena-and-hiding-it-from-her thing.

Of course, Alena called off their wedding and broke up with Loch. I don't blame her. She's hurt, but so is he.

On his weekends off, he stays in our guest bedroom, licking his lonely wounds and all the cookies I bake for him.

And ... *I told my kings this would happen, too.*

See? I'm like Dolly; listen to me, and all your problems will be solved.

But my kings don't always listen, and the secrets between us spread like venomous threads, poisoning our bonds and threatening to tear us apart.

Any day, I'm ready for Sire's secret to unravel our world.

Vale widens her eyes with the mention of my sex life. She stammers, "Do you and Sire and Loch fu—"

"Lord, no!" I laugh. "First, Sire hasn't shared me since my

initiation. Second, Loch will become a monk if he doesn't win Alena back. I lowkey pity his pity party."

"So, what did you text him?"

"My plan." I shrug, smiling. "Have the shop send this bench to my place, and I'll have Loch put it in the guest room and throw his dirty boxers on it."

Vale scoffs a laugh, "Sire will kill him!"

"Exactly. Sire will see a breeding bench and want to play stallion tonight, but his brother will cockblock. And maybe..." mischief ignites my eyes, "I'll finally convince him to get us a second place near y'all. One with a sex room."

The queens are close: me, Zar, Delphine, and Vale.

Our beautiful beasts and kings have no idea how we scheme behind their backs, all under the sage guidance of The Queen, my badass mother-in-law, Nadine.

Vale twirls one of her long black braids, crushing her Wednesday Addams look. "I feel guilty," she sighs. "Nash and I are finally happy. You and Sire live in sinful heaven. Zar and Nick are sublime. Delphine and Grant are perfection. Even The Queen has a hot toy now and—"

"What?" I perk up. "Who?"

I thought Nadine lived a sexy, celibate life. Like, she's the Fairy Godmother of Orgasms, granting all but herself a climax. I assumed it was to honor her second king, the man who died saving her and the boys, getting them out of Russia and away from Ruslan.

But apparently...

Something on the blank ceiling suddenly interests Vale. She won't tell me who.

I get it. As queens, we balance sharing and secrets. It's not easy.

"You're such a clit tease." I toss a condom packet at her. They're everywhere in here. It's like a candy store, except flavored condoms and lube fill the jars.

She bats her lashes. "Just work your Wren-magic and ask Sire. Ask about Nadine's captive."

"I heard they have a couple in the bunker."

She leans forward, gushing, "Yeah, and one of them is serving delicious sub-sin on a cracker for The Queen. Like, he worships her."

"Who doesn't?"

"Right?"

"So, Axel brought a blindfolded mystery woman to your initiation," I recap our lives. It's a lot to process. "He's in love with her but won't tell us who she is. All the while, Loch's fine ass is twerking on my last nerve, moping about Alena, instead of winning her back. And Jace? I swear, that hot man's dick is too big for his heart to be so broken."

Warmth floods Vale's eyes. Jace is her second king. They're close.

To outsiders, some may assume the queens would be jealous of each other. But you have to live on the inside—*our* inside, where the queens share beauty-mark piercings, erotic rituals, laughs, and brutal kings.

You have to be marked by danger, by our world. You have to be initiated to feel our bond. We're too alike, too caring, too committed. We have too many threats against us not to stand together and hold on tight.

Vale knows I belong to Sire: body, heart, and soul. It's the same love she shares with Nash.

Yes, Nash is my second king, and I swear, Vale acts as protective of me as he is. She does the same with Jace. Vale's protective of him.

Pressing her finger to her merlot lips, she hushes our chat, pointing toward the open door.

"What?" I mouth.

"She's downstairs." Vale mouths back.

"Who?"

"Her."

"Her, who?"

Vale whispers her laugh, "*Her*: Jace's pea to his huge carrot."

I jump up. "I gotta meet her."

Vale jumps up after me. "Oh, hell no, you gotta find a filter."

I smile, waving my phone screen at her. "Sorry. No filter. No time. Jace has to escort me to the church by seven o'clock. Sire's expecting me."

It's six forty-five, and Vale knows the queens aren't allowed to go anywhere unguarded. A king always protects us. And whenever I shop at Delta's, Jace escorts me here and home.

Before she can stop me, I grab my basket of goodies to buy and bound down the grand, wooden staircase.

Delta's is a popular, yet discreet, store in the French Quarter of Charleston. The owner, a former beauty queen turned woman with three husbands, flipped this historic three-story single house, with its iconic side porches, into a posh destination known for pleasure.

But what most *don't* know is that Jace and Grant work here as security. Vale is the manager, Nash is the accountant, and Axel made a deal with the owner, moving our throne room from his office boardroom to the majestic owner's suite on the third floor.

Fittingly, it's down the hall from the salacious room with sex furniture.

Our secret room, with its black door and ornate gold hardware, remains locked except to us. It hides the row of black leather kings' thrones, opposite our white leather queens' thrones, with a large, low, tufted leather platform in between.

Vale was the first queen to be initiated in our new throne room. I have a feeling Axel's mystery woman will be next.

And after that?

Well…

On the second floor, guests enjoy the lavish showroom with high-end sex toys and luxurious lingerie. Two former bedrooms on the same level are now a changing room and a boudoir photography suite.

That's where I find Jace.

Stumbling into a skittering halt at his feet, I drop my basket of sex toys.

Picking up the box with my new nine-inch, Suga Daddy dildo, Jace chuckles, "I'm surprised my big brother lets you use this, and not *his* dick."

I smirk. "I'm surprised you assume that *I* use the dildo, and not your brother."

Did he just blush?

I twirl, tilting my head. "What*cha*doin'?"

He slices me a guarded look. "Working."

"With *who?*"

"Every horny person in this shop."

I point toward the closed door. "Is there one in particular you wait… I mean… *work* for?"

Fighting a smile, Jace snarls, "*Vaallee?*"

"What?" She stands behind me on the stairs. "I didn't say anything."

"Uh-huh." He leans against the white plaster wall. "Then why do you two smell like a cunty coup?"

I chuckle. "As long as you're nose deep in *any* cunt, we're happy. Speaking of…" I point toward the door again. "What's her name?"

His sexy blue eyes narrow. "Missus None-ya Fuckin' Business."

I nudge his elbow, winking. "You sure are cute when you're catchin' feels."

"*Wrreenn*," he tries to fume, but loves me too much. "I swear I'll take you to Dollywood if you walk away. *Now*."

"Will we ride the Tennessee Tornado?"

"I hate roller coasters."

"But I *love* love. Deal or no deal, or I'll stand here until I meet your—"

"Jace?" The white wooden door swings open. A stunning brunette with a Nikon camera swinging from her neck asks, "Is everything okay?"

"Uh, yeah. Sorry, Viv." Jace shuffles, clearing his throat with his white-knuckled grasp clenching a giant Suga Daddy dildo. "This is... Uh. She's a... Uh. Umm."

This is painful.

I stick out my hand. "Hi, I'm Wren. A friend of Jace's." I beam, because ... *she's beautiful* and *Jace is screwed*. "Actually, I'm the wife of Jace's pastor." I snatch the dildo from his hand. "Jace's *progressive* pastor, and these are *my* sex toys, and he was just about to walk me to my husband's church. You see, I'm new in town and get lost."

No, I get knee-deep in bullshit lies and hope she's wearing boots.

"Hi, Wren. I'm Vivian Tate." Her right hand warmly reaches to shake mine, but I clock the wedding ring sparkling on her left. "And I get it. Jace is always so sweet, guarding the door whenever I have a client. He makes everyone feel safe."

"Yep, that's our Jace." I smack his chest under his dark suit. It's like smacking the Hoover Dam. "Always keeping us safe."

No, this is our Jace, breaking my heart.

He's in love with a married woman.

ON THE FIRST BLOCK BETWEEN DELTA'S AND THE CHURCH, we walk in heavy silence. Vale had the sex bench and my new toys sent to my penthouse before she sent me and Jace on our way.

Solemnly, he strides between me and the bustling road, his sad eyes making me want to pull him into a giant hug.

We stroll past Axel's law office on Meeting Street, and I can't take his pain. Tenderly, I offer, "She seems really sweet, and like she likes you, too. So, what are you gonna do?"

"Respect her marriage," he grumbles. "Even though it's a shitty one."

"Shitty?"

"Beyond shitty. I want to kill her husband, but that would hurt her, and hurting Vivian would kill me. She doesn't have a mean bone in her body. She just wants out of her crappy marriage, but he won't let her go."

"How do you know all this?"

We turn left toward the church. Palm trees line the sidewalk outside boutiques and galleries. It's quaint, but not for Jace.

"We've become close friends." He mutters, glancing down, "Well... as close as her marriage and my morals will allow."

I loop my arm over his like a little dinghy, casting her delicate rope around a cast-iron bollard. Except, I worry in this storm, Jace will drift away, so I hold on tight.

"Are you in love with her?"

"Painfully." He lifts his stare, his handsome face, stone.

"Does she know?"

"Accidentally."

"Are your morals waiting for her?"

"Impatiently."

God, I love my kings so much. When they hurt, I hurt. "When will you make a move?"

"When I get a sign."

"Mmm." I squeeze his arm. "Like, when she cuts off her pinky for you?"

Jace turns his gaze to me. "Something like that." I smile to lift his spirits. It almost works. He grins. "I'm damn glad he found you. That *we* found you. You know that now, right?"

"Yep. Just like I knew Sire's the one for me..." We turn right on Church Street. *Speak of my handsome devil.* He's standing on the sidewalk, waiting outside his chapel for us. "Vivian's the one for you. I felt it."

Jace huffs, laughing, "You *just* met her."

"You *just* believe me; you'll be with Vivian one day." I echo him, "You know that now, right?"

He unhooks his arm from mine, wrapping his over my shoulder as we cross the street. "Whatever you say, little one."

"You owe me a trip to Dollywood."

"Deal," he agrees as we reach the chapel, and I rush into Sire's waiting arms.

He smiles, murmuring into our kiss, "Dollywood?"

"Road trip," I sigh over his lush lips, loving how my husband always hooks his arm around my waist, lifting me so our lips can meet.

"Yeah, but this time: shotgun," Jace adds, giving quick hugs before leaving us, standing on the sidewalk.

Sire reaches for my hand, his worried stare watching his brother's back. "What happened? He seems upset."

"I just met his future wife and queen."

"Hallelujah," he chuckles. "About fucking time. Literally."

With a sexy smirk and warm hand, he guides us home through the graveyard.

"Yeah," I chirp. "I'm gonna have to poison her shitty husband first, but she'll be our sister-in-law."

He laughs, brushing past deadly yew-berry bushes. "I never doubt you, Angel."

Strolling through weathered headstones, with cicadas whirring around, it's a sweltering, darkening summer evening, but ... *something's off.* A sudden shiver slithers up my spine.

I look around.

Spanish moss sways from tall oaks. Blood red azaleas cling to their blooms. Ferns, coping the graves, fight for shade. Even the shadows are hot in Charleston.

I've grown used to my new home with Sire. It's so sultry and hospitable, it's like evil is welcome here, too, until Sire stops, his glare piercing the blackness under the oaks by the iron gate to our home.

"What is it?" I whisper.

Stepping in front of me, he snarls, "*Otets.*"

CHAPTER THIRTY-EIGHT
SIRE

"Father."

The word in Russian bleeds from my lips before I can stop it, because he's *not* my father.

No, he's the Devil sitting on a cemetery bench. Deep shadows cloaked his presence, but I felt his chill in the air. The stench of evil. I knew he was here.

"*Krasivaya zhena*," he jeers.

"Speak of my wife," I vow, "and I'll cut out your tongue."

When I was six, I heard my father speak the exact words regarding my mother. He made me watch him cut out a man's admiring tongue before gouging out his eyes, too.

All for stating the obvious: *beautiful wife*.

As is Wren.

She grabs my T-shirt, letting me know she's there. But she's not safe. Not with him seated before us.

A smile tugs his wicked lips, easily slipping into English. "It seems I have taught you well."

I smirk, "And it seems you're dying soon. Well deserved."

His amusement evaporates. "I die; you die. You know the rules, Sergei."

"Indeed, I do. Fracture for fracture, eye for eye, tooth for tooth; so says God. But kidney for kidney? Get on your fucking knees for it."

I've dreamt of this moment for decades. Fearing the abused child in my heart would quake. The scars on my chest would burn. The nightmares I had would reclaim my mind.

But now ... I have no fear, only fury. I'm a grown man, guarding my wife, our future, *our* family.

With his arctic eyes, raven hair, chiseled face, and snarling full lips, my father's beauty was one of his many lethal weapons. Viciously, he seduced with it, leaving the slain behind.

But Age humbles all, and Time laughs at powerful men. No one can survive them.

Dappled dusky light threatens to find his face, revealing the grey pallor of his skin. The life draining from his veins. His once towering form, crumbling.

"I kneel for no one." Still, he boasts, "Not death. Not your God. And not my son. I have someone you want."

"Give me my nephew and I'll give you what you need."

I have no patience for his games. Not when an innocent child is involved.

"Or maybe..." He drums his inked, ringed fingers over his bespoke, ash pants. "I will wait for *your* child, my *true* heir."

"Touch our child and you're dead." Wren steps out from behind me. "One drop at a time, motherfucker, I will poison you and that bitch who took Axel's son."

I squeeze her hand, so goddamn in love with my Iron Angel.

Wren's wearing the demure, white Chanel minidress my mother gave her. Her long, dark curls, an aura. A crown. She's a queen. *My queen.*

My father can see it.

"My dear daughter," he chides, "you know *not* to whom you speak."

"Someone who needs food and water," Wren flatly gloats. "We all do; even if it's deadly."

His glare slithers to mine. "You need to *tame* her."

My God, he believes that shit. That any living woman can be truly conquered. No, she's just waiting for your pathetic ass to die.

I sneer, "Like you tried to tame *my* mother? Foolish man, women will only take so much before they take everything from you. On that note: my brothers send their *Die and go to hell* regards, too."

Slowly glancing right, then left, he draws my attention to who I already knew lurked behind the trees and monuments: armed soldiers in black suits.

We're surrounded.

There's no escape.

"Doctors will prepare you to give me what you owe," he demands. "In exchange, Aleksi may meet his son. Once."

I bark a laugh. "Imminent death has made you demented, old man. Too many people in Moscow hate you and love us. They remember what you did: to my mother, my brothers, and me, and they'll whisper it to Lev. I'll make sure of it. He'll grow up like us, hating you, until he comes home to his father and uncles—forever."

He scoffs, "Lev will never leave his mother."

"A cold mother who took him from a loving father?" My nostrils flare. "I never had a good father, but if I had, nothing but death could keep me from him."

His lip curls. "I can arrange that."

"Like I can arrange yours, too, as I did Viktor's. Mutual destruction. Is that what you want, Ruslan?" I spit his name. "Your entire bloodline, dead, including you?"

Something human flits across his dead eyes. Worry? Care? It can't be. *That's not the demon who raised me.*

So what is it?

What does he want?

Sheremetev!

That's it. The intel we got from The Six about his enemy. The one on our shores. The one he keeps sending me to destroy.

"No, you don't want mutual destruction." The ground shifts. There is an escape. I have the upper hand. "You want victory. Pride. Power. You want Valentin Sheremetev. That's why you've been sending me notes. So I can seek and destroy his operations here."

"So you can seek and *rescue*," he snarls, nodding toward Wren. "You should be thankful."

At the mention of her past, Wren squeezes my hand, and I squeeze back. *We're okay. I got you.*

"Since when do you give a damn about human suffering?" I condemn, "You cause it."

There it is again.

Pain ghosting his eyes.

If I didn't know him so well, his DNA corrupting my body, I'd miss it.

I'd miss his faltering compassion.

I press, "Sheremetev controls the East Coast. Trafficking women and girls, and why do you care? And don't tell me it's for the money. You have plenty, and you wouldn't risk your operations to be caught by U.S. authorities, so why do you give a shit?" I trap his bitter stare, reading his reaction. "Is your heart finally beating as your kidneys die? Do you finally care about someone other than yourself?"

Bullseye.

He winces.

I'm onto something.

"Your kidney for my grandson," he bargains coldly. "You may have him six months a year, while you and your brothers continue to work for me."

Work to rescue sex trafficking victims? We already do it, so what's the catch? There has to be one.

Wren's hand twists in mine. She senses it too. This is the end of the lie about Axel's son, but the beginning of something else.

Of what?

"My brothers and I work for *our* queen," I smirk at the irony. "If you want our help, you need to look her in the eye and beg for her permission."

I don't know what my father really wants, but I want to give my mother this: a chance to stand before her throne, surrounded by her loyal sons, and spit in his face.

Shockingly, he doesn't protest.

Ruslan gestures to his right, to the stocky man looming in the shadows. "I will leave Yakov here. He is my new Sovietnik. He will oversee your tests and preparation before you fly to Moscow for the surgery. And when I have recovered, I will return with my grandson and meet with my wife."

"She's *not* your wife," my bark is instant. "You forced her to marry you."

"Yeah, Nadine hates you," Wren chimes in. "And *Cuntya*? That's your wife's name, right? You married Axel's second-hand pussy? Oh, she's gonna be ill as a hornet to know another woman still lives rent-free in your mind."

Ruslan clenches his teeth at Wren. "If you weren't my daughter, you'd be dead for speaking to me that way."

Wren mocks, "Yeah, well, I'm *not* your daughter. I'm Dolly and Nadine's, so I'll speak however I want, and you can kiss my country ass about it."

How does she do it? Every. Damn. Time.

My angel swoops in with her bravery, butterflies, and filterless mouth, and my heart swells, my lips fighting a smile.

"Yakov stays." I take control. "I'll pick my doctors and communicate through him, and when I'm ready, I'll fly to Moscow for the surgery and return home with my nephew in my arms."

Wren insists, "And I'll go with him."

"No!" Oddly, we bark in unison.

Why? Why does my father not want Wren in Moscow?

For me, it's obvious. I don't trust him. He may have motives, and we have leverage, but the Devil is a capricious soul. If he ever had one.

I turn to Wren. "You'll stay here, safe, with the other kings. And if anything happens to me. If our deal is broken..."

Holding my wife's hand, I aim my glare at my father. The scars on my chest, burning. The child in my heart, guarding his mother and little brothers. The man I am today, vowing, "You'll start a war for me."

CHAPTER THIRTY-NINE
WREN

I rest on Sire's chest, tracing my fingertips over the ink hiding the burn scars on his pecs. I've memorized them.

"Did you really mean it? That I should start a war?"

"Yeah." He holds me tighter, his voice low. "If I don't come home with my nephew, tell Axel. Tell The Queen. Tell everyone. They'll start a war for Lev and—"

"But that means you'll be…" I swallow, suddenly silenced, tears biting at my eyes. I know my husband. Sire will die for me, for his family.

He rolls on top of me, caressing my curls. Kissing me, it's like he has no fear, only faith. "That means we'll start our family before I leave."

We just made love. It's all Sire wanted to do when we got home. Hold me. Kiss me. Live inside me. *Come* inside me. Even though he can be so dark and kinky, sex is sacred between us; sometimes he fights tears, too.

I want a family with him. Sire *is* my family. But he's been making us wait.

Until now.

I know why, and it terrifies me. It conjures my ominous

instinct, making me plead, "Don't. Don't leave me. Please..." Tears blur my vision. "Let me go with you."

"No. You're my answered prayer, Wren." He gazes down at me as if I'm his only treasure, pecking my lips. "I'll do anything to protect you. So, I need the kings to keep you safe, because I don't trust him. For some reason, Ruslan actually gives a shit about your safety, and—"

"Because he wants to take our child ... if we ever have one."

A knowing grin crinkles the ink by his eyes. "That'll never happen. My wife is a badass. No matter what, she'll protect our child."

I sniff, "Don't say that as if you won't be here, protecting us, too."

"He will command His angels concerning you to guard you in all your ways; they will—"

"Do *not* quote the Bible to me when we're talking Bratva bullshit."

I cup his handsome, whiskered jaw with his hard, naked body over mine. He's a feral distraction, but I'm serious. Tears leave, and my determination sets in.

"You will get me pregnant, Sire Rutledge, then give a kidney to the Devil, and bring your nephew home, and get me pregnant again. Five kids and fourteen grandkids; you can't die until we're surrounded by them. That's our deal."

"*Five* of my babies?" He smiles, letting his swelling erection answer, his knees forcing my thighs open. "Deal. We'll have your IUD taken out tomorrow."

My smile mirrors his, our emotions and bodies fused. I wriggle under him. "Shouldn't you save your seed until then?"

He grabs my wrists, pinning them over my head, his gaze trapped by my stigmata tattoos before he locks eyes with mine. "I get so fucking hard for you, Wren, I have plenty of seed to pump inside you." Pressing his swollen tip to my wet entrance, spilling from minutes before, he can feel it. It makes his eyes blaze. "Your pussy is so perfect, dripping with my cum. It wants more, doesn't it? It wants my baby."

"Yes." I wrap my legs around his waist, getting wetter at how his ass cheeks flex beneath my feet, his obliques straining against my thighs. "Breed me, Pastor. I'll be a good girl for you. I'll stay full of your load forever."

"Fuck, Wren." He loses it, growling with a thrust inside me, making me cry out. "You want this dick, Angel? You want my cum?" He starts fucking me hard and not holding back, the friction against my clit forcing moans up my throat.

"Good girl," he grunts. "That's it. Take this dick. Let me fuck you and fill this tight pussy."

Our sex gets loud, wild, and sweaty before a bang on our bedroom door.

Sire stills inside me, his jaw clenched. "Go. Away."

"Sorry, bro," Loch calls through the door. "Just thought for the second round, you'd want to use your new breeding bench."

Planked over my body with his hungry dick buried inside me, Sire looks like a killer, crazed by kink. "My *what?*"

Is he asking me or Loch? Should I moan or giggle? I told Loch to do this. To cockblock. I just didn't know it'd be on a night like this.

A night when everything's changing.

"Your breeding bench," Loch answers. "That's what it is. Right, Wren? The sex store delivered it today. No way it goes in your living room, and it wouldn't fit in your bedroom, so I had them put it in mine. But maybe you should get a place with a third bedroom, cuz it barely fits."

"I'm gonna kill him," Sire snarls.

I stick with my plan, rolling my hips. "But you have seed to spread, Pastor."

"Not when my brother's at the fucking door."

"Since when has that stopped you?"

Suspiciously, Sire slants his eyes. Pulling out, his dick glistens, suspicious too. "What did you do?"

"She got a sex bench and it's kinky as fuck," Loch taunts. "You can strap her to it and fill her with your seed *all* day. But you should really get another place for it, Pastor. Your visiting parishioners will clutch their pearls if they see this perverted thing."

My lips roll over my teeth.

I'm busted and don't care.

Neither does Sire. Jumping up, he storms to the door. Angrily ripping it open, he stands nose-to-nose with Loch. "I'm about to clutch my fucking Glock and kill you if you don't go home right now and make up with Alena."

"Whoops," Loch smirks, glancing down at his brother's fuming erection. "Did I interrupt the God Rod?"

"You know you fucking did, and it's time to leave. *Now*."

"Don't make him leave. It's not his fault." I sit up, clutching the sheet over me. "I told him to do this. I just want us to get a—"

"I know what you want, Angel." Sire and his erection point my way. I swear that thing is like a giant compass, and I'm its true north. "And surprise, I'm already working on getting us a second place near Nash and Vale."

"You are?" I beam. "But you didn't tell me."

"Hence, the surprise." Only his eyes soften. "I always know what you need, Angel, before you even feel it. But you..."

He turns back to Loch, leaving butterflies bursting in my heart.

Sire knew.

He always knows me.

How did I finally get so lucky? And why is it so innocent *and* hot that these brothers can stand buck naked around each other? And why am I clutching the sheet? It's not like Loch hasn't seen my goodies, too.

"So help me, God," Sire warns him, "if you don't leave and go home and get Alena back, I'll drag your ass there."

Loch snarls, the humor leaving him, "She said to give her space."

"Three hundred fucking miles of it?" Sire deadpans. "No. Go home."

"It's time you resume Operation Grovel For Alena," I add.

Loch counters, "Groveling annoys her."

"Okay. I'll just say it..."

I flit my hand at Loch in jeans and a black T-shirt. The man has giant muscles popping everywhere.

And I flit at Sire, my jacked, inked, hot AF husband, who's *still* hard; Viagra should take notes.

"You brothers are way too hot and blessed with beautiful, big dicks. You're never annoying, even when groveling. We're just making you work for the pussy when it's already yours." I stab my finger at them. "And don't tell the queens I told you that; I'll get kicked out of their Cunty Club."

Sire smirks, crossing his beefy arms and leaning against the doorjamb. "So, I *never* annoy you?"

Oh fuck.

I'm gonna regret that confession.

Sweetly, I huff, "I love you, but don't test my theory. Just stay hard. We're not done. And you?" I aim my orders at Loch. "You love Alena, and she loves you. Grovel and make it hot. Use that big dick and smile. And if you need our help, you know we always will."

CHAPTER FORTY
SIRE

An eerie calm claims my blood.

I know I'm doing the right thing.

I'll save my family. I'll give my kidney to get my nephew. I'll get Wren pregnant before I go. I'll find out why my father gives a shit about someone more than himself. And I'll do it by finding my answers here.

"Thought you said I had to leave." Loch swings open the heavy metal door to Mom's club.

"Thought you owed me this first, cockblocker." I grin, holding Wren's hand, and escorting her inside.

It's early afternoon, the club is closed, and its house lights are on. Staff are busy cleaning as usual.

It no longer bothers me bringing Wren in here. In fact, it makes me happy when she runs, arms open, to hug Alan. Like she promised Nannie, she's protecting him.

He's been out of rehab for months. He's wearing a smile and a healthy amount of weight. He's a changed man, who's far safer here on the coast than where we last found him in the mountains, trapped in Waylon's deadly snare.

Mom gave Alan a job at the club. He's happy, sober, and rumor has it, in love with Lucy, the bartender.

Lucy glances up from slicing limes, nodding at us. "She's upstairs in a meeting."

"Thanks." I wave, leading the way. Wren and Loch follow as I call out, "Hey, Alan. Join us, please."

"Uh…" He drops a mop into a yellow bucket. "Yes, sir."

"Please, don't call me 'Sir.'" I enter the code for the door to the upper levels. "It's *Sire*."

"Yes, sir, Sire," he rushes, but I'm too focused on my plan to correct him again.

Climbing the stairs, we stop outside my mom's office door. Behind it, I hear a familiar, deep voice—*Axel*—but then there's another man's voice I don't recognize.

Who are they meeting with?

I knock, and Mom asks, "Who is it?"

"Me." I stare at her camera aimed at our group standing outside her door. "Us."

What the fuck? I know she sees us. Is she stalling? She's been so secretive lately.

Voices murmur, raising my suspicions. Finally, Mom huffs, "Oh, for Pete's sake, just come in."

Holding Wren's hand, every cell in my body tells me something's going on, and I'm about to add to it.

When we step inside her office, it takes a moment to register the sight.

Mom's sitting behind her antique desk, wearing an ivory Chanel suit, and reigning over her empire. Axel's in a dark suit, sitting on the sapphire velvet sofa.

That's normal.

But sitting beside Axel? A breathtaking redhead. *Ruby Jones.*

Axel told me about her. I've met her and like her. When

he tried to sneak her into Vale's initiation, blindfolded, it fucking amused me. But since I've violated Axel's trust already, I didn't tell Wren about Axel and Ruby.

Now, she knows.

But kneeling beside my mother? Shirtless. Covered in ink. Swole like a beast, like us. Wearing black pants and a matching leather chest harness with a BDSM collar and chain.

Is one of the captives from our bunker?

What the fuck?

We caught this man sneaking over the wall at Delta's. He's part of the trafficking ring we've been hunting this year, and now he's kneeling? As a sub for my mom?

I know she's a revered dominatrix, but him?

She reads my furious face.

"Well, no sense in burning daylight. Everyone, take a seat." Mom gestures to the empty emerald velvet sofa. "Wren, dear..." She always greets her with warmth. "Please meet Axel's future wife, Ruby."

Future wife? Good.

This shit? Not good.

Wren nestles in beside me, her smile excited, her instant connection to another queen, obvious. She chirps, "Nice to meet you, Ruby."

Ruby beams, "Likewise, Wren."

"What the fuck is *He* doing here?"

Like me, Loch seethes. He's confused. Settling in beside Wren, Loch's glare is aimed at Mom's threatening sub kneeling beside her.

But she shifts her focus to Alan, unsure why her staff is also in here. Alan doesn't know who we really are, so we have to be careful.

Then again.

Neither does Mom's brutal BDSM boy-toy, so what the

hell? And why is Axel in here with him? Why hasn't he cut his throat open and killed him with salt?

"This is Roman." Mom tugs her sub's leash, and I swear the fucker stifles an aroused moan. I want his head, but she assures, "He's trained and trusted. You may speak openly around him."

Since when? Since when does my mom let anyone outside our family, the kings and queens, know who we are?

"Alan," Mom addresses him. "Dear, I'm not sure why you've been brought into this meeting. My apologies for any awkwardness."

"No, ma'am. It ain't awkward." Alan stands, ramrod straight. "I'm here because Sir Sire asked me to join y'all."

Sir Sire? Yep, Wren heard it that time.

She snorts a laugh.

Irritably, I explain, "He's here to discuss Waylon Banks and how we found Wren. How we know Sheremetev was involved."

Axel doesn't flinch at the name. He's been intrigued by that intel from The Six, too. Ruby's stealth and calm. We can trust her. My mom was also familiar with Sheremetev. We told her what The Six told us.

But her captive? Roman?

Recognition flicks across his eyes.

I clench my molars, and Mom catches it, redirecting our attention to Alan. "And how can Alan help us?"

"Maybe you knew him," Wren speaks up, turning to him. "From when I was taken with the other girls. Did you ever hear that name?"

My Iron Angel has found her filter and an Oscar. No one has any idea the secret Wren hides for me. How she deftly protects me while getting intel and seeming so innocent about it. When really?

My Joan of Arc will start a war for me.

"Sorry, Wren," Alan frets. "I don't recognize the name. Truth is, I got big holes in my memory. I want to help ya, but—"

"It's okay." She gets up, reaching for Alan's hand. "I'm just glad you're healthy now, but if there's anything you can remember. Like I remember an accent. A Russian accent. It'll help us."

"Would you remember a face if I showed you?" I ask, taking my phone from my pocket.

Cade Bryant said Valentin Sheremetev hid behind diplomatic immunity. I found a picture of him—a news story—online. It's a few years old, but I show it to Alan.

The color drains from his face. "The Warden."

"The what?" Wren asks.

"The Warden." Alan's spooked eyes lock on my phone screen. "Yeah, I've seen him. Never knew his name, but I knew his evil."

"His evil?" Mom sounds worried.

"Yes, ma'am." Alan nods. "My dad said The Warden kept girls locked up, and my dad'd sell him more. Sorry, ma'am, but I think it's true." He turns to Wren, his eyes blinking back tears. "I'm so sorry, Wren. I never meant—"

"It's okay." She wraps her arms around him. "We're going after him. We're getting those girls."

Loch probes, "You got any idea where The Warden may be? Where these girls are?"

"No, sir." Alan lets Wren go, answering, "I mean, I got the feeling they were close by, hiding in the mountains. My dad was never gone for long, though I ain't sure. My memory and all..."

His words and chin drop.

"Alan, thank you, dear," Mom eases. "You've been a big help."

"I'll go with you." Alan looks up, offering to Loch, "If you need help findin' him, holler, and I'll go."

Loch nods, thankful.

With another hug from Wren, Alan politely leaves us.

Sitting.

Silently.

Staring at each other.

A feeling I've never had before pounds through my veins. *There's another secret in this room, and it's not mine.*

Does it mean they know about me? Dear God, I hope they trust I'd never betray them. My hand on the Bible, I believe they'd never betray me.

But deep down, I know, we're about to test our belief in each other.

Mom aims her laser focus on Loch. "Go home, *today*, and protect Alena. I don't care how proud and stubborn she is. Don't take your eyes off her."

"Yes, ma'am."

Like us, Loch's her son and soldier. We follow her orders.

"You two." She points to Axel and Ruby. "I want this NFL thing wrapped up. Yes, I want my sons happy, but more? I need y'all safe and secure. You hear me?"

"Yes, ma'am," Ruby replies with Axel.

They're working on another operation with Nick and Zar. Sometimes, I think we're fools to take on so much. Other times, I think we're saints. We have no choice. It's our calling.

"I want you initiated and protected. You need a second king," Mom presses Ruby. "Ask Wren your questions. She'll answer them and introduce you to the other queens. Right?"

Wren stands where Alan left her. Lifting her chin, she replies, "Yes, my queen."

"And Wren?" Mom drills, "You want to tell me why my eldest son is looking as dark as the devil's riding boats and acting so strange?"

Wren doesn't even glance at me, assuring, "We're trying to get pregnant, and he's the pastor, always trying to save us. That's his plan."

I swallow the lump in my throat.

It is my plan, and it's their only salvation.

Warmth softens my mom's face. "You know I want that blessing for you two. For all of y'all, if it's what you want, but what's really going on, because that's not news?"

Actually, it is.

We visited the doctor's office before coming here. Wren had her IUD taken out, though everyone thinks we've been trying for months.

We haven't.

But now?

I'll try as if our lives depend on it.

This lie, trying to protect my family, has been my cross to bear for years. I can almost lay this burden down, once and for all.

Even if I won't be here.

At least, they'll be saved.

"It's Sheremetev," I reveal. "He's our answer."

"Answer how?" Axel wraps his arm around Ruby, and she nuzzles into him.

Peace fills me. *When I'm not here, Ruby will love my little brother.*

Deliberately, I prophesize, "I believe Sheremetev has something Ruslan wants. If we get Sheremetev, we'll be safe. We won't have to hide anymore."

"What does Sheremetev have?" Axel suspects.

"Catch him and find out."

No one replies.

Warily, they exchange looks before our Queen leans back in her chair. She never says Ruslan's name. She won't give him the respect. "*That* man won't rest until he destroys us."

The spirit moves through me.

It speaks and I listen.

This time, it's God *and* the Devil.

No matter what happens to me, they need to believe this. They need to do it; it's their only way out.

"Exactly. He wants to destroy us, so catch his enemy and destroy him first."

CHAPTER FORTY-ONE
WREN

Three months later

Loudly humming the song from my winning karaoke performance, I'm trying to be like Dolly—happy and counting my blessings, not my fears.

Sire grins, his inked hand warmly holding my waist, his other swiping the keycard to our hotel suite. Steaming over my ear, he gives me goosebumps, "My beautiful angel is drunk."

"No, I'm not."

"You stood on a hotel bar, singing about bean enchiladas into an empty tequila bottle like you were on the bow of the Titanic." He holds the door open for me. "You're *drunk*."

"Since when do I need tequila to sing? Delphine and Vale emptied the bottle. I didn't touch a drop."

I flop onto our sumptuous bed while he strips down to his black boxer briefs.

This five-star Mercier Hotel in Mykonos, Greece, is paradise. Axel and Ruby's wedding tomorrow will be

perfect. The whole family is here for their joyous cele-
bration.

While I'm hiding my pain.

I've had months to fear this day. Months of watching Sire
go through tests and preparations. He's in top shape for the
surgery but insisted on waiting until after Axel's wedding. He
wouldn't miss it.

And I don't want to miss my last hours with him. I won't
sleep. I won't cry, either. But he's too beautiful, half-nude and
crawling over me. God, he takes my breath away, searching
my eyes like that. His are so blue and full of love. "So, you're
sober?"

I nod, not sure if I should tell him. Will it make this
better or hurt even more?

"But you threw up tonight."

I nod again. Is it normal to be this afraid of losing
someone?

"And you didn't drink any alcohol?" He reasons, "I mean,
you haven't for months."

He's fighting the truth, too. Sometimes, it's too precious
to dare speak it aloud.

"Wren?" He blinks. "My sweet angel?" His eyes swell. "Are
you—"

"I'm pregnant," I whisper, choking on a sob. Thankful.
Scared. Happy. Terrified.

He nuzzles his nose to mine, his breath in awe. "My angel,
you've answered my only prayer. You're having my baby."

"*We* are having a baby *together* because you're coming
home to us," I demand through tears. "You made a deal with
me. Remember?"

He groans, capturing me in a desperate kiss; that's his
answer. He makes love to me; that's his wish. He kisses my
belly, his tears spilling over my flesh; that's his hope. He holds
me all night; that's his promise.

I'm only six or so weeks along, and I know I will have Sire's child.

But someone ... please tell my heart ... I'll have my husband, too.

THE WEDDING WAS A DREAM. AXEL, OUR ICE KING, MELTED at the sight of Ruby in her stunning dress. He swiped tears away.

Standing in the line of bridesmaids, I glanced at the army of groomsmen. At each inked king blinking back tears, too.

God, Nadine raised her sons right. They're true men, not afraid to cry or kill for love.

All night at the reception, Sire danced with me. He sang with me, too. We brought the house down with our Dolly and Kenny duet while Axel danced with Ruby to it.

It was their day, and I swore to myself I'd be brave. I wouldn't make it about me. I smiled, sang, and had fun. I danced with every king and laughed with the queens. When I barfed, they thought I was drunk. When I cried, they thought it was out of joy.

It was half true.

But now Axel and Ruby are locked in their honeymoon suite. The reception is over, and Sire has invited the rest of the family back to our hotel suite.

Gathered on sofas and chairs, we're admiring the view from our terrace overlooking the sparkling night ocean. Heels are kicked off. Ties flung aside. Drinks are in hand.

All are relaxed until Sire lifts his glass, establishing his cover story.

"I'm leaving tomorrow on a mission trip to Ukraine."

Nadine replies calmly, "Bless your heart. No, you're not."

"Mom," he matches her tone, "you know I need to go where I'm called."

"Young man," she forgets his age, "you are called to keep your ass by your wife and family. Let someone else save the world."

"So, I can save the world in the States but not abroad?"

He's got a point, and Nadine doesn't like it.

"For how long?" Jace tries to smooth the tension.

"I'll be gone for a few months, helping a parish deliver food and medical supplies."

Sire's preparing for the worst. He really is going to Ukraine for a few weeks. From there, he'll text pictures to all, securing his cover story. Then, he'll go to Moscow, where we have no idea the tricks Ruslan will pull, the delays he'll force, or how long Sire will have to wait to be strong enough to travel home.

"But what about Wren?" Vale curls on Nash's lap, but worries about me, "That's too dangerous for her."

Sire nods, revealing, "She's not going with me."

"No!" Delphine protests. "That is too long for a wife. Wren will be lonely, yes?"

Delphine mirrors everyone searching my face, fearing I'll falter.

There's not a filter big enough to keep my mouth closed, but I try.

I do this for my family.

Sire swallows, squeezing my hand. He hates every damn second of this. So do I, but we have no choice. "Wren will stay home with you all. Keep her safe for me."

Nash lowers his dark brows, doubting, "So you're leaving Wren? The love of your life? For months?"

"Yeah, but he's doing it to help others." Grant jumps in, defending his brother. "Our nanny was Ukrainian. We can speak the language, and they really need help over there. Besides, Wren's strong as hell. She can—"

"Wren is a grown woman. She can speak for herself," Nadine interjects, eyeing me with compassion. "Wren? How do you feel about this?"

Feel?

It's all I can do.

It's all I can hide.

Nannie used to tell me, "Country girls don't retreat. They reload."

I lift my chin and Sire's left hand to my lips. Kissing what's left of the finger he gave for me, I vow, "I fell in love with a man who sacrificed himself for others, including me. And I won't stop loving him now. I support him. I'll be fine."

Sire cups my face, pulling me into a kiss. "God, I fucking love you so much," he murmurs over my lips.

He won't stop kissing me while the others descend into a debate about humanitarian aid versus self-preservation.

His warm lips find my ear, his ringed hand holding mine tightly grasped over my belly. *Our baby.*

"I love both of you," he whispers. "Have faith, Angel."

I do have faith.

Until seven weeks later.

When Sire stops calling from Moscow.

CHAPTER FORTY-TWO
SIRE

It's snowing, but I don't care. Back home in Charleston, two snowflakes would shut the city down. But here in Moscow? Life goes on.

I stand by a back door of the sprawling dream home that was my childhood nightmare, but I refuse to let them invade my mind. Not when outside in the gated courtyard, snowflakes fall over an empty kids' playground.

It wasn't there when I was a kid.

It was built for Lev, who's supposed to be out there, but...

"What the fuck is taking so long?"

It's all taking too long. The weeks I spent in Ukraine. The weeks I've been waiting for my father to be ready for surgery. Yakov says Ruslan needs more time.

But I don't have time.

I need to get this surgery done. I need to be home with my wife and baby. I need my nephew. I haven't even met him yet.

"Patience," Yakov urges. "One more meeting."

"Fuck these meetings." I get in his face. "I know what he's

doing. He's grooming me if he dies, but I'm not taking over. He gets my kidney, not my life."

At the sound of approaching footsteps over emerald marble floors, Yakov turns to greet the next guest. It's like I'm a prince in a goddamn royal receiving line, when all I want is to see my nephew.

With my back turned to the next guest, I hold my breath. Katya is supposed to bring Lev outside to play. As a "family friend," I'm supposed to spend the day with him, but she's been stalling, too.

Every morning, I call Wren. Every evening, too. She's my salvation, calling me home. *Soon, Angel. Soon.*

But not without my nephew.

"I always knew our godly prince would return."

I pivot to greet the familiar, smoky voice with a Russian accent. "Tariel," I smirk. "Can't say it's nice to see you again."

From his barrel chest, he rattles a laugh. "Leave us." He dismisses Yakov like a fly.

Tariel is my father's most powerful *Avtoritet*, a brigade leader. He's a brutal killer who was always kind to me as a child. He never had kids. Maybe that's why.

Standing alone, he combs my adult form, nodding his approval. "You're a soldier now, not a prince."

"I'm *not* staying."

"He will make sure you do."

"When all he ever did was make us want to escape."

Tariel winces.

I never understood why a ruthless butcher gave a damn about the abuse we suffered—me, Axel, my brothers, and my mom—but he did. Often, Tariel would distract my father by calling meetings to keep him away from us.

It worked.

But not enough.

"You do not want all this?" Tariel gestures to the compound, coveting every inch draped in opulence.

"I want my nephew."

"How is Aleksi?" he asks fondly.

"He wants his son."

"But he does not want all this, too? You were to be a priest; therefore, Aleksi was to be our next Pakhan."

"And our father wasn't supposed to beat the shit out of us and our mother, so plans changed. I don't want it. Axel doesn't want it."

Most men in the Bratva forgo family. They're a liability. My father, of course, believed he was exceptional. He forced his bloodline to continue while Tariel has nothing, no legacy except his role, power, and money.

"It should be yours," I tell him.

It's treasonous if he answers.

So I confide, "I'll give it to you if you tell me why Ruslan wants Sheremetev. *Why* is he hunting in our territory for him?"

Tariel's face falls as the thrilled shriek of a child pierces the air.

I whip around, recognition grabbing my heart at the sight outside the window. I stagger, mumbling, "Oh my God. He looks just like him."

Black hair. Blue eyes. Cold cheeks flushed with joy. It's exactly how Axel looked when we'd play in the snow as boys.

Guilt, grief, and joy rush my veins. I grab the doorknob to meet him finally, but Tariel grabs my arm.

"Do you vow?" he compels. "When the day comes, this will be mine, and you will not fight me for it?"

"All I want," I point to my flesh and blood outside, "is *him*."

Tariel swallows, lifting his chin. "He is not the only one."

"What?"

He fumes, "Ruslan wants Sheremetev because Lev is not the only child *taken*."

"Come on, Angel, answer."

The signal is intermittent. No doubt because Ruslan's soldiers are listening in, and turning it off and on to fuck with me.

But somehow, I need to tell Wren about today.

About Lev and how we made snowballs together. How I gave him a watermelon Ring Pop, and he loved it. They don't have them here. How Lev thinks I'm his new best friend...

And I am.

I need to tell her about Tariel and the deal we made. A new part of my plan to set us free.

But more, I need to tell Wren...

I love her.

I need to know my angel's okay. I need to know what song she sang in the shower. That's her new thing—singing all the wrong lyrics to her belly, *our baby*.

"Jesus, Jesus. Come on, Angel. Pick up," I huff, pacing my former bedroom, the sick irony isn't lost on me.

It's lunchtime there, nighttime here. Wren's probably busy, helping Ms. Davis with the preschool kids.

I roll to voicemail and guardedly leave her one, knowing the ears have walls.

"Hey, Angel. Call me back. No matter the time. I met Lev, and my surgery's tomorrow morning. And I love you and..."

A soft knock on the door startles me.

"And I need to hear your voice. No filters. All songs, butterflies, badassery, and my baby. Call me."

The knock demands again.

But I need to say this, "I love you, Angel. Bye."

I end the call, ripping my bedroom door open. "What?"

"Did you forget your southern manners?" Katya tries to drawl but sounds ridiculous.

"Did you forget to go to hell?"

Slyly, she grins. If she weren't an evil succubus, with her blonde hair and bold cleavage, she'd have a chance at being pretty.

"Always full of fire, Sergei." She licks her red lips. "I craved that about you. Not your brother. Axel was cold."

"Yeah, well, fucking freezing pussy will do that to a man."

"It was never cold for you." She drags her fingertip down my grey sweater, over my abs. "It's still warm, ready, and *wet* for you."

I swat her hand away. "I'm married to the most beautiful woman with the hottest pussy; I'll never cheat on my wife. I love her."

She purrs, "But I am a queen, and you are my second king. You made a vow to me, too. You bred me in front of your brothers. You made me drip for you. Remember?"

"Unfortunately, I do. But thankfully, I wore a condom and pulled out, and Delphine's sweet mouth swallowed what you never deserved. Remember?"

She purses her lips, threatening, "Does your wife know you breed men, too?"

I laugh. "She *joins* us."

Her face twists, trying another angle. "If you want to see Lev, you will give me what I want. *Tonight.*"

I see right through her. "What you want, Katya, is the love you never got from your father, so you tried to get it from *my* father, the Devil. When the truth is, if you opened your heart to your son, you'd find a new and better love as a mother."

"I *am* a loving mother," she hisses.

"Then act like it." I get in her face. "Like what my mother did for her sons. Give me Lev. I'll get him out of here and keep him safe."

She steps back. "Like how you kept my father safe?" Her chin trembles. "How you had him killed, and he did *nothing* to you."

"Exactly," I seethe. "Viktor did *nothing* while a woman and her children were beaten. Daily. Then, your father stood by and sold *your* body to the Devil, too. I'm sorry for your loss, Katya, but Viktor threatened Lev. To my *face*. He was willing to kill his grandson for power."

A tear rolls down her cheek. "You lie."

I step to her face again, staring her down. "Look your king in the eye and tell me if I'm lying."

She does, and ... she can't.

We all have a choice: will your pain make you cruel or kind?

"Look me in the eye, my king," evil fills her glare, "and tell me if you will wake up tomorrow."

Katya chose cruelty.

CHAPTER FORTY-THREE
WREN

"You're pretty, so I'm giving you wings like an angel," the little girl proclaims, scribbling on my left cheek.

Another silently doodles on my right. I don't care if the markers they're using aren't waterproof.

"*¿Qué estás haciendo?*" I tickle the girl on my right.

She giggles. "*Mariposas.*"

"*Gracias. Te amo, mariposas.*"

My Spanish isn't perfect, but Sire was teaching me some.

Moments like this are bittersweet. Like me, the girl loves butterflies. Like him, I love these kids. Like these kids, I wonder where he is, too.

Ms. Davis calls out in Spanish, and the kids rush to the playroom door, excited when their parents pick them up. After we straighten the room and clean the tables, she asks, "So, how is our intrepid missionary?"

Don't cry. Don't cry.

I swallow.

"He's loving the work, of course." The lies roll too easily off my tongue. "But he doesn't love the freezing temps over there."

"I bet not," she laughs, handing me a baby wipe for my face.

"Oh, I don't mind the doodles." *They make me think of him.* I give her a quick hug. "See ya tomorrow."

Quickly, I grab my handbag and leave. Any day, I fear Ms. Davis, or someone will see right through me.

Pain hides behind a thin mask. It can crumble, like me, at any second.

Smearing away tears, I go to Sire's office, log on, and check his emails. Dutifully, I reply to what I can and forward the rest to the staff and clergy.

I don't let myself sniff the hoodie he left on his chair. His masculine aroma hurts too much. I want to smell *him*, his warm skin, not a cold, cotton hoodie.

In the chapel an hour later, I'm not alone. A few others silently pray. I find little comfort in the desperation that brings us here.

Nodding at them, I work my way to the front pew. To my spot in front of Sire's pulpit. Kneeling, I let my gaze fall on the sacred space in front of the altar.

The place where I became Sire's.

And he became mine.

Tears fall, and minutes pass while I say every prayer and make every promise. I even call on Dolly, but fear no one's listening, until someone startles me.

"Ahem."

I turn, not seeing who I wish was there.

Him.

"Excuse me, Mrs. Rutledge."

No, it's Karen, aka. Mrs. Cabot.

"Yes?" I rise, dabbing my eyes with a tissue.

"I'm sorry to interrupt your prayers. I'm sure we share the same ones, for his safe return."

For once, I nod, agreeing with her.

Awkwardly, she shuffles in her plaid Lilly Pulitzer heels. "I just want to say that... Well, I've been praying, too. For him *and* for you."

I blink, not sure if there's a judgmental back slap coming.

"You've been so graceful and strong, the perfect First Lady for this church in his absence. We see you with the children, and at service every day. You're doing a great job, organizing the nativity play and holiday market in advance. And well..." She twists her lips before they confess, "I misjudged you, and I'm sorry."

The words he'd say spill from my heart, "Judge not, and you will not be judged. Forgive, and you will be forgiven." I touch her arm. "Thank you, and I accept your apology."

If I were happy, I'd be inwardly twerking. All triumphant, savage, and classy with Megan Thee Stallion.

But I'm not happy.

I'm barely hanging on.

I let Mrs. Cabot ramble on about the holiday market and what her bible circle has planned. It sounds like pastel plaid Christmas bows are the trend. *God, help us.*

Finally, I escape her mind-numbing chatter, wishing her a good night.

Walking home through the graveyard by myself doesn't scare me. My fears are far worse than ghosts.

Usually, Jace escorts me home, but I lied to him and said Grant was doing it tonight.

I just don't have the heart to look my kings in the eye without spilling my soul.

Why isn't he calling?

Twice a day, Sire has called. First, from Ukraine, where the signal wasn't reliable. Then, from Moscow, where we could sometimes do a video chat.

But I missed his call three days ago. One of the preschool kids threw up, and that caused another to do it. *The Exorcist* would've been proud, and by the time I tried to call him back, he didn't answer.

His voicemail said his surgery was the next day and now... Nothing.

Yakov texted with an update, but I don't trust him. He said Sire is in recovery, but if that were the case, Sire would call me. He'd never go a day without talking to me.

Something's wrong.

I know it.

I feel it.

I don't think I can breathe through it.

Pushing open the iron gate between the graveyard and our building's parking lot, I chew my trembling lip, not sure if I should start a Bratva war or book the next flight to Moscow.

What if I'm being impulsive? Naive? Even immature? Patience has never been my virtue. What if I pull the trigger on Sire's secret and ruin everything? What if I—

"Wren."

A husky voice makes me jump. Reaching for the gun in my bag, it's training; I whip around, my thumb flipping off the safety, my aim landing on a shocked face.

"Whoa, whoa, my queen."

My shoulders sag. "You scared the shit out of me."

"Same." Loch grins with his hands up. "I need to borrow a pair of his boxers now."

At the mention of Sire, I twist my lips, blinking back tears.

"You okay?" Loch reaches for me.

"Yeah," I lie with my cheek smushed against his marble pecs.

"Where's Jace?"

"I don't need an escort everywhere I go."

Lowly, Loch warns, "Wren, you know better."

"I'll give you cookies if you don't lecture me."

"Deal."

Once we're inside, I open the laundry room, and Onyx mewls at my feet. Courtesy of Axel and Ruby's mama cat, Sparky, this orange tabby kitten has been my one joy. Well, two joys, counting our little secret no one knows about.

I pick him up, nuzzling the wet, black spot on his nose. "Hey, buddy. You hungry?"

"Fucking starving," Loch answers for him, making himself at home, searching through my refrigerator. "What is this shit? Rabbit food?"

"No, it's salad and rotisserie chicken."

For the baby, I make myself eat healthy meals. Otherwise, I'd have no appetite.

"Where's all the biscuits and ham and mashed potatoes?" he huffs, frustrated.

"Okay, DoorDash." I flop down on the sofa, letting Onyx crawl over me. "Next time, call ahead with your dinner order."

Grabbing the tin of cookies I made for the church kids, Loch falls into Sire's black leather chair. "What time does he usually call?"

It used to be any minute. But now? I won't blow his cover. "Some nights he doesn't call. He can't get a signal."

Angrily, Loch chomps a cookie. "I need his advice. He's the only one who can calm me down."

"Calm you down from what? Murdering my Snicker-doodles?"

"No." He swallows. "Murdering someone over Alena."

I lean forward, relieved for the distraction. "What happened?"

"I resumed Operation Grovel For Alena like you told me to, and it was working."

"Yeah, I saw you two sneak away at Axel and Ruby's wedding."

"Exactly." He stacks his tactical boots on the coffee table. I don't care. All the kings do it. "We had some hot, kinky nights, and I thought we were back together, that we were good. But then she said we needed to talk."

"Uh-oh."

"No, shit," he agrees. "I don't have to lie to Alena anymore. I was fine with it, answering all her questions about us, the kings and queens, about Delphine, too, and how she trained me."

Don't do it.

I'm dying to raise my hand and blurt questions about how Delphine trained Loch, too. God, I bet it was hot. But I suspect that's not the burning issue.

"Honesty's the best policy." Instead, I win the gold medal in hypocrisy, but I'm trying to help him.

"Yeah," he glowers, "but then Alena got *real* fucking honest with me."

The hinge of his granite jaw flexes.

Usually, Loch's lush lips smirk, relaxed, while his sexy blue eyes murder. It's a lethal, panty-melting family trait the brothers share. Forget how well-endowed they are, too. Their look alone could inseminate.

But tonight, it's not seductive. It's scary.

"Honest about what?"

"Her first," he seethes.

"Okay," I ease. "Almost every woman has a first. I mean, unless she's a nun, and even then... It's not a crime."

His nostrils flare. "Is it a crime if her first is your brother?"

Cue heart seizing. "What?"

It's not Sire. It's not Sire. I know he protects his brothers' secrets—I don't mind—but between us, there are none. Especially about sex and his past partners. Sire would've told me.

So, which one is it?

Not Nick. He's gay. Is it Jace? Or Grant? I mean, Grant's got the freest Willy of all the kings, but even he isn't dumb enough to fuck Nash's daughter.

Hell, Loch risked his life to get Nash's blessing, and Nash *still* growls about it. To Nash, Alena is like a plastic Barbie doll with no holes.

Carefully, I venture, afraid I'll poke the Grizzly named Loch. "Who was her first?"

He shakes his head like he can't believe it, baring his teeth like he's ready to maul.

"*Axel*."

The room starts spinning. I grab the sofa. "Axel?" I gasp. "Like, Alena's godfather, Axel? Like, Nash's grumpy sidekick, Axel? Like our king? Our leader? Axel?"

Loch huffs, ready to attack, "Like my big brother, who I've always trusted, who's been lying to me for years. Yes, *Axel* was Alena's first fuck."

Holy second-worst-lie-in-this-family drama. What would make Axel do it? Fuck his best friend's daughter?

And forget about his best friend. Look at his not-so-little brother. The rage churning with pain in Loch's eyes is scary. I fear what he'll do.

So, what would Sire do?

"Okay, hang on. I need some context." I pet Onyx. It calms me. "When was this?"

Loch shrugs like he doesn't care. It's done; Axel's dead. "Six years ago."

"Did Axel know you were in love with Alena?"

"No one knew."

"And Alena didn't know *you*?"

"We had met, but she had no idea who I was."

"So, she didn't know that you were Axel's baby brother?"

"Not until she found out about everything else, no."

"Okay, with all due respect..." I let Onyx chew on my curls. "This is all B.U."

He jerks back. "B.U.?"

"Yeah. *Before you*. No one is guilty of who they fucked before you."

"But Axel should've told me."

"Maybe. But maybe he had a good reason not to."

The veins on his inked neck pop. "A good reason for *lying* to his brother?"

I swallow. For a second, I had forgotten my pain. My lie. Sire's lie.

"Maybe your brother did it to protect the family," I hint. "To protect Alena. I mean, how did it happen? Because I can't ever see Axel betraying Nash."

Loch sighs, falling back in the black leather chair. He fills it like a king, just like his brother.

"Alena said it was her, that *she* came onto Axel. She was tired of being a virgin, and she trusted him."

I slap the leather sofa like I'm wielding a gavel. "As a former virgin myself, I can testify in her defense. I get it. Some say virginity is a gift, but for others, it's a burden. Or it's a process when we're ready to mature. And despite his many flaws, Axel is hot as fucking hell to ... uh ... *process*."

"Not helping," Loch huffs at the ceiling. "Where's my pastor when I need him?"

Don't. Don't cry. I need him so much, too. I need Sire to be okay. I need our family to be okay.

"He'd tell you the same thing." I choke, "To forgive."

That draws Loch's scrutiny. He aims his sexy eyes at me. "What did I say? Shit, Wren, are you upset?"

"Yeah." Tears bite at my eyes. "Because you love Alena. You can have a life with her, and it's that simple—be with her."

"What about killing Axel?"

"Based on what you just told me? Nash will beat you to it. Does he know?"

"Not yet. Alena doesn't know if she should tell him." He cocks a thick brow. "I think she should, but—"

"But it's her body, her sex life. We're not men's property anymore. She doesn't have to tell her father who she fucked, or—"

"True." He nods. "But Nash is more than a father. He's a king. He's like our brother. We don't lie to each other. That's what makes this hurt so much; Axel lying to me."

This is what Axel was hiding.

That evening on the yacht with The Six when Axel said he'd hope for forgiveness from his family, it was for this. For Alena.

"Do you think Ruby knows?" Loch asks what I'm wondering too.

Mentally, I run through every hug, laugh, tear, and more I've shared with Ruby. She's perfect for Axel; twice as smart and three steps ahead of him. She's like us. She's a queen.

"Yeah, Ruby's gotta know. Axel loves his balls too much to lie to her."

"And yet," Loch shakes his head, "Ruby hasn't said anything."

Onyx has fallen asleep on my belly. I know it's probably not possible, but I swear our kitten senses it. He's already sleeping next to...

Our baby.

I lift my chin, but it trembles. "Ruby's protecting her king, and Axel would do the same for her. He'd die for her. They're in love. Just like you and Alena. Just like me and..."

I can't.

My voice breaks.

So does my mask.

Tears burst, streaming down my cheeks.

"Fuck, Wren." Loch jumps up to sit beside me. "I'm sorry. I came here, all about my shit, when you're dealing with it too."

Sweetly, he hugs me. He assures, "It'll be alright. He'll be home soon, and I'll tell him all about how you stopped World War Three."

Stop a war?

Or start one?

I don't know what to do.

CHAPTER FORTY-FOUR
WREN

T\ EXTS.

That's what I get from Sire after four days. No calls. No videos.

Septicemia? It means sepsis. I looked it up.

Antibacterials? We'd say *antibiotics*.

This isn't Sire. It's a translation. It's not my husband. He'd be sweet. He'd be bossy. He'd say he loved me and call me Angel.

And I'll kill you myself

An agonizing hour later, I get a picture of Sire in a hospital bed with an oxygen tube under his nose, an IV in his arm. His beard, grown out. His skin, mottled and pale with patches. His blue eyes, open. His loving gaze, gone. He's alive, but barely there.

I choke down tears, my hands shaking as I text:

Prove the date to me

Now Yakov!!!!

With a newspaper

I want proof of life

Today

More painful hours pass as dawn creeps into my room. Onyx curls beside me in bed. Grant snores in our guest bedroom. He and Delphine stayed the night to keep me company.

I appreciate their love, but it makes this worse. I don't want an audience for my lies, for my demise. I don't want to see their faces when they find out about Sire.

Finally, I get a text. It's the same photo of Sire with a newspaper in the foreground. Of course, I can't read the headline. It's in Russian. But our current president, gloating, is the cover story. I zoom in, and if I'm reading the numerical date correctly, it was...

Oh God...

No...

Four days ago!

A sob hits me so hard, I bolt for our bathroom, kneeling in front of the toilet. I don't know what I'm losing. Meals. Water. Time. Tears.

Life.

Love.

Four days ago? Four days with an infection that can quickly kill him.

"No! Please, God, no!" I think I scream it.

In a rush of French, Delphine is behind me, holding my hair. I heave, but nothing comes out before Grant picks me up. Like a doll, I dangle over his mammoth arms.

"We gotcha, princess," he soothes. "Hang on."

In a blur, I'm in Grant's Tahoe. In a daze, my head rests in Delphine's lap. We're in the back row. She's caressing my curls, consoling me in soft French. Onyx is in his carrier on the floorboard. My suitcase is packed.

I have no idea where they're taking me, but I know they won't leave me.

I just *don't* know if I should tell them why I'm dying, too.

CHAPTER FORTY-FIVE
WREN

When I was little, all I had was a voice talking to me from the clouds, or the trees, or the butterflies, or from Dolly, of course.

Folks thought I was crazy.

But I wasn't.

I was just lonely and listening to God. She kept me company.

But now, a mighty voice lures from the pillow beside mine. "You need to tell me what's going on." Nash lies next to me in his guest bed. Brushing a curl from my face, he urges, "I never believed for a second he'd leave you."

Nash is dressed and lying on top of the covers, while I'm buried underneath them with Onyx swatting at my curls. They're my kitten's chew toy, and I don't mind.

I need something to keep me anchored to this world. If not, I'd slip away into my nightmares.

Vale is downstairs, cooking breakfast with Delphine. I can smell the bacon. Grant's giving us privacy because I'm supposed to trust my second king. I'm supposed to let him protect me.

"I'm pregnant," I confess.

"Congratulations." His brown eyes glow, a sexy smile tugging at Nash's beard. "And that's another reason why I know he'd *never* leave you."

"He's helping others."

"He's sacrificing himself as usual, and I need to know why and where."

Nash met Sire first. He became his brother first. They went from juvie to being married kings. He knows him too well.

The ink Nash hides under his starched white button-up peeks through. I spot the tiger, snarling at the lion on his carved chest.

All the kings are marked with lions. All the ways they honor their bond; all the ways they honor their queens; I'm losing track.

I wedge my hands under my cheek. Nash mirrors me, as if he's trying not to scare me when I know the man has killed with his bare hands. Anyone who lays a finger on Vale has signed their death warrant.

And when he finds out about Axel with Alena?

There will be blood.

Lots of it.

"I'm protecting him," I answer.

"You are, and you're making him proud. But something's happened." When Nash is serious, he's threatening, but not to me. "We know you, Wren. You're our queen, too. We've felt you. We know you're strong, and the only reason you'd collapse is if something is wrong."

I can't answer, but I feel our bond, too. All the ways I'm tethered to Nash and the kings.

And something is wrong, but what if I make it worse? What if I start an unnecessary war and get my family killed?

He cups my cheek. "Please. I love him, too."

"I don't know what to do."

"Let me help you; that's what you'll do."

Sire's alive. I know. He has a fighting chance. I hope. He holds the only way to make this right, including Axel's son in his arms, if I trust he'll be okay. That Sire will come home.

Have faith, Angel. I love you. Always. It's the last thing he said to me, with his kiss, before he left me in our hotel suite.

Okay.

Faith.

"Can you give me time?"

"I'll give you my life, Wren. You know that." Nash confronts my eyes. "Just tell me he's okay. Tell me he's alive and I'll give you time."

"He's alive."

NASH GIVES ME A WEEK, AND I BARELY LEAVE HIS guest bed.

Vale takes care of me. She knows asking only makes it worse, so she gives hugs. She makes me smile. We watch our kittens, Milo and Onyx, fluffy little orange brothers, pounce on the bed.

They're a cute distraction from the daily texts I get from Yakov with updates about Sire. Each one, a translation. Each one, a daily newspaper. Each one, a picture of Sire looking dazed.

Delirium is one of the life-threatening symptoms of sepsis. I looked it up. I've scoured every online resource I can find.

Sire probably got it from a used needle. Or a contaminated instrument. Or his surgical wound. Organ donation is usually very safe. But trusting his father and associates to take care of my husband? That was the risk.

Deep down, that instinct tells me to hang on. To have faith as Sire asked me to. To take care of myself and our baby.

It's news I can't expect Nash to hide from The Queen.

With a gentle knock on the guest bedroom door, she enters wearing a blush Chanel skirt suit and carrying a giant bouquet of blue hydrangeas.

"Not that I assume you're having a boy," Nadine assures, setting the vase on the dresser. "I'd love a granddaughter to spoil. I just like spoiling you, too. And from your sweet engagement video, I know these are your favorites."

I sit up, alone with Onyx, and smooth the sheets and my hair. "I'm sorry. I should've told you sooner."

She sits on the edge of the bed, reaching for my hand. "Your body, your business; you know I believe that, dear. All I want is for everyone to be okay, but I need to know..."

She blinks back tears. She can barely whisper, "I need to know if my son is okay."

I squeeze her hand. "He's okay."

"He's with *him*, isn't he?"

Sire always said I had no filter. But maybe I just couldn't hurt good people. They deserved to know the truth.

I open my mouth to answer, but I pause too long.

Nadine reveals, "I know more than you think I do, but dear Lord, I need to know that my son hasn't betrayed me."

"Never," I rush, leaning forward. "He'll die before—"

She gasps.

"I mean, he's alive, but..." I start swiping my falling tears. It's useless to stop them. "Ruslan found Sire years ago, through his criminal record, and he's been threatening him ever since."

She nods. "That man threatened to kill me, so my eldest son bent to *his* will to protect me. Am I close?"

"Yes, my Queen."

She pats my hand. "Keep going."

"Ruslan wanted an heir, so he told Sire to give him one. To get a woman pregnant, and give him the child, and he'd leave y'all alone. Sire agreed and secretly planned to never have kids. That bought Sire years until Ruslan sent Katya to get Axel and—"

"Say less." Nadine rolls her eyes. "This wicked part I know."

"You do?"

"Yes, darlin'. That man wants an heir. He wants my royal blood and believes his sperm is made of gold, when actually, it's all gurgle and no guts. He thinks all of my boys are his, when probably, most belong to my second king, the man I truly loved."

"Are you serious?"

"Deadly," she clarifies.

Bombs couldn't kill more than Nadine's pissed off face right now.

"So, you know about Axel's—"

"My sweet grandson, Lev? Yes, I know about Katya taking Axel's son. And now, let me guess; that's where my other son is, trying to get his nephew back."

How did she know?

I don't have the breath to ask while relief floods me. "Yes, my Queen. But he's..." The fear, too. "But Sire's..."

Dammit, I'm trying to be brave, but the tears won't stop. Please tell me it's pregnancy hormones and not premonition. Please tell me I won't be a young, widowed mom. I will. I'll live on in Sire's honor, but I don't want to.

"He did what, darlin'?" Nadine jostles my hand. "I need to know. That boy would sell his soul to save me or his brothers, so what did he do?"

"His kidney," I sniffle.

Nadine closes her eyes. "I should've known. It's in *his* family: a genetic kidney disorder."

"He was going to take Lev's," I explain, "but his organs are too small, and Sire was a good match. He had all the tests done. The surgery was days ago, but then Sire got sepsis."

Her pause scares me while calculations click behind her eyes. Her sons get that same lethal look. "So, he can't be moved right now?"

"No, he can't. The risk is too high. He needs to fight off the infection. He needs to get stronger."

"Who is your contact over there? In Moscow, right?"

"Yes, and it's Yakov, Ruslan's new Sovietnik."

She sits taller. "You let me handle this. Okay? I got more contacts than LensCrafters over there. We'll get my medical team into that hospital. Our people who know what to do. He'll be alright. You understand me?"

"Yes, my Queen. I understand." I sit taller, too. "It's just that..."

Sure, I had Nannie.

And I still have Dolly.

But I never had a real mom. I never had anyone tenderly shush away my tears after the kids made fun of me.

From the moment she wrapped a warm blanket over my shivering shoulders on the night I was rescued, Nadine has been the closest I've ever had to one. The only hug, smile, laugh, or tears I've ever shared with a woman who cared more about me than herself.

I don't want to lose her.

I don't want to lose my found family.

But I will protect my husband. Pinky for pinky. Soul for soul. Our love against the world. I'll risk it all for him.

"You can't tell Axel," I demand. "You can't tell anyone about any of this until Sire comes home. You're not the queen in charge of this." I lift my chin. "I am."

Nadine pulls back, silent.

She wrests her hand away, leaving mine empty.

But I keep going. I keep risking. "I mean it. This is everything Sire has fought for, all by himself and for so long. *He* will be the one to tell Axel, and no one else. Give him the chance to make this right with his brother, to feel redeemed. You understand me? *I'm* handling this."

With a stony face, she blinks.

Slowly.

Deadly.

Weighing my warning.

I sit up even taller, meeting her glare.

It lands on the diamond she gave me—the Monroe piercing above my lip. On the day of our initiation, Nadine gives a diamond to each queen. It's her vow to us, before the kings forge their bonds with us, too.

"I don't want to disrespect you," I press, "but I *will* protect my husband, my king, the father of my child, and if this means I've lost my fam—"

"Hush." She could silence a hurricane. "A queen expects; she does not explain."

I swallow, nodding.

"*I* expect to bring my son home, and *you* can expect to protect his family."

She offers her hand again, her fingertips always adorned with a flawless French manicure.

Formally, I take it, fearing a distance, a loss, but she tugs, gently pulling me into a hug.

With a choked voice, she whispers proudly in my ear. "Spoken like *my* daughter."

CHAPTER FORTY-SIX
SIRE

The dream is never-ending, sweet, and torturous.

Kids crawl over me in bed. My kids. *Our kids*. Five kids with Wren's dark curls and my light eyes. *They're so beautiful.*

I can see them, but I can't move.

I can feel them, but I can't say, *"I love you."*

They poke my cheek. They tug at my hand. One, my daughter, traces the broken heart inked on my cheekbone with her little fingertip. It's the softest touch I've ever felt.

Another, my son, bravely lifts my eyelid. "Is he sleeping?"

From my soul, I scream, *"I'm awake!"*

But they can't hear me.

More hands crawl over me with tubes and probes, making my children retreat.

"No!"

I want to scream, but my bones ache like liquid bruises. My muscles are on fire, my heart thundering, trying to feed my dying insides. My brain, I can't control it.

"Wren! Angel!"

I pray, and she appears in a white silk slip. Her long curls, a heavenly aura.

Through the beeps, bright lights, and barking orders around me, she leans down, warmly smiling. Her beauty, ripping my last breath away, as she vows, "I told you we'd fall in love."

Lightly, she kisses my lips before I'm swallowed by darkness.

CHAPTER FORTY-SEVEN
WREN

For so long, I never understood Dolly's most famous song. Especially the iconic Whitney Houston version.

Both sing of always loving someone. *That* someone. They love him so much, they wish him well ... and they let him go?

Why?

How?

As a lonely little girl, I'd belt the song, but I swore, if I ever had love like that, I'd never say goodbye. I'd never let go.

I rub my belly. I sit on my pew. Staring at the baby in the manger scene beside the pulpit, I'm not alone in this empty church.

I will always have love like that.

I understand the song now.

You don't keep love.

You give it away.

That's Sire. He gave everything to me. He gave me a love so great, something some never get to feel; how can I be anything but grateful?

The Christmas Eve service is over. The parishioners have

left. Evelyn, the Minister Emerita who married us, told the staff to leave the lights in the apse on for me.

She knows I won't stop praying for him.

Tucking my earbuds in, I tap the song to loop on my phone and close my eyes, praying. I can't help it. Lowly, I sing the song with Dolly.

Maybe because it's a holy day, I sing through tears, smiling. Or maybe it's because I just felt the baby move.

Or maybe ... that was gas. I had bean enchiladas for dinner.

A tap touches my shoulder. I don't even jump.

Goddammit, sweet, Jace. He's supposed to wait for me outside.

I yank my buds out, whip my gaze to the side...

And freeze.

The man is huge. The shadows around him, even larger. His ribbed, cable-knit grey sweater clings to his muscles, the ink on his neck peeking out from its thick, rolled collar. His dark jeans look worn. His black tactical boots, brand new.

The diamonds piercing his ears catch the nativity light. Same for the diamond in his nose.

His hair is cut and styled, but darker, as if it hasn't seen the southern sun in months. His beard, neatly trimmed, frames his lush lips. He licks them at the sight of me, a slight smile crinkling the tattoos on his high cheekbones, while his blue eyes look like they're ready to murder the months we've been apart.

Sire says softly, "I'll always love you, too, Angel."

I can't stop my sobs. I can't bolt up fast enough. I can't fling my arms around his neck—he's too tall and I'm too tiny —so he wraps his arm around my waist and lifts me to meet his lips.

"I'm heavier," I warn, sighing into our kiss salted by happy tears.

"I should fucking hope so." His smiling lips brush over

mine. "You look so goddam beautiful having my baby, Mrs. Rutledge."

His kiss. "Fuck, I love you, Angel." His voice. "Fuck, I missed you." His smell. His warmth. "Goddamn, I'm never leaving you again." Sire takes me with it, and I lose time to his lips on mine, his breath finding mine again.

But then I remember...

"Put me down."

Quickly, he sets my feet on the floor. "Did I hurt you? The baby?"

He gazes down at my emerging bump. At five feet tall and in a white sweater dress, I look pregnant from my chin to my ankles.

"No. You," I rush, gently touching below his waist. "Your kidney. You shouldn't lift anything heavy."

He cups my face. "That was months ago, and the least of my worries. It's my mind and strength I needed to get back because all I worried about was *you*."

With the shock gone and my tears drying, I can see it in his face, arms, and chest. He's lost weight and muscle. He was jacked before and still looks amazing now, but a wife knows.

He's been through hell.

I take his left hand, the one with half a pinky and wearing our wedding band. Pressing it to my belly, I anchor to his eyes. "We had faith. We're fine. I promise."

It's his turn to blink back tears. "You're everything I fought for, Wren. I swear to God. Every fucking day until I was strong enough to come home to you."

Looping my arms around his waist, I cling to him and our future. He wraps me in his arms, too. Cupping my head to his chest. Kissing my hair. Murmuring prayers.

I don't want to let him go, but he sighs, "I have so much to tell you."

"Not yet," I insist. "Just take me home and be my greatest gift on Christmas morning."

CHAPTER FORTY-EIGHT
SIRE

I can't stop smoothing my hand over her beautiful belly and making wishes. I can't stop kissing her soft lips and making her moan. I can't stop the urge to climb between her legs to get her pregnant with twins.

I know it's not possible but tell that to my heart. It's so goddamn alive again beside her.

"God, I missed you so much." I have her in our bed and trapped in my arms. My legs ensnare her, too. *I'll never let her go.*

She lingers her fingertip across the fresh scar, from left of my belly button, down to my pubic hair. It tickles, and I warn, "Angel, keep touching me like that and we're going for round three."

"Does it hurt?"

Damn, I missed her voice.

"Not when it's getting hard again."

"Be serious." She props her chin on my chest. "How weak do you feel, and don't lie to me."

"Okay." I sit up a bit. "After months in a hospital bed, a twelve-hour flight, and two rounds of hot sex with my beautiful wife and queen?" My voice drops an octave. "Angel, I'll admit..."

She tilts her head like a nurse, ready for my maudlin medical update.

"I got a bad case of a breeding kink. Seeing your belly with my child makes me spike a fever in my dick for you."

"Uh, Sire."

She slaps my chest, making me laugh. "It's the truth, and I'm fine. I swear."

"You're still recovering."

"No, I'm still and will always be so in love with you, Wren Chapel Rutledge, you're my cure."

She fights a smile, but I see her fighting tears, too. It kills me to guess how many she's cried while I was gone.

With my fingertip, I lift her chin higher. "The only thing I feel is my vow to never leave you again. I promise I'll give you five kids and fourteen grandkids. I saw them in my dreams."

She beams. "You did?"

"Yeah, they had your curls and my eyes. Our kids will be beautiful."

Kids.

My heart clenches. "But Axel. I need to talk to him. *Today.*"

"They're with Ruby's sisters for Christmas," she reminds me. "I'll call her and set up lunch tomorrow."

"Alright."

My mind lags, processing everything. It's a symptom from the sepsis but it's getting better. Much better. Or maybe I'm just overwhelmed. There's a lot about to happen.

Wren fills the silence. "What did Jace say when he saw you last night? No one but your mom knew you were coming home. You're lucky he didn't shoot you."

I let my fingers twirl through her soft curls. "He drew a

gun, then saw it was me and gave me a back-slapping hug before shoving me into the chapel to be with you."

"No one knows." Her topaz eyes widen. "I swear, I told Nadine that *you* had to be the one to tell Axel how Ruslan bribed you and no one—"

"You told The Queen what to do?" Impressed, I grin. "And you're still alive?"

Her smug look melts my heart. "I told my *mom* what to do, and she said she was proud of me."

I brush my fingers over her cheek, relishing her velvety skin. "For such a cute former foster kid, you sure got this family drama thing on lock."

"Speaking of... He has lots to tell you."

"Let me guess: Loch knows about Axel and Alena."

She perks up. "You knew?"

"Yeah, Axel told me earlier this year. He wanted to tell Ruby but didn't want to betray Alena's secret."

Her brows bend, worried about her second king. "Does Nash know?"

Add it to the million things I love about her, because I worry, too. "If Axel's still breathing, then no, Nash doesn't know. But first, I need to talk to Axel and pray he doesn't kill me first."

"He won't kill you." She kisses my chest. "I won't let him."

"I sure hope so." My heart starts racing at the wheels I've put into motion. "Not with what I have coming."

OUR LUNCH WITH AXEL AND RUBY AT THE MERCIER Hotel is like the slice of three-layered red velvet cake Wren and Ruby split.

The top layer is all sweet.

I'm so goddamn relieved to see my little brother again. Ruby's pregnant, so he's happy, too.

Our wives banter about what to name our daughters or sons. It's a sugary subject, hiding another layer to this conversation.

Axel has no idea where I really was, why I was there, the death I escaped, or why I need him to forgive me.

I sense the bottom is that he's hiding something from me, too.

You can't be brothers who shared a bed because you were scared you wouldn't awake the next day and not sense when the other's heart is breaking over someone.

Is it Alena?

No. Axel's madly in love with Ruby, and the truth is, it was never love between him and Alena.

Is it Nash?

Maybe. It's a matter of time before that ticking bomb explodes. But I'll be there, defending my brothers and family. Always.

"Oh, shit." Ruby jumps up after a belly laugh with Wren. "Excuse me. I gotta hurl."

"I'll go with you." Axel jumps up after her, but Ruby insists, "Please. I don't need an audience for version two point O of my chicken salad. I'll be right back."

She races to the elevators, whisking her to their new penthouse apartment in The Mercier.

"Those are rough days," Wren sighs. "Morning sickness doesn't understand the assignment; it hits at any time of the day."

I reach for Wren's hand, regretting I missed every day, every hour she went through to get this far along.

We try to make small talk with Axel, but he keeps glancing toward the elevators, worrying about Ruby.

"Sorry, folks." He tosses his linen napkin on the table. "My wife needs me."

"Hey." I catch his wrist before he leaves. "We need to talk."

"Sure, man. We'll catch up."

He thinks I want to testify about my missionary work in Ukraine and would rather get a root canal. I know my brother, but I'm running out of time.

"Tomorrow night," I insist. "At the church. Meet me there at seven."

He's dismissive. "Yeah, if I can."

Fuck, Axel's a bulldog with his priorities: his wife and kid. He won't commit to anything else.

"No." I stand, still holding his wrist, and pulling him toward me. "Tomorrow night. Bring Ruby. You have to be there. Promise me."

His eyes narrow like I'm about to be cross-examined. He's a goddamn good lawyer that way.

But silently, I cock my eyebrow, because I'm finally a goddamn good oldest brother.

"Alright, man," he huffs. "Tomorrow night. Seven. The church. Got it."

CHAPTER FORTY-NINE
WREN

It *is* our baby kicking, not bean enchiladas.

The flutters are distinct, making me rub my belly. Our little one must feel how nervous I am. My heart is racing—my pulse, climbing.

Tonight can go a dozen ways, beautiful or bloody.

"What are we doing out here?"

Axel gestures to the entire family, all the kings and queens, gathered in the hallway outside the preschool playroom of Sire's church.

No one else is here. The school is closed for the holiday week.

Cotton-ball Santa Clauses, paper chain garlands, felt Christmas trees, and toilet paper roll ornaments adorn the bulletin boards around us.

Grant and Loch grin, inspecting the kids' art while Nick, Zar, and Jace suck on candy canes. Nash wraps around Vale, kissing her cheek. Delphine stands with Nadine, their arms looped, but their worried eyes are locked on Ruby and Axel, who's losing his patience with Sire.

"Why are we here?" Axel challenges him again. "For a

PowerPoint presentation on your missionary work in Ukraine? The mighty savior, all while you left your wife and child behind? No thanks."

Axel's been brusque with Sire since he's been home. Sure, the brothers talk shit; I like that part. But acting cruel and even judgmental?

What's wrong?

It's like Axel already knows.

But he can't.

Nadine promised me Sire would get to tell him. That's why we're here. Don't ask me why we're in the auxiliary building and not the chapel, but I have faith and assume Sire doesn't want blood on the Bibles.

"You mad at me?" Sire steps to him.

"Yeah." Axel chest bumps him like they're about to brawl.

I glance at Jace and Loch, their broad shoulders drawing up, about to pull them apart.

"Good." Sire stays in Axel's face. "You should be mad at me. You should hate me. You should never want to talk to me again, and I deserve it." His voice breaks. His handsome face, falling, too. All the pain Sire's been hiding, he lets it go. "I'm sorry, brother. I'm so fucking sorry from the bottom of my soul."

Axel pulls back, coldly raging, "So, it was *you*? You're the one who sold us out to our father."

Grant barks, "What the fuck are you talking about—he sold us out?"

"We've been found?" Nick fumes. "The fucker knows where we are?"

Jace growls, "Goddamn, I suspected it. I heard—"

Nadine lifts her hand, snapping her fingers.

Silence falls over the family and the brothers, standing nose to nose.

Sire won't let go of my hand, either. Does he think I need comfort? Or does he?

"You knew?" Sire asks, sounding calm.

"Yeah, we fucking *knew*." Axel doesn't. "Our captive? The one who climbed over the wall at Delta's? Roman: he's our half-brother and told us we'd been found. But we didn't know who ratted us out." His lip curls. "*You.*"

"What the fuck?" Jace thunders. "Roman's our half-brother? And you ratted us out?"

The circle of angry brothers tightens around us, but Nadine turns to them with one eyebrow raised.

They stop.

"Ruslan raped my maid's daughter." It's the first time I've heard Nadine use his name, explaining, "She was fourteen, and Roman is their child. He was raised to kill us, but is on our side instead. He hates Ruslan and told us what he knew."

"Like how Roman used to be married to Katya," Axel adds, not breaking his deathly stare with Sire. "But our father made Katya leave Roman and come after me instead. To marry me. To get pregnant by me. To leave me and take my *son* as his heir." His nostrils flare. "Our father knew where to find me. How?" He grabs Sire's throat. "Because *you* fucking told him where we were."

Ruby tugs Axel's arm. "Don't. Don't do this. Let him go."

But Axel's not listening. This is why he's furious; he's had time to feel the pain. He knew half of the secret.

"Yes." Sire doesn't flinch. "It's my fault. It's my fault he found us through my criminal record. It's my fault he took your son."

"No, it's not." I try to wedge between them. "Tell him, you had no choice."

"What is she talking about?" Axel snarls, "You had no choice? No choice but to let him take my *son*?"

"He wanted *my* son." Sire lifts his neck, letting his brother choke him tighter. "He wanted my heir, so I offered my unborn child to keep us safe. And I secretly vowed to never have one. It kept him away from us for years, until he came after you and he took…"

A tear falls down Sire's cheek, over his broken heart tattoo, confessing, "He took Lev, your baby boy, and I'm so fucking sorry, brother. I'd rather die than hurt you or him, and I've been trying to get him back."

"He gave his kidney," I blurt, joining Ruby, tugging on Axel's flexed arm. "Let him go. He almost died trying to get Lev back."

"Lev." I hear Nash invoke the name to Axel. "You have a son, my brother; that's his name. So be a better man than your father. Be a father Lev can admire. Forgive your brother."

Axel swallows, slowly dropping his hand.

But Sire doesn't move. His chin, lifted. His throat, open. It's as if he's willing to stand in Axel's pain for as long as it takes to end it.

"What does she mean you gave your kidney?" Ruby asks. Like me, she looks worried about our kings, our kids, and family.

"Show him," I urge Sire. "Show him your scar. Show him why you almost died trying to save Lev." I turn to Axel. "That's where he's been. Not Ukraine. Not abandoning me or us. He went to Moscow to sacrifice his life to get Lev back."

"Fucking hell, I knew it," Nash mumbles.

"Did our nephew need a kidney?" Grant asks, confused.

"No," Nadine sighs. "*He* did. The man who thinks he's your father. He has a genetic condition, and he used my grandson as leverage to get a donor, to force your brother, once again, to sacrifice for this family."

"You've been in Moscow?" Loch frets, stepping toward Sire. "This whole fucking time, and you almost died?"

"Yes," Sire reveals. "I think Katya tried to kill me. Somehow, she gave me sepsis because she knew I tried to take Lev, but—"

"But you're here?" Axel steps back, his eyes shifting, not knowing what to think. He's been so betrayed. So hurt. It's heartbreaking to watch. "You made a deal with the Devil to save my son. You almost fucking died doing it, so where is he?" Axel blinks, his tears falling, his voice booming, "Where's my son!"

I feel it in my soul, too, the pain of a parent. I hold my belly while Axel's pain echoes down the hall, reverberating in every heart gathered who loves him, mostly his brother's— the one who's held his pain the longest.

Sire palms his chest. "He's here. It's okay, brother. I brought Lev home to you."

I gulp.

He did? When? How?

I glance at Nadine. Tears stream down her smiling face.

The Queen did this.

I glance at Sire. Finally, his face looks peaceful.

My king did this, too.

"They're bringing him up the back stairs, into the playroom," Sire assures him. "We don't want to scare him. Calm down."

Under his brother's patient hands, Axel's chest heaves. I don't blame him. I'm crying. I look around. Everyone is crying.

"How?" Axel can barely speak. "Who?"

"Roman and his mother." Nadine reaches, holding Axel's arm. "She was Lev's nanny and traveled with your brother to bring him home. We helped him adjust yesterday. He can't speak English, only Russian." Her voice chokes. "He's a sweet little boy. He looks just like you. You need to be tender with him."

Axel wipes tears away. He's barely able to ask Sire, "Does he know about me? Who I am?"

Ruby clutches Axel's arm, smiling through her tears.

Proudly, Sire sheds a tear with his brother, too. "You're his father. It's your blessing to tell him. No one else."

Axel swallows, turning to nuzzle his forehead against Ruby's. It's like he can't breathe. He can't believe this.

"How did you get him out?" Jace wonders what I don't even know. "Why did our father let you leave Russia alive? And with our nephew?"

I guess Sire was protecting me when he came home. He needed to make sure I was safe and our baby was okay. He wanted our reunion, our time, and tears, too, while he was guarding this secret.

"I left him no choice." Sire cups Axel's shoulders. "Lev is yours now. Forever. He's not going back. You get to keep your son."

Axel shakes his head, aiming his eyes at Sire. They're burning bright blue with tears. For all of Axel's ice, he has the warmest heart.

"That's too easy," he doubts. "It's too good to be true. My son is mine? Without a fight?"

"It *is* true," Sire answers, "but it won't be easy. I made a deal, and there *will* be a fight."

"Here we go," Grant mumbles.

"Damn, right." Sire lifts his stare from Axel, ordering his other brothers, "Here we fucking go. All of us. For our nephew. Our mom. Our wives and kids. You better fucking believe we're about to go."

"Go where?" Jace nods his chin, ready.

"I—" Sire starts to explain, but the cutest kid's squeal explodes through the air, like sparkling, happy fireworks, turning our heads toward the playroom door.

Sire glances through its glass window and smiles. "Lev's here."

All step forward but Axel.

He doesn't move.

He can't move.

I've never seen a menacing man look so damn beautifully afraid.

"Come on, brother. Just me and you." Sire reaches for him, leading him. "We'll play with him. He'll warm up. We'll—"

"We'll scare him," Axel worries. "He doesn't know me."

"He'll love you." Ruby lifts on her toes, kissing Axel's cheek. "You're going to be a great father. Twice."

"Here." Sire reaches into his suit pocket, pulling out a pink Ring Pop. "Give him this and he'll be your best friend."

Sire turns to grab the doorknob, but Axel yanks him back.

For a moment, I fear he'll punch Sire. It's everything Sire's feared. Axel's pain. His rage. His anguish. All the years with Lev that Sire can't give back to Axel. It's not Sire's fault, but my man was born to bear a cross. For his family, he'll carry it, standing tall.

But Axel wraps Sire in a hug. "You fucking dick." He squeezes him tighter. "Thank you." He whispers through tears. "I love you, man."

HUDDLED AROUND THE OPEN PLAYROOM DOOR, WE'RE LIKE a huge family in front of the window of a hospital nursery.

Except there's only one little smiling boy, sharing his hot pink Ring Pop with a jacked and tatted man, while his other little hand scribbles doodles on the man's face.

His father's face.

His father's *smiling* face.

The little boy's uncle, all jacked and tatted, too, sits in a tiny red plastic chair. Strumming his guitar, he softly sings about a bullfrog and "Joy to the World," before he looks over ... and gives me a sexy wink.

Hey, Dolly, we've come a long way since the last time we stood in the doorway like this.

The proof?

Mr. Muscle hovers beside me, mumbling, "It had to be a *pink* Ring Pop for my badass nephew?"

I backhand Jace's chest. "Shut up." It's like backhanding a Mack truck.

"Pink is sexy for a man, no?" Delphine corrects him.

"I look hot in pink," Loch boasts.

Grant laughs. "Wearing it or fucking it?"

"I heard both." Nick piles on.

"Don't tease me, Daddy," Zar drawls.

"That's my line," Vale coos.

"And that's *my* cue," Nash mumbles, aroused.

"Sweet Jesus," Ruby huffs. "We can't go anywhere without you kings getting hotter than blue blazes."

Jace chuckles. "As long as it ain't blue balls."

"Speaking of blue balls..." Vale turns to Jace. "Where's Vivian?"

Delphine taunts Loch, "And where is Alena?"

"Leave my daughter out of this," Nash warns.

"She's one of us," Vale debates. "Alena's a queen and—"

"No," Nadine snaps her fingers, "*I'm* The Queen telling y'all to cork your pistols." She points to the tender sight before us. "Whatever we must do, we fight to keep this deal. I expect to keep our family together. You understand me?"

"Yes, ma'am." We answer in unison.

She arches a brow. "Excuse me?"

We try again. "Yes, Queen."

Looping her arm around my pregnant waist, she gives me a warm squeeze. "And *that's* how you do it."

CHAPTER FIFTY
WREN

"Dear God, make them stop praising you," I mutter, grabbing my back. "These wooden pews are killing me."

Sitting beside me, Delphine whispers her laugh, "I am sorry you suffer, but this is proof God is a woman, no? Only she can make us sit on hard wood and praise the Lord."

I giggle. Grant chuckles. Then, I roll my lips, hoping we're not busted.

The church is full. Everyone is here for Sire's return sermon. The kings and queens hide amongst the crowd, not making it obvious they're our family, but I can't help it.

I steal a glance over my right shoulder and spot Ruby and Axel, sitting across the aisle and one row back.

Sweet little Lev. He's asleep on his father's shoulder. Proudly, Axel wears his son's drool on his suit.

Nick and Zar sit beside them. Many eyes are on Nick, our famous NFL king, who proudly came out as one of the first top-tier gay players in the league.

But Nick's too focused on smoothing his sleeping nephew's dark, sweaty curls. After Ruby and I, Nick and Zar are ready. They're trying to have a baby with a surrogate.

For now? My fellow queen feels me. Ruby winks, then rolls her eyes, suffering the hard wood pain in her pregnant ass, too.

Yep, I'm giggling again.

Vale, sitting with Nash behind me, leans forward, whispering, "What's so funny?"

We're supposed to be listening to the other clergy droll on about how amazing Sire is, *and he is*, but I don't need a sermon to praise my husband.

I do it almost every night.

"We're thanking God; she's making us sit on hard wood for an hour," I whisper back, and Vale snorts.

Another snort echoes her. I glance over my left shoulder, happily twiddling my fingers at Alena, sitting beside Vale.

Alena twiddles back, her other hand holding Loch's. I twiddle at him too, and he blows me a cute kiss.

Silently, I pray for a glitter bomb, not a bloody one, when their story explodes.

I clock Nadine, sitting with Roman behind them. *I want to be her when I grow up.* Roman's hiding his sub's collar for Nadine under his suit.

Only a trained eye could clock it, and thanks to my husband, I've been lustfully trained.

Speak of the handsome devil.

Finally, it's his turn to speak.

I turn around, politely clasping my hands, sitting tall like a proper First Lady of the church.

But my clit doesn't understand the proper lady assignment.

She tingles like a bad girl every time Sire wears that dark grey suit. He's been home for a few weeks. Thanks to my cookies and the gym, he's put some meat back on his bones.

Bones he loves to give me every night; he really does have

a hot breeding kink. I'll be wearing maternity dresses for the next ten years.

I expect him to take his place behind the pulpit, but he surprises me. Approaching the choir and band, he grabs the microphone.

"Thank you for the kind words today, my fellow clergy." He opens his palm to the parishioners. "My brothers and sisters, too."

He clears his throat.

I swallow the lump in mine.

Sire's looking at Axel. "Thank you for coming today to welcome me home. But this praise isn't about me. It's about *us*; what we do for one another outside of these walls. 'Let us not grow weary of doing good, for in due season we will reap'…" He chokes again. "'If we do not give up.'"

I glance back and choke up at Axel cradling his son … and fighting back tears.

"That's from the Book of Galatians," Sire continues. "It's about the work we're called to do for our brothers and sisters. But I must confess … I almost gave up on my work. And what kept me going and brought me home wasn't you…"

He turns, gesturing to the giant crucifix. "No offense, Jesus. We're good."

Softly, the congregation chuckles.

"It was my wife." He turns to me, and I gasp. "Always and forever, I come home for her."

He takes a step my way, owning the crowd, owning my heart.

"She was shy and wanted a small wedding. And I was smitten…" He grins. "Still am, and will give her whatever she wants. But I always wanted to do this for her. Because, you see, there are some romantic love stories in the Bible."

He takes another step my way.

What is he doing?

My heart is racing—my palms, sweating.

"And me and my angel? We were like Isaac and Rebekah. It was love at first sight. Now, in the Bible..." Sire smirks at the crowd. "Rebekah fell first. She lowkey asked Isaac's servant about him. *'Who is that in the field coming to meet us?'*"

He pitched his voice like a woman, all sassy like it's a "Housewives of Charleston" show, not the Book of Genesis.

The congregation laughs.

I chew my lip.

Falling deeper in love.

Feeling our baby kick.

"But in our story?" Sire stands before me. "I fell first. I fell fast and hard and found salvation in this Iron Angel. She may be small, but don't underestimate her." Warmly, he nods at his mom in the crowd. "Don't underestimate any woman. Proverbs say of women, 'Long life is in her right hand.'"

He offers his, asking for mine.

But humility hits me. Shyness, too.

Funny, I can sing karaoke standing on a bar, but be the center of love, of family, of no one laughing at me? Of all this adoration?

I don't know how to do this.

With his inked hand, Sire gives that sexy *Come to me* gesture.

I could falter, but Jace, sitting on my left, stands and helps me rise, offering my hand to his brother.

God, give Jace his love, too. He's the only king who's alone.

I send up the prayer.

"I wrote a song for my wife while I was away." Sire takes my hand, gently rubbing his thumb over mine. *You're okay. I got you.* "It kept me going on dark and lonely nights."

He won't take his eyes off me while he tells the crowd, "It's a bit unorthodox, but so am I. It's soulful, but how I feel for her. It's a little sexy, but we're all adults here. Right? The kids are in Sunday school?"

He winks at the laughing congregation. He's got them and me: hook, line, and sinker.

"Trust me," he smirks, "you don't want Mrs. Rutledge, our fine First Lady of this church, messing up these lyrics. Because she will." I shake my head, smiling. "But every word is for her."

The band kicks in.

The beat drops.

Sire sings how God went crazy, making me for him, and him for me... and I get lost in his eyes and the lyrics. I'll never forget them.

Sure, all hell will break loose.

I'm married to a Bratva prince who'll cut off evil heads.

But I'm in love with a hot, inked pastor, who gave me his pinky, heart, body, soul, and child.

So, there's a lot of heaven for us, too.

EPILOGUE
SIRE

Seven months later

"Since when are you shy about this?" I reach over, tickling Wren's waist.

"Since it's been a minute," she giggles, tugging on the belt of her white trench coat. "The last time we were here was for my test, and that was before I became a mom and—"

"So, moms don't have sex?" I laugh, "If so, please inform mine. As you'd say, she didn't understand the assignment."

"It's too easy for dads." Wren turns nervously to the limousine window, the nighttime lights of Atlanta whizzing by. "You bust a nut in a minute, wait nine months, and ta-da—instant parent. While women..." I love her non-filtered mouth. "Our poor little pussies go through a lot."

I reach for her cheek, turning her eyes my way. "You're beautiful. From the moment I met you, I couldn't believe my eyes: my angel. And when you had our baby, I couldn't breathe. You're *that* perfect." I grin. "You and that hot little pussy."

She searches my eyes for a lie. She'll never find one there. My wife gets everything from me.

"But if you want," I flop back in the seat, sighing dramatically, "we can just fuck in the limo and go back to the hotel. Nash and Vale will be disappointed that their babysitting gig was cut short, but they'll get over it."

"No." She grabs my hand. "I want this night for us. I asked for it. It's just that…" She glances down at her cleavage. "What if I leak?"

"Damn, I'll bust a nut right there."

"Sire." I love it when she swats me. Maybe I'm morphing into her sub. Roman would be proud. "I'm serious. I'm still breastfeeding Bluebelle, and Vale said this bra would hide it, but what if it's obvious?"

"Hey." I grab her neck. Softly, she gasps. "What will be obvious tonight is that I'm married to the hottest woman in the club, who's having her fantasy fulfilled. And I happen to love this woman even more, with every day I'm alive, and I'd really like to fuck her for all to see how much."

She chews her lip. "Are we using condoms?"

Shit, she's already making me hard.

I pull her lips to mine. "With others? Always. Between me and you?" I kiss her, my tongue teasing hers, my dick swelling. "Fuck, Wren. Angel, you know I want to breed your pussy again."

She pants. Her smile, the sexiest I've seen in months.

Yes, it's heaven beyond my wildest dreams being a father. I cried when our baby girl was born. Now, I carry her and my Glock in a back holster.

Our daughter is beautiful. Like her mother. Like my dream. Black curls. Light eyes. Long lashes. Her soft skin, a blend of our love.

Wren's the best mom. A natural. She wears Bluebelle in a

baby sling, singing and fucking up songs to her while she bakes cookies.

But like every mom, she deserves a break.

And like every woman, she's even sexier now. I just need to prove it to her.

She nuzzles my nose. "You want to start trying again?"

"Angel, I'll never stop trying with you."

"Okay, no condoms for us but..." She reaches for my crotch. "What's his name?"

I'm already hard for her, as usual, but with her requests for tonight, I'll need to pace myself. It's been a long minute since we've done this.

I smirk. "You won't believe it."

"Try me."

Wren asked me to find a man for tonight—someone I want. I had to create a new profile on an app I trust, one that caters to ethically non-monogamous and sexually fluid adults. It took me a few weeks to find a play partner we could trust —one who would be a hot surprise for her, too.

"Christian."

She pulls back, laughing. "Seriously? His name is Christian?"

I tease, "And he really wants to worship his pastor tonight."

"Does he know about you?"

"Yes, and he's bi." Her eyes light up. Thrilled. Aroused. *God, my woman's hot.* "I had to tell him a few things about us and find out about him, too. I won't let some piece of shit lay a hand on my wife."

"So, you trust him?"

"Yeah. I looked him up. He has a job he needs to protect, too. He travels. Doesn't have time for love or relationships and..."

Her eyes widen. "And?"

"And I think he's worked with Redix and Daniel. Like he's in the film industry and goes to the club, and he heard about me."

She frets, "But you didn't show your face on the app, right?"

"No. It's my hand with my wedding ring. I wanted it to be clear I'm proudly married and looking for a play partner only."

Her teeth snag her bottom lip. "So, how did he know you?"

"When we chatted online, he shared one of his fantasies, something he saw at a club in Atlanta and—"

"And it was *you*," she sighs, climbing to straddle me as the limo stops in front of the private entrance to the discreet club.

I lace my hands through her hair. "But this is for you, too. You can change your mind or tell me to stop. You're my priority. No one else."

"And you're mine." She nips my bottom lip. "You know what I want. You know our boundaries. They haven't changed."

"Mine have." I'm getting harder just thinking about sharing this with her. Only her.

"What do you mean?" She nuzzles her forehead to mine.

"I want everything you want," I grab her hips, "and then I want to try something new for us. Together."

CHRISTIAN SITS BESIDE ME ON THE TUFTED LEATHER SOFA, sipping water while Wren's on my lap.

It didn't take long to find him in the club. How many men

are six foot six and clearly a model or an actor? I'm not sure, but he's something.

He hints, "Should we bother with small talk?"

"No." I reach down to where Wren's grinding on me, her back to my chest. Spreading her legs, draped over mine, I expose her pantiless pussy and my jeans' zipper. Dragging it down, I didn't wear boxers, either. "There's nothing small about tonight." I free my hard cock and order Christian, "Now be a good boy and eat her pussy and suck my cock."

Clearly, he wants this. Licking his lips at the sight of my swollen dick, he lowers to his knees.

We're in the VIP section of the club. I called ahead and made sure to reserve a sofa surrounded by red velvet ropes and gold stanchions, cordoning off our area. It's more selective. More private, but still a few gather by the ropes, watching us.

"Oh fuck," Wren gasps into our kiss while her pussy is licked. I groan into her mouth and grab her neck. Claiming her tongue, I try to stifle my jealousy, letting her fulfill her fantasy.

It's been a long time since I've shared her, and that was with the kings.

But so many things have changed. For better. For worse.

Nash versus Axel. Loch and Alena. Jace, fighting for Vivian. Sheremetev and the hunt. Our deal. Our family. Our freedom.

Honestly, I needed a night off from the shit we're dealing with.

And this man's hot, hungry mouth sucking my hard dick and licking my wife's pussy is exactly what I need.

"Fuck yeah." I palm his skull. "You're such a big, strong boy, aren't you?" He sucks Wren's clit, then licks my tip. "But you love tasting pussy and sucking a big dick, don't you?"

"Yes, Daddy." His green eyes ignite, his mouth plunging down my shaft until he gags.

"God, that's hot." Wren watches between our legs.

His broad shoulders are bent over. My thick dick is in his big hand. His whiskered lips stretch around my shaft. My hips pump, my tip fucking the back of his moaning throat.

"That's it. Good boy. Suck this dick." I fist his light brown curls for minutes, letting him indulge. "Now lick this sweet pussy that belongs to me. Sucking my cock made it wet. Now, fuck it with your tongue. Taste what a dirty girl she is for me."

He moans into Wren's sex, spearing her cunt. She writhes on my lap, her panting lips hovering by mine, her proud lust making me lose my goddamn mind.

"Fuck, Angel." I see our little crowd, horny couples watching us, and tug on her sexy coat. "I want you nude. I want everyone to see what's mine. What I get to fuck."

Quickly, she unties the coat, squirming to free herself and tossing it aside. But her black bra, I respect her body. It's her choice, and she leaves it on.

It's enough exposure of her gorgeous body for Christian to moan, "Fuck, your wife's hot."

Gritting my teeth, I won't be my father. I won't cut off his head or slice his tongue out for that.

Instead, I take what's mine, shifting Wren's body so she can fuck me in a reverse cowgirl position. Pinning her back to my chest, I reach down, pressing my swollen crown to her slick entrance. "Whose hard dick is this?" I steam over her ear.

"Mine," she sighs. "Now show them how you breed me like a good girl, Pastor. How I stay full of your cum."

"Aw, fuck yes, Angel." She knows what to say. I grunt, thrusting inside her.

She cries out while I take my other hand and palm his

skull again. He said he wanted it rough, so, "Eat our fuck," I command. "Lick my dick while I fuck her pussy, and suck her clit while I pound her cunt."

He obeys, and it feels so fucking good to hold my wife, leaning back and moaning into each other's mouths while we indulge in what I only trust to share with her. A hot outsider, we let join us for our pleasure. A stranger's tongue, licking our union. A foreign mouth, sucking the juices of our fuck.

"Fuck. Fuck. Fuck, Sire." Wren bucks, coming so fast and hard, I clench my teeth, fighting mine.

I have to pull out and gently lie her down, lengthwise on the wide sofa. Our playtoy lifts away, kneeling and licking his glistening lips while he shucks his pants down, his hard cock, springing free.

"Spread your legs, Angel." I stand up beside him and tug off my white T-shirt. Shoving my jeans down next, I kick them and my shoes free, while I gaze at the prettiest, wet, pink pussy I've ever seen. "That's it. Spread those lips for me. Show us how wet you are."

Wren obeys, the lust in her eyes my dark salvation.

I point to the bowl of condoms on the end table and tell our plaything, "Roll a Magnum on my dick so I can breed your ass while you eat my wife's pussy like a good boy."

Wren moans as his eyes droop with lust, obeying.

"Is this what you want, Angel?" I focus on her while he preps my hard cock to fuck him. *Damn, it's hot.* "You want to see how hard I can make his dick while I fuck his ass?"

"Yes, my Lord." Wren starts fingering herself, and I grin, the goddamn luckiest man alive.

This is not our toy's first time. Quickly, he kneels on the sofa, putting his ass up for me, and his face between Wren's spread legs.

Taking a bottle of lube from the table, I pour it down his crack. I set the bottle down and fist my base, climbing between his muscular legs, admiring his puckered, shaven hole as I tease it with my sheathed tip. "Tell me what you want because I'm going to fucking give it to you and get my wife off."

"Breed me, Daddy." His voice is gruff and deep, his back arching open for me. "Pound my ass with that big dick."

Wren moans, and I give her and him what they want. For minutes, we're in a lewd daze. Her eyes, glued to mine. Her stare, combing my flexing body while I grab a man's broad shoulders and fuck his ass as hard as I can.

He grunts into her pussy, licking it. She sinks her hand into his hair, making him do it. I sweat, growling, wanting to fucking kill him for touching her as she writhes, moaning and coming on his face, and that only makes me fuck his gaping ass harder.

"Come here, boy." I yank him up, snaking my arm around his neck, choking him just enough to get us off. "Do you have my wife's cum on your lips?"

"Uh.... Uh..." He doesn't know how to answer as I thrust into his ass. He cries out, screaming, moaning, gasping, satisfied with each thrust, my skin, slapping his cheeks.

"Do you?" I squeeze his neck harder. He's as tall as me, as big as me, and that makes this even hotter, sweatier. A fight like we want it—a helluva show for those watching us. "Answer me, boy," I hiss into his ear. "Did you taste my wife's pussy? The pussy that belongs to me?"

"Yes, Daddy," he cries out, jerking his hard cock off.

Wren's watching and writhing, her fingers strumming her swollen clit.

Fuck, I'll kill for her. Fuck, she's mine. Goddamn, I'm fighting one urge and fucking the other.

"You need to fucking pay for it," I growl. "You're lucky I don't kill you. Want me to breed your ass instead, for touching my hot wife?"

"Oh fuck, yes, Pastor," he groans, jerking faster. "Punish me. Breed me with that big dick."

I swat his hand away. "Don't touch it." I hammer my hips, snarling in his ear, "I'm going to breed this ass so hard, you can't fight me. You're gonna show them how sweet her pussy tastes, you wanted to take my big dick for it." Wren moans. "You're gonna come for us, aren't you?" I choke him harder. "Say *God*. Say my name while you come so hard with my dick pounding your ass."

"Oh fuck. Oh, God. Oh fuck, yes, I'm coming. I'm coming." His bouncing hard cock spurts everywhere. Way too much and making me murderous.

I palm his skull. "Clean it up. Lick your cum off my wife. Now."

Wren loves this. I've lost count of how many times I've seen her come, watching me do this for her. For us. Even our toy is moaning.

He licks, his impressive dick barely deflating while he cleans his cum off Wren's thighs and pussy.

"That's enough." I yank him away. Then I pause, checking his eyes. "You good?"

"Very. Thank you." He licks his glossed lips, grinning. Sweating. His massive chest, heaving.

"You ready for my turn?" I ask him.

He grabs a condom. "Give me a few minutes, and yeah, I will be."

"Your turn?" Wren asks, curious, while I snap off my condom.

I didn't come. I always save it for her. With the wipes on the table, I clean myself before climbing on top of her. Kissing her. "We're going to try something new tonight. Me and my wife."

She reaches up, cupping my jaw. "New?"

"Yeah." I kiss her again. And again. And again, before I reveal, "I'm going to fuck you while he fucks me."

"Oh my God, Sire," she sighs over my lips. "You want that?"

"It's been a long time since I've bottomed, but yeah. I want it. I told him to do this, that I want to feel this with you." I nuzzle her nose. The crowd disappears. The world falls away when I stare into her eyes. "Everything, Wren. We share everything until the end. Promise me."

"I promise." She rises for me, kissing me. Then, she reaches, surprising me as she tugs the cups of her bra down, exposing her full breasts. "Everything, Sire," she sighs. "Everything I have is yours."

"Oh, fuck, Angel. I love you," I sigh at her vulnerability with me. Her bravery with me. How she's given everything to me, too. Trusting. Loving. She's mine.

Wren kisses me again, our mingled breath going from tender to heated when she reaches down, stroking my hard dick. "You sure you want to do this?"

"Fuck yeah, I'm sure."

I'm very sure when our toy starts licking my ass. I'm damn sure when she teases my swollen tip over her hard, slick clit at the same time. We play and tease until our toy asks, "You ready?"

I gaze down at Wren, at my world. "Yeah, I'm ready." He pours lube over my ass while I slowly thrust inside her.

"Oh God," Wren cries out. "Oh God, Sire, I'm gonna come."

"Wait for me, Angel. I won't last long."

She grabs a breath, nodding, edging. With her tight wet heat clenching my dick, once I feel his sheathed tip, teasing into my ass, I groan, "Fuck. Fuck."

"Tell me." Our toy is good. He echoes my taunt, "Tell me

what you want because I'm going to fucking give it to you while you get your wife off."

He grabs my hips while I thrust into Wren. I kneel with my arms braced, my body planked over hers. I watch as she palms my chest, hanging on. *Fuck, she's beautiful.* Her eyes, anchored to mine. Her legs, open and trembling. Her lips, parted and shaking. Her pussy, wet and taking me.

My lips shake, too, feeling him breach my entrance. "Fuck," I grunt. "Fuck yes. Fuck my ass hard and make me breed my wife."

"Oh God," Wren arches, her orgasm threatening.

"Edge, Angel. Edge," I urge, but then I can't breathe, feeling the invasion. The stretch. The eye-rolling pain that burns into pleasure because Wren's pussy chokes my cock while I take a long dick in my ass.

"Fuck, yeah, Pastor," he sighs. "Oh fuck, your tight ass is hot."

He slowly thrusts inside me, and for a moment, I can't move until we find our breath. Our rhythm. Our bodies, receiving. Taking. Connected. Me and Wren, together, until she's shaking. I'm shaking. My legs. My lips. This pleasure will make me fall into a million pieces for my wife, and it's where I belong. With her, whole. With her, broken. With her, dying. With her, alive.

"Harder." My dick swells. The pleasure in my ass is too much. I'm at the point of no return, needing it to be our end, our beginning. The white heat in my spine, ready to burst. My dick, my voice, demanding, "Fuck my ass harder. Make me come so fucking hard inside her pussy."

"Sire, I'm coming." Wren thrashes, sinking her nails into my straining pecs. "Uhh. Fuck. I can't stop it. I'm coming. Oh, God!"

She screams, crying out, her orgasm making her buck, and

I lose it. All time. All place. All pain. It's gone while I groan, letting go inside her. Only her. Only Wren. Only us. Forever.

Carefully, he leaves my body, but I don't leave hers. I roll us onto our sides, my back to the club, her head to my chest. "Fuck, Angel," I sigh into her curls. "Fuck, I love you. Only you."

Panting, she kisses my sweaty chest until she's softly laughing.

I lift her chin. "What's so funny?"

She climbs up, reaching her lips for mine. "We need to make this a *bi-annual* thing."

I laugh. "Good one."

Getting dressed, Christian laughs, too. "Damn. I hope I find my angel, too, one day."

Wren pops her head up, answering him, "You will. Go to Dollywood. You'll find her ... or him there."

"Dollywood? Really?" He chuckles. "Okay, I'll check it out."

He leaves while I nuzzle her neck. "I'm surprised you didn't sing a little Dolly for him, too."

She sighs, "No, I save my piña coladas and getting caught in the rain for you."

I jerk up, gazing down at her. "*What* did you just say?"

She bats her lashes. "Nothing."

I narrow my eyes. "So, you *do* know the right lyrics? You just fuck 'em up to make us laugh."

Her fingertip shhhs my lips. "I don't know what you're talking about." With a kiss, she demands, "Let's go. I miss her already."

Quickly, we dress because I'm missing her, too. This is our first night away from Bluebelle.

But yeah.

This will be a bi-annual thing.

Taking her hand, we work through the crowd. On a Saturday night, it's a big one.

I'm focused on the door, but Wren halts, yanking my hand.

"Oh my God," she gasps, and I turn to see her frozen, watching a couple with a crowd gathered around them, too.

It's hot. It's a big man in a black spandex fetish hood. No shirt. Just worn jeans and a jacked body.

He's playing with a woman, standing naked and wearing a fetish mask, too. It looks like he's using every toy to please her for their audience.

"Look," Wren chokes, almost in pain. "It's him!"

"Who?"

"*Loch!* The devil on his chest; I'd know one of my kings anywhere. Oh my God." She shakes her head, covering her eyes. "That asshole. He's getting his pleasure Dom kink off and cheating on sweet Alena."

Squinting my eyes, I look closely, reading the ink down his body. The seven lions across his obliques.

Yes, I'd know one of my brothers anywhere, too. Sure, I knew Loch had his kinks. Never did I think he'd cheat on his innocent woman, though. She's practically our princess.

"I'm gonna fucking kill him." Charging across the room, I elbow people aside. In seconds, I'm grabbing his arm and whipping him around.

"You fucking dick," I seethe. "You're dead."

Under his mask, his blue eyes shock wide open. It takes him a second to see me.

"Shit, man," he huffs. "It's not what you think."

"I don't need to *think*." I get in his face as Wren joins me. "We can fucking *see* what you're doing."

"I can't believe it. You? Of all my kings." Wren shoves him. She's so tiny, he doesn't move. But her fury makes him flinch. "I can't believe you'd do this to her, and don't think I won't tell her. Don't think I won't beat your ass for hurting her too, and—"

"Wren." A woman's voice calls from under the fetish mask. Yanking it off, a cascade of thick tawny hair tumbles down. "It's me."

We stammer in unison.

"Alena?"

NOT THE END

Please leave your honest review. It's the greatest gift to an author. Xoxo, **Kelly**

Thank you so much for reading SIRE!
This is their happy ending,
but the epic story continues.

Find out what happens next in **LOCH,**
where more shocking secrets and
forbidden romances are revealed.

For free hot bonus scenes teasing Jace's story and The
Queen's toy, visit kellyfinley.com/freespice

Enjoy Loch's shocking teaser next.

Please take a moment to leave your honest review, too.
It's such a gift to authors.
Thank you!

TEASER - LOCH

THEY SAY THE DEVIL COMES AS EVERYTHING YOU'VE *wished for.*

But isn't there another saying? About being careful what you wish for?

Yeah, because I'm getting butterflies and shit. Like, I'm not a grown man, knocking on thirty. No, I'm back in sixth grade and about to get my first kiss from Kristen Morris on the school bus. Never did, though. I punked out. Sorry, Kristen. Wasn't you. My first boner grounded me in my seat.

But I'm not punking out this time.

I've wished for this moment since I was eighteen … but I suspect Alena Allen isn't wishing for me.

Hell, she doesn't even know I exist.

Yet.

"What do you say, Mutt? I get a do-over on the sixth grade? This time, we control our boners?"

Mutt gives me a half-ass bark. Sitting in the passenger seat of my truck, my golden shepherd is more interested in the squirrels eating peanut shells by the garbage can of the gas station than the woman I'm here to stalk.

I mean ... secretly bodyguard.

I check the time. It's 5:22 p.m. Alena should pull up any minute. I really should warn her about her schedule. She moves like clockwork. She's disciplined. I like that about her.

But it makes this stalking shit too damn easy.

Woof! Mutt Damon goes apeshit when another truck pulls into the lot. This one has a hot husky in the bed of the truck.

"Settle down." I scruff his head. "That's not who we're here for."

No, we're here for a beautiful woman who has no idea she's in danger.

Problem is, is she at risk because she doesn't know that her father is secretly in the mafia? Well, ex-mafia? Like me?

Or is she at risk because I've secretly been in love with her, and said father would fucking kill me if he knew? He's really into eye-gouging.

No, thanks.

I like my eyes, but...

They really like Alena. She's got this smile with her friends that frickin' makes my chest explode. My eyes get all blinded, too. Maybe it was the wind on the beach. That's where I'd go, and she'd happen to be there, too. Every weekend. Noon until sunset.

Yeah, I'll be ticking all the this-shit-is-crazy boxes on this bodyguard assignment. But blame it on my brothers. They're making me do it. I'm the baby brother of seven, who usually gets away with murder, so they put me on this detail— guarding Alena.

They're really twisting my arm.

Making me watch a woman I've been watching for years.

The suffering is real.

They don't know I'm in love with her. They'd kill me if they knew, but that's what it is, love. Sure, I've never really spoken to Alena. I wasn't allowed. So maybe it's been an obsession.

For over a decade.

But I'm a closet romantic. I read romcom books. They're fucking hilarious. And hot. So, let's go with *I'm in love with Alena Allen from afar*.

It's less stalkery.

Finally, the white SUV with a black front push bumper, light bar, and a US Forest Service door emblem appears. It parks in front of the 7-Eleven.

A tall woman in a light green shirt and darker green uniform pants emerges from the driver's seat. Her long, tawny hair in a messy braid, falling from her baseball cap. Her face, that profile, those lips, like a doll. Her curves and that ass, goddamn killing me.

Fuck, I'm in sixth grade again.

Boner wants to play.

A Forest Ranger uniform is about as sexy as a stomach flu. But damn, Alena Allen makes her uniform look dangerously hot.

She waves to the elderly couple, filling up their Subaru. She ignores the three teenagers leaning against their truck, catcalling with their bullshit, while I note their license plate and how big their graves will need to be.

Swinging the glass door open to the store, she disappears inside, and it's showtime.

"Stay here," I tell Mutt. "And don't hump my dash over that husky. You hear?"

If dogs could roll their eyes, Mutt just did.

Sliding out of my truck, I flip my dark green baseball hat backwards. I'm going for cute, not scary-as-fuck. I'm tempted to issue death threats as I stalk past the teen hecklers. I should tell them their small-dick-energy is showing every time they catcall a woman.

But I'm on a mission.

The chime above the door sounds as I enter. I nod at the cashier behind the counter; Jesse and I have a little arrangement.

On cue, as I'm aiming for the far wall with the soda fountain machines, days-old hot dogs spinning on a rotisserie, and rock-hard muffins, Alena brushes past me, telling Jesse, "Hey, um. You're out of cups for the Slurpee machine."

"What? Really?" I whip around, sounding surprised. "Yeah, man, I'll need one, too."

"Just a moment, please. I will get more cups." Jesse acts as animated as a corpse. He pivots to go in the back, while I turn to Alena.

Heart, pounding.

Dick, stirring.

Soul, exploding.

Face, calmly grinning. "Guess Slurpees are popular here."

That's it? That's my opening line? Goddamn. Stick to swiping right, Loch.

"Yeah." Alena steps back, guardedly giving me a covert glance.

That's all she says. Not that I blame her. She's trained to observe, to be suspicious. And I stole all the swagger from the air with my Captain Obvious comment.

"Here are your cups." Jesse emerges from the back, carrying a sleeve of neon cups. Woodenly, he proclaims, shoving them in my face, "Sorry. About. Being. *All* out of cups. Can you please *help* me? And load them up? I am. Busy. With customers."

No, he isn't. We're the only ones in the store.

Clearly, Jesse isn't taking drama classes at his local high school.

"Sure." I grab the sleeve, fighting an eye roll. "Got it. Thanks, man."

He pivots again, marching to his place behind the counter while I slide the row of cups into their designated dispensary hole.

Saving the last two, I hand one to Alena like I'm presenting a red rose, not a DayGlo forty-ounce tankard. But I keep my mouth shut. It's not the skilled part of my body working right now. No, that part twitches in my pants.

Damn, she has pretty brown eyes.

Quit staring!

"Thank you." She takes the cup. I hold my breath. Because she has manners, my silence forces her to comment, "Guess the Slurpees *are* popular here."

Houston, we have lift off.

Now, play it cool.

"Can't blame 'em." I gesture for her to go first while I calmly quip, "A Slurpee a day keeps the assholes away."

What did I just say?

Since when am I a poet? Maybe I should let Boner do the talking after all. He's been trained. My mouth hasn't.

Alena stifles her giggle, reaching for the handle of the diet cherry soda flavor, filling her cup. "Never thought of it that way," she grins, "assholes and Slurpees. But if you say so."

Don't! Don't say it! I don't care what kinky vision you just got of how your tongue could show her, don't you fucking dare!

I clench my jaw, nodding. Admiring her pour, I say, "Classic choice. Cola and cherry." I reach for the handle on the machine beside her, filling my cup with neon green, then fluorescent yellow. "But I gotta go with this new combo—watermelon lime mixed with lemonade. Read about it in *Bon Appétit* magazine."

Alena stops short, staring at me, her jaw dropping. "You read about Slurpees in a culinary magazine?"

"Yeah, I'm a loyal fan."

So is Alena.

She gets one every day around 5:30, 7:30 on the weekends. Back home in Charleston, she'd go to the 7-Eleven near Folly Beach, where I happened to be filling up my full gas tank.

This goddamn gorgeous woman has no idea how much I know everything about her, how I used to watch her study the sand on the beach, and how much I'm not supposed to want her like my next breath.

I understand why her dad needs to keep her safe. What our enemies could do to her makes me murderous.

What I could do to her? Makes me want to kiss those lips.

"Me, too." She finally gives me her real smile, and my chest explodes, my eyes blinking. She keeps talking, while I'm staring at the sun. "I get a Slurpee every day. They remind me of my mom. She loved them. Coke and cherry. Classic, like she was."

Sorry, Alena.

I know your mom died when you were ten. I know it almost broke your spirit.

But now it's time for my dick-move.

Trust me.

It'll seal our fate.

Women like their men, all unattainable-yet-theirs, all aloof-but-attracted, all dark-and-mysterious-though-not-murderous, unless it's to unalive their evil ex. I borrow my sister-in-law's smutty books. They're like instruction manuals for heteroflexible men.

Lucky for me, most men don't get it. They mock romance books, so that leaves more women for me. It's like shooting fish in a barrel.

When I only want this one.

This one, killing me with that smile.

"Yeah, well...have a good one, Ranger." I nod toward her uniform. Turning toward the counter, I call over my shoulder, "Slurpee's on me."

My heart clenches, knowing I just left Alena standing there. All happy and vulnerable and like what-the-fuck?

This was our meet-cute.

She just doesn't know it yet.

I'm about to move in next door to her. I'm about to shadow her every move. I'm about to pretend to be her colleague, maybe even her trusted friend, while I'll be guarding her shoulder and looking over mine for threats.

Alena faces more dangers than the black bears up here. She's the daughter of a ruthless mafia king. She's the princess to my family, my Russian family, who escaped the Bratva. She's not related to me, though my brothers think of her as their little sister. Hell, even their goddaughter.

She has no idea who we are, how she belongs to us, or how she's a prime target for our enemies.

And I have no idea how I'm going to be her secret bodyguard, as her father insisted, without everyone knowing that every time I close my eyes—in bed, in the shower, on the beach, or in a gas station—I see her.

I want her.

Can't you tell?

I'm in love with Alena.

For now, I hear the keys on the carabiner hooked to her utility belt jangle as she silently walks behind me, leaving through the glass door.

Slapping a fifty down, I tell Jesse, "Thanks, man. Good performance with those cups."

"Look, man..." Jesse warns, swiping up the Grant, "Fucking with a ranger can get you killed around here."

"Yeah, I know." I turn my hat back around, revealing the Forest Service emblem. I reach, grabbing the Slurpee, my T-shirt lifting to reveal my hidden gun. "I'm a ranger, too."

Order **LOCH** Today

Dear Reader,
There's more to come with the Belles & Bratva
Beasts. **Loch**. Jace. The Queen and some surprises.
More secrets will be revealed. More spice will be
shared. More snark will fire. Oh, and the hot,
crazy, contract-killer cousins are coming, too.
For More visit KellyFinley.com

ALSO BY KELLY FINLEY
"THE QUEEN OF SPICE"

-Interconnected Books & Audiobooks

Available in Kindle Unlimited and Audible-

BELLES & BRATVA BEASTS

NASH

AXEL

SIRE

LOCH

JACE

A Not-Mafia-Mafia, Dark RomCom Series

SHAMELESS PLAY

SHAMELESS GAME

featuring Blair, Beau & Colton

A Frenemies to Lovers, Why Choose, Football romance

MAKE HIM

featuring Luca & Scarlett with Zar and Nick

A Billionaire Dom, MMF, Why Choose Romance &

Audiobook

TEMPT HER

featuring Stacey & her husbands

MMMF, Why Choose Revenge Romance & Audiobook

HOLIDAY FOR SIX

HALLOWEEN FOR SIX

with cameos of MCs from characters above and below!

Very Spicy, Lots of Friends to Lovers RomComs & Audiobooks

ALL FOR HIM

featuring Silas & Eily Van de May with Cade and Redix

A Forbidden Cinderella Retelling Poly Romance

AFTER HIM

WITH HIM

An Angsty Second Chance to an MMF, Why Choose Duet

PROTECT HER

PIERCE HER

HUNT HER

CHASE HER

A Spicy, Romantic Suspense, Bodyguard/Celebrity Trilogy

Join my newsletter.

I share sneak peeks, giveaways, and more.

KellyFinley.com

ACKNOWLEDGMENTS

My husband and silver fox: Thank you for understanding you're a hot distraction. I miss you so much when I go away to write romance because *you* are my love life.

My Book Team: Big hugs to my BTS fam: Ashley, Brit S, Anja, Cat, Jay, Kimberly, and more. Y'all make my author life so much easier. Deborah, Lizzie, and Heather, my proofreaders! Thanks for fixing my goofs. Thank you, Lori, for another stunning cover design. Holy breathtaking photo, thank you, Michelle Lancaster, for this perfect photo of Kally.

My Beta Team: Brit F, Kayla, Lauren, Madison, and Thorunn. I love it when you send me long emails! I truly cherish you.

My Content Queens & ARC Team: Your edits, posts, reviews, and support melt my heart. I'm always so inspired. I live for your DMs and keep writing for you. Like. Legit. Thank you!

#Bookstagram, #BookTok, and FB Book Babes: I love hearing from you! I get all teary at your edits and comments. Thanks for your love.

Local Romance Bookstores! I found you! I love supporting you or just popping by. Here's to filling shelves and hearts with smut.

Author Friends & Mentors: Particularly Eva, Maggie, Rachel, and Trisha! I'm not alone with book besties like you.

Best for last - You, my reader: Thank you for sharing this story with me. I welcome your messages, posts, and emails, and promise to keep giving you more spice.

Please leave your honest review. It's the greatest gift to an author.

Xoxo,
Kelly